"*The Memory Garden* meshes the secular and holy in a palatable and believable way that challenges our faith and how we live out that faith in the world around us. It is brilliant and realistic, capturing the nuances of Southern dialectal beauty and touching the soul of humanity with truth and light, while pushing us toward renewed thinking and transformative living. Meshing culture, race, age, and status into an intricate weave of oneness, the book is a stroll down Main Street USA with vivid and memorable characters from familiar places we call 'home,' or wish we could. A must-read. Jessica Brodie is a writer for all times and does so with great insight, depth, reach, and compassion. She is the female Nicholas Sparks. We will be hearing from her for years to come and gladly!"

Connie Davis Rouse, columnist, author
and cultural diversity consultant

"Jessica Brodie is a gifted writer. She is unable to write a dull sentence. Those who read the first few pages will not be able to put this book back on the shelf."

Rev. J. Richard Peck, former editor, General Commission on United Methodist Men, *International Christian Digest*, and *Circuit Rider*

Praise for The Memory Garden

"As I read through a book, my head searches for the appropriate emotion—the right feel of where I think the author fits. Jessica Brodie falls headlong into comfortable, tender, and earthy. Her characters are real, reaching from the page to grasp your hand and pull you into their fictional bubble. Well thought and smooth as a warm cup of hot chocolate, you walk alongside the characters of Dahlia, welcomed into their lives with open arms. Brodie sets a new pace, one that demands you keep in step. Beautifully done."

Cindy K. Sproles, bestselling author of Appalachian novels *Mercy's Rain, Liar's Winter, What Momma Left Behind,* and *Coal Black Lies*

"*The Memory Garden* intricately weaves the seemingly unrelated threads of her characters' lives into a stunning tale of new life and hope. Jessica Brodie is a masterful storyweaver. In a culture where anyone armed with a computer can thrust themselves into cyberspace as a storyteller, commentator, or writer, Jessica is oh-so different, possessing that rare ability to bring wisdom and compassion to complex issues of life and faith."

Missy Buchanan, internationally acclaimed Christian author and speaker on topics of faithful aging

"Jessica Brodie is a master at weaving mystery, tension, and true-to-life scenarios into a tapestry of faith. In *The Memory Garden*, she's crafted a story that is as real as the neighborhood I live in. Like a litter of puppies dropped on my doorstep in a snowstorm, her characters wormed their way into my heart from chapter one. I found myself rooting for them, lamenting over their woes, and hoping for a satisfying conclusion."

Lori Hatcher, bestselling author of *Think on These Things, Refresh Your Faith, Refresh Your Hope,* and other devotionals

"Jessica Brodie has a beautiful, captivating voice and a skill at crafting stories with the perfect blend of depth, nostalgia, Southern charm, and hope."

"Unforgettable. *The Memory Garden* leaves a deep impression on the soul. Characters rise from the ashes, summoning strength to start again. Faith in family, community, and Christ restores hope and blazes unexpected paths for the future. Engaging and heart-stirring. This book is an irresistible page-turner."

"A charming, affecting novel. Jessica is a wizard at creating settings for her stories. I would move to Dahlia in a heartbeat. You want to live in her settings and be best friends with her characters. She is a remarkable talent."

"Jessica Brodie is an immensely talented person. Her ability to write in several genres with comfort and fluidity is remarkable. She is able to weave complex and immense truths into accessible stories and accounts."

THE MEMORY GARDEN

Jessica Brodie

Book One in the Dahlia Series

THE MEMORY GARDEN

a novel

Jessica Brodie

VALOR
PUBLISHING GROUP

Valor Publishing Group, South Carolina

First published in the United States of America in 2025

Library of Congress Cataloging-in-Publication Data
The Memory Garden
p. cm.

Cover Design by Hannah Linder Designs

ISBN 979-8-9929008-0-4

To my husband, Matt, with all my love forever.
You inspire me to be open, honest, faithful, and true,
and your love and support give me wings to soar.

To our children, who are as different yet as beloved
as possible: Cameron, Avery, Allison, and Will.
I know our future is in good hands because of people like you.

And to my Lord and Savior, Jesus Christ. I am yours, forever.

"Never hurts to take a risk when it comes to growing things. In my experience, sometimes the worst mess of nothing can sprout the most vibrant testament to life."—Helen Chastain

CHAPTER 1

Rebecca

THE VOICE WAS urgent and low. "Rebecca."

For a moment she wanted to dream it back to its neat little corner, the flat slate-blue landscape where she'd been safe, floating on air, moments before.

But then the beeps came, and the soft intermittent puffs. The hum from a machine to her right, or behind her. The cold antiseptic smell that twitched at her nostrils, tickled her throat. Her body ached everywhere. Rebecca cracked open an eye, then shut it just as quickly.

Oh, dear God. What have I done?

The hospital. It was all coming back to her now. She wiggled a toe, just enough that she could feel the tight sheets tug and press against the top of her ankle. A finger next. Movement was good. Movement meant she'd be okay. Of course she'd be okay. She had to be.

"Rebecca Chastain."

Louder now.

She steeled herself. She wouldn't think about it. Not yet. There was plenty of time for that.

"Mmpf." The word felt odd on her tongue, and she swallowed

past the dry mouth, squinted as she tried to sit up. The room was at once too bright and just right.

The nurse stood at the foot of her bed, a helmet-haired thirty-something with gray eyes far too close together, her yellow scrubs dotted with tiny farm animals. She moved to Rebecca's side, keeping a firm hand on Rebecca's collarbone—settle down—as she pressed a lever on the bed.

The room went from far off to front-and-center in an instant.

"Do you know why you're here?" The nurse's voice was softer now, no trace of impatience.

Rebecca's heart began to pound. She nodded. "Th-the pills." Her voice sounded nothing like her own, like she was either twelve years old or sixty.

"Thirty of them, to be exact. You're very lucky they found you." The nurse fluffed the pillows behind her, added a small one behind her neck. "Up for visitors?"

Rebecca's expression must have said it all.

The nurse tsked, but it was a good-natured tsk. "Your granny just stepped out for some coffee. She'll be back in a moment."

Granny. Rebecca's eyes filled with tears. Stupid. Stupid to think she could do this, this one ridiculous thing, and keep it from the people she loved. Of course Granny was here. Her parents, too. Of course they would be. And Sarah, and Marisol.

She looked at the nurse, unable to form the words.

And Peter.

Oh, please. Please not Peter.

All she'd wanted was sleep, escape. Silence.

Now everything she feared was crashing in around her like a massive wave, as if she were six years old again, floundering beneath the surface, unable to break free.

The tears came, coursing down her cheeks, ugly thick tears that made her eyes swim and her lips swell. Her breath came out in awful, hoarse, hiccupping sobs.

"There, there, honey." The nurse stood close, patted her back.

Rebecca found herself resting her head on the woman's soft bosom, cradled in her fleshy arms as if she'd done this a thousand times before.

The nurse fished atop the table and handed over a tissue. "Here."

Rebecca mopped at her face, grabbed for another tissue.

"I bet you're one relieved lady," the nurse said over her head.

Rebecca looked up to see Granny standing there. Her Granny, petal-pink pocketbook clutched in her hands with her old, familiar Bible poking out between the handles, spring straw hat, the same hat Rebecca remembered from her childhood, crooked atop her gray curls.

And her eyes. Those dark, deep eyes. Indian eyes, Granny called them. Watching. Waiting.

But instead of judgment and disappointment, Rebecca saw worry, concern. Even a little fear.

Most of all, she saw love. The years melted away.

Hours later, the room was quiet, the warm glow of the setting sun smoothing out the lines and spots on Granny's arms as they sat, hand-in-hand, in the hospital room. Granny smelled of peppermint and lavender, the scents of home.

"Was he worth it?" Granny asked quietly, and Rebecca didn't even have to strain to hear the South Carolina twang in her words. "If the pills had worked, if you'd died last night, would he have been worth it all?"

Rebecca let out a breath. "No."

It was the truth. Peter wasn't worth it at all. And right now, he seemed like he was a million miles away, as if she'd imagined him, an artificial replica of those perfect men she and her cousin used to conjure up in their bedtime make-your-own-husband games, where they'd invent the ideal man they'd one day marry. Vikki's was usually blond and outdoorsy, occasionally an artsy type or a politician thrown in here or there. Rebecca's, however, was always tall, dark and brooding, charming and dashing, always rushing out to handle the next big thing and then coming home with flowers and romance.

She'd gotten what she'd asked for. Peter was certainly dashing. And ambitious. And everything else she'd thought she wanted.

Until he broke her heart. Until he didn't come home at all, except to pack his bags and inform her he was moving in with what's-her-face.

Alyssa.

Rebecca had set herself up for failure from the start.

"It was everything, Granny." She swallowed hard. "Peter, losing my job, not being able to dig myself out of the pit. Everything I built my life on, it all just crumbled down to nothing. I just feel so … so empty."

The last word was so soft it could have been a whisper. Rebecca squeezed her eyes shut, willing the tears back, but one slipped past, tickled her cheek as it rolled to her chin.

Granny just arched a brow, patted her Bible, which now rested beside her. "Sounds like it's time to build your house on solid ground."

A long silence fell over them, so long Rebecca thought Granny might have fallen asleep there in the hospital chair. Surely Granny was tired. She'd taken an early flight to come here, had sat all day keeping watch, taking care.

Rebecca peered out the window, straining to see the bustle of city outside. All she could glimpse was amber sunlight glinting off concrete. New York had been her home for fifteen years now, and sometimes she still felt like a tourist.

A knock came at the door, and she and Granny both sat up. The lights flicked on.

"Hi, Rebecca, I'm Dr. Carter."

He was a tall thin man in a white coat, his balding head shining like a beacon framed by thick brown domes of hair by his ears. When he smiled, his eyes crinkled at the edges, and the hair domes bounced.

"Head of psychiatrics here. We met earlier, though I don't imagine you remember. And you're her grandmother?"

"Yes. Helen Chastain."

They shook hands and then went through the details—the backstory, the pills she took, the stomach pumping, the counseling she'd need. It had been Sarah who'd found her. Sarah, her best friend who lived clear across the city now, who was supposed to be driving upstate for the weekend with her new fiancé. Sarah, who'd had a "bad feeling" and used her spare key to let herself into Rebecca's loft apartment, found her passed out cold on her computer desk. She hadn't even written a note. The empty bottle of pills and glass of wine said it all.

"I didn't mean to kill myself. I didn't want to die." Her voice was small, cracked on the last word. "I—I was just tired of it all. Tired of the game, the mess everything had become. Tired of hurting all the time." A bitter laugh escaped, which turned into a sigh.

"You're a journalist, right?"

"I was assistant editor. On the fast track." Her lips twisted, and for a moment she remembered how it felt to rise. And fall.

"It's a hard market."

"You can say that again."

He cocked his head, looked first at Granny, then at her. She decided she liked him.

"So why the pills?" He leaned in. "You know better."

She did know better. Rebecca shivered.

"It sounds really dumb, but in some skewed corner of my mind, I guess I'd convinced myself that if I took enough pills I could, I don't know, maybe somehow restart my life. Like I'd restart my laptop."

"You're not my first patient to say that."

She shot him a look, and he shrugged.

"A call for help, hm?"

"In retrospect, yes." Rebecca looked him straight in the eyes.

He blinked, then smiled. "I like an honest patient." He scooted his chair a bit closer. "Want to know my theory?"

She nodded.

"I think you're suffering from post-traumatic stress disorder brought about by the breakup of your relationship and the loss of your job, all fueled by what we psychiatrists like to call a deep depressive state."

She sighed, sank into the pillows. Depression, indeed.

"I've never been depressed before."

"It runs in the family," Granny said quietly, and Rebecca glanced over, questions swirling.

"And you've had quite a whirlwind, Rebecca." Dr. Carter's eyes softened. "In, what, twenty-four hours, you lost everything you associated with your identity in one fell swoop. When the depression took root, you had nothing else to temper it, nothing else to help you cope. It was only a matter of time before you went looking for Plan B."

Plan B in the form of a bottle of pills. Rebecca pressed her lips together, cheeks hot, warding off the tears.

All those years. All that time.

And now she had nothing.

And Peter was on top of the world.

Peter. Her "why" when he'd told her sounded pitiful even now. She remembered that "why," remembered how badly it hurt, how physically rotten she felt, everywhere. It was a wheezy, plaintive "why," raw and not remotely appealing. She'd almost made herself sick hearing it come out of her mouth, but she'd said it, again and again.

"Why" was all she could manage. She'd hit him, then, and he'd let her. Hit him with a vengeance, with her whole body, like she did the punching bag at the gym. As if hitting him would wake him up, make him see. Make him realize how much she loved him, how much he loved her.

But he didn't love her.

And the job. The job that had been everything. Gone, too. Weeks of going through the motions, fruitless job searches. That last interview, the one for the doe-eyed Ken doll with side-swept bangs and a fuzzy collar, he'd insinuated she was perhaps a smidge too old for the hustle. Old? Her?

Now she was empty. Stuck in this hospital bed with unwashed hair, her granny and Dr. Carter staring at her like she was glass, so fragile she might crack before their eyes.

Sniffing hard, she swiped at her cheeks. Thought about Ken doll and his dumb, patronizing smile. No. This is not how I'm going down.

"It's not going to happen again," she told them, looking first at Granny, then at Dr. Carter.

I'm going to make it on my own two feet. My own way. No pills, no pity party, no bones about it. I've got to.

Dr. Carter looked genuinely happy. "That's the spirit. So here's what we're going to do." He firmed his lips into a line as he scribbled something on a prescription pad. "We'll try Prozac, for starters. Next is the support network." He looked at Granny. "She's going to need you, you know."

Granny just nodded, squeezing Rebecca's hand like she'd known that all along. "That's why I'm here."

"I mean, need you around the clock. Preferably far from here, where she won't lapse into her old ways."

Rebecca opened her mouth to speak, but Granny held up a hand. "Already on that."

Rebecca blinked. "Granny?"

"Problem solved." Granny tucked her Bible into her purse, then clicked the clasp shut with a loud snap. "Rebecca's moving in with me."

"Wait, ah—what?"

Dr. Carter smiled. "Good. Where?"

Granny gave a small smile. "Dahlia, South Carolina. About as far from New York City as a body can get, heart, mind, and soul."

"We'll have to line up counseling there, of course," Dr. Carter said.

"Of course. Charlotte's an hour away. We can go there if needed."

"But—but what about a job? And Granny, I can't leave my apartment. I have fixed rent, and—"

Granny just smiled. "Don't you worry about a thing, sweet girl. I have it all worked out."

CHAPTER 2

Devon

He shut the back door with a light click, padded his way down the concrete steps and over the soft blanket of leaves that had fallen during the light rain the night before. The rain was so gentle it didn't even wake him, though when he'd woken on his own in the night and peeked out the curtains, he'd seen the water trickle like a miniature river down the driveway and to the street beyond. The tiny river comforted him somehow. Water was always a comfort.

"Have a good'un, sugar," his Memaw said from inside the house.

He looked up to see her standing at the cracked-up window, white curtains around her shoulders like a cape. He gave a wave, got a toothy smile in return.

Today would be a good day.

He hadn't even realized she was awake yet. He tried to be real quiet in the morning, tiptoe so she'd stay fast asleep. Memaw stayed up long into the night now. Aching bones, she said, and the summertime made it worse. When her asthma got to flaring up, she'd stay awake a long, long time, listening to her portable radio and reading her large-print Bible, the one her church friends had pitched in and bought her when her eyesight got real bad.

9

Often he woke up in the night now. It started way back when Mama was in the hospital. After the funeral, after he came back to Memaw's alone, he kept it up. He wasn't awake long, usually. Long enough just to peer out the window, see the moon or the stars, take a full deep breath and let it go. Let it all go. The burden's heavy, Mama liked to say, and sometimes you gotta put it down. But it's your burden, Devon Robinson. It stays where you stay.

God spoke to him the strongest in the night. Then he could more easily drown out the noise and the bustle and the pace, hear God's words, know his strength. Sometimes, if he was lucky, he'd sense just a little bit of Mama, too.

Last night was one of those God nights—no moon, stars tucked behind thick clouds, the only light coming from Mrs. Brown's porch across the way, shining onto the street and, just barely, onto Mama's memory garden, the stones and the cross and the tiny little plants like a beacon in the wet night. Maybe that's why he stayed up awhile, watching the river of rain in the glow from her porch light, waiting for God to give him a word, something so he could go back to sleep for the night.

At least Uncle Terrence hadn't come around last night, bringing his bad news and smoky clothes, picking through Memaw's wallet for whatever he could get his paws on. For that, Devon could be grateful.

Devon's own porch had no such light. They only ran power a little while in the afternoons and evenings, when Memaw had the strength to cook. Social security checks only ran so far. When she didn't feel up to cooking, they just opened up some of the pop-top cans he got from the backpack program at school. They didn't need much.

Last night, maybe it was thinking of Mama and the memory garden so much before bed, or maybe it was that they'd only had some of the leftover oatmeal packets mixed with warm water from the sink, he found himself up an unusually long time. He'd finally pulled out the Bible, the one she'd given him, the one that had been hers with all the underlines and notes in the margins. Now his underlines were in there, too. He used blue pen for his, so he could tell which were his markings and which were hers. Hers were black and far more numerous, but in the two years he'd had the Bible, he'd done his share of blue, so that now when he flipped through, the black and blue markings jumped out, mixing together. His words were in there, too, mixed with hers.

"Be content with what you have, for he has said, 'I will never leave you nor forsake you,'" was last night's verse, from Hebrews. He thought about it now as he walked across the leaves and onto the rutted pavement. That verse was one of Mama's favorites, the one she'd clung to at the end, in the hospital bed. The soft prayer shawl knitted by the grannies at church had been tucked around her thin bones, blues and pinks and greens like springtime against her caramel skin. She'd looked so small those last few days, and he'd known what was coming. Mama had told him, and Memaw, and the grannies from church. Rev and Marla, too.

But it was one thing to know and one thing to see. And some nights he remembered the seeing all too well.

No matter. One day he'd be with her again. Jesus himself had promised that.

For now, he had living to do. Surviving. Taking care of Memaw. Him and her.

He passed the memory garden, making sure to kiss his fingers before bending down and gently touching the small wooden cross, the one Mama had helped him set in the center. So you'll remember me, she'd told him, and remember I'll always love you, and remember that one day we'll be together.

He reached the stop sign early, tugged on the cords of his backpack while he waited for the school bus. Theirs was the middle stop, so he didn't have too long to wait. And he'd get the hot breakfast when he arrived. That would calm the rumbling in his belly for sure. Today was eggs day.

"Yo, Dev, seen your uncle lately?" came a voice from behind, and some laughter, the bad gonna-get-you kind. Devon's heart skipped, then settled into a dull thud. It's nothing. Someone cursed in Spanish, and Marquis, who used to be his friend and now hung out with the mean kids, gave him a good-natured smack on the head, shoved by.

Devon just nodded hello, walked past to stand on the corner. He caught Shenise's eye, gave her a smile.

CJ walked up then, stood by him. In no time, the bus pulled up, and they all piled on.

Devon didn't need to pay those guys any attention at all, didn't even look at them. He just needed to focus on school and keeping his nose clean. Just like Memaw always said.

Today would be a good day. He'd make sure of that.

CHAPTER 3

Rebecca

A SUITCASE IN EACH HAND, Rebecca stood there on Granny's white-painted porch, the sharp click of the key turning in the lock matching the thrum of her heart.

I'll be fine. I'm always fine.

No. Not always. Memory hit her hard and fast—the neat pile of pills, the bitter taste as they slid down her throat, catching on her tongue until she forced them all straight down. One at a time, then five at a time, into the pit. Her pulse pounded in her ears, her throat, so fast and thick she thought for a moment Granny could hear it, standing there next to her.

She'd never be fine. Never be all right again.

"There!" Granny said, and the world slid back to Dahlia as the front door opened wide and Rebecca felt herself and her suitcases ushered inside, the feel of Granny's hand steady and almost too warm on her back. "Home sweet home. Welcome back, sweet girl."

A loud thwack made Rebecca jump as the screen door swung shut behind them, her neck prickling even as she reminded herself: It was a sound straight from her childhood. The sound of summertime.

Get it together, Rebecca. It had been four weeks. Surely she was getting a little better. Coping. Wasn't she? She'd nailed the interview, even. Gotten the job in Dahlia like it'd been meant to be. It was a far cry from New York, but it was something.

Granny bustled ahead, flicking on small lamps, her low heels clicking over the hardwood floors and thin rugs, then the linoleum in the kitchen.

Swallowing hard, Rebecca set her two heavy suitcases down in the foyer and let her oversized handbag sink onto the bench by the door. The floorboards creaked as she did, and Rebecca peered around in spite of herself, gasped.

"Granny, it's almost as I remembered it."

Rebecca stepped to the old-fashioned settee, pressed down on the brocade, ran a hand over the smooth wooden armrest. Her lips felt tight against her teeth, and she realized she was smiling.

Granny laughed, called from the kitchen, "I'm not sure if that's good or bad."

"Oh, it's good."

Rebecca scanned the living room, taking it all in afresh—the crown molding and antique rose wallpaper, the smattering of lamps and doilies interspersed with Gramps's old leather recliner. Even though Gramps had been gone years now, died when Rebecca was in her twenties, she still thought of it as "his" recliner, just like she still thought of it as "his" office or "his" tool shed. Closing her eyes, she breathed in, imagined she could still catch the faint scent of his pipe, hear the low murmur of the television in the background.

A lump settled in her throat, the tight-teeth smile gone. She swallowed past the burn.

"Is Gramps's tool shed still out back?"

She forced sunshine into her voice, stepped into the living room fully now. One of the lamps, the peacock one with all the blues and greens, still had the crack in the corner from where she'd once tossed a marble by mistake. Granny had said then that the crack added character. Looking at it now, Rebecca felt badly about it, about how cavalier she'd once been. She'd been cavalier about a lot of things.

"Sure is." Granny reappeared, this time with a faded blue dish-towel in her hands. "You probably still have your old tool bench and apron out there. Remember the summer he tried to teach you woodturning?"

"Talk about a disaster." Rebecca remembered the way he'd patiently showed her how to hold the wood and use the lathe, and how desperate she'd been to get the lesson over and done with so she could run off and go fishing. Funny how now she'd give anything to do those years over again, stand in the musty shed shoulder-to-shoulder with Gramps as he guided her hands, pointed out the difference between wormy chestnut and teak, oak, and pine.

A quiet settled over her, the gloom hard like a rock in her stomach.

Her parents had sent her from Washington to Dahlia every summer, hoping to instill some small-town morality in their too-big-for-her-britches city kid, especially after she'd discovered boys and a rebellious streak. She'd hated it at first, hated Dahlia and the heat and the lessons, hated being in the middle of nowhere away from her friends. But the lessons stuck, and by the end of the summer she'd completed a few pieces. One she still had, a pretty little mahogany box, used it to keep her rings.

Her chest tightened. Rings.

Was everything going to remind her of Peter? She didn't think she could bear it.

Rebecca willed herself not to think of him. To think instead of Sarah, and the spring wedding her friend was planning. No. She wouldn't spend her life pining over him. This was supposed to be her fresh start. Wasn't it?

The memory of the pills came again, the ugly dome of tiny white ovals against the smooth oak of her computer desk. All the pain. All she'd done.

"He did love teaching you." Granny's voice sounded almost too light, and she felt rather than saw Granny studying her.

Rebecca met Granny's eyes, tried to smile, but her lips wouldn't cooperate. Sighed instead.

"I loved it, too. And you—Granny, I loved being here with you, too. I hope you know that."

"Ah, girl, I know it." The light tone was gone now. Silence fell, heavy as night.

To think she'd almost let it all go. Given up. Guilt swirled—for Sarah finding her, for Granny dropping everything and coming to her. Rescuing her. Tears pricked.

"Granny … thanks." Her words came out in a tumble, and she swallowed thickly. "For letting me come here, for getting on that plane with me this morning, for making me leave all that mess behind—"

"Sweet girl, I'd do it a thousand times over."

She would. Rebecca knew that without question. Suddenly, all she wanted to do was sleep.

A moment passed, then another. Granny motioned to the staircase.

"Why don't you take your bags up to your old room and get settled. I'll see what's in the icebox for supper."

"You're sure? I can come right back down and help."

Granny waved a hand like she was shooing a fly.

"I have so many premade suppers I'm swimming in them. Go on." Granny waved again. "Get settled and I'll get things started."

Shouldering her handbag, Rebecca started up the stairs with her first suitcase. Her legs felt like lead—no, rubber—as she pictured the bed in the guestroom at the end of the hall, imagined herself rolled up in the soft summertime quilt. Alone and still.

She stopped after a few steps, gazing up at the embroidered scriptures above. "Seek the Lord while he may be found; call upon him while he is near—Isaiah 55:6," read one. At the landing, she read another: "Have I not commanded you? Be strong and courageous. Do not be frightened, and do not be dismayed, for the Lord your God is with you wherever you go—Joshua 1:9."

For as long as Rebecca had remembered, Granny's faith had been a cornerstone of her life—and, judging from the décor, a tangible part of this house. Even when Gramps had died after a short battle with cancer, Granny had seemed to wear her faith like a suit of armor.

Years later, Rebecca still marveled at her strength—the same kind of strength and determination she'd shown propelling Rebecca to Dahlia, from lining up job prospects to booking their flight. Granny liked to call it gumption, and Rebecca knew her dad, Granny's only son, had it too. It served him well in the courtroom and even stronger behind the scenes, working the system, climbing the ladder.

Her parents thought her coming to Dahlia and taking the newspaper job was a good idea. Sarah and Marisol thought so, too. After all, Granny seemed to have it all worked out. In no time, she'd lined up a tenant for Rebecca's apartment and, perhaps most remarkably, the job in Dahlia. It turned out the former editor of the *Dahlia Weekly* had stepped down due to heart issues, and the local newspaper needed someone pronto. Granny called it a "God thing," pulled a few strings, and lined up a phone interview.

Rebecca just called it coincidence.

But she'd aced the interview, and with a glowing recommendation from her former boss—Ed owed her that much, after all his broken promises—and a portfolio of award-winning articles to her name, not to mention a willingness to work for the ridiculously low salary they offered, Rebecca had the job.

It was almost too easy. Scary-easy.

"Take it, work your magic, and enjoy this time with your Granny," Sarah had told her in the hospital room as they were waiting for Rebecca to be discharged, her blue eyes sympathetic. "I know it's not what you wanted, but after everything … well."

"Yeah. I know." After everything, indeed.

"We'll get you back to normal soon. This will open doors. It has to."

As she reached the top step, Rebecca had the sinking feeling nothing would ever be quite normal again. Her stomach churned, and she shook her head, steeled her jaw.

Swallowing hard, she headed down the hall to her room.

The next morning, she woke in a tangle of bed sheets, one sock on, the other who knew where. She lay still a moment, listening to the steady tick of the clock, which felt off-kilter with her own heartbeat. The smell of bacon and coffee had her pulling on a robe, padding downstairs.

Granny was nowhere in sight.

A note beside the coffeemaker caught her eye. "Louise drove me to church for the knitting circle. Bacon and eggs warming in the oven, keys are on the hook. Can't wait to hear what you think of the *Dahlia Weekly*. Love you. Granny."

Rebecca clenched her stomach, her chest tight and itchy beneath the light cotton. Today was meet-the-staff-day, always awkward anywhere, but especially here, where she barely knew the dialect, let alone what to wear. She pictured her closet full of suits and wrap-dresses, the labels that used to mean so much. Somehow she doubted they'd matter one bit here. Granny was letting her borrow the Buick. Car shopping would come later in the week, after she had a day or two to get her bearings. All she needed to do now was muster the get-up-and-go.

Except she had no get-up or go.

The heaviness settled again like a cloak. How in the world was she going to run an office, even one in the middle of nowhere, when she couldn't even keep the job she'd had? Peter had seen it, cut his losses. Jumped ship. If she was being brutally honest, she had, too. Weren't the pills proof of that?

She managed two strips of bacon and a forkful of eggs, slid the rest in the trash beneath the coffee grounds. Even the thought of food made her queasy right now. Sleep, when it finally came, had been restless and sporadic, filled with dreams she couldn't remember and a deep pool of dread in her belly when she woke.

The coffee cup felt slick in her palms, and she forced herself to breathe.

You're not the first person to start a new job in a new city, Rebecca. Not the first person to rebound after life's tanked beneath you.

But it just felt too soon. She wanted to run back upstairs, bury her head in the feather pillows.

Instead, she gulped down the rest of the coffee and headed to her room. Extra concealer hid the dark circles, and she slid on a pair of black trousers, a lavender silk blouse. Not too dressy for Dahlia. A coat of lip gloss and some blush, then she faced the mirror, gave her best nice-to-meet-you-this-will-be-fun smile.

You've got this. Except ... she didn't.

The dread sank ever deeper.

At the newspaper office, she slid out of the car, surveyed the squat wooden building set back from the road, baskets of pink and yellow petunias flanking the entry. The sign out front looked like it'd been scrubbed down with sandpaper, and the last "a" in Dahlia was so worn it looked like an "o." Dahlio? For a moment, an un-bidden image of the elegant glass-and-steel high-rise, her daily backdrop in New York, filled her mind. No.

She bit her lip, stepped inside. The brown fake-wood paneling had to be straight out of the seventies—sixties, even—and the place smelled like mildewed paper, dry-erase markers, and some-one's gardenia perfume.

The staff wasn't impressive either. The reporter, Tiff, looked six-teen and sounded eleven, with a breathy voice and stilettos so high Rebecca took mental bets whether she'd fall flat on her face stand-ing up to shake hands. The ad representative, Dinah, had a spray-on tan and cracked her gum when she talked. Millie, the secretary, pursed her lips so tight Rebecca would have sworn she'd just eaten a sour pickle.

"Pleased to meet you," Millie said in a thick Southern accent, sounding anything but pleased.

Rebecca's throat tightened. "Likewise."

She got out of there as fast as she reasonably could, mentally berating herself as she drove toward Granny's and the solace of her guest room. What in the world did I get myself into? She surveyed the homes as she drove—pretty wooden houses, all of them at least sixty years old, a few renovated surprisingly well, nearly all with porch swings and rockers and wide expanses of lawn that boasted tree houses and gardens and tire swings, everything wholesome and sweet and classic Americana.

Everything she was not.

The early summer sun was high and bright as Rebecca navigat-ed the busy Main Street, making a mental note to remember the coffee shop, Joe Mama's, a surprisingly chic little place for Dahlia. It was nestled between a frumpy boutique and the hardware store her Granny and Gramps used to own before he died.

As she drove, she peered down a side street, caught a glimpse of water. The Wahca River, where she used to spend hours fishing, first with Gramps and later with her pal JJ, a freckle-faced, chubby, pimply kid who'd taught her to net the fish without killing them and hung out, mostly content to let her talk at him while they baited hooks and cast lines. Fishing. She didn't think she'd done that in twenty-something years.

She glanced down at her sleek trousers, her leather briefcase in the passenger seat next to her—both entirely wrong for Dahlia, she knew it—and felt light years away from the girl she'd been in those summers. She didn't even have the same hair color anymore, all blond and streaky now, thanks to her colorist. Had that summertime girl ever really existed? Sometimes she felt like she was living in a dream, like she was completely separate from her body, swimming an inch above her skin. Treading water. Holding her breath. Like she wasn't even real.

A wave of longing for her old life back in the Big Apple struck her like a gut-punch. Sarah and Marisol, the bustle of the streets, the galleries, the restaurants, the pace of the city, everything. Now here she was in Dahlia, South Carolina, about as far away from New York as she could possibly get. While Granny and Dr. Carter thought that was a good thing, Rebecca had some serious doubts.

Forget doubts. This was a mistake. A Class A, one-hundred-percent mistake.

She gripped the steering wheel, heart thrumming as she stared at a man in overalls in the car next to her, a woman on the corner in a bright yellow "Jesus Is My Co-Pilot" T-shirt.

What on earth am I doing here?

CHAPTER 4

Devon

AFTER SCHOOL GOT OUT, Devon hurried to the corner store to help Mr. Allen awhile before heading up to the church. Mr. Allen usually gave him a dollar or two and whatever leftover muffins he had from the morning, the ones that wouldn't be good enough to sell the next day. Today, Mr. Allen tucked an extra juice box in the plastic grocery bag, his knotted-up hands shaking a little as he tied the bag up tight.

"For the sweeping." He patted Devon roughly on the shoulder, leaned hard on the cane. "You're a good boy. Your mama would be proud."

Mama had worked for Mr. Allen since she was a young woman. Had even met Devon's daddy there, too, though A.J. Robinson wasn't much cut out for life in rural South Carolina. Mama'd said the lure of the city was too much for any woman to keep his daddy pinned down. Who knew where he was now. No matter, she'd always told Devon. She said Devon's love was more than enough for any woman, worth more than three good men put together. Devon believed her. Mama had a way of making him feel like a million bucks and then some.

Devon took the shortcut to the church, cut through some alleyways to avoid Marquis and his gang. He didn't need to, but it was better that way. Easier to avoid temptation than confront it head-on.

Sweat pooled at his lower back as he walked, beading his upper lip, soaking his brow. At the corner, his knees felt weak as he scanned the street—all clear—then let out a breath he didn't realize he was holding. No sign of Marquis.

He sucked at the juice box, the sugar making the heat seem not so bad. His dark shirt didn't show much sweat, thankfully, and by the time he got to the top of the hill and past the row of rundown houses and the one barber shop, he was ready for a break. "The Reverend Mack Bryant, Pastor" the sign out front proclaimed, along with "Dahlia Community Bible Church" and the ten o'clock Sunday worship time.

"Hey, hey, hey," came the melodious voice, and he looked up to see Rev walking toward him, a grin on his face and his hand out for a shake. Rev's shirtsleeves were rolled up, and his dark skin made the light yellow fabric stand out. Rev mopped at his brow with a handkerchief.

"How's it going, Devon?" Rev asked, and Devon shook his hand, thumbed toward his backpack.

"Got the papers right here."

"Awesome, my friend. Most awesome." Rev gestured to the little brick church, and its open door. "Come on in and cool off. We'll have some sodas and go over it."

Devon took a seat at the table in Rev's office, pulled out the blue two-pocket folder with three full pages of signatures front-and-back. The bottle caps made a long hiss as Rev twisted them off and tossed them in the trashcan. The room was cool and dim; Rev didn't like to work in harsh light, said the fluorescents gave him a headache. Instead he kept the window curtains open wide, letting in natural light. Long rays of afternoon sun beamed across the room and onto the table where they sat.

"Three hundred signatures, Rev. I counted them twice." Devon slid the papers over. "All parents and guardians."

Rev reviewed the names, nodded here and there.

"Suzanne Lawson signed?" His mouth opened a little when he got to the name.

"Yessir. Said she had a change of heart, didn't want to stand in the way of progress. Especially if it was going to be free."

Rev threw back his head and laughed, a long, loud laugh that Devon himself couldn't help but join.

Devon had worked for two weeks to get those signatures, and tonight Rev and Marla and some of the other church folk were going to link up and take the idea, his idea, to the town council. The West Dahlia Leaders Summer Enrichment Camp. Though it'd probably always be Fun School in his mind.

No one knew but Devon that it was CJ who'd really started it. Even CJ didn't know it. CJ, who'd been bullied and picked on since kindergarten, who wouldn't even leave the house now except for school. Last summer, CJ'd spent the whole nine-week break indoors, terrified of Marquis and Johnny Vasquez and Big Ty, Marquis's older brother. Johnny had thought it would be fun to name a target for the summer. Every time CJ set foot out of the house, they were waiting. Sometimes they threw stuff at him. Soggy, rotten trash from the dumpster. The last time it had been a dirty diaper. CJ didn't even go to the free lunch up at the community center.

Devon had tried to talk to Marquis about it but Marquis had just laughed at him.

"Wanna be next, Dev?" he'd asked, bouncing the basketball over and over. Thwop. Thwop. Thwop. Brows raised, more of a challenge than a question. "We're always looking for volunteers. Volunteers for something else, too. But there's time on that."

Devon knew what that meant. Drugs. Marquis's older brother already had him dealing on the side. But that was one path Devon planned to steer far, far clear of. He was nothing like Uncle T. Nothing. Never would be. Not ever.

When school started back in August, CJ had lost so much weight his pants were hanging off him. Devon asked around, found out a lot of other kids had had a rough summer, too. There was nothing to do but get together in the big field and play soccer and basketball and stuff, or hang out on the corner, but the fighting and bullying was a problem. Del Dominguez got busted for stealing candy at the dollar store. One of the girls from a lower grade got her hoop earrings ripped out after she called another girl a freak for insulting her sister. Devon stayed busy helping Memaw, and Mr. Allen at the store, but most of the other kids didn't have anything.

And then Ms. Haywood their teacher started in on dipping test scores and summer slump and that's when the idea had hit him—a summer church camp, but with a school side, too. Teachers could help, and he knew the church folk always liked to pitch in. Rev said so all the time. Parents wouldn't say no if it was free, and the kids would have someplace safe to go each day. James Watkins was one of the poorest schools in the region, an inner city school—the teachers were always talking about it. Said it was part of the Corridor of Shame or something.

Rev and Marla thought the camp was brilliant. They'd gotten all of Dahlia Community Bible Church on board and even brought it to their big Dahlia churches group for help.

Rev thought if they could get the town council on board tonight, especially with all the church support and all the signatures Devon had collected, they could maybe get the program rolling as soon as school let out. Devon even had the kids write personal notes about why they wanted the program. Marla'd already drafted a curriculum and lined up the teachers. All they needed now was the final go-ahead for the meal funding and the okay to use the school.

"You can still come tonight? To the town meeting?" Rev asked. "Marla and I can pick you up, do some dinner first. We can go to Sally's. It's all-you-can-eat fried chicken night."

"Sure." Devon didn't want to seem too eager, but he was already salivating over it. He couldn't remember the last time he'd had fried chicken. Yes, he could—four weeks ago, at the church Homecoming. Fried chicken, and corn on the cob, and mashed potatoes with a little cheddar cheese mixed in, and collards and lima beans and Miss Nessie's bacon green bean casserole with the little crunchy onion things on top. Memaw had even managed to make a chocolate cake, though at the last minute her hip hurt too much and she had to stay home in the bed while Devon walked it up the six blocks to the church.

Rev hugged him when he left. "Pick you up at five thirty sharp."

As Devon darted down the steps, he could see a few of the guys from Marquis's gang sitting on the stoop across from the gas station. One of the guys looked straight at him, and Devon's heart did a slow somersault until he felt Rev's hand on his shoulder.

Rev cocked his head, stared hard at the boys till they looked away and started flipping a half-empty bottle of Mountain Dew instead. Devon could hear their laughter. Hard. Like they'd laughed at CJ.

"See you, Rev." Devon gave a little wave.

And he ran home as fast as he could to help Memaw and do his homework and chores, feeling Rev's watchful eyes on his back, hoping against hope that tonight was a night Uncle T would stay far, far, far away.

CHAPTER 5

Rebecca

Rebecca sat at her desk at the Dahlia Weekly, reviewing news copy and fanning herself with last week's paper. It had been three weeks since she'd moved here, three weeks of sweltering heat and frizzy hair and shirts that always felt damp against her lower back. Millie, the office manager, had the air-conditioning on full blast and the fans going, and Rebecca still felt like she needed an ice bath.

Three weeks of pretending she was getting into her groove, like she didn't take mini-breaks in the bathroom pressing her head into her hands and wondering why-why-why-in-the-world she'd ever agreed to uproot her life and move to this—this town named after a flower, where everyone sounded like an extra in *Gone With the Wind* and bandied about "bless your hearts" and "how's your mama 'n' thems" every other minute. Not to mention running a barely-hanging-on-newspaper.

Oh, right. Granny. And that bottle of pills. And Peter. Her mouth suddenly felt like a desert, and she realized she was clenching her red pen so tight her knuckles had started to ache. She loosened her grip, forced herself to breathe.

A fresh start wasn't bad. It was just, well. Different. She could say it a million times over, try to convince herself all she wanted, but at the end of the day, living in Dahlia was about the most frustrating thing she'd ever experienced. People were nice. She shouldn't complain. It could be so much worse. But it wasn't New York. Wasn't anywhere near New York.

"Why bless yer heart, sugar," Millie was saying into the phone, like whoever was on the other end was a relative or close friend. Maybe it was. "You really think she did that?"

Get off the phone, Millie. Rebecca literally had to bite her tongue to keep from saying the words. Making nice on the phone was customer service after all, even if it was production day, and they were already behind, and the sooner Millie got off the phone, the sooner they could finish the classified layout.

The door jangled then, slammed open so hard the frame rattled and the doorknob bounced against the doorstop, and Rebecca looked up, her heart beginning a slow, uncomfortable thud. It was an older man, his face red and his eyes squinted.

And he was heading straight toward her.

"You've got some nerve."

The vein in her head began to throb as she stared at the man. He was no taller than her reporter, Tiff Steadman, in heels, and almost as skinny, but between the balled fists and the hot gleam in his eye, it didn't take rocket science to figure out he meant business. Outside, someone in a waiting pickup gunned the engine.

She squared her shoulders against the roar in her ears and stood to face him. She could feel the eyes of her staff upon her, saw Millie hang up the phone.

"Beg pardon?" Rebecca managed in the most ladylike voice she could muster, fingernails digging into her palms so they wouldn't quiver.

"You heard me." His voice was a hiss, and she wanted to take a step back. "That was my mother, hear? I don't know what they did up north where you come from, but 'round here, we take last respects serious in our town paper."

She recognized his voice. He'd called that morning. Hung up on her, in fact. She leveled her shoulders, spine straight and chin raised. Her childhood ballet teacher would have been proud. A flame of anger began to push past the fear.

"Mr. Calhoun, with all due respect, we're a business, not a charity, and as I tried to explain on the phone before you cut me off, we cannot run obituaries for free in this newspaper any longer. We're just losing too much money." She softened her tone. "I'm sorry for your loss, truly I am, but—"

"Sorry?" The man barked out a laugh, lips tight behind his grizzled beard. He loomed closer, and she could smell bitter coffee on his breath. "You're sorry?"

Rebecca swallowed, pressed sweaty hands against her thighs. Her heart was pounding so hard she imagined he could see it through her thin summer blouse. She raised her chin, opened her mouth to speak, but he waved a hand and pressed on.

"We're family here, not some outsider-run business. I don't care who your granny is. Mark my words, Miss Yankee. You're gonna make some enemies in this town if you keep this up—"

"Now, Jim." A quiet but stern voice spoke up from the far side of the room. Millie.

"Don't you 'now Jim' me, Millie Jeffers." He glared over his shoulder at Millie, then pointed hard at Rebecca. "We don't need you in this town. Remember that."

And with that he was out the door and climbing in the passenger side of the pickup, wheels spinning out as they pulled onto the main road.

Rebecca closed her eyes, took five slow, deep breaths, jaw tight to keep the shaking at bay, every exhalation punctuated with the unspoken thought: I will not let this get to me. She opened her eyes to find all three of her staff staring at her—Millie, Tiff, and Dinah the advertising representative. The smallest staff she'd ever had. Tiff let out a nervous giggle, and the vein in Rebecca's head began to pound anew.

"Okay, back to work, people. We go to press in an hour." She clapped her hands, made shooing motions. "Don't tell me you've never had a complaint before."

"Not like that."

Millie kept her tone low, but the emphasis on the word "that" was not lost on Rebecca.

"They'll get used to it." Rebecca's voice was tired.

She felt rather than saw Millie press her lips into a line. "Lot of changes lately."

"And lots more coming." Rebecca rubbed her neck. "Look, Millie, they hired me to turn this paper around and make some money, save everyone's jobs, and keep the paper afloat. That's what I'm trying to do, all right? And I'd appreciate it if you'd try to get on board with that."

Millie tensed, appeared to consider whether to say more, then let out a soft sigh. She turned back to the reception desk, roller-chair creaking.

Rebecca closed her eyes and turned back to her own desk, willing her emotions under control. She pictured the bottle of antidepressants in her purse, her new therapist's number printed in bold black on the label, and gritted her teeth. Once she'd prided herself on her ability to brush off insults and confrontations like they were nothing. Now everything meant more. Stung more.

She missed her old life so badly she could almost taste it. She knew she didn't fit in here, knew only Granny lent her legitimacy, though that was marginal at best and quickly wearing thin.

As Rebecca was leaving an hour later, paper done, Millie stopped her.

"Honey, I give you this in love." She handed Rebecca a pale-blue scrap of paper. On it was printed in a precise, firm hand: Do not be overcome by evil, but overcome evil with good. Romans 12:21.

Rebecca raised her eyebrows.

"Don't let them get under your skin, is all." Millie's voice was quiet, the words soft as butter and the accent just as smooth. "But remember: If you do the right thing, you'll come out on top."

"Thanks." Rebecca tried to smile. "Well, at least for tonight, I'm going to make like Madonna and celebrate. The paper is done, it looks fantastic, and I'm ready for a bubble bath and a good book."

"Who's Madonna?" Tiff blurted from her desk, then looked immediately like she wanted to eat her words. Even Millie turned to look at Tiff this time.

"Madonna, the pop star? You know—'Material Girl,' 'Vogue,' 'Lucky Star?'" Rebecca waited for Tiff to remember. Nothing.

"Sorry." Tiff blushed, tapped way-too-high stilettos against the base of the chair in a nervous click-click. "Before my time?"

Rebecca bit back a barb. "See you tomorrow."

Pocketing the scripture, she slung her purse over her shoulder and headed out.

Back at the house, Rebecca found Granny on her knees in the rich brown dirt, her face shielded from the late afternoon sun by an oversized straw hat and her gloved hands buried in a mass of tangled roots and soil. She looked supremely, gloriously alive—nothing like her eighty-four years on this earth. She hummed to herself as she worked, occasionally speaking to the delicate baby plants.

"There you go, little one, into the soft ground where you'll stay snug and safe," Granny murmured as Rebecca approached, smiling a little as she guided the young plant into the dirt and patted the excess back around, just right.

Granny always said talking to her plants made them grow faster, stronger, and healthier than when she didn't. She also said when you earned your wrinkles you earned license to do as you darn well pleased. Well, within reason.

Rebecca watched as Granny scooped up the rest of the leaves and one sad, squished half-root and piled them into a mound, then seemed to decide to bury them, too, and see what happened.

Her face broke into a grin as she looked at Rebecca.

"Never hurts to take a risk when it comes to growing things. In my experience, sometimes the worst mess of nothing can sprout the most vibrant testament to life."

Rebecca grinned back. "I like that philosophy."

Granny offered her cheek for a kiss.

"How's the newspaper? Did you finish layout?" She peeled off her gardening gloves and slipped them into the bucket, along with the rest of the tools and scraps.

"Thankfully, yes." Rebecca sat on the edge of the porch, briefcase at her feet, and rubbed her neck. "It wasn't difficult so much as tedious. And it takes forever to do layout here. The computers are old, and my reporter is just out of college and—I don't know, Granny." She paused, unsure of how much to say, then shrugged. "It's not what I'm used to."

"I know, honey." Granny gave her a sympathetic smile.

"You do?"

Granny cast her a look, settled on the porch step next to her granddaughter.

"I know what it's like to be a long way from everything you're used to, feeling like a square peg in a round hole, where everyone knows the customs and ways and manner of dress, and you're left stumbling along, figuring it all out on your own."

Rebecca looked over at her, remembering.

"It was hard for you, wasn't it? After your parents died."

"That's right. I was fourteen, and my sisters and I were lucky enough to be taken in by our aunt and uncle here in Dahlia, though all of us were far more accustomed to farm work than town life. But you sink or you swim. I swam. Though it doesn't make the process any easier. And Dahlia, well, I know it's a long way from the Big Apple."

"It really is." Rebecca nodded, throat suddenly tight. "I know it'll take time. But some days, Granny ..."

"The paper needs a lot of work."

Rebecca's eyes flashed. "Yes. And my reporter is a kid. She needs training on absolutely everything. The ad rep practically requires a shove for me to get her out of her chair to sell ads, unless it's to her five best friends in town. And the secretary always gives me these disapproving glares or 'helpful suggestions.' It's like I'm fighting an uphill battle."

Granny laughed. "Sweet girl, you've been a fighter since the day you were born. You weren't breathing, and your dad turned bone white he was so worried. The birth nearly killed you and your mom, but you both made it."

"Dad always said I was handful enough for three kids, even though he and Mom couldn't have any more after me." Rebecca said it lightly, like there wasn't a bucket full of psychoanalysis down that well. If they would have had more kids, it might have made her life easier, taken some of the pressure off. But she didn't have to think about that now. Ever, really.

She leaned back and closed her eyes, savoring the afternoon sun. Little gnats buzzed around her legs and arms, but she paid them no notice.

Granny ruffled Rebecca's hair lightly and Rebecca smiled. "Those summers you visited me and your grandfather were wonderful, but yes, I do remember a young lady full of gumption, ready to take on the world."

She reached over, clasped Rebecca's hand. Love you, Granny squeezed twice. Love you back, Rebecca squeezed in reply.

"Thanks, Granny. For being there." Rebecca swallowed, eyes moist.

"Always, Becca." The moment lingered, tender and sweet.

"Granny. Becca?"

Granny giggled.

"Old habits die hard."

"Hey, Granny—thanks. For everything"

"I'm here if you need me." Granny softened her words, looked deep into Rebecca's eyes. "There's nothing I won't do to help."

The moment drew out, like a deep, consuming breath. Then with a little shake, Rebecca squeezed her hard and kissed her hair.

"I know, Granny. Believe me, I know." She stood. "I'm going to head to my room, do a little work, and try to clear my mind. I'll be down in a bit to help with supper."

Later that evening, after dishes were done and Granny had headed out to whatever food mission she was doing at her church, Rebecca sat on the full-sized bed in the upstairs guest room, laptop on her legs and four neat stacks of paper piled around her. The mattress creaked as she shifted a bit farther back against the antique headboard, the feather pillows pressed snugly as she made her little nest. She'd updated the newspaper's website earlier with a teaser about next week's articles, and now she was trying—without success—to get back online for the third time that night.

"It's like the Dark Ages in this town," she muttered and jabbed in the Wi-Fi password one more time. She forced her eyes off the screen and across the room, the old saying about the watched pot firm in her mind. Her eyes fell on one of the embroidered scriptures Granny had framed and scattered throughout the house: "If you abide in me, and my words abide in you, ask whatever you wish, and it will be done for you—John 15:7."

Rebecca glared at the words. *I wish I could get a blasted Internet connection. What do you say to that?* She knew she was being petulant, even if her therapist had told her anger was not a bad thing—at the very least a more active way of dealing with her feelings. But there were millions of people starving around the world, or dying from a preventable disease, and all she could think of was getting online. She couldn't even connect through her cell phone hotspot because for some reason it didn't work here. Even the cellular carrier couldn't explain it. Dahlia truly felt like the middle of nowhere.

Five minutes later, she shut the laptop with a hearty smack. She'd wake up early tomorrow and handle it at the newspaper office. At least there they had a decent wired connection.

She piled the paperwork in alternating stacks back into her briefcase, then picked up her cell phone and started exploring social media from her phone's data plan. She could connect that way still, thankfully. No one even seemed to notice the slow Internet but her, and that made her feel even more like an anomaly. Even Tiff, who was probably used to being able to search the internet, stream music, and shop online simultaneously, waited patiently for a slow-as-molasses webpage to load as though the pace here in Dahlia was no big deal.

She scrolled through the feed, relaxing now that she was connected to the outside world in some way, liking some posts, commenting on others. And then she couldn't help it. Her mind said no, but all the willpower in the world couldn't stop her fingers from typing his name in the search box.

Peter Montclair.

In an instant, he was there on the screen, dark full hair and gorgeous teeth, looking larger than life and impossibly handsome. She could feel her heart pound beneath her T-shirt. Squeezing shut her eyes a moment, she forced herself to count to five, then looked again. Maybe it was her imagination, but the grin seemed a bit smarmy. Fakey sincere. She looked closer, decided his hairline was receding. Serves you right. She scrolled down, and her stomach clenched. There he was again, covered in glow paint, his arms around a younger woman, the "other woman," both grinning their sickeningly white smiles at the finish line of some hip nighttime 5K run in the city.

"You two are the perfect couple!" Someone had commented below the picture. Her stomach roiled and she gritted her teeth harder, kept scrolling.

There they were again, at a gala dressed to the nines, and again somewhere in Central Park with a little yapping dog on a leash at their feet. Peter hated tiny dogs, their little mouths and beady eyes. Called them snake food. What was he doing with this woman?

She stopped after the final set of photos: Engagement Party. At one of his and Rebecca's favorite restaurants. The one where she'd hoped he'd propose to her, and instead where he'd proposed to someone else. She'd seen the photos before, but it still stung to know how quickly he'd moved on. Like she was nothing.

Now he was getting married to someone else. Someone who looked a good ten years younger, who looked cute and charming and fun and, well, vivacious was the word that came to mind. Rebecca scowled at the woman, at her pert nose and friendly green eyes and long, wavy red hair. He didn't even have the decency to pick someone a little bit like her. He'd picked the polar opposite, like he wanted someone as far away from Rebecca as he could possibly get.

Rebecca swallowed hard, a wave of heat coursing through her, then fished in her purse and pulled out the antidepressants, turned the bottle so she could see her therapist's name and number. "Call anytime," the woman had told her. "I'm here for you."

Her fingers started to punch in the numbers on the cell phone, then she jabbed the "off" button and tossed the phone aside.

No. I'm doing this on my own. It's my head, my problem, and I'm the one who needs to be sorting it out, not my therapist. She liked Nancy, even liked their weekly sessions. She probably should have been in counseling years ago. But she was darned if she was going to start relying on someone else to save the day.

I'm going to make it, and I'm going to make it my way.

And with that, she piled all her work and her laptop on the nightstand, turned off the light, and willed herself to go to sleep.

CHAPTER 6

Devon

THE SOUND WAS SOFT at first, then louder, calling to him in the underwater world of his dreams. Devon buried his head deeper in his pillows, but he couldn't ignore it.

Then came the slam of the car door, the chirp of the alarm.

He'd know that sound anywhere.

Uncle Terrence.

Quickly Devon slipped out of bed and to the door of his room, listening. Maybe he'd dreamed it. He ducked his head around the corner, peered into Memaw's room. Faint snores, then a long stop, then snores again.

Outside, he could hear the crunch of shoes on gravel, the telltale pop of twigs.

For a moment, he debated sliding the deadbolt, keeping him out, but he knew Uncle T would only pound on the door, hard, then harder, then holler until he woke Memaw and the neighbors and anyone else within earshot.

If he let him in now, maybe Memaw would at least stay asleep till morning.

"Uncle Terrence?" He crept to the door, whispered.

The sound of cursing echoed faintly from behind the door as his uncle dropped something, scrambled for it.

Devon sighed, switched on the porch light. He turned the lock, creaked open the door.

"Ain't you s'posed to be 'sleep?" Uncle T said, squinting his eyes at the light.

"Woke up to go to the bathroom and heard your car." Devon stepped back to let him in, then bolted the door after him and stepped aside, keeping a wide gap between them. He knew better than to get within grabbing distance.

T cocked his head, and Devon could smell the night on him—booze and cigarettes, something else sour behind the cologne. He staggered, and Devon realized he was drunk. Or something.

"Memaw's asleep, Uncle T. Do you need a place to sleep? Want a pillow? Some blankets?"

"Shoo, ain't tired yet, boy." He fumbled in his shirt pocket, pulled out a cigarette. "Want one?" T laughed at himself. "Started myself when I was your age, you know what I'm sayin'? What're you now, fifteen?"

"Eleven. Uncle T, you're not supposed to be smoking in the house. Memaw's asthma."

T sighed, flopped down on the couch, looked around like he was missing something.

Devon waited.

"Wha—where's the TV?"

"It broke."

"What the—you don't have a television?"

"Not anymore, sir."

T made a face, upped his voice an octave. "'No, sir.' Somebody rob y'all? What kind of house is this? Sound like Uncle T need to be steppin' up round here."

"Honestly it's fine." Devon peered at the wall clock. After two o'clock. He stifled a yawn. "I'm gonna head to bed. School tomorrow."

He left T on the sofa muttering and looking at his cell phone. Quietly, he snagged Memaw's purse from the hall table, tucked it safely in his closet. Last time T came by, his uncle had helped himself to a couple of fifties from her purse, said he'd come back the next day with more. That was weeks ago.

Devon twisted the little lock on his bedroom doorknob and got back under the covers, but sleep wouldn't come for a long, long time.

In the morning, he tried to slip out without waking anyone, but he found Uncle T and Memaw in the kitchen. Memaw was pouring him a cup of coffee, her gnarled hands shaking with age. T had stacks of bags and money lined up on the kitchen table, counting.

"Morning," Devon muttered.

"Hush up, now, you made me lose count." T shot him a glare, went back to the stacks.

Memaw kissed his head and motioned to the counter. She looked happy.

"Your Uncle T brought doughnuts. Help yourself, sugar."

"No, thanks, Memaw. I'm not hungry."

T brought a fist down on the table. "Too good for doughnuts now, boy? That's straight-up whack. This the thanks I get for showin' up, trying to take care of my family? What're they teachin' you down at that school?"

Devon watched Memaw lay a gentle hand on T's shoulder.

"Now, Terrence, Devon's said he's not hungry—"

"How can a person not be hungry for a doughnut. You feel me? It's a dang doughnut, for g—"

"They feed us at school, Uncle T." Devon slipped his backpack on, gave Memaw a peck on the cheek. "See you tonight."

"Got the Friday Night Giveaway tonight, Devon?"

"Yes, ma'am."

"You be safe now."

Uncle T's voice, going on and on about church and the giveaway, faded as Devon crunched down the driveway. Left it all behind.

He paused at Mama's memory garden as he went, kissed his fingers and touched the smooth wooden cross. He blinked hard as he gazed at the cross, at the tiny heart that used to be red and was now a faded brown, painted into the center. Miss you, Mama. Miss you like mad. Carefully, he tugged at some of the thicker plants at the edge of the memory garden, the ones threatening to move in and overwhelm the others. The bigger plants were like bullies, growing wild and fast during the hot months, trying to exert their might and power over the smaller ones. But unlike bullies, these plants you couldn't ignore and they'd get bored, go away. You had to deal with these, rip them out at the root, or they'd take over.

He tossed the scraps into the trees, brushed his hands on his shorts, then headed for the bus stop.

"Uncle T's bringin' you into the family business, huh." Marquis pursed his lips and jostled him as Devon approached.

Devon ignored him, crossed the street to stand by CJ and Shenise and her friend, the Latina girl with the braids and the skull and crossbones pin on her backpack.

"What's that for?" he asked her, pointed to the pin.

She shrugged. "My tio gave it to me when we moved here. Don't mean nothin'."

"Just asking. You going to the enrichment program this summer?"

She gave him a look like he was crazy. "What enrichment program?"

Shenise rolled her eyes. "You know, Gabby. The thing I was telling you about yesterday. It's free, right Devon?"

"Yeah. Rev Bryant set it all up with the town. Starts the Monday after school lets out. Free lunch, free everything."

"Oh, that." Gabby let her tongue loll out of her mouth. "Who wants to go to school for the summer?"

"Hey mamasita, careful with that tongue," one of Marquis' friends called out, laughing. Gabby held up a fist, and they laughed harder.

"Come on, Gab. Everyone's going. I mean, what else are we gonna do? Beats hanging out with them all summer." Shenise shot a glance at the trio on the corner.

CJ looked at Devon. "I'll be there."

Devon nodded. "Cool. Me, too."

The bus pulled up, and as they piled on, Devon could see his uncle's car cruise slowly by, low bass pumping from the speakers. Then T gunned the engine and roared off.

Devon watched the car until it turned the corner and the bus passed it by.

Don't come back. We're fine on our own.

CHAPTER 7

Rebecca

THE JUNE SUN WAS STILL LOW in the sky Saturday morning as Rebecca eased her run from a full throttle into the cooldown. Her feet made slapping sounds as she jogged the wide loop of sidewalk from Main Street past the post office and turned right onto Church Street, where the newspaper office was nestled. Despite the early hour, it was blazing hot. Her hair was matted to her head and neck, her T-shirt drenched, and the bugs nipped at her ankles already.

Her therapist said she needed to get regular exercise, said the release of endorphins would help keep the depression at bay. And she didn't disagree; she'd packed on a few extra pounds the last couple months between the binge eating during crying jags and the Prozac, which made her feel puffy and nauseous. She knew as well as anyone she needed to get better, get her "me" back. Get back to normal and, as soon as possible, get back to New York.

She took a mouthful from her water bottle and surveyed the street. She supposed some people would call it idyllic, and truly it was pretty. The sidewalks were the older kind, chunky not-so-perfect concrete, and little tufts of grass peeked up from the cracks in places where property owners hadn't stringently clipped them back. The slabs were uneven here and there, which was murder on her joints, and in one spot, the sidewalk wrapped around a tree, its roots gnarled and older than the town itself.

Church Street wasn't the most creative name, but it was apt. Lining the street was church after church—Baptist, Presbyterian, a tiny Church of God on the left at the end. Granny's church was there on the right, and she studied the cheerful brick façade, marveled that while the church looked like any other, with its stained glass and statues and cutesy little sign advertising worship times and the requisite soul-save, within those walls at any hour could be any number of happenings. Granny had told her that while the church was technically part of a denomination, that aspect of it had almost been forgotten. It had become such an integral part of the town that people just called it Dahlia First. There was even talk of a name change.

Granny was active in church. Rebecca supposed with Gramps gone, her only child moved away, and most of her friends active in church, too, Granny would naturally gravitate there as a home away from home, but it seemed like every day she was dropping off yarn for the prayer shawl knitters, popping in to organize the preschool art supplies or teach some Bible class, or delivering food for the church's once-a-month teen dance party, like she'd done last night.

How did they all fit in that place? Rebecca cocked her head as she took her slow jog to a brisk walk. She was out of breath anyway, felt a twinge in her hip that made her recognize she was definitely not in her twenties anymore. Or her thirties. A flash came of Peter and his new fiancée at the 5K, and she scowled as she forced herself to think of something, anything else. Who cared if Peter and Ms. Bouncy Hair Pert Nose had the energy of two kids? She had more important things to worry about.

Like her paper. Or making it to the office before she collapsed from heat stroke.

She studied the pretty sanctuary and the no-frills fellowship hall, then realized too late she was also staring at the pastor, who'd come out of the parsonage and was waving at her like he meant it.

"Hey there, Miz Rebecca!" Granny's pastor Dave Benson, an older stick of a man with so many freckles she knew his pale hair had once been red, held a hose and was busy watering the church landscaping. Somehow the rubber slip-on shoes and khaki cargo shorts looked entirely out of place on this man of God, whom she half expected to be wearing some sort of collar or robe at home, and she stared a moment before remembering to respond.

"Hope to see you in church tomorrow with your granny," he called. "We'd love to have you."

"Thanks," she managed with a wave and kept walking. "Maybe so."

She had absolutely no intention of attending, but she'd found it was far more polite to be noncommittal than admit the truth: unless it was Christmas, Easter, or somebody's wedding, she'd rather be scanning headlines in her bed than dolled up in some flowery dress making niceties and drinking bad coffee after the service. God was fine, but she preferred a more solitary way to explore religion. Besides, the music drove her nuts.

And nuts was the last thing she needed to be feeling. She was sure her therapist would agree.

Her skin felt mildly cool, her cheeks returning to a semi-normal flush by the time she made it to the newspaper office, dug out the key from her running shorts, and let herself in.

"Well, good morning, Miss Becca!" The saccharine voice from behind made her jump, and she turned to find a woman with steel gray hair and vivid red walking shorts, already coiffed at seven o'clock. "I know your granny. Lib Pauling." She gestured to herself and beamed, one manicured hand firmly on her well-apportioned bosom, the other on the open newspaper office door.

"Please, call me Rebecca. Nice to meet you, Lib." Rebecca held out a hand, conscious of her sweat-drenched T-shirt and short running shorts, which Lib Pauling gave the once-over while still somehow maintaining eye contact. Becca. Would she ever escape that?

"I was just going to leave this outside, but here." Lib reached into her purse and pulled out an envelope, began to slide several glossy photos and a handwritten sheet of paper from it. Rebecca could see a wide-eyed, chubby-cheeked baby, and Lib grew animated. "My new precious grandbaby! Annette Lynae Richardson, after her mama's great auntie who passed two months ago, bless her. Would you look at those cheeks?"

Rebecca rolled her eyes inwardly and made nice over the pictures.

"You must be so proud! We'd love to run them. You do know our new policy, Lib?"

Lib smiled winningly and fanned herself with the envelope.

"Well, since I'm your granny's best friend and all, I figured that didn't apply to me."

Best friend? Not likely. Rebecca gave her most sympathetic expression.

"I really wish I could, but we've had to make a lot of changes to keep our numbers up. I'm sorry, but we have to charge for birth announcements and obituaries across the board now, no exceptions. Here, let me get you an ad sheet."

Lib's face pinked, and she fanned herself faster.

"I—charge? For a picture of my newborn granddaughter in my own town's newspaper?"

"Sorry, Lib." Rebecca tried a smile.

"It's Mrs. Pauling to you, and I hope you will reconsider that awful new policy." Lib straightened and snapped her purse shut with a sharp click. "You have no business charging for major town events like this. Why, half of us are kin to each other. Births and deaths are important." The words came out in a hiss. "That's, why, that's downright wrong to go and do something like that. Your Granny should be ashamed of you."

Here we go again. Rebecca pressed the ad sheet into the woman's hand. Lib took it, her head high. She turned and left without a backward glance.

Rebecca locked the front door after her and made sure the office sign was still turned to closed. Then she walked to her desk chair and slumped into it, taking a deep, centering breath. Despite what some people had insinuated, she had zero malice in charging for births and obits. But the paper was in serious trouble. They needed to cover their bottom line somehow.

She couldn't fail again. Not after New York. Not after—everything. If she did …

No. She couldn't allow the thought to even begin to form. You're not going there, Rebecca Chastain. Not now, not ever again.

She turned her attention to the stack of mail Millie had left for her yesterday. On top, printed on a pale blue sticky note in the secretary's firm, no-nonsense hand, were the words, "God is our refuge and strength, a very present help in trouble—Psalm 46." She eyed the note as she tore open the bank account statement, swallowed hard as she realized how low their reserves had dipped. At this rate, unless they managed some new ad accounts, they wouldn't have enough to make it till fall out of their checking, and continuing to rely on savings wasn't sustainable. She did some quick calculations, then opened a file on her computer, plugged in a few numbers. Better for now, but it still didn't look good. And she didn't want to lose any staff, at this point. Not that they had that many to lose.

She glanced at some of the "extreme measures" she'd listed—cutting the ad rep and charging for calendar items—and knew they'd go over even worse than the births and obits ruckus, but it felt good to have a plan.

A loud knock came, and she started. A middle-aged man stood at the door, peering in, clearly unsure if anyone was inside. She froze. The last thing she wanted to do right now was talk to anybody. After a minute, he decided the office was indeed closed, slipped an envelope through the mail flap, and walked back down the sidewalk.

When he was long-gone, she fetched the envelope.

> Dear editor,
>
> I don't normally write to the paper, but I have been a reader and subscriber of the *Dahlia Weekly* for twenty-seven years, since I got a free year as a delivery boy when I was fourteen. My parents and their parents read the paper. All my neighbors and friends read the paper. Or did.
>
> We all know the paper has taken a downward slide in the last few years, but these latest changes are the last straw. Charging for announcements like we are some big-city publication goes against everything that makes Dahlia what it is: a community-first kind of town where you are proud to know and love your neighbors. And your recent policy limiting what you call "features" in favor of "hard news" is completely backwards.
>
> People in this town like reading good news about our friends. Call it old-fashioned, but we like stories about Mr. Johnston's pick-your-own blueberry farm, or the annual pictures of the end-of-year field trip, which you decided to nix. It hurt my son's feelings pretty bad when he didn't get to see his friends in the paper. I tried to explain, but frankly,

I don't understand either.

I highly recommend you reconsider your policies or you will find yourself entirely out of subscribers—and a job.

Sincerely, Joshua L. Jamison

He'd printed an address and phone number, all by the book, the whole thing far less than three hundred words, which meant it met all the standards for publication as a legitimate letter-to-the-editor. The other letters she'd received had either been anonymous, or way too long, or contained name-calling and other slams, so even though she'd gotten her share of nasty calls and complaints, she'd actually been able to avoid printing anything in the paper. But this letter was fair game.

Well, fine, Joshua L. Jamison. I'll publish your stupid letter. This isn't the first time I've had to face the flames, and I've always come through.

She remembered the slams she'd gotten for months in New York over outing the senator's daughter's drug habit, or the time her old managing editor had gone to bat for her after she'd embarrassed the publisher's wife with an expose of her law firm. In a strange way, she sort of admired Joshua the Letter-Writer. His name sounded familiar, but she couldn't place it. Still, it was a good letter. Objective, fair, pointing out the issue while allowing just enough emotion so others could relate.

And not even a single derogatory comment, while still managing virtuous outrage.

Well done, you self-righteous jerk.

She filed the letter in the typing stack for Tiff, then listened to her voicemail to find a cancelled subscription, two more complaint calls, and the most atrociously hokey story pitch possible, suggesting she do a profile on somebody's great-aunt who'd gone to college with Meryl Streep. As if. She gathered her keys and refilled her water bottle. Time for some coffee and a walk the long way home. She'd show Peter and his 5K-running fiancée.

"Well, hey, honey!" The high-pitched voice accosted her the moment she stepped into the sunlight. She peered and saw a track-suited older lady waving vigorously from a trim house two doors down. "Aren't you the workaholic—in the office at eight on a Saturday morning!"

Rebecca's smile felt dry and tight over her teeth. "That's me. Hello, Mrs. Blackwelder."

"Have a good day, sugar. I'm praying for you. Oh, now look out!"

Look out? Rebecca whirled to start down the steps and almost ran straight into a very tall, very well-built man who looked almost as taken-aback as she did. He wore a crisp blue and white button-down and a bowtie that somehow managed to look good on him, not in the least bit pompous.

"Good morning!" He grinned, an arm out to steady her.

"Good morning, yourself," she said, breathless, self-conscious for the second time that day. "Can I help you with anything?"

"Well, I was just looking for the new editor, Rebecca Chastain." He looked sheepish. "I know it's a Saturday, but I guess I was just hoping to catch her and pitch a business idea."

"I'm Rebecca," she said, then took a step back, realizing she was gazing up at him. She motioned to her running clothes, forced a confident laugh. "Obviously I'm not dressed for work, but I have a few minutes if you want to talk now. Or we can chat next week."

He was even more handsome than Peter, if that was possible. The morning sunlight glinted off golden hair that was professionally styled, yet somehow tousled in a boyishly appealing way, and his biceps ...

Stop it, Rebecca. Stop it now. Dating is off-limits, Nancy had reminded her in numerous therapy sessions. She needed to work on herself. Not that she wanted to date anyone anytime soon. But she certainly didn't need to allow herself to get giddy over some perfect stranger.

"I'd love to talk now, if you really don't mind." He grinned again, motioned to the folders in his hand. "I won't take long, but I'd love to show you something. I'm Erik, by the way. Erik Wennerman."

"Nice to meet you, Erik." She shook his hand, plastered on her professional smile.

She unlocked the door and motioned him inside, leaving the door open to send a clear message: All business.

Sitting back down behind her desk, she gestured to the chair in front of her.

"Have a seat. So, how can we help you?"

"Well, I'm hoping it will be a mutually beneficial arrangement." Erik sat up straight as he pushed one of the glossy folders before her, a well-designed logo for Wennerman Incorporated emblazoned in bold blue, black, and yellow on the front, with a yellow circle a bit like a setting sun on the horizon. "My family runs a number of retirement communities in the area, and we partner with the local newspapers group to place advertising in every one of their newspapers in a three-hundred-mile radius."

"Wow."

"It's a big reach." He smiled again. "They offer us a good deal, and in exchange we commit to consistent weekly advertising support for every one of their papers. I got to thinking that your paper, even though it's private ownership, might be interested in a similar arrangement."

"How much are you talking?"

He slid the pricing sheet toward her, and she tried to keep a neutral face. It was significantly lower than the *Dahlia Weekly's* normal ad rate.

"But it's weekly support," he said, eying her. "It would help us reach seniors in this area, which could be a strong market for us, and it would help you drive sales, which I'm sure you can use."

The newspaper's bank account balance flashed in her mind, and wheels began to turn.

"I'll have to think about it—"

"Of course! There's no rush. I happened to be in Dahlia today visiting my great-aunt and thought I'd pop by, introduce myself."

She took the folder and the pricing sheet, slid it into her stack. "I'm really glad you did."

His smile widened. "Me, too."

Rebecca felt her cheeks begin to flush, and she stood, offered a hand.

"Well, it's nice meeting you, Erik. Can I give you a call next week?"

"I'd love that."

He stood, and they walked to the door together. He waited at a respectful distance as she locked up, then stood to watch her go. She noticed his car parked on the street, a new-model black Audi convertible—much nicer than the one Peter had kept in the garage—and gave a goodbye wave.

And turning to head home, she decided to skip the coffee in favor of a pounding all-out run.

She was out of breath and drenched by the time she got back to the house and found Granny in the kitchen, stirring something in a big pot over the stove.

"Gracious, girl, sit. You're soaked!" Granny motioned to one of the wooden chairs at the small kitchen table, and Rebecca did.

"I'm fine," she huffed out, laughing, but Granny brought her a tall glass of water, and she drank it gratefully.

Granny gave the pot one last stir and then joined her granddaughter at the table, where she had a big pile of string beans laid out on a dishtowel. She snapped the ends off a bean neatly into a big metal bowl and eyed Rebecca.

"So what's on your agenda today?"

Rebecca shrugged and forced a smile, her breath coming easier now. She thought about Erik Wennerman's ad pitch, carefully avoiding any thoughts about his physique, hair, and smile, and the bank account numbers, which were far less appealing.

"I don't know, work?"

"Oh, hon. You remind me of your Gramps." Granny snapped the ends of the string beans one by one, popped the good ones into the bowl, the action almost a percussion beat. Snap-snap-ting. Snap-snap-ting. Rebecca grabbed a bean and joined in, the motion coming back quickly, like riding a bike.

Granny used to force her to help when she was a miserable, anxiety-ridden teen, and she remembered that first summer how angry she'd been about it, wanting to escape upstairs to read or write a letter to a friend back home about the injustice of her parents sending her away for the entire summer. By the end of that summer, the bean-snapping had become their time. Girl Time, Granny had called it, where Granny would share about customers, or Rebecca would regale her about the bass she'd caught in the lake or the progress she'd made fixing up Gramps's tool shed. Granny and Gramps had paid her well that summer for helping part-time in the shop, claimed they needed the extra help, but looking back, Rebecca didn't think they needed much help at all. It was she who'd needed the help, the escape from all the sophomoric melodrama back home, even though she didn't think so at the time.

Her rhythm was smoother now, and Rebecca smiled at her granny.

"You mean the workaholic tendency? Some lady accused me of the same thing. Mrs. Blackwelder of the ever-present tracksuit? Lives by the newspaper office? 'Aren't you the workaholic—in the office at eight on a Saturday!'"

Rebecca exaggerated the accent in a clear falsetto, and Granny laughed out loud, not missing a beat as she snapped the beans.

"Well, Becca, I'd say she's probably right. You did a full run, then went to work?"

Rebecca shrugged. "I couldn't sleep. And besides," she said, pausing mid-snap to pat her thigh pointedly, "I'm forty now. Staying in shape isn't as effortless as it used to be."

"Oh, sweetie, you are beautiful. But I won't stop you from running. It's good for the body, good for the soul. Just take it easy. Life is not a marathon."

"I don't know, Granny. Sometimes I feel like when I slow down, I can't help but think of, well, everything." Rebecca bit the side of her lip as she snapped a bean. She cocked her head. "Ever feel you have to work sometimes just so you can't think? So you can't give yourself time to get depressed?"

Granny continued bean-snapping, but her eyes shifted to the window, scanning the pretty yard beyond like she was searching for something.

"After your Gramps died, I did that for a long time. Threw myself into work at the shop, work at home, work cleaning out his old tools and those dusty books he couldn't bear to throw away." She turned back to Rebecca. "But you know I was putting off the inevitable. Even though it felt right at the time. So I get it."

Rebecca nodded, not trusting her voice yet. After a moment, she whispered, "I thought Peter and I would be married by now."

"I know, girl." Granny's voice was soft. "You get through the best you know how. The sunshine is coming. Believe me."

Rebecca wished she could.

CHAPTER 8

Devon

UNCLE T STAYED AWAY for three weeks, long enough for Devon to finish ironing out the last details of the camp plans with Marla and Rev and get the flyers passed out to all the kids at James Watkins, and even at Dahlia Elementary in town, too. T stayed away so long Devon thought he'd finally gotten the message and wouldn't be coming back.

Truth be told, Devon knew nothing about planning this kind of stuff, but it felt pretty nice to be included. They always took him out for ice cream after, and dropped him off at home so he didn't have to walk.

"Didn't you use to have a bike?" Rev asked him last night.

"Someone stole it from the bike rack."

"At school?" Rev's mouth hung open.

"Yeah." He couldn't tell him Uncle T had thrown it against Me-maw's big oak tree out back last month, bent the frame so badly it was worthless. He couldn't even remember why Uncle T was mad. No good reason, most likely. Mama had gotten him that bike. Back then, it used to be too big.

Rev shook his head. "I'll see if I can round up another for you, and a lock, too. We always seem to be getting our hands on extra bikes and stuff here and there. Between the Friday Night Giveaway and everything else we do."

Devon just waved, hoping he didn't look as desperate as he felt. He'd love a bike, love a lot of things, to be honest. But sometimes it was better not to want. It made the not-having easier to deal with. If you never wanted anything, you didn't ever have to feel bad about what you didn't have.

But deep down, he wanted so much. Wanted it all. Wanted his mama back. Wanted a house with air conditioning and good food. Real food, not the kind that came out of a box or a can. Wanted not to have to worry about whether Memaw had enough money for medicine or whether Uncle T was going to show that night, digging for dollars and whatever else he was looking for.

Uncle T was Memaw's oldest child. Her only living child, now that Mama was gone. She and Mama had been quite the team, Prayer Warriors, they'd called themselves, and for as long as Mama had been alive, T stayed away.

"We don' want none a'that drug business, hear?" Devon had heard his Mama yell late one night, when he should have been in bed. "Get on now, T. You get outta here. You might be blood, but what you bring here is bad news, all around. Go and stay gone. You won't bring this family down. You won't bring my son down."

Her voice had been rough and raggedy, like she'd been crying. Devon knew he shouldn't have been listening, but he couldn't help himself.

"Your son's gonna be just like me, Arnetta," T had hollered back, but he'd gotten in his car, rolled down the window so he could holler some more. "Just you wait, hear?"

T was wrong. Devon would be nothing like Uncle T. He didn't care how much stuff T's drug money bought or that they were blood.

Once he was grown, Devon didn't plan to ever lay eyes on his uncle again. Not even at T's own funeral.

Memaw was a different story, though. Uncle T was her son, her only child left, and she had a soft spot for him, even though he used her and she full-well knew it.

"You think your Memaw knows Uncle T steals money from her purse?" CJ had whispered to him late one night. They'd had a sleepover, and the two boys had huddled in Devon's room with the lights out when T made one of his surprise visits. CJ's mom didn't let him come back after that, though Devon was always welcomed over at CJ's house.

"I don't know." But Devon imagined she probably did. Memaw was the kind of woman who'd give you the shirt off her back if you asked for it. Decent people wouldn't ask for it. Memaw was old, and her twisted-up knuckles were painful even to look at. Between the cane and the asthma and everything else, she was the kind of person you should be giving to, not taking from.

But Uncle T wasn't a decent person.

"Saint Devon," T'd taken to calling him last time he was there.

Devon tried to ignore him and steer clear, hoping against hope that he'd eventually go away. So far, he always did.

But tonight his luck had run out. When he got home from school and Mr. Allen's, Uncle T's brown Cadillac was in the driveway.

Devon tried not to drag his feet as he walked in to the smell of cooking meat and spices. Not only was T there but his friend, too, a man with a patch over one eye who T insisted Devon call Uncle Ray. The two were laughing and clinking glasses when Devon walked in.

"Where's Memaw?"

"Whassa matter wit'you, boy? Got no manners? Say hello to your Uncle Ray here."

Uncle Ray grinned, the silver on his teeth all shiny in the kitchen light. Devon saw a line of coiled, viney-looking tattoos run clear up the length of the man's arm. All black, except two blood-red eyes. Right in the head of a cobra.

A shiver ran down Devon's back. He tried to move past them, but T blocked the way.

"I said say hello to your Uncle Ray." T's words were like ice, and a hand reached out then, clamped Devon by the neck. Squeezed so hard Devon almost thought he was going to have to yell, but at the last second T let go, and all he let out was a breath.

"Hi, Uncle Ray. Hi, Uncle T." He muttered the words, wouldn't meet their eyes, just hoped they couldn't see the pounding of his chest beneath his shirt.

T stepped aside, and Devon slipped past, clutching the cords of his backpack.

"No respect, these kids," Devon could hear T mutter to Ray. "Gonna hafta teach 'im a thing or two, you feel me?"

He made a beeline for his room.

Memaw wasn't on the couch. He dropped the backpack on his bed, then tapped gently on her bedroom door.

"Memaw?"

No answer.

He tapped again, then gently opened the door.

Memaw was in bed, the covers drawn to her chin. Devon looked at the clock on her wall. Five-thirty. Memaw was never asleep at this time.

"Memaw?" He approached the bed. Still no answer.

He could see her chest rise and fall, but when he reached her, he saw she was shivering. Touching her brow, he pulled back. She was burning up. Fear fluttered in his belly.

"Memaw, are you okay?" He shook her slightly, but she didn't budge.

Darting out to the bathroom, he rummaged through the drawers and then the cabinet, looking for Tylenol or Advil. Something. Anything that would help bring down the fever. He looked in the trashcan, saw an empty bottle.

Heart pounding, he dashed back into Memaw's room, searching.

There. In the corner, he saw her familiar black pocketbook. Digging inside, he grabbed a few bills, stuffed them inside his pockets.

"Memaw's sick," he told T back in the kitchen.

"Shoo, when's she not?"

"Uncle T, she's burning up."

T's jaw set. "She's fine."

"Do you have any medicine?"

Ray laughed, a low, knowing laugh, and Devon sighed.

"Forget it." Starting for the door, he called over his shoulder, "I'll be back in a bit."

But at the drugstore, the pharmacist wouldn't give him antibiotics, not unless she came in and saw the clinic doctor or brought a prescription. He almost didn't sell Devon the Tylenol, pointed to the "no sales to minors" sign, but he must have noticed the look on Devon's face.

"Give her some ice chips, too, and plenty of water," the pharmacist said, ringing up the Tylenol. He was a big man, with giant frizzy sideburns and tiny rectangular glasses. "If she's not better tomorrow, call me and I'll see if we can get someone to go to the house. I know your Memaw doesn't get out."

"Thanks," Devon said, and ran the ten blocks back to the house.

When he got back, Ray was gone, and T was on his cell phone on the back porch, yelling at someone. Devon tiptoed into the kitchen for a tall glass of water and plenty of ice, then down the hall to Memaw's room.

"Thank you, honey," Memaw said, when he got her upright and put the pills and the glass of ice water in her hands. A little water sloshed out and onto the bed, but she didn't seem to notice. "You're a good, good boy. Good like your mama."

He slept in there that night, at the foot of her bed, reading his Bible for a long while.

Proverbs, mostly, and the psalms, and part of Kings, at one point. Psalm 28 was the one he read over and over. It was the one his Mama had read when she was so sick: "To you, O Lord, I call; my rock, be not deaf to me." And later, "The Lord is my strength and my shield; in him my heart trusts, and I am helped."

When he woke in the night to use the restroom, he felt Memaw's forehead. Thank you, Jesus.

The fever had broken.

He looked down at the Bible in his hands and back at the woman, his only link to Mama, his own mama's mama, there in the bed. What would happen to him if she got too sick, or worse—if she died? A rush of warmth hit him in the gut like a punch. He couldn't stay with Uncle T. He'd run away before he'd let that happen.

But what else was there? Foster care? He'd had friends who were bounced around in the system, spit back out like unwanted rags. Shane and T.C. That girl Lily. Horror stories.

He sank to his knees.

Please, God. Please let Memaw be okay. I can't go to foster care. Please—I'll do anything.

But God didn't answer.

CHAPTER 9

Rebecca

"WITH A MASTER'S IN JOURNALISM from New York University and a bachelor's from Syracuse, now all the way from New York City to run the *Dahlia Weekly*, please help me welcome Ms. Rebecca Chastain!"

Obligatory applause followed the gravelly voiced Rotary Club president's introduction, and Rebecca rose from the round breakfast table in the Baptist church fellowship hall to make her way to the front of the room, stand before a neat brown podium. Stay confident. Reigning in her nerves, she shook the older man's hand, then turned to smile at the room, the aroma of bacon and diner-style coffee so thick she could almost taste it. She searched the faces. Thirty-two of Dahlia's best and brightest business and community leaders there before her, and not one of them seemed remotely interested in what she had to say. She felt like the new kid in school.

She cleared her throat, gave her warmest grin, and tried her best to calm the shaking her hands wanted to do. She clutched the edge of the podium.

"Thank you so much for having me, and on behalf of the *Dahlia*

Weekly, I am grateful for your support of our newspaper institution and its critical role in this community."

Her pat speech lasted fourteen minutes—the history of the paper, the new price increases, the focus on bigger and more important hard news over some of those mindless features that used to eat up the front page. Only she didn't call them mindless. "Lighter" was the euphemism, and she inwardly applauded her tact. Everyone had loved Ron Stone, who'd been the editor since the eighties, but after he'd passed away and they'd hired that string of new editors, the paper had dwindled to a bunch of nothing, in Rebecca's private opinion. The last editor had taken what was already bland and ho-hummed it to a state of near irrelevance. She only hoped this crowd would see her efforts for what they were: a true attempt to save the paper.

"You, in the gray? Mr. Collins, is it?" She gestured to the balding man on the far left with his hand raised. She was pretty sure he was Reynolds Collins, president of Dahlia First Bank.

"I appreciate what you are saying, Ms. Chastain," he began in a slow drawl dripping with a healthy dose of fatherly patronization that made her wince, "and I'm sure it costs a lot of money to run your operation, but why take sections people love and cut them down to practically nothing? Like the high school sports section. My boys didn't get their picture in the paper once this spring. I don't know about the Big Apple, but that means a lot to us here in Dahlia. This town, and this Rotary Club, has a vested interest in what's going on at that paper."

She heard murmurs of agreement, and her heart thudded. Keep it together—they're not the enemy. They don't want to run you out of town. They only want a strong paper.

"You're right—it does cost a lot to run a paper." She made her voice as warm as she could. "We felt a six-page school sports section was a lot, so we're trying two pages, tightening photos, until we can grow advertising and circulation to the point where it's sustainable to run a bigger section."

A neatly coiffed woman in a beige pantsuit lifted a finger.

"Marge Dawkins, president of the Dahlia Historical Society. I understand charging for lengthy obituaries. They can get tedious, and perhaps not as well read as other sections." Her husky voice was gentle. "But I do question the wisdom of charging for birth announcements, which are short and, well, far more interesting. The last thing new parents need after an expensive birth is to have to shell out twenty-five dollars to have a new member of this town get proper recognition."

Rebecca's smile in return was genuine. "I understand. And I know this is hard for everyone. We will continue offering a basic listing, for free, of everyone who has died and been born, as a courtesy to this community. But as you said, standard obituaries are long, and baby pictures take a lot of room. In this business, space is money."

A man waved an arm. "Will you accept news suggestions?"

"Definitely. Call or email me," Rebecca said, and pointed to the short stack of business cards on the front table. "My contact information, including deadlines, is on that card."

Polite applause filled the room and she made her way to her seat, trying her best to still her nerves and be approachable, stay poised.

After, filing out with the others, she stopped to snag a banana from the breakfast table.

"Thanks for speaking with us," a voice said, and she turned to see a sandy-haired man in a button-down and khakis, his hand out for a shake. He looked familiar, really familiar. She found herself smiling almost on reflex, and grateful her talk had at least resonated with someone. "Can I offer some friendly advice? Just be careful."

"Careful?" Rebecca raised her eyebrows as she shook his hand, took a half step back.

His palm felt almost too warm against hers, and calloused. She tried to place where they'd met before, though in this town, with so many people related, it could merely be that she'd met his brother or father.

"You don't want to tighten your belt so much you cut off the blood flow and lose the whole thing. Take it from me," he said kindly. "I run a building company, and I've seen that happen on houses. You put in cheap tiles, cheap siding, and cheap carpet, scrimp on labor and cut too many corners, and pretty soon you wind up with a house not even worth the land it's on."

Rebecca considered the analogy. "Well, I'll definitely take your words to heart, but there's a difference between cheap and short."

"Not in this town. You cut out too many things and you're gonna find people don't even want to read it anymore. Just my opinion." He shrugged, and she peered at him closer. He definitely reminded her of someone, but who? "Anyway, I'm Joshua Jamison. Jamison Contracting."

His name jumped out at her. Jamison. The letter-writer. Her eyes glinted.

"You turned in a letter-to-the-editor Saturday."

A small smile hinted. "I'm one of those readers. And I mean no offense."

"None taken," she said like she meant it, then gave him a sideways look. "You know, Mr. Jamison, I remember that field trip photo. We have thirteen grades in Dahlia School, not to mention James Watkins Elementary on the edge of town, plus the preschool. Running field trip photos for all of them isn't easy."

Why wouldn't people understand the paper was a sinking ship, and she was trying her best to get it back on track? She let her hand trail into her purse, fingered the small bottle of Prozac.

He nodded. "I understand. I'm sure it's not newsworthy on a big scale, someplace else. But here in Dahlia, it's news to us. And it's tradition. You walk a fine line, and I don't envy you your job, but you've gotta weigh pictures of people's kids over, say, that national news roundup you started. They can get that on the Internet. Put yourself in our shoes a moment."

She let out a breath. "I'll try."

She was trying. But the last editors had left her with a colossal mess, and she needed to fix that before the paper could make any kind of strides whatsoever.

He smiled, again that something familiar nagging at her.

"Give it time. Get involved. You'll see what I mean." He turned to go, then paused. "Oh, and that letter wasn't meant for publication. It was just for you. To be helpful."

"I'm happy to print it, Mr. Jamison." Her voice was even, but inside her heart did a happy dance. She would love not to run it. She'd been in the business a long time, but the embarrassment of being publicly called out never got easy.

"Josh. And no, I'd rather you didn't. Just pray on it." He gave a half-wave, walked off.

She peeled the banana and took a bite, puzzling over his words. And frowning, she stepped out into the bright morning sun and decided Dahlia was quite possibly the strangest place she'd ever lived.

Back at the office, Rebecca had put out two sales fires and had finished giving a new article assignment to Tiff when the little bell over the door tinkled. She looked up to see two suited men walk in and survey the flurry of activity—including her ad rep on the ground with a pile of paperwork and her shoes off.

Her stomach dropped. Stuart Hansler and Buck McCafferty. The owners.

Rebecca plastered on a smile. "What a pleasant surprise! Staff, I hope you remember Mr. Hansler and Mr. McCafferty, our owners."

Tiff wiggled her fingers, and Dinah waved cheerfully. Millie stood and, to Rebecca's shock, gave both men a big hug.

"It's been a long time! How's that newest grandbaby of yours, Miss Millie?" Buck McCafferty's smile was open, sincere.

"Almost two now," Millie said with the biggest grin Rebecca had seen since she'd met the prim-faced woman. "Potty training," she stage-whispered, and the men chuckled.

"Mine turned three last week. What a love." Buck patted her shoulder. "You keep up the good work, and make sure to hug that baby's neck next time you see her."

"Sure will." Rebecca couldn't be sure, but it looked like Millie was downright blushing.

The men turned to Rebecca, shook hands all around.

Stuart Hansler jammed a thumb out, motioning to the conference room. "Got a minute?"

"Always." Her heart was pounding. It felt like New York all over again. She half expected Ed to walk in, cock his head, and say, "Sorry, sister," like he did last time. She gritted her teeth and followed them into the cramped wood-paneled room.

Stuart shut the door behind them, swiveled the blinds shut. Once they were settled at the round oak table, he laid some papers in front of her, sat back, and crossed his arms.

Financials.

"Gentlemen," she said smoothly, after a show of glancing at the papers and then deliberately setting them aside, "you hired me to turn this paper around. You knew the numbers were dismal before I started. They're still dismal. That doesn't change in mere weeks. What's going on here?"

She gestured to their circle around the table, leaned back. Be confident. She eyed Stuart first, then Buck. Both stared right back.

"Ms. Chastain, the numbers are even worse than before you started." Buck rubbed his hands on the legs of his tan suit, a large brass belt buckle peeking through. "We didn't expect a turnaround, but a twenty-percent drop this month is significant."

"I'm doing some radical changes to try to help numbers grow. Look at the expenses line." Rebecca tapped at a column on the paper. "Printing is way down."

Stuart pointed slightly above, his thin gray hair looking even thinner in the harsh fluorescents. "And look at circulation. Subscriptions are the lowest they've been in the history of this paper."

"For now, yes, but that's the initial fall-off of the wishy-washy subscriber base. The hard news we have lined up, the big investigative stories I've assigned our reporter, means they'll be climbing and even exceeding by—"

"I don't think you heard me." Stuart leaned forward, made sure she was looking directly in his eyes. "Subscriptions are the lowest they've been in the history of this paper." His voice grew softer with emphasis. "Why are we here if not for the readers?"

Her lips twisted. "I assumed this was a money-making endeavor for you."

"Money, yes, but we have a passion for small-town papers, Ms. Chastain," Buck said, his cool blue eyes unreadable. "And frankly, I'm not so sure you understand what makes this one tick. We thought with your Dahlia connection and the fact that you'd spent some summers here you had some sort of instinctive grasp of this town, but perhaps we were wrong."

"The calls I've been getting daily—yes, daily—from dissatisfied readers would knock your socks off, Ms. Chastain," Stuart said.

His eyes she could read. Hard, with a hint of red-hot anger.

"What we want is your action plan," Buck said, his voice tired. He pulled his cell phone from his front shirt pocket, scrolled through, then set it down before her so she could see the calendar view. "By Friday, we need to know exactly what you plan to do to turn this paper around in a way that is uniquely Dahlia. I need lists, concrete examples, and if it's what you call 'radical,' I need references to other papers where this has worked."

Rebecca's jaw was tight. She nodded.

Buck scrolled through the months view, got to December. He pointed, then gazed at her. His eyes were soft, and he looked genuinely troubled now.

"If we don't have hard progress by this date, the first of December, you're out of a job. That's six months." Buck held up a hand as she started to speak. "But not only that. If we don't make those numbers, we're closing the doors of the *Dahlia Weekly* forever. We've had offers to buy out, merge this paper with a bigger publication that wants a local offshoot of what they're already doing. The readers won't be left in the dark." He shrugged. "They just won't have the *Dahlia Weekly* anymore after decades of existence."

Closing the paper. Out of a job. Failing—again.

Her mouth was bone dry. She nodded.

"We don't want to let this paper go, Ms. Chastain. But it's been failing a long, long time. Since Ron Stone passed away, really." Stuart shook his head. "That was an editor, let me tell you. You might read up on him, see how he did things. You may bring twenty years of big-city experience, but Ron knew Dahlia, knew small towns."

Rebecca gritted her teeth. "Just bear with me, gentlemen. I have big plans for this paper. We're upping the quality of articles and photography, quality of paper, and—"

"Quality means little when there's no one left who cares."

Stuart rose. Meeting done.

Buck stood, too, and gathered the paperwork. He paused before opening the door.

"We're not playing games here, and we're not out to micromanage you. We'd rather have this paper open than closed, but frankly, we don't have time to babysit an operation that's on the way out. Stuart has four grandbabies, my daughter's due in November with her second, and we'd rather sell out now and focus on what really matters in life than throw shovels of dirt over something half in the ground." Buck raised his brows at her. "If you catch my drift."

"I catch your drift, Mr. McCafferty."

They opened the door, made nice with the staff, and were gone in their two-tone Lincoln within five minutes flat.

"What was that all about, Rebecca?" Tiff looked nervous, her skinny legs crossed tightly under her short skirt.

"One second, ladies—quick bathroom trip. Then we'll talk."

Rebecca fled to the restroom, locked the door, and willed her pounding heart to subside. She washed her hands carefully, then splashed a bit of cool water on her still-flushed cheeks.

She couldn't tell the staff, could she? Morale needed to stay high, and if they thought they were on a sinking ship, they'd bail out now. At least, she would if she were in their shoes.

No. They needed to know. If she was going to make any headway, they'd need to pull together like their lives depended on it. Their livelihoods did, at any rate. So did hers.

She took a breath, stared at her reflection. She thought she could see fine lines peeking through the makeup on her forehead, and dabbed a bit of restroom hand lotion, smoothed it in. There.

She knew what she needed to do—she needed to make her staff care. Make them want to step up. This wasn't going to be New York all over again. Not if she had any say.

Grabbing the door handle, she put on her show face.

"Okay, ladies, gather round." She snagged a chair and pulled it to the center of the room, perched as naturally and confidently as she could muster. "As you can imagine, the owners haven't been happy with the numbers. Ads are down." She looked at Dinah, who bit her lip. "Circulation is down." Millie had the sense to look down before Rebecca could meet her eye. One of Tiff's stiletto heels started its nervous tap-tapping. "They've given us six months to turn this thing around or they're closing us down."

Tiff gasped, and Millie's lips tightened, her expression unreadable.

"But—six months? I mean …" Dinah's face flushed, and her chest turned an odd shade of plum.

"We're going to do this." Rebecca held up a hand. "I didn't come all the way from New York with all my experience to run this thing into the ground. We're making great strides to improve quality right now. We just need to up our game."

Millie's face darkened. "I knew those complaint calls were taking a toll. I've been working here going on thirty years. The last thing I need to be doing is job hunting."

"I know. And I don't want to see that happen, either." Rebecca met their eyes. "I'm going to do everything in my power to keep us afloat. Got it?"

They nodded.

"So let's think about what we do have going for us." Rebecca gave her most reassuring smile. "For starters, the paper is a good product. Readable. Now we need to make sure our numbers reflect this, and that we're generating a product that is so stellar people can't help but subscribe. Tiff." She turned to the girl, who looked like a deer caught in headlights. "I'm promoting you to assistant editor. This means you have a bigger stake in this paper, so you need to work a lot harder seeking out big news. The kind of news that sells."

Tiff flushed a pretty shade of pink and nodded vigorously.

"Dinah and Millie." Rebecca turned to them. "I'm increasing your commissions ten percent each." Millie gasped, and Dinah's eyes were wide. "New sales only, but still, a sizable increase."

"That's double what we're making!" Dinah bounced a little in her swivel chair, her color returning to normal. "Thank you, Boss!"

"My pleasure." Rebecca clapped her hands. "So let's hop to it. I know we have some new changes around here, and yes, a lot of complaint calls. But we need to weather things a bit longer. People will get on board, and we'll make this happen. The sooner the better."

The circle scattered, and she was pleased to see Dinah pick up the Chamber of Commerce directory, no doubt scouring new businesses to contact. Millie looked energized, and Tiff seemed ready to burst with pride.

You just bought yourself three months of staff motivation with that little speech. Rebecca smiled inwardly, her stomach roiling. Now let's hope it works.

She looked down at her desk, and the Wennerman Incorporated folder caught her eye. Desperate times call for desperate measures, she reminded herself. She slid it out, thumbed through for Erik Wennerman's business card.

He answered on the first ring. "Erik, it's Rebecca Chast—"

"Rebecca! I've been hoping you'd call." Erik sounded genuinely pleased, and she found her cheeks were growing warmer.

"Erik, I've been doing some thinking, and I'd love to take you up on the advertising offer."

CHAPTER 10

Devon

MEMAW WAS WEAK after that fever, much weaker than she'd ever been. Devon took to making all the meals now. He knew how to make box meals, like mac n' cheese or those rice-and-bean combo things, but he'd figured out how to fry up chicken, when they had it, and after a few failed attempts, scramble some eggs.

T came and went. He was like a shark, Devon finally decided. Circling for the scent of blood, waiting for the kill.

He came home the last day of school to find T flipping through the mail.

"What are you doing?"

T whirled, clutching an envelope. "Social Security," Devon read on the return address.

"You're taking her checks, aren't you." He didn't mean to say it, but the words tumbled out, like they couldn't help themselves.

"Easy now, hustler. You think you all that? You at the bottom. You're living here rent-free. I'm her son. I deserve a cut, too."

"A cut? Is that what you think this is?" Devon heard his own voice turn up at the end, like a little kid's would, and he was mad for a minute, mad that his voice would betray him, mad because T would know he'd always win. Because at the end of the day that's all he really was, and they both knew it.

A little kid.

T shoved the stack of mail back at him, stomped through the house. "Don't you dis me."

Devon followed. Memaw's door was closed. Good—she was asleep.

"That money's for food, and medicine." He couldn't stop now. Had to see this thing through. "Besides, what do you need the money for, anyway? I thought your 'business' made lots of money."

T set his jaw. "You better watch your back, boy."

"Just leave her alone, all right? I'm trying to take care of her. Come on, Uncle T. Please?"

"You're nothing. She's my Maw."

"Then act like it."

He didn't even see it coming, just felt the roar of pain on the side of his cheek, by his ear. The room spun.

T's fist was clenched now, and he loomed above Devon, fire in his eyes.

"More where that came from, you little punk. I shoulda taught you some respect a long time ago. Your mama spoiled you rotten, and my mama's doin' the same thing. You walkin' 'round here like you're God's gift to the world and all that. Pfff. Uncle T's here to stay now. Mark my words."

Devon clutched at his cheek, heart thudding, and slowly backed away toward his bedroom.

He slipped out that night and down to the church. The Friday Night Giveaway was in full swing by the time he arrived.

"Thought you weren't gonna make it, doll baby," a tall woman with caramel-colored skin and a massive silver necklace said, pulling him in for a hug.

She moved back, caught a glimpse of his face in the fluorescent church lights.

"What in the world?"

"Long story, Miss Marla."

Marla frowned, grabbed his chin to peer at the mottled skin. "Long story, my foot. You been fighting? Don't lie to a preacher's wife." But she gave him a little wink and rubbed the top of his head. "Seriously—you all right?"

His mouth felt as dry as a sock, but he forced a shrug. "It was a dumb accident. I'm fine."

He couldn't tell her about Uncle T. Couldn't tell anybody what really went on at home. If they knew, they'd come fishing, and pretty soon he might find himself in a home like Shane and T.C. They said too much, someone from the state came snooping, and that was that. And then who'd take care of Mama's memory garden? Who'd take care of Memaw? They'd put her in some home, where she'd be a number, not a person. She needed to be with family.

Needed to be with him. They needed each other. Besides, he'd promised Mama.

He shook his head and realized Marla was looking at him still, gave a little laugh.

"Sorry, Memaw always says my mind likes to wander. So what can I do tonight?"

"I'm guessing the kitchen. You know the drill. Head on back."

He did know the drill. Giveaway Night was held every Friday in the fellowship hall of Dahlia Community Bible Church, and people from just about every church in town came to volunteer in one way or another. Even a couple people from the synagogue over in the city drove over a few times a month to help. He liked that word, synagogue, liked to imagine Jesus speaking to the people in one, like in the picture Rev kept in his office, propped against the long row of church books on his bookshelf. Jesus was just a kid in the picture, a kid like him, and he liked to think they would have been friends, him and Jesus, or at least that he could've followed Jesus around a bit. Like the boy who brought fishes and loaves. He could've been Jesus's helper. Mama always said it didn't matter how old you were. Even kids like him could do big things, good things. Important things.

To the right, the far wall was lined with folding tables that held pitchers of sweet tea and that night's dinner—tonight, chili and cornbread and big bowls of green salad. A handful of people were working in the kitchen, and against the back wall were several huge tables. There he saw Mr. Mike, who was passing out a bunch of mini bottles of shampoo and other products, and next to him, a lady in a green T-shirt and jeans was neatly stacking some clothing. Papa Toe was playing something on the big black piano, and the guests were all lined up in the front corner near the windows. In the center of the room were rows and rows of tables and chairs, people in almost every one, plates piled high.

"Hello, there, Devon," a woman's voice came from his left, and he waved and continued back to the kitchen, slipping on an apron and jumping right in.

Nearly two hours later, he, Marla, and Rev were relaxing at the tables with a handful of the other volunteers, the last dregs of chili and cornbread before them.

"That was Nelly Driggers's recipe," Marla said, spooning in her last bite and sighing contentedly.

"What's on the menu for next Friday?" a man at the end asked.

"Spaghetti and meatballs, and a great big cake," Rev said. "We'll be celebrating the first week of our brand new West Dahlia Leaders Summer Enrichment Camp, thanks to Devon here, who gets all the credit for the idea and the initiative."

Applause went up, and Devon hunched his shoulders.

"I'm proud of you, kiddo." Marla patted his shoulder. "Thanks to you, local kids can stay off the streets and get some academic direction."

"I hear they're even going to do some college prep for the older kids. Helen Chastain's got that part set," a woman, Annie somebody, said.

At the end of the night, Rev and Marla called him out back.

"Check out what just happened to roll in here this morning," Rev said.

And then he was wheeling out a black ten-speed bike from behind the shed. An actual ten-speed, with a basket in the back and a bell on the handlebars. It was a little beat up, but the tires looked full of air and the frame appeared straight.

Devon's jaw dropped. "You're kidding!"

"No joke, my friend. And a lock, too." Rev held it out to him, a shiny metal lock and chain. "The lock's a gift from me and Marla, and the bike is all yours. Consider it a thank you for all you've done for Dahlia and the kids. And for this church."

Devon blinked fast. The words wouldn't come at first, and it felt like he had a ginormous lump in his throat. But he swallowed past it, tried to smile.

"Wow. I—I don't know what to say."

Rev laughed. "Thanks is fine. Now, let's get you and your new bike loaded up. It's too late to bike home. We'll drop you off."

"I—uh. Thanks." The bike. It was his. He almost couldn't believe it.

"You're welcome, honey." Marla came up from behind her husband, wrapped Devon in a hug.

When they dropped him off, T's car was still out front. Devon's heart thudded. As soon as Rev and Marla were gone, he planned to lock his bike out back, far from where T could see it. No telling what "lesson" Uncle T would dream up if he saw Devon suddenly had a new bike.

"Did Memaw get a car?" Marla peered, squinting through the trees.

"Nah, that's Uncle T. He's visiting tonight." Devon busied himself gathering his lock and the bike, then gave them a wave. "See you Sunday."

"See you. Tell Memaw we hope she's feeling better, and we're prayin' for her."

Their car slowly backed out and down the long road, back to the parsonage.

A breeze swept through the trees, and Devon shivered. If he was lucky, T was on the phone, or even better, passed out. And crossing his fingers, he rolled the bike around back.

CHAPTER 11

Rebecca

"Come to church with me, Becca."

Granny set the last of the cookie trays on the Formica counter-top, the aroma taking Rebecca straight back to childhood.

"Pastor Dave's preaching on his mission trip to Guatemala. We can do brunch after! Dahlia's version of what you did in New York."

Rebecca inhaled deeply. She was huddled in her robe at the breakfast table, a huge mug of coffee before her. The soft morning sunlight cast shafts of white everywhere she looked—on the cookies that smelled simply amazing, on the morning paper before her, on Granny herself.

"Granny, this is the first morning I haven't gone anywhere in possibly two weeks," she said and smiled up, doing her best to project an exaggeratedly pitiful air.

Granny ruffled Rebecca's hair softly, pulled out the chair next to her. "You've been working like a madwoman lately."

Rebecca shrugged, slid the biscuits and plate of butter and rasp-berry jelly a little closer to Granny.

"You know why."

Granny twisted her lips. "You're gonna keel over before you even have a chance to save this thing."

"So says the woman who's awake at dawn most days, cooking for the homeless and wayward teenagers and some men's breakfast group and who knows what else." Rebecca elbowed her. "If you're not volunteering somewhere, you're working your tail off in the garden or that Zumba class you've been taking."

Granny suppressed a grin. "It's an exercise ministry, but you're right, I could slow down a hair."

"Workaholism runs in the family. At least that's what Daddy always said."

"Work is good for the soul, true, but there's a fine line, honey." Granny looked serious now. She put her hand over Rebecca's, her soft, dry palm patting gently. "I know you have a lot of pressure. I just don't want you to burn out. You're still meeting with Nancy each week for counseling?"

Rebecca made a face. "Yeah, and it's going well, but some weeks it's hard to find time."

"I hear you. But please, come to church with me. It's a beautiful day, and I'd love the company."

"Ah, Granny." She weighed her words and sighed. "Look, we've talked about this—organized religion isn't for me. I believe in God, I'm not saying I don't, but church and all that …."

She shook her head. The thought of going to church, dealing with all those people, made her palms itch.

"Maybe next week."

Disappointment flashed in Granny's eyes, but all she said was, "I hope so, sweet girl." Then she stood, kissed Rebecca on the top of the head. "I'm going to shower and get dressed for worship. See you in a bit."

An hour later, Granny out the door, Rebecca was in her room plotting this week's paper. The last few weeks had been a flurry of fast-paced, high-energy news gathering, writing, and production, peppered with a healthy dose of marketing and nightly number-crunching. She'd assigned Tiff the town beat, and the girl was cranking out political digs and deeper stories about what the latest votes might mean for Dahlia residents.

"No meeting is just a meeting," Rebecca had instructed her reporter. "The news isn't the meeting—it's what the action means for the readers. Why's the mayor touring two new businesses next week? Are we getting new industry here?"

For her part, Rebecca had delved into investigative pieces: Why was Dahlia still struggling with decent Internet speed? Was the economy worse off than people imagined? Still, for all the hard work, Dahlia's reaction to the harder news had been lukewarm. At least the complaints had tapered off.

Rebecca tucked the pencil behind her ear and leaned back against the pillow. She glanced out the window at the pretty summer day beyond, realized she was restless. A good run—maybe that was what she needed. Besides, Granny was right. It really was a beautiful day.

And with that, Rebecca stood, slipped off the robe and into a pair of running shorts and a T-shirt, laced up her sneakers, and pulled her hair back into a ponytail.

Fifteen minutes later, drenched and out of breath, she found herself on the banks of the Wahca River. Gramps had told her long ago the river was Dahlia's namesake—"wahca" meant flower in the Native Siouan language spoken by the Catawba tribes here hundreds of years ago. Rebecca flopped down on the riverbank and closed her eyes, breathed in the dark scent of soil and fish and river water. Did the Native Americans have any idea, all those years ago when they lived off the land and prayed to their Creator, that one day they'd be long gone? That this beautiful territory would soon get named after a fluffy, vibrantly colored blossom smuggled to America by the same European settlers who'd later chase the Native people from these parts forever?

She gazed across the river into the piney woodlands beyond and imagined herself a Native woman, there on the riverbank. Wondered how it might have felt to know your home was being taken over by strangers who wanted you gone, far away. From where she stood, she could see no sign of the town beyond, hear no cars or other sound indicating another soul for miles. Loneliness washed over her, and for a moment she could almost smell New York again—her favorite bakery on Barrow Street, the Japanese cherry trees in Central Park in late April, even the food vendors and exhaust from the taxicabs up and down the streets as she'd make her way into work. She felt utterly, completely alone.

What am I doing here? A lump gave way to tears. She brushed them away, but they came harder. Finally she gave in, let them take over for a moment, let the memories slide back. Peter. Her old life. Her old world. Her boss Ed Bannister and the look on his face the last time she'd seen him, the day she'd packed up her office and left it all behind.

Deep gulps of air came like an onslaught, and she covered her face with her arms, blocked out the sun and the easy breeze.

She'd had it all, and it was taken right out from under her. And now she was nothing. A failure in the middle of nowhere. Only Granny probably cared if she lived or died. Her parents? That was a joke; they'd probably come to her funeral and be right back playing tennis or in the courtroom the next day. It had been years since she'd last been home, and except for a quick phone call while she was in the hospital—when she'd assured them she was absolutely fine, thank you, no need to come visit—eons since they'd even talked. She and they were as different as night and day, and frankly, she didn't think she could stand job advice from her dad or the press of her mother's thin lips.

The only child of two self-absorbed workaholics knew when to stay far, far away. Even Granny couldn't argue with that.

Sitting up, she wiped her eyes and peered across the river. Years ago, twenty-six to be exact, she'd flung flat rocks across the smooth surface, watched them bounce and zip along while her Gramps strung fishing line and hooked a worm before he cast out, wide and perfect into the water. Bass, bream, and catfish swam in those waters, she knew. Later it was she who'd cast the lines, Gramps in his work shed or at the shop downtown.

She remembered the exhilaration she'd felt when she got that unexpected tug of line—she'd caught one!—and wished now she had a pole with her. Sometimes she'd throw the fish back, and other times she'd bring a few home for dinner. Granny and Gramps had even taught her to clean and cook them, something she hadn't done since she was a teenager. Maybe that's what I'll do. Come down here later, after dinner, and fish awhile. Back then, it had been a balm for her melodramatic teenaged heart and mind, the smooth feel of the fishing pole in her hands, the zing of line as it whipped gracefully over her head and into the water, the satisfying plop as it landed way out in the Wahca River. Maybe it would be the same kind of balm now.

She heard whistling behind her and whirled to see a man and young boy walking up the path, looking straight out of an episode from *The Andy Griffith Show*. Quickly she wiped her eyes and tightened her ponytail.

It was the boy whistling, and the man ruffled the kid's sandy hair as they walked. The tune sounded majestic, and their steps were in sync with the song. A deep brown dog followed, tail wagging as it sniffed at tree roots and tufts of grass. They were still far off—the path from the main trailhead was a long, relatively straight one— but Rebecca felt there was something familiar about the pair.

"Dad, what do you think Pastor would say about that song? 'All creatures of our God and king, lift up your voice with us and sing.'

Does that mean people and animals sing? Like when Choco howls at the fire sirens?" The boy thumbed back at the dog and whistled the tune some more.

Rebecca gathered her keys at the same time the pair noticed her. "Nice day."

"Don't leave on account of us," the man said with a smile. She noticed a pair of fishing poles slung over his shoulder.

As they got closer, she felt a glimmer of something—recognition?—and then her heart sank. Ugh, the letter-writer. Josh Jamison. Rebecca felt her smile tighten.

"It's okay, I really have to get back to work. The water looks good today."

"Work? On a Sunday?" The kid stared up at her, freckles dotting nearly every half-centimeter of his face.

"JJ, some people do have to work," Josh said. He gave Rebecca a wary but friendly look. "Say hello, son. This is the editor of our local newspaper."

"Did you say JJ?" Rebecca's eyes widened, and she shook the boy's hand. It couldn't be.

"That's his name, short for Josh Jamison Jr." Josh peered at her closely, and she met his gaze.

Years fell away as they stared at each other. A sharp staccato began in her chest then, and suddenly she remembered fishing on these same banks with a freckle-faced, overweight, acne-riddled teenaged boy named JJ, who used to bring apples and Hostess cupcakes to share after they'd caught a bucketful of catfish to bring home. The staccato became an all-out thrum. This had to be the same JJ.

Josh broke into a grin as Rebecca saw the recognition suddenly match her own.

"Should be Triple J, but Dad says that's a mouthful," the boy said, oblivious to the looks his father and Rebecca exchanged.

The Josh Jamison of today looked nothing like that pimply, chubby kid. Absolutely nothing. I mean, this Josh was downright cute. Handsome, really. If she was being purely objective.

"I'm nine," the kid prattled on, "definitely old enough to hook my own worm this summer."

"Becks? It is you, right? I should have realized." Josh's smile was as open as his son's, his shoulders doing that familiar half-shrug he'd done as a teen. The wary look was gone, as though it had never been. "You look so different. I mean completely different. All blonde and ladylike and professional-looking. No offense, but back then you were almost a tomboy—brown ponytail and baggy T-shirts and none of that makeup stuff. And of course, there's the whole 'Rebecca' thing. If you didn't have the whole ponytail hair-do deal going today, I might not have even made the connection. Well!" He took a breath, held out his hand for their old handshake. "Good to see you, Becks."

She returned the handshake, smiled in spite of herself.

"Becks. I haven't heard that in years. I can't believe I didn't realize it was you at the Rotary breakfast." She looked at young JJ, his freckles gleaming boldly in the late morning sun. His boyish face open and kind. "Your son looks just like you."

"Minus the craters and the flab. He takes after his mom in that area, thankfully."

Rebecca laughed, tried to imagine what kind of woman he had married. Probably pretty, athletic, good-natured. Fun like him.

"You weren't that bad."

"Please." Josh gave her a "what-you-talkin'-bout-Willis" smirk, and she laughed again.

Josh looked down at JJ, put his hand on the kid's shoulder. "I used to fish this very same river with this lady here, back when I was a few years older than you are now, son."

"Fish with us now!" JJ said, his smile all teeth and a gumball.

"I can't. I really do need to get some work done today." Rebecca winked. "Rain check?"

"My dad says that! Yeah, rain check. And I'll hold you to it." JJ winked back at her. "And maybe you can come to church with us next Sunday! Dad and I, we always fish the river or the pond behind our house after church. We even brought a picnic." He patted his backpack.

She was still laughing to herself as she walked off down the path. Good for JJ—Josh. A family, a business, and a house in his own hometown. Living the nice, clean, wholesome life. It suited him.

She wondered about the woman he'd married, where they lived, what it would have felt like to have stayed here in this little Southern town, where they spent their Sundays going to church and their Fridays at the high school football game instead of rubbing elbows with the Who's Who of the city.

She sidestepped a thick branch in the path. Two invitations to church in one day. She gazed up as she walked, peered at the sun behind a big mass of white. God was out there, in the clouds somewhere, sure. But how in the world people got from this abstract higher power notion to daily prayer and what Granny liked to call "a personal relationship with Jesus Christ the savior" was beyond her.

It all sounded like a bunch of wishful thinking.

Early the next morning, Rebecca was fumbling with the house key, locking up on the front porch, when her cell phone rang. Granny.

"Hi, Granny, what's up?" Her shoulder jammed the cell phone to her ear.

"Honey, I left a box of school supplies that I desperately need sitting right there on the kitchen counter. Have you already left the house? Do you see it?"

Rebecca set her workbag down on the porch and headed back to the kitchen. The big brown box was there, filled with neat little stacks of crayon boxes, notepads, and a healthy clutter of glue sticks, rounded-point scissors, and mechanical pencils.

"It's here. You're already out and about?"

She'd been tiptoeing around all morning, trying not to wake Granny, not realizing she'd had the house to herself. Clearly being an early riser runs in the family.

"First day of the summer enrichment program at James Watkins Elementary, and we've got fifty-three kiddos set to arrive in less than an hour." Granny sounded breathless. "Would you mind terribly? It's the school way down on the outskirts, out toward Aberville. Should take you ten minutes. I'd come myself, but—"

"No problem, Granny. Just come in the main doors of the school?"

Rebecca hoisted the box onto a hip, her heels clicking briskly on the linoleum and then the wood floors and thin carpet as she walked through the small house and out to the porch again. The sun was already bright and unwavering, even at this early hour, and the birds had some sort of song competition going from the big oak tree in Granny's front yard. The door slammed with a sharp bang.

"Yes, come to the admin office. You can't miss it."

It took less than ten minutes to navigate the quiet Dahlia streets and turn onto Aberville Road, and Rebecca noticed how the town changed as she drove. In Dahlia proper, the houses were bigger, with great expanses of lawn and forested areas in patches between the homes. Lawns were well manicured, and the houses themselves were those pretty old Southern masterpieces, the kind with dormers and big porches and lots of cleanly painted wood exteriors, usually a crisp white, though there was one pale pink at the corner of Elm and Main, and someone had done some creative colorscaping with the shutters of a house on Granny's street. The maples and crape myrtles stretched out overhead like a soft green roof, and the drive soothed her, made her feel like she was somehow snuggled within the trees. Safe.

The houses got smaller as she drove, then closer together, the older homes replaced by some newer models and a few squat brick ranch styles. Out toward Aberville, the landscape changed markedly. Smaller houses gave way to well-tended trailers and cottages, then the not-so-well-kept. A handful of closed-down businesses, rusted fences, overgrown yards, and gutted concrete homes came next. One neat trailer stood in the middle of a shabby-looking street, the lawn trimmed back and a cheerful "welcome" sign with large yellow sunflowers posted at the front. Someone had kept up lush bushes at that house, and potted flowers lined the front steps.

But on either side of the house it was a different story—rundown, unkempt yards, and one shirtless man stood smoking a cigarette on his front porch and glared at her as she passed. A "condemned" sign with some yellow tape warned her to stay away from a house two doors down. The neat, well-kept house stood out like a sore thumb, made her sad. She wondered why the owners would bother to stay, why they didn't sell and move to a classier neighborhood, where people seemed more like them. Then again, she wondered why anyone would stay in Dahlia, period. Little industry, lots of farms, a half-hour drive to the nearest small city—if you could call it a city. The so-called city had a mall, at least. Dahlia had, well, churches. And pretty old houses.

By the time she pulled into the parking lot of James Watkins Elementary and got to the front walk of the school, the heavy box of supplies was slipping, and she had to juggle it several times to keep it from tumbling all the way to the ground. She couldn't imagine how Granny might have done it on her own.

"Need some help?" a young male voice said, and she felt part of the weight taken from her. She couldn't see her helper over the big cardboard sides, but together they carried it to the front door.

"Thanks," she said, as he held open the door. They walked inside. "I'm going to the front office with this."

"It's this way, on the left," the helper said, and she followed him down the spacious hall.

The woman at the counter, a pale-skinned lady with an enormous red belt and matching earrings, greeted her with a warm smile. "Helen's granddaughter? You're a dear." She took the box, waved Rebecca on—"I'll see she gets this. Keep up the good work at the newspaper!"—and disappeared down the hall.

Rebecca turned to her helper for the first time. "Thank you," she began to say, and realized he was a kid. He had close-cropped hair, soft dark eyes rimmed with long lashes, and skin the shade of rich creamy coffee. In another few years he'd be a heartbreaker. "I appreciate the help."

"You're welcome," he said and tilted his head, gave a small smile. There was something in his eyes, something about the quiet hunch of the shoulders that tugged at her.

"I'm Rebecca Chastain, but Ms. Chastain's a mouthful. You can call me Becca."

What in the world had motivated her to say Becca? She hated that name, went to great lengths to get all former friends, family, and acquaintances to stop using it, and now she was tossing it out like everyone called her that.

"I'm Devon Robinson." He ducked his head and gave a shy little shrug. "Nice to meet you, Miss Becca."

"My granny helps with the enrichment program here. I should probably go say hi. You know where it is?"

"I'll walk with you."

"Thanks." She grinned down at him as they walked. There was something about his stride, upright, with a thin form but a bit stooped in the shoulders, that made her think he'd be very tall one day. He wore a huge blue backpack, and as they walked, he tugged at the cords on the pack, the zip of the material against nylon matching the rhythm of their feet.

At the door to a classroom, he stopped. "I think she's probably in here. Your granny's Miss Helen?"

"Yeah. Hey, thanks!"

He scrunched up his face, like he wanted to ask her something. She waited.

"So, you work at the newspaper?"

"I do," she said. "I'm the editor, which means I run the whole paper."

He nodded. "Maybe you could do a story on us. The program here." He gestured to the school around him.

The classroom door opened then, and Granny stepped out, her face lighting up with surprise and joy.

"I see you've met one of my favorite people in Dahlia!" Granny grinned, catching Rebecca in a hug. "And yes, I think you should definitely do a story on the program. In fact, your first interviewee should be this young man right here. Devon started the program."

Rebecca's eyes widened. "What … ?"

Devon shrug-ducked again. "Sort of."

"Pfff, sort of." Granny made a face and elbowed Devon. "It was his idea! He laid it out, and the rest of us ran with it. You do a story, you definitely need to start with Devon here. Though you'll need to wait till around three o'clock, when the program gets out. Devon's in the enrichment program, too."

Wheels began to turn. "Wow!" Rebecca eyed him. "I'd love to interview you. Really. Would you mind?"

Devon tugged at his backpack cords, head down. "Um, sure, I guess it's okay."

"I could take you to Harold's, the diner? Maybe drop you off at home after. Would your parents mind?" Rebecca remembered the paper had a big supply of parental waiver forms above the copy machine. "Could you get them to sign a waiver form saying it's all right?"

"It's just me and my grandmother, but I know she wouldn't mind. She'd sign the form."

"Great!" She held out a hand. "I'll pick you up at four. Right out front."

He shook it, then gave her a small smile. "See ya then." He turned, gave a little wave back at Granny. "See you in a bit, Miss Helen."

"Bye, Devon." Granny gave a wave. "I'm glad you and my Rebecca here got a chance to meet!"

They waited until Devon was in the next classroom and the door had shut before Rebecca gave Granny a look.

"Are you just being nice to make the kid feel good, or did he seriously come up with this whole idea?"

"No, he really did. Girl, that child is something else. You'll see when you talk to him today." Granny wrapped Rebecca in a big hug, then put her hand on the doorknob. "Got to get back in class. We'll talk later, and I'll give you the whole story."

And blowing Granny a kiss, Rebecca headed off to work.

CHAPTER 12

Devon

AT FOUR SHARP, Devon was waiting outside the school. The news-paper lady was right on time. She pulled up in a little gray sedan, tires squeaking.

"Hop in!" She grinned through the open car window, clicked the automatic door locks. "I hope you're hungry, 'cause I'm starved."

He was, too.

Twenty minutes later they were seated across from each other in the big plush red booth in Harold's Diner, the seats that smooth leathery kind that made his legs cold, a huge plate of half-fin-ished fries between them and her notepad before her. He'd already finished a gigantic, drippy cheeseburger, which he'd decided was probably the best thing he'd ever tasted in his life. He'd had burg-ers before—I mean, who hadn't—but that burger was in a whole new class. Devon hadn't done any interviews before, but he de-cided that if they involved food this good, he was all in.

"So, you don't talk a whole lot," the newspaper lady said, study-ing him.

He felt his cheeks get hot. "Quiet, I guess."

"Is it weird, talking about yourself? Or maybe it's just being a

91

kid. To be honest, I don't know a thing about kids. Except having been one, of course. And that was a long time ago."

He couldn't help himself. He laughed.

She smiled. "What?"

"You're funny."

"Funny, as in weird?"

"Just funny." He laughed again, and she laughed this time, too, grabbed another fry. He liked this lady.

"So Devon, tell me about the camp. How'd you come up with the idea?"

Devon gulped the chocolate shake, wincing at the loud sluuuuuurp, but the newspaper lady didn't seem to mind.

"Well, I got to thinking one day about how a buncha kids my age don't have much to do once school lets out. Me too—and it gets really, really boring. When you get to be my age, most of the grownups decide you're old enough to stay home alone. But some of the kids get into trouble."

"Like, fighting?"

"And drugs, graffiti, all that stuff."

"Drugs? In Dahlia?"

He gave her a look. She raised her eyebrows, jotted some notes.

"How old are these kids? Like, teens?"

"All ages, high school down to elementary."

"Wait. Kids in elementary school stay home alone in the summer all day long?"

"Well, yeah. Grownups have to work." He fiddled with the stripy straw in his shake. "The churches offer free camps when you're little, but those end after second grade."

"They don't have any other camps in Dahlia?" Her eyes were wide.

"Those cost lots of money."

She frowned. "So you decided the kids needed someplace to go."

"Yeah." He grabbed another fry. "I figured the churches are always looking for ways to help, but older kids like us can be hard. And I know the teachers are off all summer, so I thought maybe we could do something at school. Not like regular school, more like fun school, only in the summer."

"Fun school. That's pretty genius."

"Thanks. Anyway, I went to my pastor, we got the school and the other churches to say they'd help, and presented it to the town council last month. That's about it."

"I'm impressed." She snagged another fry, wrote furiously. "So the name, West Dahlia Leaders Summer Enrichment Camp."

"I wanted to call it Fun School, but they all thought this sounded better. And besides, they call all the kids 'leaders' in the camp." He shrugged. "You know, to make us feel important. I've gotta admit, it does feel good being called Leader Devon all day long."

"Expectation breeds success," she said.

"That's what Miss H always says." He gave her a smile, and she smiled back. "We've got fifty-three kids this year, from eight years old all the way to the end of middle school."

"And I hear the staff is all-volunteer—no one gets paid at all. Retired teachers and a handful of regular schoolteachers, right?"

"And some high school helpers. They get summer school credit for it. It's a pretty good deal."

"I'll say." She wrote all this down.

"It goes from nine to three all summer long, with reading and some brain stuff in the morning, and the state feeds us lunch and two snacks cause we're a poverty school. Your granny helped get us that. She's on the committee with me."

The newspaper lady opened her mouth a little. "She never mentioned it. So, it is fun? Do your friends like it so far?"

"Yeah, I mean, there's soccer and tag and recess stuff to keep the kids happy, book stuff to keep the grownups happy, and the town's happy cause it keeps all us kids off the street. We even have a Bible study, but a kid version."

She finished writing, tapped her pen against her chin as she looked at him closely.

"So, Devon Robinson," she said, her words soft and news-reportery, like he'd seen on television. "Why do you care? Why go to all this trouble?"

He looked out the window, thought a long time. She was patient, though. Waiting.

Finally he bent down, reached in his backpack, and pulled out his Bible. He was almost embarrassed to show her—it wasn't a brand-new good-looking Bible but old, really old. The black leather was worn in places, and the pages were dog-eared. It had "Bible" stamped on the cover in gold letters, but even those were peeling.

Still, it was his Bible, and Mama's. Thinking about it made his throat go all scratchy, but he swallowed hard, rested his hand on the book, and looked the newspaper lady straight on.

"For Jesus."

She chewed her lip. "Jesus." He couldn't read her expression.

Devon nodded. "He's my savior. He died on the cross for me. For me and for you, and for everyone, really. So we could have eternal life. And he thinks I'm important. That's a pretty big deal to me. If I'm gonna call myself a Christian, a real one, then I want to step up and actually be one, really do stuff for him, to make him happy. Like caring for the least."

"The least?" She scribbled fast, turned another page.

"Yeah. 'The least of these.' You know, the people who have a really hard time in life, like widows and kids whose parents died, like me, and super-hungry people, the people who don't have anything. Rev calls it being Jesus's hands and feet in the world, and it's up to me to do it, me and other people who believe, too." He tapped the book. "It's all in there."

"Sounds like you've got the world on your shoulders."

"Somebody has to. Why not me?"

She shook her head, ate a fry. "You're one amazing kid, Devon. I've seriously never met anyone like you."

"And I've never met another grownup like you. You're a neat lady, Miss Becca." She was.

Afterwards, he showed her the shortcut back to James Watkins. "Drop me right here," he said, as they got closer to the school. He could see his bike was still in the rack, locked up with the new lock, safe and secure. Even better, there was no sign of Marquis. He breathed a sigh of relief.

"At least let me take you home!"

"No!" The word was loud in the small car, and she gave him a sideways look, his stomach flopping back to normal. "I mean, thanks anyway."

"You're my last appointment today, and it's really no trouble."

He shook his head, already grabbing the heavy backpack and sliding out of the car. "Nope, I'm supposed to meet up with my friends, but thanks." He gave her a no-biggie wave. "And thanks for taking me to Harold's. It was nice meeting you."

"You, too, Devon. Oh, and don't forget—make sure you get that form signed. I can't run the story without the parental waiver. Send it over with my granny tomorrow, okay?"

"I'll do it, Miss Becca. See ya."

He watched as she drove away in her little gray car, then turned to unlock his bike and head home. He only hoped Uncle T wouldn't be there when he arrived.

He wasn't so lucky.

CHAPTER 13

Rebecca

A Ministry for "the Least"
New enrichment camp helps kids' bodies, minds
while providing safe summertime haven

By Rebecca Chastain

Devon Robinson sits in the red leatherette diner booth, his mouth crammed with burger and French fries like any other eleven-year-old as he chatters excitedly. Only instead of video games or his latest soccer match, Devon is regaling the Dahlia Weekly *with stories of the non-profit ministry he founded in one of the poorest schools in the region: James Watkins Elementary.*

The ministry, West Dahlia Leaders Summer Enrichment Camp, features a daylong slate of mind-, body- and spirit-centered programming designed to keep elementary and middle school kids off the streets in a safe, fun environment.

"These kids had no place to go during the summer," Mayor Jimmy Ballentine said, applauding the program, which started Monday and runs all summer. "They were tearing up the soccer field, getting in fights

and causing a ruckus, and our town desperately needed a solution. Thanks to young Devon and our caucus of community churches, Dahlia now has that solution."

Volunteer Director Jane Scott said the fifty-three kids—dubbed "leaders"—range from second to eighth grade. They spend their mornings engaged in reading comprehension activities, often debating higher-level topics such as racial justice, bullying, substance abuse and more in college-style circle discussions.

"They call all the kids 'leaders' in the camp," Devon said. "You know, to make us feel important. I've gotta admit, it does feel good being called Leader Devon all day long."

Lunch and two snacks are provided by the Department of Social Services, and the day winds down with computer time and physical play.

"I love the program," said Tasha Smithers, 11, jumping rope with a friend. "Before, I didn't have nothing to do all day long but sleep and watch TV and get into trouble with my friends. But this is fun!"

Twelve-year-old CJ Samuel said he didn't want to go to the program at first, but his mother forced him. "I'm glad she did," he said. "I'd probably be sitting at home bored out of my mind. Now we can all hang out together here."

That's what it's all about, Devon said—helping kids have a good time and enrich their minds while providing a safe place during the summer months. He, too, attends the enrichment program, but also helps in a visionary role to guide lessons and logistics.

Devon said he just wants to "serve Jesus," and the West Dahlia Leaders Summer Enrichment Program is one way for him to do that.

"If I'm going to call myself a Christian, a real one, then I want to step up and actually be one, really do stuff for him, to make him happy. Like caring for the 'least,'" Devon said, noting underserved children, along with widows, orphans and others in need, require extra attention and care.

The program is all-volunteer and subsidized by donations from local churches and community members. For more information, call James Watkins Elementary at 555-7000.

On Wednesday, the latest *Dahlia Weekly* in her hands, Rebecca read over the article once more. All around her desk, the phones rang and people popped in to check their subscription or buy a single copy of the paper. She'd come to love Wednesday mornings in the newsroom; the hustle and bustle reminded her of the paper in New York, all that energy and noise and flurry of activity that spelled relevance, life.

She'd put the Devon piece on the front page in spite of it being a feature story—figured the quote from the mayor and the community service angle gave it heightened importance—and ran the photo of the kids in book discussion a full five columns. Running it as lead photo was purely coincidence; she'd had to pull one of Tiff's meeting stories last-minute and needed a filler. But now, looking the paper over, she was glad she'd done it. It looked good, and it had been a while since she'd had kids pictured on the front. It made for nice balance, plus was good play against the in-depth economy piece.

"Boss?" Tiff raised a hand nervously, then realized what she was doing and quickly lowered it.

"Yes, Tiff. And please—call me Rebecca."

"Okay, Boss. Um, Ms. Rebecca. So I've been thinking. Along with the economy stories we've been running, what if we did a story about the people behind the meetings? You know, deeper features about our elected officials."

Rebecca made a face. "Sounds like campaign stuff."

Tiff shook her head, eyes wide. "I wouldn't do that! More like human interest. Besides, they're not up for election this year."

"I don't know. We have to be really careful about that stuff." She gave Tiff a kind smile. "But I'll think about it. Thanks for making a suggestion."

"Okay. Um, you're welcome. Oh, and I really liked your story on the summer camp." Tiff blushed and tucked a stray lock of mousy brown hair behind her ear, the phones ringing loudly around them.

"Rebecca, line one." Millie called out, and Rebecca gratefully swiveled her chair away from Tiff and picked up. The girl irritated her beyond belief and she didn't know why—something about the combination of sweet shyness and drab run-of-the-mill prettiness blended with that whole I'm-a-startled-doe act.

"Rebecca Chastain."

"This is Lib Pauling," a huffy-voiced woman began, "and I want you to know your piece on the town's financial standing is way off-mark."

Lib Pauling. Rebecca recalled the steel-gray hair and walking-shorts-clad proper Southern lady who'd claimed to be Granny's best friend. "I'm sorry to hear that, Mrs.—"

"Forget it," Lib barked. "Just be careful about what you're doing with those articles. You have no idea the kind of impact your stories can have in this town. Now, for the real reason I called." She paused, took an obvious breath. "That story about the ministry at James Watkins Elementary was perfect. My church helped get that program started, and even though I didn't see any mention of any of our churches by name, which in my opinion was a sore oversight, that article was wonderful and will do a lot to help community morale and PR for the ministry."

"Mrs. Pauling, thank you, but it wasn't intended to be a PR piece—"

"No, no, no, that's not the point." Rebecca could visualize the woman waving her hand dismissively, held her tongue. "Anyhow, I have to go. Tennis in an hour. Just keep doing those kind of stories and keep away from that exposé garbage."

The line went dead, and Rebecca stared at the phone in her hand a moment, then replaced the receiver. One of Millie's sticky note scriptures had gotten caught underneath the headset, and Rebecca distractedly crumpled it, not bothering to read the words, and tossed it in the trash. She stifled a giggle as she realized that might actually have been the first underhanded praise call she'd received since she'd taken the helm of the *Dahlia Weekly* three months ago. Well, well.

"Rebecca, line four," Millie sang out from across the room.

Three hours and four complaint calls later, plus two praise calls, Rebecca had put out a handful of advertising fires, charted the news budget for next week's paper, and gone over Tiff's assignments with her. Dinah the ad rep had seen a marginal boost in advertising, but she'd messed up sizing on a real estate ad and forgotten to note a placement request on another, so Rebecca had needed to talk down a grumpy business owner who didn't like that she'd not put his ad in the youth sports section.

"Here," Millie said, and Rebecca looked up, startled. The prim-faced woman in the pale-blue polyester blazer was standing over her, a neatly tucked brown bag in her wrinkled hands. "A turkey and cheese from Sam's Sammies, and those healthy chips you like."

"Oh, thank you! You didn't have to—"

"Nonsense," Millie said, her voice brusque. "I figured you wouldn't eat, and you've been skin and bones lately."

"Thank you," she repeated, touched by the gesture even if Millie hadn't been exactly friendly about it.

She opened the bag and pulled out the sandwich and chips, the aroma already making her mouth water. The sandwich was still warm and toasty, the cheese that just-right kind of gooey. She took a huge, satisfied bite and sighed contentedly.

Millie was back in her chair, and Rebecca realized they were the only ones in the room. Dinah was out making the rounds, she knew, and Tiff must have run off to grab lunch or do a story, maybe both. Millie opened her own bag and bowed her head a moment, mouthed some words Rebecca couldn't hear.

"So how are things going?" Rebecca asked after the prayer was done.

"Same old, same old." Millie shrugged, took a bite. "Got my grands on the weekends while their mama works and my church summer clothing bazaar next week. Between that and work, there's never a moment's rest."

"I hear you." Rebecca tried to make her voice sympathetic. "Well, you're doing a good job on the bookkeeping and customer service. I really appreciate that."

"It's my job," Millie said simply. "And I heard some of the calls this morning—you really did do a nice job with that story about the summer camp."

"Thanks."

"No, really—that's the sort of thing people like around here. It's news, but it's news people actually care about. You do more stories like that and you'll see your numbers start to pick up again. People need to see we care about the community, that we're not only out for a profit."

Rebecca wrinkled her nose. "I'm not so sure that's going to drive numbers. Didn't the last editor do that stuff? And the guy before him?"

Millie snorted. "TJ Banks did the bare minimum. He was a nice person, don't let me tell you wrong, but the stories were blander than potatoes with no salt and butter. You might try some of what he did but taking it up a notch."

"We'll see."

"Rebecca, with all due respect, what worked somewhere else

isn't necessarily the right recipe for Dahlia." Millie's cheeks had little points of color at the center.

"Thank you, Millie," Rebecca said, her tone clear: Conversation closed. Millie's mouth pressed into its familiar thin line.

When Rebecca left that day, the stack of mail had a blue sticky note on top. Instead of scripture, Millie had scrawled four words: I'm praying for you.

Rebecca balled it up and jammed it in her purse.

"Rebecca!"

She looked up from her car to see Erik Wennerman waving from the coffee shop up the road. Joe Mama's. She could almost smell the coffee beans from here. Erik was grinning at her, his shirt sleeves rolled in the afternoon sunlight, and she had to tamp down the sudden sear of attraction. She waved back as casually as she could manage.

"Got a minute?" he called. "Can I treat you to a cup of coffee?"

Millie and the anger she'd felt moments ago instantly faded, and the flame instead became a little ember of thrill. Why not? It's just business.

"Sure." She smiled back and clicked the lock on her car, quickly crossed the street.

"Good to see you," he said, holding open the door to usher her in.

Popping her sunglasses atop her head, she stepped inside. He stood a little too close, and she brushed against him slightly. The spot where their bodies touched felt warm and buzzy as she moved inside the café.

The cool air and nutty, slightly bitter aroma of French roast swarmed her senses, and she felt herself begin to relax. Joe Mama's was a charming shop, with books, high-end lotions, and artsy collectibles stacked neatly on the shelves. A few metal tables were scattered around the room, one taken by the town's sole hipster pastor, a goateed twenty-something guy who wore a massive wooden cross, surf shorts, and flip flops and pored through the Bible like he was searching for the meaning of life. Two older ladies sat at another table, discussing a book and laughing like sisters.

"I don't know about you, but their lattes are my favorite," Erik said as they approached the counter. "After the day I've had, I can use a pick-me-up."

"Sounds good to me." It really did. She smiled at him.

"Two lattes," he said. "With whipped cream."

Minutes later, they'd taken a seat at one of the cute bistro tables and he was regaling her with tales of his day. She found herself laughing like she hadn't in days.

"The kicker came when I called on this one shop and accidentally asked for the owner—who'd died the month before."

"No!" Rebecca covered her mouth with her hand.

"Oh, yes." Erik shook his head ruefully. "Like I said, one of those days."

"I'm all too familiar with those days."

"Oh!" He reached into his leather satchel, pulled out today's paper. She glanced at his hand as he did. No wedding ring. "I loved your story on the camp, by the way. I bet you've gotten a million calls about it."

"Thanks." She flushed.

"Seriously, you're an incredible writer." He looked straight into her eyes, and her stomach gave a flip-flop. "I mean it."

She gave a shake of her head, glanced at her watch. I've got to get out of here.

"Got to run." She downed the last of her coffee. He'd been right—the lattes were amazing. "I promised I'd help my Granny with something. Oh, and hey—thanks for the ad partnership. I'm really grateful you're on board with us."

"I feel the same." His smile lingered again, and suddenly she felt uncomfortably nervous. Almost date-like.

Which was the last thing she should have been feeling, at least per her therapist. Note to self: "Just coffee" is never "just coffee."

"See you later." She stood, gave a little wave.

And fled Joe Mama's as fast as she could possibly maneuver.

As she got to her car, she glanced across the street and saw a familiar form. She squinted. Devon Robinson, peddling slowly along First Street, shoulders hunched and backpack on.

She turned left instead of right when she pulled out onto the street, rolled her window down, and tooted the horn.

Devon looked startled, stopped the bike.

"Hey, Devon. Thanks again for the story the other day." Rebecca smiled, gradually realizing it was her real smile.

"No problem, Miss Becca. I hope it helps." He straddled the bike.

"I'll bring some by maybe tomorrow. Papers, I mean, to the school. Is that okay?"

"Sure." He shrugged but smiled, and Rebecca motioned to the bike.

"You're a long way from your neighborhood. Want a lift?"

"No, um—I'm visiting a friend. Thanks, though."

"Okey doke. See you around."

"See you."

She drove off, watching him get smaller and smaller in her rear-view mirror as the distance between them grew.

CHAPTER 14

Devon

DEVON HOPED TO MAKE IT home before Uncle T, slip in to check on Memaw, maybe grab a quick snack to take to his room for later. But as he pedaled closer to the house—making sure to go the back way so T wouldn't pull up behind him and see the new bike before he could hide it behind the clump of trees by the shed—he saw not only T's brown Cadillac but two others. One was a beat-up yellow convertible and the other a slick black machine with silver rims that gleamed in the afternoon sunlight. Ray's car.

His stomach got all quivery, reminding him of eggs in a pan before they scrambled up right.

T spotted Devon as he was walking over from the yard. There was a woman with him. Girl, really, with giant hoop earrings and shorts that looked so tight and tiny Devon had to blink to make sure he was seeing right. The girl was laughing and swaying, like there was music playing except there wasn't, and her long blue fingernails scratched playfully against T's arm.

"Terry-baby, come on now. Play nice."

She slitted her eyes like a cat.

Devon cleared his throat.

T tossed him a glare. "What you doing sneakin' up the back like that, tryin' to get blasted?"

"No, sir."

T thinned his lips, one hand on the girl's hip. The girl didn't seem to mind.

"You come tiptoeing in with your crusty ol' head, get yourself beat down or shot if you're not careful. Best go easy now, boy."

Devon swallowed and eyed the door, tried to decide whether to edge past T and the girl or go around to the front door. He figured T was liable to take it as some sign of disrespect and get mad if he went around. Slowly, he climbed the back stairs, keeping as much distance between him and his uncle as he could. The girl had her arms around T's neck now, doing a little dance. Whatever she was smoking smelled foul, skunk-like. T didn't seem to care.

But when Devon got to the top of the stairs, T's hand shot out, clenched Devon's arm. The girl laughed and wriggled, but T held on, stared him down. His arm hurt, and he knew T wanted that, wanted to show off.

"Aw, leave 'im be, Terry-baby. You're scarin' the poor kid." The girl squeezed T's bicep.

T flicked a look her way, and she laughed nervously.

"Hear me?" T's voice was cold. Devon managed a nod. The eggs in his belly began to slip and slide again, and his knees felt weak.

"Yessir," Devon muttered, and then T released his arm and Devon half-fell past, slipping into the house and the smoke-filled kitchen.

Two dirty frying pans were on the stove, and a man in an undershirt and blue jeans was passed out at the kitchen table, his head turned slightly to one side. Devon could see the man's tongue poking out just barely, saw a line of yellow and white pills and what looked like powder on a tray. Ray was nowhere in sight, but he could hear giggling down the hall and the squeal of some girl.

He scooched closer to the sound, realized they were in his room. Great.

Quickly, he opened the door to the pantry and grabbed a half-empty bag of chips and a pop-top spaghetti and meatballs. He stuffed them into his backpack, then grabbed a couple of juice boxes and headed down the hall to Memaw's room. The TV was on in the living room, the new flat-screen T had brought, and Devon switched it off. So much for saving on the power bill. He sure hoped T would be around when the bill came. Then again, he hoped he wasn't.

"Memaw?" He tapped softly at her door, stepped inside.

Her room was quiet, cool, and the overhead fan ticked softly. The curtains were drawn, but a thin strip of rectangular white light came from the bottom of the roller shade, just enough so he could see where he was going, see her sleeping form on the bed.

He tiptoed in, and she stirred at the creak of the floorboards.

"Devon, honey, that you?" She coughed, a weak, raspy cough, and he went to her.

"Yes, Memaw, it's me. How are you feeling?"

"Oh, my sweet, sweeeet boy." She struggled to sit, and he saw she was in her nightgown, hair still pinned up in back the way she wore it at night. She hadn't moved all day, then. "So sweeeeeet."

Her voice sounded funny, and he peered at her. Her face looked droopy.

"There are people here." His hand gestured to the door. "Memaw, T's got some friends here. Girls, too, and they're all up to no good."

But Memaw only shrugged, settled back against the pillows.

"Ah, hungh," was all she managed, and then her eyes closed, and she was snoring softly, and he was alone again.

Tears pricked his eyes. What was going on? Memaw never slept this much. She needed a doctor, he knew it, needed someone to figure out what was happening here. But how could he bring a doctor here, to this place, with all this mess going on? And how could he get her out of the house in this condition, to where she could get help?

He could ask CJ, maybe. But CJ would tell his mom, and then who knew what would happen?

Leaving his backpack in her closet, he opened the door, marched out to the patio. The girl was in the chair now, lighting another smoke.

"She needs a doctor, Uncle T."

"She don't need nothin'." He set his jaw.

"So you're just—just gonna let her die? A doctor could do something to help, figure out what's going on. She might've had a stroke or something, or an aneur-whatever it's called, or—or something. Please, Uncle T."

All the trying in the world couldn't stop the hot tears from pooling. He squeezed his eyes tight so they wouldn't fall. If they started, he knew they wouldn't stop, not for a long time, and T'd never let him hear the end of it. You big baby. Get it together for Memaw's sake. For Mama's sake.

T shook his head, thumbed at the girl. "Missy's got her. She works part-time. An aide, at the old folks' home. Said she sees this all th'time, a'ight?"

Devon whirled on her. "Did you give my Memaw some pills or something? Something to make her go all wacko?"

Missy half-stood and blew out a whoosh of smoke. "I di'nt give her nothin'." Her voice was like a hiss. "I don't know where you come off, kid, but I don't go 'round feeding grannies pills or nothin'. That's not how I do people."

"Missy, shut it." T sighed. "Look, kid, she's old. You know what I'm sayin'?"

"She deserves better." The words were tight in his throat. "Will you at least drive her to the doctor?"

"No—"

"Or let me call Doc Kittredge? He makes house calls some-times. I'm sure he'd come."

"Nobody's comin' here. Got that, boy? I mean no one. You cross me on this, it'll be a big mistake. Hear me?"

His words were soft, but Devon knew a threat when he heard it. He held T's eyes a long moment.

"Let it go, boy. Nothin's gonna happen. We're family. I got this."

Devon didn't even bother to answer. He just let the door slam behind him and dashed back to Memaw's room, where he locked her door and buried his face in her bedcovers. She didn't budge, just slept on. The tears came for what felt like hours.

Please help, Jesus. Help my Memaw.

CHAPTER 15

Rebecca

REBECCA STOOD AT GRANNY'S kitchen counter that evening, chopping carrots into thin strips and popping them into the giant stockpot on the stove as Granny herself washed long stalks of celery, cabbage, and peppers in the sink. Low music played from the CD player on the counter—something semi-modern, with a peppy beat—and Granny hummed as she worked, her hair pulled back into a cute mini ponytail. Rebecca smiled over at her, imagined a much younger version of Granny, with a child at her feet and a husband, all clamoring for dinner and attention.

"You do realize you look like a kid with your hair tied back that way?" Rebecca waggled a carrot at Granny's hairdo.

Granny laughed and shook her ponytail. "You're only as old as you feel, sweetie." Her hands expertly rinsed and snapped. "Honestly, most days I'm downright stunned I'm this age. Eighty four! I was eighteen just yesterday, falling in love with your Gramps and setting up house here. Still feel eighteen half the time. At least in my head."

"That's better than I can say. I feel every inch of forty." Rebecca made a face. As for the love part, no thanks. The coffee encounter with Erik that afternoon had left her feeling awkward and un-settled, like she was a high school kid sneaking out her bedroom window with some bad boy.

Though why she felt that way about someone like Erik Wenne-rman was actually rather bizarre. He was handsome, smart, nice, funny, and unmarried—if you judged by the lack of ring. Nothing like a bad boy. And handsome was really an understatement. She felt her cheeks flush.

Maybe that was the problem—maybe he was all right, and she felt all wrong.

Granny laughed again. "Well, you don't look forty. And besides," she said, turning off the water and drying her hands on the thin blue dishtowel by the sink. "It's all up here, anyway. Age is only a number." She tapped her head, winked saucily.

"I believe you." Devon flashed in her mind. "That kid from the summer camp—Devon Robinson?—he's like eleven going on forty."

"Oh, I believe it. That child has the world on his shoulders. Going to be somebody very special someday, if he can rise above his home life."

Rebecca started cutting the green peppers now, the motion soothing. Granny joined her, their rhythm smooth, practiced, like Rebecca hadn't been gone twenty-three years and Gramps was still out in the living room, watching the news and sipping his nightly glass of sweet tea.

"So what is his home life, anyway?" She gave Granny a sideways look. "He said his mom died, and he lives with his grandmother?"

Granny shook her head. "It's a pretty sad situation. Arnetta Robinson was a good lady, very involved at the church, but took ill two, three years ago. Stage four ovarian cancer. Apparently she'd not been to a doctor in years, went from running Mr. Allen's convenience store out on the highway to the coffin in six weeks flat. Devon was her only child."

Rebecca shivered, imagining a young Devon at his mother's funeral, his stoic little face watching everything, not able to understand.

"There's no dad?"

"Not that I ever heard about. Devon lives with his grandmother, but she's got a lot of health problems. Asthma, arthritis, diabetes, blood pressure. The church helps out when they can. There's an uncle that comes around, but he's a little, well ..."

Rebecca pursed her lips. "He doesn't want the help?"

"Not sure he likes the poking around, or the charity."

Rebecca frowned. "So how do they stay afloat?"

"I imagine they do okay. Dolores Robinson gets social security, and there might have been some life insurance money, though I can't be sure on that. Believe it or not, you can make it work if your house is paid for and you keep your bills down. They have a quiet life, live in one of those small cottage homes off Aberville Road. Devon's one of our backpack kids, in fact."

"The ones who get the extra food sent home in little bags over the weekend so they don't get hungry?" Rebecca felt a pang, remembering how Devon had wolfed down the fries and burger at Harold's Diner. At the time she'd thought it was a typical boy's voracious appetite. Now she wondered how often he got the chance to even go to a diner, eat a burger and fries like a regular kid. She remembered how skinny his arms were. How serious he'd seemed. Driven. Determined.

"It's a lot more kids than you think," Granny murmured, watching her.

Rebecca shook her head. "I just ... ." She stopped, realized she didn't have the words.

They worked in silence a moment. The rest of the vegetables went into the stockpot, and Granny stirred the pot and set the lid on top. Drying her hands on a dishtowel, she kissed Rebecca's hair softly.

"Hard to reconcile, the thought of kids going hungry. Kids you know."

"Yeah," Rebecca said quietly. "Makes me want to—I don't know." She dried her hands, too, gripped the towel. "It kind of makes me want to go buy his family groceries, take him out for dinner every night."

"It's just life, sweetie. Life for lots of people. All you can do is try to help."

"How do you do that?" Rebecca squinted at Granny, folded her arms. "You work all day, every day. Making soup and chili and holding clothing drives. Hosting those free dinners. How do you keep from trying to save them all?"

Granny gave a half-smile. "You can't rescue the world. You can just be Jesus to them."

"What, like read them the Bible?" Rebecca shook her head. "I'm pretty sure that kid knows more about the Bible than I do."

"No, Becca. I mean *be* him. Actually be his hands and feet. Treat them like he would have done when he walked the earth. Love them no matter what they look like or where they come from or whether their hands are dirty or their clothes smell. Give them food and clothing, a warm blanket, help them get their lives in order if they need it, offer two strong arms to hug them when they need comfort. Be an ear. You can't save everyone. But you can be kind. You can help."

When they came, the words were small. "How do I help someone like Devon?"

"You could start by being his friend. Spend time with him." Granny's words were gentle. "And sweetie, it never hurts to ask God to guide you. Try it," she said simply. "He knows what we don't."

Rebecca reached out a hand, clasped Granny's cool, dry fingers in her own. "Thanks, Granny. I'll see what I can do."

The next morning, six copies of the *Dahlia Weekly* on her front seat, Rebecca drove the ten minutes from the house out to Aberville Road and then to James Watkins Elementary. She parked the sedan out front and clicked the locks, headed toward the doors.

"Heyyy, mamasita."

She turned, the sharp smack of a bouncing basketball on asphalt filling the air. Three preteen boys in low-riding jeans and those ribbed white tanks leered at her. What looked like yellow rags or handkerchiefs were stuffed in their pockets, the edges poking out, and one had a bright yellow bandana wrapped around his head, doo-rag style. Mini-gangsters. In a couple years when they were older, she might have been afraid of them. For now, she just smiled and quickened her pace. Gangs, in Dahlia?

"Hi, boys."

"Boy?" One of them, the one in the middle, puffed out his chest and grabbed at himself. "I'll show you 'boy.'"

"Shut up, Vasquez." The skinny one shoved at him.

"You shut up, Marquis."

They all stood and stared like she was a platter of fresh meat. The hair on her neck prickled, and she froze. Then she remembered sharks, and prey, and forced a smile, waved like it didn't bother her. Never let them smell your fear. Even in apple-pie-in-the-sky, wholesome-as-it-comes Dahlia.

Inside, her heels click-clicked on the school's linoleum. She remembered her own elementary school, six hours north in Arlington—the classrooms with their uncomfortable metal and plastic chair-desks, the school lunchroom with its ever-present aroma of buttered corn and floppy pizza, her fourth grade teacher Mrs. Boudreaux, with her huge teased hair and rayon pantsuits. The way it felt to be young and desperate to fit in and aching to grow up and get started on life. She wondered if the boys outside had ever felt that way.

Or the kids inside. Kids like Devon.

"I wanted to leave these for Devon Robinson?" she said at the front desk, and a tall, attractive woman with rich caramel skin and an oversized emerald-green necklace smiled, held out her hands.

"You can leave them here. I'll see he gets them."

"Actually," Rebecca considered, "is there any way you can call him out front a moment? I was hoping I could ask him about a follow-up story. I'm Rebecca Chastain, from the *Dahlia Weekly*."

The woman's eyes lit as if she recognized her. "Of course we can buzz him." She crossed the tiny reception area to the intercom, pressed the button. Over the loudspeaker came her voice: "Devon Robinson to the front office."

She turned back to Rebecca, smiled again. "By the way, I'm sure you've been hearing this all over town, but your article on the summer camp was really good. I hope it opens some eyes, gets people realizing what goes on out here."

Her voice was warm and melodic, like she was singing instead of talking, and Rebecca found herself returning the smile, relaxing.

"Thanks." Rebecca met her eyes. "I hope so, too."

"These kids, shoo." The woman shook her head, her breath exhaling in a quick little puff. "They have a hard time of it. Those houses in this neighborhood outside," she waved her hand, gesturing, "you don't know half of what goes on there."

Rebecca thumbed toward the front. "I saw three boys outside who looked like they wanted to jump me."

The woman made a face. "Them again. I'll call the police. They've been warned one too many times."

"Well, they didn't actually do anything but grab themselves and give me the eye, but it was a little unsettling."

"No, no, it's better if I call. We've had enough of that loitering nonsense, and in this neighborhood, you give an inch and they take a mile." The woman gave her a smile. "I hope you don't think they're all like that. Most of the kids around here are good kids. They just have it rough, most of 'em."

"I believe it."

"These kids, they show up looking mostly like regular kids, but some of their stories would make you cry."

Rebecca leaned on the counter thoughtfully. "Is that why you help out?"

The woman gave a firm nod. "Absolutely. I'm Marla, by the way. Marla Bryant."

"Nice to meet you."

"That boy?" Marla nodded toward the hall beyond the closed reception doors. Rebecca turned to follow her gaze, saw Devon walking slowly toward them. "He's one of the good ones."

Rebecca grinned, raised her hand to wave as Devon caught her eye.

"He sure is," she said over her shoulder to Marla as she stepped into the hallway to meet him.

"Hey there, Miss Becca." Devon looked genuinely pleased to see her. He wore athletic shorts and a vivid blue T-shirt, no yellow gangster symbols anywhere, and she noticed how his permanent teeth still had those telltale jagged edges of childhood. It made her remember again what it felt like to be eleven, that gawky completely out-of-place middle ground between kid and teen. Tweens, they were calling them now—someplace in between—and knew there was a whole universe of specialized marketing to appeal to hundreds of thousands of kids like him.

Except maybe those kids had plenty of food.

"Hey, Devon!" She held out her hand, and he shook it carefully, his little fingers cool against her own. They took seats on the brown bench outside the administration office.

"Miss Marla showed me your article this morning. You did a good job!"

Somehow hearing those words the last two days from a dozen adults couldn't top the overwhelming rush of pride she felt when Devon said them.

"Thanks," she said, surprised to feel her face heat. "Well, I brought you a bunch more so you can have them for your family, maybe give them to other people you think should read about this?"

"Awesome."

Rebecca took a breath. "So I've been thinking."

"You want to do more articles. About the program." Devon nodded. "I think that's a great idea."

She laughed again. This kid was something else!

"Yes, Devon, that's exactly what I was going to suggest. The article went over well and made for a nice front page, but more importantly, the story resonated with our readers. I think we have the chance to do some real good here."

"I think so, too. Mama always said shining the light keeps the darkness out."

Rebecca thought about that, nodded slowly. "I think your mama was right. So, do you know anyone who might talk to me? Maybe we can weave some of their lives in as we do a series on the program, how it's making an impact."

"I was thinking." Devon scratched his chin like he was deep in thought. "Could you let them tell their stories, one by one? Like, a story a week? And at the end of it all you could do some big article about how the summer went?"

She sat back, visualized it. That might be brilliant. She considered the implications—how the stories would look on a page, how she might tie in an editorial, even a photo page midway through.

"You think they'd do it?"

"I think so. Maybe if you gave them a gift card or something, not much, like five bucks or whatever, it'd help."

Five bucks wasn't much. She would've done it for five bucks when she was a kid.

"Yeah," she said, deciding. The excitement began to build. "Yeah, I think we can do that. We could change their names, some of the details to protect their privacy. Run some photos from time to time. Maybe a few voices from the volunteers. But yes, I like this. A lot."

She made her face look serious a moment. "But there's one catch."

"What?" Devon gave her a guarded look.

"I need your voice in there, too. This program was your idea. People like hearing stories from the visionary, too, not just the people who are getting the help. So once a week, I wonder if you and I can meet around four or so, and maybe I can take you for burgers and shakes, and I can interview you."

Devon shrugged, but his eyes sparked. "Sure. That'd be great! So …" He gestured to the hall behind him. "Want me to start talking to the kids, see who might wanna do it? I can even pass out some of those waiver forms if you give me some."

Rebecca laughed again, feeling light years more relaxed than she'd been in a week. Like a kid, almost. Being around Devon Robinson made her feel good. She wasn't sure why—maybe it was because he was an oddball, like her, or maybe it was encountering someone who could relate to her drive and passion.

In fact, she realized that for the first time in ages, other than when she was with Granny, she wasn't playing "Social Rebecca" anymore—that trained bright smile and let's-do-business handshake. She was smiling her real smile at him, the kind that stretched her face and exposed all her teeth.

"Devon Robinson," she pronounced, shaking her head. "You seriously are the most 'together' person I think I've ever met."

He smiled. "I like you too, Miss Becca."

"So," she said conspiratorially, crossing her legs on the bench to match his. "Want to grab those burgers this afternoon?"

CHAPTER 16

Devon

AFTER CAMP THAT AFTERNOON, Devon walked the long corridor from the classrooms toward the front office. His blue backpack was heavier now, with his books from the program wedged next to six cans of something Miz Johnna from the cafeteria had tucked in, after Devon had helped her stock the shelves in the lunchroom. He'd gotten to go inside the kitchen doors all the way to the back room to do the work, sent by Miss Becca's Granny because Miz Johnna was getting up there in age and didn't need to be lifting in her condition.

While they'd worked, Miz Johnna had kept up a steady stream of chatter about her grandkids and the collards and oven-baked mac-and-cheese she'd be fixing that weekend when they came to visit. Had talked so long about it that by the time they were done his tummy was growling and he was starting to get hunger pains for real when he remembered that afternoon, and the burger and shake Miss Becca would be buying him.

All for sharing his story.

He'd write the story himself for the burger and shake, but she didn't need to know that, and besides, she was nice. He liked being with her. When he talked about the kids at camp and his Mama and the stuff at church, she listened to him with her whole self, like he mattered. Like Rev and Marla listened. And once a week? That was almost too good to believe in.

When he said bye to Miz Johnna, she'd bent down real quick-like beneath the counter and pulled out a thin plastic bag. He could see through, see a few ravioli pop-tops inside.

"Extras," she said to his questioning look as she turned him around, unzipped his backpack while it was still on him, and stuffed the bag in. She zipped him back up again and motioned to the shelves. "Can't fit 'em on the shelf, and I sure rather you take 'em home than I send all them cans back to the state."

"Thanks, Miz Johnna."

"It's my pleasure, Devon." Her brown eyes were big and a little watery in her face, and she blinked real fast. "You're a good helper. God's got big plans for you."

He smiled a little at that, because that's what Rev always said. He told her as much.

"I hope you're listenin', young man, 'cause that preacher of yours is right."

"Yes, ma'am. I believe it."

He felt a little guilty taking the extras, though, and as he walked down the corridor to the front, wondered if he shouldn't give them to someone else.

T was there every day and night now, and Missy and whoever else, too. His posse, T liked to say, and T liked to eat. Steaks and greasy sausages fried up sometimes late, late at night. Devon smelled them when he woke in the night to use the bathroom. Last night the party was still going strong when he'd gotten up at one o'clock in the morning and heard them in the kitchen, clinking glasses and cooking something that smelled so good he almost wanted to wander out, see if they'd share.

But he knew better. So he'd just finished in the bathroom and darted back to Memaw's room before they could see him, back to his nest of blankets by her closet. He'd taken to bunking in her room now. Ray used his room too much. He liked it in with Memaw, anyway. It was the coolest room in the house, and no one came in after six o'clock.

But in the mornings when everyone was passed out, he tiptoed to the kitchen on his way to camp and usually struck gold. This morning there'd been two burgers wrapped in foil, and he'd eaten them cold as he pedaled to school.

Still, the extras from Miz Johnna meant he wouldn't have to scrounge for supper from the pantry or fridge and deal with Uncle T's friends.

Memaw wasn't talking much, and Devon still didn't know why or what to do. But she sat up a little, and ate what he gave her, and nodded some when he read to her from Mama's Bible. His Bible. Mostly she just slept. This morning she stirred as he was leaving for camp.

"Sweeeet boyyy." The words were little more than a whisper, and still sounded weird, like she was talking underwater or something, but he'd kissed her forehead and promised to be back that afternoon.

"Aaff-noooon." Memaw had nodded and slid back down on the bed, turned her face to the window, where a slim shaft of morning light was beginning to touch her pillow.

He wasn't stupid, knew what was going on, knew she'd had a stroke or something. But he didn't know what to do for her without drawing attention to their situation, making things worse. She wasn't going downhill, at least. There was that.

He gritted his teeth at the helplessness, realized as he walked the school hallway that his fists were clenched, too. Slowly, slowly, he released, then exhaled.

He reached the door to the school and was just starting to open it when he heard giggles and a "See ya, Dev" from behind. He turned to see Shenise, her friend Gabby, and a little Gabby looka-like coming from the front office. Gabby still had the braids and the crossbones pin, and she smiled at him too, ruffled the head of the kid beside her.

"This's my mini-me." Gabby gave a lopsided grin, tugged at the girl's ponytail. "Mariana, this guy, Devon, started the camp here."

Mariana looked impressed. "It's an awesome camp. I like that book we're reading, the one about the kid from Haiti? Beats hang-ing out at home all summer." She made a face.

"Got that right." Shenise looked at Devon. "How's your Me-maw?"

"Oh, fine."

Shenise raised a brow. "Fine? Haven't seen her at church in, like, a million trillion years. Some'a the guys been saying she's dead, but nah, I woulda heard. She's a nice lady, your Memaw."

She waited for the explanation, but Devon shrugged. The less she knew, the better.

"Her hip makes it hard to get around, but she's good. We do home church."

The corner of Shenise's mouth quirked. "Aunt Lou calls it that. Home church. I see your Uncle T's been staying up there a lot."

That he definitely didn't want to talk about. He waved a hand like it meant nothing.

They reached the doors, and Devon looked out, saw Miss Bec-ca's gray car at the curb. His stomach dropped as he also saw Mar-quis and Johnny Vasquez and a couple of older guys, maybe high schoolers, bouncing the ball by the bike rack. He stopped short, still inside, and turned to the girls.

"Hey, ever feel like sharing your story for that series? Being in the paper?"

Gabby hooted, slapped her knee. "Like that newspaper you passed around in circle time today? Capital N no. My parents would freakin' kill me if I aired our dirty laundry like that."

Shenise elbowed her. "You get to change your name, dodo." She eyed Devon, bit her lip. "I might be interested. It's a good way to get other people in this stupid town to open their eyes and see how the rest of us live. You should, too, Gab. You're always sayin' how people don't know what it's like, how they think your whole family's from Mexico or something and works the farm."

Mariana nodded fast, piped up, "Yeah, sis, Shenise's right. You got a chip on your shoulder about that."

Gabby rolled her eyes, but she shouldered her purple backpack and gave him a grin.

"Just playin', Dev. I might."

She pushed open the school doors and stepped out into the summer afternoon. The hot air hit him like a shove after the air-conditioning, but Shenise, Gabby, and Mariana didn't seem to feel it, just slid by, headed down the block past Marquis and his friends, past Miss Becca and the bike rack, where his new-old black bike from Rev stood with its shiny lock. Marquis called something after them. Devon couldn't hear what, but Gabby turned and flipped him a crude gesture, and Shenise laughed.

"See you got your little sister," one of the older guys called. "Couple more years and she'll be ready for me."

Devon could see Miss Becca's head swivel from where she sat in the car, take in the scene. He quickened his pace, heart bouncing like the tallest kid's basketball. The last thing he needed was for her to get creeped out by Marquis's gang, never want to come back again.

"Shut up, Choo." Shenise said over her shoulder, a warning hand on Gabby's arm.

Gabby had stopped and turned full round, her eyes narrowed.

Devon saw her hands were tight balls.

"Couple more years and you'll be in the slammer."

"Oooooh, she burned you," one of the guys said.

"Watch it, Shenise."

"Or what, you gonna do something about it?"

"Maybe."

"Yeah, yeah, keep talking."

The girls moved off, down the street to where he knew Shenise lived, and the boys stayed behind, Marquis bouncing his basketball. Thwack. Thwack. Thwack.

Devon knew Marquis was watching him now, watching him walk to the little gray car.

Probably watching Miss Becca.

If he didn't hurry, they'd probably say something to Miss Becca, and then she'd really never come back, never want to take him to Harold's for burgers and shakes.

Devon tapped on the car window. Miss Becca started, but she flashed a smile, clicked the locks unlocked.

"Hey, Devon!" She grinned as he slung his backpack onto the floorboard and climbed in. "How was your day?"

He waited till the door was shut to answer.

"Pretty good. How 'bout you?" He could feel Marquis's eyes on him, felt all the guys' eyes on him, as they drove away. He wished he could pile his bike into the backseat, too. He closed his eyes for the briefest of moments, gave it to God. Can you keep my bike safe? Please?

Then he opened his eyes, smiled at Miss Becca. "Did you write a lot of news stories?"

"Not so much, today, I'm afraid." She made a face but looked happy as she pressed the gas and turned the wheel, pulled out to head down Oak Street toward the diner. "It was one of those number-crunching days, plus a bunch of meetings."

She paused at the stop sign, turned to face him. Her eyebrow was creased in the middle, and she looked worried.

"Devon, do you know those guys?"

He shrugged like they were no big deal. "Yeah, kids from the neighborhood."

She took a breath, like she was trying to figure out what to say. "Do they … bother you? I mean, if I hadn't been there, would they have done something to those girls, or to you?"

Devon shook his head fast, mouth dry. "No, no, nothing like that." The last thing he needed was her sticking her nose in. That would guarantee his head on the bully target for sure, not to mention maybe cause problems for her, too. "Really, they're okay. They were playing. We're all kinda like … friends. Sorta."

They were still at the stop sign, and he turned to look back at the school. The guys were a good distance off, but Devon could see they'd stopped and were watching their car. Miss Becca needed to put the pedal to the metal. They didn't need to draw attention. Maybe next time he could meet her on the corner, or early, while there were still lots of kids around. And teachers.

Rebecca looked at him a long moment, finally nodded. "Okay."

She looked like she wanted to say more, but he rubbed his belly. "I can't wait for one of those Harold shakes. They're the best! So what's a number-cruncher day?"

She opened her mouth, then shut it and smiled, stepped on the gas. They turned onto Aberville Road, and he let out a breath he didn't realize he was holding.

"I'm trying to raise more money for the newspaper, but it's not always easy."

He'd never considered that before. The newspaper was a business just like Mr. Allen's store, and Mr. Allen was always complaining about customers and sales. He thought a moment.

"You could do a sale. You know, give stuff away when people buy stuff, and then they come back for more?"

She glanced at him. "We don't have anything to give, really."

"Give a newspaper. You know, get a subscription or something if you buy an ad."

Her lips twisted. "That's not a bad idea." She tossed him a look. "You're a smart kid, Devon."

The way she said it sounded like she meant it, like she wasn't trying to baby him, and he was still smiling a few minutes later as they pulled up to Harold's and took their seats at the diner booth.

After they ordered, she leaned in. "So who do you think I should interview next? Got any ideas?"

Devon dug in his pack, pulled out a square of notebook paper. He unfolded it and spread it out on the table.

"These two here said they'd definitely talk to you. Cheyenne wants to ask at home first, but Diego said his mom wouldn't mind and you can call him tonight and set something up."

Miss Becca leaned back. "You got me names already? How in the world—"

He shrugged. "We had circle time after lunch and I showed them the paper, and some of the kids said the story was cool. So I asked them at recess."

"Nice! I'll give Diego a call tonight, and then when I go to the school to talk to him, I can chat with Cheyenne, see what she thinks." She started writing on the paper, making notes, and he grabbed one of the Saltines from the little white box on the table. "What kind of gift card should I get for him, McDonald's or something?"

"Nah, that's too far for some of them. A lot of the kids go get candy and sodas and stuff from Mr. Allen's shop. I help out there, and I've seen Diego come in a few times. I bet Mr. Allen would do a gift card. Want me to ask?"

"That's a great idea. Thanks!"

His burger and shake came—Miss Becca just got fries—and she told him stories while they ate, about where she used to live, all the way in New York City, and the paper she used to run. He told her about the safe stuff, like Mr. Allen's shop, and Rev, and the camp.

The door tinkled, and he looked over to see a man and a boy about his age come in. The boy had more freckles than anyone he'd ever seen. They walked past him to a booth, but when they passed, the man stopped short and was smiling down at Miss Becca. It was a big smile, the kind that showed all his teeth.

"Well, hey there, Becks. How've you been?" The man turned to the boy. "Son, you remember Miss Rebecca, from the river?"

The kid waved at her, cast a curious look at Devon. "Hi again! Catch any fish lately?"

"Would you believe I haven't been back to that river since the day I saw you?" Miss Becca motioned to Devon. "This is my friend, Devon Robinson. Devon, meet JJ and, well, JJ." She laughed and looked up at the man. "I guess I'd better start calling you 'Josh' now, huh."

"Nice to meet you." Devon shook their hands, and then the man, Josh, started talking to Miss Becca about fish and stuff, and Miss Becca looked really happy. Devon tried to study the kid without him noticing. The kid had on good shorts, the kind that looked like they came from a real department store, and one of those soft mini backpacks with the cords that sucked in the top tight, and shoes with fresh white laces. The ends weren't torn up, either. Not a single bit.

"How old are you?" he blurted to the kid.

"Ten today. It's my birthday." The kid smiled at him. He looked nice. "How old are you?"

"Happy birthday! I'm eleven."

"Cool. You like to fish?"

Devon shrugged. "Never been."

"You've never been fishing?"

Devon felt embarrassed then, but the kid must've noticed, because he shrugged, too.

"Hey, it's okay. My buddy from school didn't go till three weeks ago. He caught a huge bass, too. Guess they call that beginner's luck, huh."

"Guess so."

The kid talked fast, like he'd just had a bunch of sugar. Devon decided he liked him. JJ.

"Maybe you can come with us sometime. We usually go every week after church, but today, Dad got the day off, on account of it being my birthday'n all, and we always go to Mama's grave and put flowers on so she can say happy birthday, too. And now it's— burger time!" JJ held out his arms wide like he was saying ta-da.

Miss Becca seemed to pick up on that last part, because she stopped talking to the dad, turned to look at JJ. Her mouth hung a little open. "Your mama's grave…?"

"Yeah, she died giving birth to me," JJ said matter-of-factly. "She had a heart condition, so my dad gets to be mom and dad. It's a boys' house. Me, Dad, and Choco."

"The ultimate man cave," Miss Becca said and smiled, but her eyes looked sad. "Well, you and Devon here have something in common."

"My mama died too, two years ago." He tried to sound as casual as JJ. JJ gave him a surprised look, and then a nod. The No-Moms Club.

JJ and his dad moved off a few moments later to their own booth, but not before JJ invited him again to come fishing at the river on Sunday. It sounded like fun. It would be a good long ride on his bike, and it would get him out of the house for the day. Between that and church and helping Mr. Allen, he could probably manage to stay out all day long and avoid Uncle T.

As they walked off, Mr. Josh slung his arm around JJ's neck, and Devon felt a pang of something settle in his stomach. For a moment he wished—no. No matter. His dad didn't know what he was missing, like Mama had always said.

"You got kids?" he asked Miss Becca after JJ was long gone, and she laughed.

"Not me. I'm too busy at work to be anybody's mom."

"Mama used to say the work would always be there, said if she'd known before how great it was being a mom, she would have had twenty more."

"Twenty!" Miss Becca giggled, and for a moment, she sounded like a kid. "Your mom sounds like one amazing woman. I wish I'd known her."

Mama would have liked Miss Becca. He told her as much, and her cheeks got a little pink then.

"Thanks, Devon. I know I would have liked her, too." She clicked her pen. "So talk to me about how the camp is going? You're, what, two weeks in now?"

After, she dropped him at the school. To his relief, the guys were long gone, and the afternoon had settled into that soft glowy time, when the evening was just starting to build and the sky was changing, like it had whispers at the edges. He spotted his bike still in the rack, and the tightness that had gripped his chest a moment ago was suddenly gone in a flood of gratitude. Thanks, God.

"See you tomorrow, maybe?" She smiled at him. She had a nice smile.

"Hope so." He meant it. "Thanks for the burgers, Miss Becca."

"Thanks for the help with my story. You want a ride home?" She glanced nervously at the small clump of trees up ahead past the school, like she was worried someone was going to come jumping out of them like in the movies or something. "Those guys won't come back and bother you, will they? I can fit your bike in the back, I'm sure."

"Nah, thanks, though. Besides, I'm supposed to meet my friend, uh, CJ here." He made a showy move of looking around, like he expected CJ to walk up any second now. He felt bad for lying. He was doing a lot of it lately. But there was no way he wanted Miss Becca bringing him home, seeing Uncle T. Or worse, Ray or one of the other really rough guys. "It's fine, I promise."

She bit her lip. "If you're sure. Bye, Devon."

He watched her drive away, watched her little gray car turn right at the stop sign. JJ and his dad came to mind then, and the arm slung around JJ's shoulders like they'd walked like that a thousand times before.

And suddenly Devon felt very, very alone.

CHAPTER 17

Rebecca

A WEEK LATER, Rebecca sat at her desk, skimming this week's paper. All around her the newsroom bustled with noise—Dinah schmoozing with a customer on the phone, Millie chatting with a subscriber about tomatoes, Tiff's stilettos tap-tapping in time with the click of her computer keyboard. The smell of fresh coffee swirled, and reminded of the half-empty cup before her, she took a long sip.

Next to the cup sat a thin vase with one chunky blossom perched neatly above. The rounded white and burgundy flower looked almost like a lollipop atop the long, skinny stem, but for the spiky, graceful petals. A "Rebecca's World" Dahlia, the older farmer had told her that morning, when he and his wife had popped by to renew their subscription and bring her the vase.

"Used to think they'd named it after my wife, here," he'd said, gesturing to the white-haired lady with the soft smile and wispy bun who stood next to him, holding his arm like she needed the balance. "But that's just the name of it. Did you know they have forty-two different names for dahlias? Why, there's a Jessica Dahlia, and a Clara Marie, even a Bahama Mama Dahlia, if you can believe it!"

"You're doing a fine job, dear," the older Rebecca had told her, looking straight into her eyes and smiling as she patted her husband's arm. "Plucked this flower right from our garden, just for you. Welcome to Dahlia."

Rebecca smiled at the memory, fingered the stem as she read this week's "Voices from James Watkins" piece, made possible thanks to her new pal Devon Robinson. Devon had lined up the interview, even helped her get three more this week alone. The kid was like a goldmine, plus he was sweet, to boot. She thought she'd enjoyed their second diner trip even more than he had, and they had another scheduled for tomorrow afternoon.

She reread the article now, remembering the little blond-haired girl she'd interviewed, Cheyenne, the way she'd swung her legs against the green hard plastic of the playground swing set as she'd told Rebecca her story, the thick Carolina accent lending a rhythm and cadence to her words.

Lisa's Story
As told to Rebecca Chastain

Editor's note: The following is next in a series of true stories from some of this community's most struggling members: the children at James Watkins Elementary School. James Watkins is one of the twenty-five poorest schools in the state, statistics say, with more students per total enrolled in the government's free and reduced lunch program than most of the schools in South Carolina. Names and identifying details have been changed to protect the storyteller's privacy.

My name is Lisa, and when I heard about this series in the newspaper, I wanted to be a part of it, too. I wouldn't ever say this stuff if you used my real name. Mama would kill me if I ever talked about our family business in public. I don't mean actually kill. She'd probably pull out Daddy's belt and then lock me in the bathroom a good long while. But this here is safe. It's almost like the poetry I read in class last year, only this time I get to tell it.

Some things you should know about me: I'm poor. I know this sounds dumb, but I just realized this recently. Like maybe six months ago or something. I know, pretty dumb to be twelve and only now getting it, but that's the plain truth. None of my friends have much stuff, and I'm too busy taking care of what Mama calls "my responsibilities" to think much about it. But now that I know, it's hard not to think about it, hard not to wonder if it's always gonna be this way. It probably is. I don't know if I mind that or not. Anyway, I'm the oldest kid in the house, and I've got a lot to do, so I don't worry about it too much. It is what it is.

My typical day is basically I wake up, get my little brothers and sisters dressed and out the door to school or the free summer camp they go to, at the Presbyterian church. Mama's usually still asleep. The baby's been sick, or up at night, and he gets real fussy, so it's my job to look out for the others so Mama and the baby can get a little rest. If she'd go to bed a little earlier maybe it'd be easier on me and her both. But nighttime is her time, she says. Her friends come over and stay up late, and even though me and my brothers and sisters keep the door shut in our bedroom and the covers over our heads to drown out all the music, it can be a little hard to sleep.

I guess you can say my mom and I have "issues." Whatever. Sometimes I wonder why she even had kids. But she loves us. I know she does. I mean, it's not something we talk about, but she's there. She cooks for us and asks us about our day. She's just a regular mom, I guess.

After I drop the littles at school, I go my way. By this time my stomach's usually growling. When we split ramen noodle soup the night before, or some of that canned stew, I usually have a real bad stomachache, but anyway, I get my breakfast at school and then do my school stuff all day. Then I get the kids, get home, help fix them snacks and dinner and do homework, and then it's another day.

Being poor isn't so bad. Except when it's your birthday, and you want a party and a cake like the regular kids so bad—a big store-bought cake with thick gooey frosting and some of those frosting flowers, the good kind that make your teeth hurt—but you know you'll be lucky to get the homemade crooked small one Mama makes. If you get a cake.

Christmas used to stink, but then the local churches put our name on one of those angel tree lists or secret Santa-type things, and now we get some great stuff and food, real food like a turkey or a ham.

I don't wish this on you, though. It's hard being poor. Maybe one day I'll get out of here. But then who'd take care of the little ones?

Rebecca finished reading and shuddered. The kid had broken her heart—that limp hair all pulled back in a ponytail like pretty was the last thing on her mind, those big blue eyes that should have been shiny and bright but were flat, like she knew what to expect from the world already. Even her teeth looked dull.

Twelve years old, all long limbs and hollow acceptance. It is what it is, she'd said again after the story was told and they sat there, Rebecca fumbling for the right words.

When Rebecca was twelve, she already knew she wanted to grow up as fast as possible and move far, far from home. Make straight As in college and land a killer job that involved travel and suits and great hair and fancy dinners, like Maddie Hayes on *Moonlighting*.

"Rebecca?" Tiff's voice was hesitant. Rebecca looked up. "Nice job on the little girl story."

Rebecca waved her hand. "Thanks, but I didn't actually do anything except write down what she said."

Tiff shrugged. "It was good. So," she said, chewed her lip and tap-tapped her stilettos, "I wonder if maybe I could do something similar?"

"Write some of the kid stories? I don't know—"

"No, I mean with a whole different angle. These local businesses." Tiff gestured to the street outside. Beyond the window, Rebecca could hear the sound of horns or revved engines from cars cruising by, and the blazing sun was already hot and bright even at this hour of the morning. "I could go try a different business every week. Sit down with the owner, ask a few questions about why they started it." Her words spilled out faster as Rebecca shook her head. "I mean, these people are from Dahlia, most if not all of them born and raised. It'd be neat to hear their backstory."

Rebecca's "no" was vehement. "Sorry, Tiff, but it's called advertorial. We need to be selling the ads, not giving them free ads disguised as news. We're already tight on space."

"I was thinking it could help business a little. Maybe do a little package deal—you know, advertise with us, get a 'how you got here' story."

Rebecca considered. The last thing these business owners needed was an ego trip courtesy of the *Dahlia Weekly*.

"I don't know. Maybe in a few weeks."

Tiff looked like she wanted to say more, then apparently thought better of it. She swallowed visibly and nodded.

"Okay," she said quietly, and turned back to her chair.

Rebecca did her best to ignore her conscience, which was pricking. But business is just that—business. Still, Tiff's tight shoulders bothered her, somehow.

"Thanks for the idea, though, Tiff," she offered. "I really will think about it."

Rebecca stood, gathered her purse. Fresh air and sunshine beckoned. "Going to scour some stories. Anyone need anything?"

The room was quiet. "No thanks, Rebecca," Millie said from the front desk, her voice gruff. "Got your mail for you, though."

Rebecca took the stack, Millie's familiar blue sticky note right on top. "For I know the plans I have for you, declares the Lord, plans for welfare and not for evil, to give you a future and a hope."

"Thanks," she said drily, tucked the mail into her purse and headed out the door. She left the blue sticky note crumpled on her floorboard.

Joe Mama's was packed when she arrived. Apparently, the whole town had precisely the same idea as she, though with the heat, why anyone would actually want a hot beverage was beyond her. The power of caffeine addiction, apparently.

But Joe Mama's was cool and comfortable, the aroma of coffee beans thick and soothing, and Rebecca felt her shoulders begin to relax. The lights were dim and cozy, making the coffee shop like a little midday oasis neatly tucked away from the hustle and bustle. Someone's perfume smelled really, really good, almost edible. She scanned the menu, realized she was subconsciously looking around to see if Erik Wennerman was there. Of course he wasn't, he didn't even work in Dahlia, but the thought had come nonetheless, unbidden. She pushed thoughts of his tousled hair—thicker than Peter's, even—and irreverent grin aside.

"Rebecca!" Someone was standing and waving from the back of the room, and she peered, took a step forward to see through the dimness. It was Josh Jamison, and he sat around a table with a handful of other people, all varying ages, a friendly smile on his face.

Her stomach gave a little tumble. Must be hungrier than I think I am, she told herself, and lifted her hand in a small half-wave.

"Hi, Josh," she said from the line, realized she was smiling. The others at the table—a slightly older black-haired woman with a vivid streak of white in her hair; a couple of men, one in a polo shirt, the other in overalls; an African-American woman in a long striped sundress and chunky earrings; two young people who looked to be college kids, one with a massive Afro—all looked over with interest. The woman with the black and white streaks smiled warmly.

"How've you been?" Josh asked, then without waiting for a response, "Want to join us? I've got extras."

He held up a big floppy book and she suddenly realized what they were doing: Bible study. The diverse gathering now made sense.

"No, thanks," she said automatically, smiled to soften the words as she motioned to the line before her. "Just grabbing a quick bite—have to get back to work."

"Hey, that's okay," Josh said, eyes still friendly. "Listen, we usually gather Wednesdays at lunch. All of us work, too, so it's just a quick little lunch group. If ever you want to join us, come on by. We're doing Luke, and it's really easy to jump in."

Rebecca nodded and smiled as though it could happen, though she knew it wouldn't. "Thanks!" She waved again at the little group, who smiled and turned back to their meeting.

She ordered an iced latte and a tomato-mozzarella Panini, ate quickly at a side table near the door.

She still couldn't believe Josh was a widower. Somehow, the thought of her superdad childhood friend and his little son in a house without a mom seemed horribly, unbelievably wrong. JJ came to mind then, and then Devon, and she found herself wondering how in the world good people like them got such a bad deal out of life when all the jerks seemed to have it made—and how in the world God could let that be so.

If she turned her head just right, she could see the Bible group across the room. The black-haired lady seemed to be the leader, but the others would jump in here and there. At one point, one of the college kids said something, and she could hear Josh's loud unmistakable laugh—his childhood laugh, a mix between a cackle and hoot, which had always gotten her rolling.

For a moment, she wished she'd joined them after all.

But what in the world would I do at a Bible study? She'd probably join the group and they'd be pressuring her to go to worship on Sunday and put money in the church offering plate so some pastor could buy a fancy robe or put in new stained-glass windows or something.

She shuddered, fiddled with her iced coffee straw. All of a sudden her stomach felt like she'd eaten a bowling ball. She stood, snagged the empty paper bag and, without glancing back at the Bible group, left.

In the car, she pulled out her cell phone, scrolled through the names until she found Sarah in the text messages list.

"Heard about any job openings yet? I've got to get out of this town," she jabbed at the letters.

But then she stopped herself, deleted the text, and set the phone down.

She sat a moment in the sun, letting the warmth of the day wash over her.

Truth be told, she wasn't sure she actually wanted to get out of town—at least not yet. She'd made a commitment to Granny. And now there was Devon, and the new series, and she had to admit it was pretty neat to reconnect with her old pal Josh and his son, JJ. She had some unfinished business to handle before she left Dahlia for wherever life would take her next, and she certainly didn't want to leave before she'd turned this paper around and left on a high note.

And with that, she shifted into reverse and headed back to the office.

CHAPTER 18

Devon

Marla flagged Devon down as he was leaving the school the next afternoon, a small white envelope in her hands.

"Give this to my sweetheart for me, would you, honey? Something for the collection plate from Mr. Sam. You're still going by the church to help Rev with setup?"

"Yes, ma'am." Devon took it, and she came around the counter to give him a hug. She smelled like vanilla and spice, and he closed his eyes, let himself relax.

"How's your Memaw?" Marla cupped his face in her hands and tugged him back so she could look at him, and his throat got all scratchy and he wanted so badly to tell her then, just lay it all out—T and the house takeover and Memaw in the bed and even what had happened last night, and what had come after.

But the moment passed and he shrugged, smiled, told her Memaw was fine, just fine, and he hoped she'd be in church this Sunday.

Truth be told, Devon wasn't sure if she'd ever set foot in church again.

"Alrighty, then, but you tell her she'd best get to feelin' right as rain or I'm bringing Doc over personally."

He could imagine the look on Doc Kittredge's face, on Marla's and even Rev's, if they stepped one toe inside the house. They'd wrinkle their nose at the smoke, step over pizza boxes to open the blinds, and then they'd see. See it all.

Maybe that would be for the best. Maybe if he said something they would come. Some days he thought even foster care might be better than this, even if no one would be around to take care of Mama's memory garden and they'd put Memaw in some home and he'd never see her again. Never see anyone.

His ribs ached then, deep inside, and he didn't know if it was from where T had shoved him or from the worry. No matter.

He forced a smile, waved the little envelope.

"I'll tell her. See you later, Miss Marla," he said, and then he was out the door with the other kids, heading for the bike rack.

Only today he'd timed it all wrong. And there was Marquis, standing smack in front of Devon's bike with his arms crossed. Johnny and Big Ty were over near the clump of trees, and Devon saw Big Ty wrap his fingers tighter around something in his hands. A baseball bat.

A thin line of sweat trickled down Devon's back.

"What do you want," he muttered, head down as he tried to slip past Marquis to unlock his bike.

Marquis clamped a hand on the seat. "Where d'ya think you're going?"

"Church."

"Chuuuuuurch." Marquis's voice pitched higher, and he laughed at his own brand of humor.

"You should go, too. You need it," Devon said before he could stop himself, but Marquis just glared.

"Shut up, Devon. Hey, whatcha got there?"

He snagged the little envelope before Devon could move, tore it open. A ten-dollar bill slid out.

"That's for the collection plate!"

"Tell the church I said thanks." Marquis jutted his chin. "You know the church gives to people in need. I'm in need of some lunch."

Devon wanted to cry, wanted to punch him right in his stupid throat, but all he could do was stand there, frozen. Even his lungs felt frozen. Empty. Turn the other cheek. But sometimes it was so hard. And who was he kidding, anyway? He was no match for Marquis. Certainly no match for Johnny Vasquez and Big Ty.

"You pickin' on people again, Marquis?" came a girl's voice from behind, and he turned to see Shenise, Gabby, and Mariana. Shenise's hands were on her hips, and she was staring Marquis down like she was a tiger and he was a snack.

"And?" Marquis stared back.

"Give him back his money."

"What money?"

Shenise pursed her lips. "You know what I'm talking about. Don't play dumb."

A loud whistle came from the front of the school, and they all turned. Marla was there, a silver whistle to her lips, and she held out a cell phone, looked at them pointedly.

"Just talking, Miss Marla." Marquis held up his hands, slid sideways away from the bike rack, toward the clump of trees and his friends. He pressed the ten back into Devon's hands, said in a growl to him, "You better not say anything."

Gabby tugged at her friend's arm, and Shenise moved, too, in the opposite direction.

"See ya, Devon," she said.

"Thanks." Devon's mouth was dry, but his palms were damp, and the bill felt sticky in his hand. He turned back to the front entrance, and Marla gave him a little wave, watched as he got on his bike and pedaled off, toward Rev and the church.

His ribs hurt worse as he rode, probably because he'd been clenching his stomach so tight. Breathe, Devon. "Let not your hearts be troubled, neither let them be afraid," came to him, from the Gospel of John.

"It does no good to worry your heart about things you can't control, Devon Robinson," Mama'd told him from her hospital bed. "God has a plan, and he'll see it through."

She was right. He knew she was right. But some days it was hard to see that plan.

Yesterday was one of those days.

He'd come home from Mr. Allen's shop a little after six, filled with relief that he hadn't run into T as he slipped in the back door. Missy was on the couch with another girl, watching some dumb reality love show on TV, and he'd grabbed two packets of oatmeal and headed down the hall when the door to the bathroom had opened and then T was standing there.

He tried to hide the oatmeal behind his back, but T was too quick, had spotted him and was prying the packets from his fingers.

"It's only oatmeal, Uncle T."

T hissed out a breath. "For a second there, I thought you were tryin' to rob me." He tossed the oatmeal packets over his shoulder, and his eyes turned cold then. T bent down, hands on his knees so they were eye level. "I'll warn you once. Don't you ever, ever, ever try to rob me. Missy'll tell you what happens to people who do me dirty, right Missy?"

He'd raised his voice over the TV, and suddenly Missy was there, a nervous laugh on her lips. She slid past Devon, wrapped her blue-tipped fingers around T's bicep. Her nail polish was starting to peel at the tips. Up close he could see her right eye was purple.

"Come on, baby, come sit down. I've been missing you."

"Tell Devon here what happens to people who try to rob me."

Missy looked from T to Devon. Then, her eyes losing all spark, she slowly sliced a finger across her neck.

Devon swallowed. "Got it."

"Got it, sir."

"Got it, Uncle Terrence sir."

T nodded, and for a moment Devon thought he'd be free, be able to continue on his way to Memaw's room.

But his uncle had other ideas.

"Come on in here, Devon. Time you learned the family biz'ness."

At the table, T made him sit there and watch as he counted out ten small white pills into tiny plastic bags, then pressed the air out with a contraption.

"This here's called a food sealer. Stick the bag in, press the lever, cha-ching. Product done. Time fo' the dividends. Next."

Devon watched his uncle. "Memaw would have a fit if she saw you."

"Memaw can't even get out tha bed, so I guess we don't have to worry about that, feel me?" T's lips were thin as he sealed another bag tight. Devon glanced at the kitchen stove, wondered how many minutes he'd have to watch before T got bored of playing uncle and let him go. "Your turn."

"Wait, wha … ? Uncle T I can't do tha—"

"You can and you will." The words were clipped.

"I—no."

The chair screeched on the kitchen linoleum, and T loomed over him.

"Oh, yes."

Somehow, the whisper was scarier than if he'd yelled. Devon's heart thudded.

"I'm not doing it."

"You are doing it." T's hand shot out, clamped his arm tight, then tighter, until it was so tight Devon wanted to scream. But he held it together. "Sit."

Devon didn't move.

"I said, sit." T shoved him roughly into the chair, pressed both his hands on the top of Devon's shoulders. "My guy didn't show, so tonight you get to work for me. Hop to it."

Devon's eyes started to burn. God, please don't let me cry.

"Uncle T, please—" He hated the way his voice cracked. Hated the lump in his throat.

"Uncle T nothin'. You eatin' my food, you gonna earn it like everyone else. Go."

And so he did, counting them out, sealing them in, pressing them tight. Twenty-five in all before T's guy Neeson showed, and T got bored and yanked Devon up and pushed him out of the kitchen.

"Go on, run to your Memaw and tell her how T turned you to the dark side," he said as the push took Devon so far he stumbled, crashed hard into the end table, knocking over one of the aluminum cans. The fall hurt bad, and Devon lay there a moment, wondering if he'd broken something, watching pale liquid pool from the can onto the carpet. Missy and her friend just watched their show and laughed at whatever was on the screen. They didn't even waste a glance his way.

"Remember—you're an accomplice now," T said from the doorway to the kitchen as Devon slowly got to his feet. "You go running to the cops, ratting me out, it's your neck on the line, too. I got your fingerprints. I got juice. We'll call it collateral."

T held up a baggie and grinned, and Devon felt like he was going to throw up then. Barely made it to the bathroom in time before everything he'd eaten for afternoon snack came out in a tumble.

He rinsed his mouth out with cool water from the bathroom sink, and stood on his tiptoes to lift his shirt and see in the mirror if there was any damage. So far so good, but he imagined there'd be a huge bruise tomorrow.

Then he crept down the hall on tiptoe, looking over his shoulder, sure any second T would drag him back out for more and worse.

But T didn't. And Devon found the oatmeal packets right by Memaw's door, and then he was inside her room, and it was locked and he was safe.

Safe.

He took a shuddery breath and winced at the pull in his side, then another breath.

Memaw was asleep, a soft snore escaping her lips, and he stared down at her, watching her chest rise and fall, watching as her bony, twisty hands rested peacefully against the thin white blanket wrapped snugly around her.

Too late he realized he'd left his backpack with his Bible out in the living room, hoped against hope that T and his friends would leave his stuff alone and he could sneak out later for them when everything was over and done with.

Accomplice. T's words came back to him when he was huddled against Memaw's dresser, carefully pouring a packet of oatmeal into the water glass from her bedside. There had been a spoon, too, and he stirred the mixture quietly, not wanting to wake her just yet.

T was no dummy, that was for sure. Not that Devon had been planning on telling. But now he knew he couldn't, and the feeling made him feel trapped, like a turtle in a tiny box, stuck. Alone.

Helpless.

He swallowed, and his throat burned, ached. Tears began to well, and he fought them back, but then they were there, silent and thick, sliding down his cheeks, and he was gasping for air, stilling himself. Crying didn't work. He'd known that for a long time. But he had yet to figure out what did work.

The next morning when he woke, T had taped a note to the bathroom door.

"P.S. Got you on video, too."

Now, as he pedaled toward church to help Rev with setup for tomorrow's Friday Night Giveaway, ribs aching from the fall and from another night on the floor, he racked his brain for a comforting scripture, came up dry. Help me, God. Help me and help Memaw.

"You okay, Dev?" Rev asked him when he caught him wincing as they scooted one of the long tables against the wall.

"Yeah, slept wrong last night." Devon made a face and rolled his eyes, tried to act like his ribs weren't killing him.

The pain was worse now that he was moving around, shifting tables this way and that. But he'd promised Rev, and if he begged off early, Rev would have to do it alone or worse—ask questions. And the way he was feeling today, he was scared that if he got asked too many questions, he'd break and the whole thing would be out in the open.

He'd almost let some stuff slip Sunday, when he'd biked out to the river to that fishing hole to see JJ and his dad. They'd gone off to JJ's hiding spot after lunch, the two of them, on the north end of the river, and JJ'd asked him about his Memaw, told him about his own granny, who'd passed a couple years ago. Devon had come this close to saying too much. Had almost wanted to.

But he hadn't. He didn't want to, not really. He just needed to keep it together. Tough it out. Talking wouldn't help anything. T would leave eventually. He always did. He had to.

Now, wiping his brow, Rev laughed. "You're too young to get those kind of aches and pains. Got to be at least my age, though don't you go telling Marla I said that. She near has me off to the doctor every time my knee acts up."

Devon forced a laugh. Fifteen minutes later and they were done, and he and Rev were sitting in the kitchen. Rev grabbed two soda bottles from the fridge and twisted off the tops, set one in front of Devon.

"To cheerful labor." Rev tapped his bottle to Devon's.

They rested a moment in silence, then Devon found himself telling Rev about the camp and some of the books they were reading.

"Miss Helen has us talking about kids during wartime. Some of the kids said they wished we had a war now, wished they were old enough to go fight. Can you believe that?"

"Sure can," Rev said, and Devon looked over, surprised. "It's in our nature, the desire to prove ourselves in the face of adversity. We like to imagine how we'd handle it if the Redcoats came riding through right now, or if soldiers were gathering on the banks of the river ahead, what we'd do, how we'd manage."

"I think most kids would flat-out run."

Rev laughed, a big deep laugh. "I don't doubt that, but they'd like to think they'd stand strong, face the fight head-on. And that's not a bad thing. Adversity builds character, and there is joy in adversity, too."

Devon thought about that. "Because we know heaven is our prize?"

"And because deep down we all know it builds character. James wrote in scripture that we should consider it a joy to face trials because we know the testing of our faith produces perseverance, and perseverance helps us be mature, complete." Rev raised a brow, smiled at Devon. "Show me someone who's learned how to weather a storm, and I'll show you someone who's come to trust in God. At the end of the day, my friend, that's what it's all about."

Devon bit his lip. "So our struggles are meant to bring us closer to God?"

"In a sense, yes. You know what someone's made of when they experience adversity. Do they crumble, or do they stand tall? I think we all know that some way or another, and I think that's why so many kids play war, and say they wish they could go fight in one."

Devon remembered how he'd felt last night, when Uncle T had loomed over him in the hallway. He'd crumbled. Standing tall wasn't even an option.

And yet, here he was today. Having a soda with his pastor, talking about a camp he helped start.

"I think that's what Miss Helen must've meant when she said wartime taught people to understand what was truly important. A lot of the kids thought she meant staying alive versus the silly stuff in life, but I bet she meant the spiritual stuff. Counting on God. Keeping the faith."

"All that in one lesson. Helen Chastain is one good woman." Rev's smile was broad.

"Her granddaughter's pretty great, too. She runs the newspaper."

"You don't say!"

"Miss Becca's real nice. Though she doesn't know much about God yet."

Rev cocked his head. "Well, then, maybe that's why God brought you two together."

Devon coached himself on adversity the whole way home, even stopped at the curb twice to thumb through the Bible, reread the section in James about joy in struggle.

But he couldn't see it. Deep down, he knew if he had another night like last night, he'd crumble again. Like that chunked-up concrete in JJ's hiding spot. And maybe this time wouldn't even be able to pick up the pieces.

His head was down by the time he pedaled to his street, and he almost didn't notice until he was in his own yard, passing by Mama's memory garden to park his bike out back.

T's car was gone.

The house looked empty, quiet.

Closed up.

Maybe … ? His heart began to pound.

Inside, there was a note on the kitchen table.

> Out of town on business. Missy's with me so you're on your own with Memaw. Don't forget what we talked about. I mean it. I have proof. —T

His breath, which he realized he'd been holding off and on since he turned into his neighborhood, let out in one giant whoosh, and a flood of energy spread over him from head to toe. He stepped through the kitchen, into the living room, bathroom, his room, even Memaw's room. No T. The house was empty save for his Memaw. He didn't even care about the threat.

"Mmpf…?" Memaw cracked open an eye while he was doing a happy dance at her door.

"Everything is great, Memaw. Just great."

"Okay, h-honnneeey," she managed, and he went to her then, kissed her cheek.

"I love you, Memaw."

"Y-yoooou too."

And he danced out the door and into the kitchen to fix supper.

CHAPTER 19

Rebecca

SUMMER WAS THICKENING into a damp, heavy heat that kept the roses, dahlias, and hydrangea lush with life and the townspeople sluggish and lackadaisical.

"Hottest summer we've had in a decade," she'd hear at the grocery store, or, "Gonna hit one-oh-four this afternoon, Mavis. Better keep that fan on high."

She kept her own air conditioning on, her runs to dawn, and her water bottle filled. Summers in New York were always hot, but this was the South, and being so far inland, the heat seemed to gather and pool so it almost seemed Dahlia was coming to a slow simmer.

She even started to forego the light makeup she wore to diminish the faint lines on her face. It all turned to sweat the moment she walked out the door, so why bother? And yet this summer, for the first time in ages, she felt like the years were going backward instead of forward. She felt younger and stronger and, if not a beauty, downright pretty. She didn't even need to streak her hair with the blond highlights; the sun did that job for her.

This morning she was almost tempted to chuck the bottle of Prozac, too. You don't need it, her inner voice whispered. You've got this on your own.

But she did need it. Deep down, she knew it all too well. She still dreamed about the hospital sometimes, still woke up thinking it had all been a nightmare. Except it was reality.

At the paper, numbers were holding steady, for now. People loved the "Voices from James Watkins" series, had even started writing letters to the editor in praise of it. Complaint calls were down to maybe two a week instead of several per day. People were saying hi to her in the grocery store like they meant it.

It almost felt like she'd achieved some sort of Dahlia grand prize of semi-acceptance: "We Are Getting Used to You." Or, "You're Not Messing Up the Paper So We'll Tolerate You." Or perhaps, "Not Bad, Rebecca."

Skimming this week's front page as she sipped coffee at her desk, the last one echoed: Not bad at all. The lead story was on plans for a new recreation plex at the town square, with an indoor walking track, basketball court, and rooms they could rent out for meetings and parties. Plans for a pool had been scrapped—too expensive—and Dahlia residents were decidedly unpleased. Rebecca had a small wager going with Tiff about how long it would take for town council members to backpedal and figure out how to fund the pool after all.

Tiff's piece on a local boy turned big-league baseball coach ran below the fold, and she'd done a good job with it. Rebecca liked the quotes Tiff had gotten, and the lead was strong and creative without being hokey. The headshot of the coach balanced nicely against the four-column lead photograph: four commissioners gathered with a shovel at the rec plex, the fifth waving a check from the state. Grant money to fund the rec plex. All of them grinning like fools.

At three-thirty she was parked outside James Watkins Elementary, waiting to pick up Devon.

She saw him in her rearview, a little kid with big eyes and a bigger backpack walking toward her. A few people stopped to say hi as he walked, and three girls—a pretty African-American girl in a tank top and denim shorts and two Latina girls, one tall and slim with long Pocahontas-style braids—stopped him and chatted a moment.

Devon was a nice kid, a lot nicer than she'd been at his age. She clicked the locks as he got closer, and she thought he looked happier than usual, like there was a weight off his shoulders. It must be tough in his shoes—only his elderly grandma to care for him, and she imagined he probably did as much caregiving for her as she did for him. And there was the money situation, too, or lack thereof. Her family hadn't been super wealthy, but she'd never wanted for a thing in her life.

Maybe that was the problem. Everything had come too easy, and she'd expected that, never built the character needed to tackle things when the going got rough. Here she'd been, sunk into a deep depression after a failed relationship to the point where she'd almost taken her life. And yet all around her, kids were dealing with dead parents and hungry bellies and, somehow, they had the strength to carry on.

She could learn more than a thing or two from them, and from Devon, she realized. Already had, in fact.

"Hey, Miss Becca!" Devon climbed into the seat, a big grin on his face.

She'd missed him, she realized. "Hey, Devon! I hope you're hungry."

"Starved. So did you get a chance to talk with Tamika for the series yet?"

Twenty minutes later at the diner, the waitress appeared with their burgers, plus a huge chocolate shake for Devon and a coffee for Rebecca.

"Your usual," the woman said, smiling kindly at them, blue eyes surprisingly bright in her well-lined face. She brushed her hands off on her waitress apron and leaned down with interest. "What are you two debating today? Last week it was the dinosaurs, right?"

"So far it's whether life exists beyond earth," Rebecca said, eyes twinkling. "Louanne, what do you think. Do you believe in aliens?"

"Aliens!" Louanne cocked her head and folded her arms, the movement causing her pouf of well-hairsprayed bangs to sway. "Could be. I wouldn't be surprised if they did exist. Hard to think of God going through the trouble of designing this great big world with all its people and animals and stopping there. I bet he kept at it."

"That's what I said." Devon grinned. "He's God—he can do anything!"

Rebecca dunked a fry. "I was coming at it from the perspective of life generally and the odds of this planet being the only one of all the billions out there. I think the odds are slim we're the only planet with life. But whether those other life forms travel the universe, land on our planet? Who knows?"

Louanne laughed. "You two. You crack me up."

"Solving the problems of the universe one week at a time." Rebecca winked at Devon. "That's what we say, right, Devon?"

"Right, Miss Becca." Devon took a huge bite of burger as Louanne wandered off to check on her other tables.

The room was close to empty this time of day—one man at the counter, a few other booths occupied with pairs like them. Outside the sun shone fiercely, but inside, Harold's Diner was cool and comfortable. Rebecca could already feel the tension of the day melting from her shoulders.

"So how have you been doing? Anything new with the camp?"

Devon nodded, swallowed. "Everything's good. The kids like it. Oh, and they really like your stories in the paper. Miz Peters reads

them to us. Neesa, the one with the sister with all that stuff going on? She likes you. She said she never gets to talk about it with
people, and she was embarrassed at first, but it was really easy to
talk to you. I mean, we have a school counselor, but they deal with
the regular stuff. You know, bullying and being too loud in class
and all that."

Rebecca chewed her lip. "That's a good point. When I talk to
people, even my friends back north, you can say only so much
without feeling like you're dumping all your troubles on them. I
bet it does feel good to just unload."

He shrugged. "Guess that's why I spend so much time with
God. I just give it all to him."

She peered at him. "What does that mean, exactly? Give it all to
him. People say it all the time."

"I don't know, I go sit with my Bible, shut my eyes, and tell him
about my day. What's bugging me. You know."

"Like a regular conversation?"

"Yeah, real natural. Like, 'Hey God, some kids were bugging me
at school today, what do I do?' That sort of thing."

"Hm." She took a small bite of her burger and drained her coffee, marveled at how easy Devon made it sound. She'd tried once
or twice to talk to God like that, but it felt weird. Stuffy and stiff
and ultimately like she was speaking to a blank wall. Which she
actually was.

"Mama taught me." Devon's voice was quiet, and she looked at
him, searched for grief or anger or anything. But there was only
that little wistful acceptance. Her coffee suddenly seemed too hot
for her throat.

He cleared his voice. "Well, really she showed me, at first. She
was always doing that stuff—you know, praying out loud with me
in the car, or like one time the power company was going to turn
off the lights and she just took the power bill and she sat at the

kitchen table and said, 'Jesus, I'm giving this mess to you.'"

He slurped his milkshake, the woooooshst loud in the small diner.

Rebecca fell silent, picturing this mom who prayed in front of her son, this son who watched and followed her example.

"So you started doing the same thing?"

"Yeah. Before she passed, she said, 'Baby, your friends and your family are gonna let you down, but God and Jesus are always there for you.' She said if I don't learn to give them my bad stuff in prayer, I'm gonna be looking for the answers in all the wrong places. You should try it." He looked at her. "It's pretty easy."

Rebecca wondered what it was like to have a mom with such faith. Her own mom liked to solve problems on the tennis court or out for a little shopping therapy. Work it away, she used to say. Rebecca had forgotten that. She wondered what it would feel like to not deal with all your troubles alone, to do that simple mystery, that thing she couldn't actually ever figure out how to do: Give it all to God. It sounded way too easy.

"So ... would you like to come with me tomorrow night?"

She cocked her head. "Come with you where?"

"I help out with something every week at my church called the Friday Night Giveaway. For people who don't have a lot. It's getting pretty big, and Rev said we need more volunteers."

"What do you do?"

"A bunch of things—food, free clothes, sometimes toothbrushes and those little tiny shampoo bottles, whatever the churches collected this week. We hang out, give it to people. Miss Marla, at the school? She's Rev's wife, and she helps, and a ton of people from churches all over town. It's more of a Dahlia thing than a my-church thing. You could maybe do a story."

She resisted the initial no, made herself really think about it. Maybe she could go. Just because she helped out a couple times didn't mean she actually had to worship there or anything. It was just, well, being a part of the community. Something she frankly needed to do more of, anyway, if the *Dahlia Weekly* was going to resurrect. Which at the moment seemed could possibly happen. At least it did this week. In this town, she'd learned things could turn on a dime.

"What time?"

He gave her the details.

After, as they were gathering their belongings to go, she stopped him a moment. "Why, Devon? Why do you do all these nice things for other people? I know plenty of Christians who go to church on Sundays and recite a bunch of Bible verses and call it good. Why do you go to all this extra trouble?"

He shrugged. "It just says so in the Bible."

She mulled that over, not really understanding. Devon dug in his backpack, pulled out his thick black worn-leather Bible, and turned to the first page. Rebecca gazed at the pages, slightly yellowish with age. It was the kind of book that looked like it'd been really handled. A brown stain, maybe coffee or soda, was dribbled at the edge, and on the right side, Rebecca could see births, deaths, and marriages written in a neat hand. On the left, written in bold hand, were more words. Devon turned the book so she could see. The pages looked delicate, but Devon handled it like it was a tool, not some fragile artifact. The births and deaths page had a strip of Scotch tape over a large, diagonal tear.

"Faith by itself, if it has no works, is dead. James 2:17," Rebecca read aloud.

"That was Mama's favorite scripture." Devon traced the words with his finger. "She said you can't earn your way into heaven, but if you really, really believe, then you oughtta want to do some good things to help people. Like Jesus did."

"Wouldn't it be nice if people actually did that," she muttered.

"Most of the Christians I know spend a lot more time judging instead of doing good stuff in the world."

"Not your Granny." Devon's eyes were wide, and she knew she shouldn't have said that. He was a kid, for goodness' sake. Plus, he was right.

"No, definitely not my Granny." A little stab settled in her chest. "And not you, either, clearly. You know what, I shouldn't have said that. It's not true."

"I know some people like that too, Miss Becca. Just 'cause you're Christian doesn't make you perfect. It only means you're going to heaven someday. But the way I see it, you got to do stuff. And even though I'm a kid, I can do a lot."

"I wish more people felt the way you do, Devon."

He shrugged, snagged one last fry.

"Most people I know do," he said. "Most people are pretty good deep down. That's what Mama always said. You just gotta get to know them."

When she got home, Granny had already headed to church for her knitting circle. The four o'clock burgers meant Rebecca wasn't hungry, and she wandered the house, restless, though from the day or the talk with Devon, she wasn't certain. She didn't feel like working, and she'd already done her run that morning.

Climbing the stairs to her room, she glanced at the framed Bible verses and pictures on the wall, and her eye fell on a photo from that first summer in Dahlia, when Gramps had taken her fishing and she'd caught her first largemouth bass, a fourteen-inch fish Granny had cooked for supper that night. That had been a good day, she remembered, one of the first truly happy memories they'd made that summer.

Then she realized exactly how she wanted to spend her evening.

The Wahca River was deserted when she arrived, and she breathed a sigh of relief. It was her first time fishing in twenty-three years, and she didn't want anyone to see how rusty she was. She set her rod and tackle box down, closed her eyes a moment to savor the silence and the scent of loblolly pines and cedars.

A crackle startled her, and she looked up to see a squirrel bound out of a tree, notice her, then scramble back quickly. She grinned at it. Hey, little guy. I won't hurt you. She didn't blame him. She'd run, too.

Like Gramps had taught her all those years ago, she found a branch and dug a foot-and-a-half-deep hole in the ground. She propped the fishing rod in the hole, ratted through the mini tackle box for a red rubber worm, and secured it to the hook. Then she flipped the reel to release the line, swung her arm back and cast in a decently smooth arc right where she was hoping to land. Nice. Sometimes, it really was like riding a bike.

She settled the rod back in its little prop hole, dug in her backpack for the thin blanket, and spread it out on the ground.

But forty minutes later, she didn't have a single nibble on her line. She was bent over, sifting through the tackle box for another fishing lure, when she heard voices behind her.

"Hey Daddy! Isn't that your friend?" a boy asked.

She looked up to see Josh Jamison and his son JJ, the sandy-haired, freckle-faced mini-Josh, approach. Their dog nosed behind them, a bright blue collar and tags jangling merrily as he sniffed and pawed at moss and smells galore. They, too, had fishing rods, and JJ carried a big white bucket. Josh smiled apologetically.

"Mind if we crash your party? I'll share." He held up a large Styrofoam container labeled "live bait" and raised his eyebrows in question.

She found herself grinning back at them.

"Sure. Nothing's biting, though." She motioned to the river, where her line was still drifting somewhere in the depths of freshwater.

"Whaddaya have on it?" JJ peered up at her.

"A red rubber worm. That's probably my problem." She shrugged sheepishly.

"Oooh, oooh, Dad, can I put one'a the worms on her hook? Please? Please, can I?" He hopped on one foot, clasped his hands together dramatically, and Josh and Rebecca laughed.

"He's totally your kid," she said.

Josh's smile looked mischievous. "Got that right. Of course, kiddo. As long as Miss Rebecca's okay with it."

Rebecca reeled the line in, held out the hook to JJ, and watched as he grabbed a slippery fat worm from the Styrofoam container and expertly guided it onto the hook.

"There!" JJ held it out to her, pride filling his young eyes.

"Thanks, JJ." She surveyed his work, impressed. "You did a good job."

JJ put worms on his hook and his dad's, then they stood in a loose line on the riverbank.

"One, two, three!" Josh said, and they cast sure and true into the water. Rebecca marveled at the pure delight she felt as the line zinged through the air and landed with a satisfying plop into the Wahca.

"We don't normally come here in the evenings. It's so weird that we're here, that we saw you!" JJ said, jiggling his rod as he talked. "We usually come Sundays after church, but this Sunday we gotta go to Aberville and fit me for some soccer cleaves. I start soccer camp Monday." He puffed out his chest.

"Cleats, buddy. Not cleaves," Josh said, not unkindly.

"Cleeeeeeeats," JJ pronounced, heavy emphasis on the T. "Got it, Dad. At least this time, we get to have some girl help with the shopping."

Rebecca raised a brow at Josh, and he blushed.

"He means Aunt Lissa," he offered, and Rebecca clamped a hand over her mouth.

"Oh, my goodness, I forgot about your older sister!" Rebecca remembered how Josh would gripe on and on as a kid about his sister Melissa Jamison, Lissa, who was two years older and so boy-crazy she'd become their private joke. She was also somewhat of a drill sergeant when she came stomping up to the river, scaring the fish and demanding Josh come home with her this instant for supper or a trip to Grandma's house or wherever else he had to be right then. Rebecca had a flash of a pretty, spiral-curled, braces-wearing teen who'd been Josh's worst enemy.

"You and Lissa survived childhood, huh?" She grinned at her old friend, and he grinned back. Warmth spread through her. It felt good to be here, to be with him again.

"It's funny how you go from worst enemies to allies like that," he said, snapped his finger. "She also keeps me on track with some of the mom things. She's got four kids of her own, and she teaches third grade to boot. JJ's pants get this high over his ankles or his nails get this long and it's Aunt Lissa to the rescue."

"I'm glad you have each other."

"Me, too."

"Though she can't cook much. Not like Dad. He's the absolute bestest cook in the whole entire universe," JJ piped up, rubbed his belly with gusto. Choco the lab wandered over, sniffed at them all in turn, then did three spins and settled down for a nap on Rebecca's blanket.

"Chef Josh? Wow."

Josh patted JJ's back with his free hand, the other still gripping the fishing rod. "I wouldn't say chef, but the crockpot and I are on very intimate terms."

"Dad says the crockpot is his BFF." JJ nodded solemnly.

"I'm still in awe."

JJ gave a shout, and his fishing rod pulled hard. Josh reached over, held it.

"You know what to do," he told his son as JJ furrowed his brows, clamped down hard on the rod, and slowly, steadily began to turn the reel handle clockwise. Shortly, an eight-inch freshwater bass began to emerge from the waters, its grayish-green-and-white scales shimmering as it fought hard to survive.

But father and son had clearly done this before. Josh slogged into the water and grabbed the line and fish, JJ held steady, and together they maneuvered the fish and some water into the bucket.

"Well done!" Rebecca exclaimed.

"First catch of the evening. Kid: one. Grownups: zip," JJ said and wiggled his brows.

"Just you wait," Josh said and stuck his tongue out at JJ.

An hour later, they'd caught four more, one by Rebecca, who felt positively exultant at the achievement. Once she would have scoffed at catching just one, but twenty-odd years later, it felt like a huge victory, like she was saying "still got it" to life and anyone else who brought her down. If only Peter could see her now, she mused a little wistfully, then promptly pushed that thought away. If Peter could see me now, he'd probably think my outfit was ridiculous and I needed to wash my hands before touching him. A wry smile twisted. No thanks and good riddance.

"What are you smiling about?" Josh asked as they gathered their belongings to leave.

"Happy, I guess. It's been years since I've done this." Rebecca carefully wound her line and hooked it to a rung on the rod. She folded the blanket and shoved her tackle box back into the backpack, then zipped it all up neatly.

Josh knelt down in the soil, piling his and JJ's belongings into a plastic grocery store bag. "You should do it more often," he said, pausing to look over at her thoughtfully. "Why not?"

She gazed back at him a moment, struck by how golden and open his brown eyes looked in the late afternoon sunlight. Why not, indeed? She should have been out here fishing that very first weekend she'd moved back. What in the world was she waiting for?

"Oh, Miss Becca, I forgot to tell you. I like your friend Devon a lot!" JJ said, packing the remaining items. "He came out and fished with us on Sunday. He came the Sunday before, too!"

"No kidding! Good for him."

"He's a nice kid," Josh said.

Rebecca smiled. "He sure is. He invited me to some giveaway ministry this Friday night. Said it's more of a Dahlia thing than a church thing?"

"Oh, yeah, the Friday Night Giveaway. I've helped out once or twice when JJ did a sleepover with his cousins." Josh nodded. "It's a lot of fun. They have music, and all the volunteers stay after and eat together."

"We should go this Friday, Dad," JJ said. "You said I could go next time."

Josh got to his feet, ruffled his son's hair. "That I did." He smiled at Rebecca. "Maybe we'll see you there? If you promise to come, I'll bring my guitar."

Her eyes widened. "Josh Jamison: superdad, master chef, and guitar player?"

He elbowed her. "Hey now."

Driving home, she realized she was not only smiling but humming along to the radio. It had been a good day, she thought, best she'd had in a long time.

As she approached Church Street, she remembered she'd left her laptop on her desk at the newsroom, decided it wouldn't hurt to swing by and snag it. It helped ward off insomnia when she knew she could do a little work on the paper, and besides, Sarah had texted earlier about a job possibility. Even if things were getting better in Dahlia, she needed to keep her options open. Anything could happen between now and December.

She'd slid out of her car and was fumbling with the office keys when she heard a loud zoom and another car, a black Audi, pulled up right beside her.

Erik Wennerman.

A clutch of something—attraction or nerves, she didn't care to know which—settled in her belly, but she forced a smile. He was an advertiser, after all. A very cute one, but an advertiser nonetheless.

She swiped a hand through her messy hair but decided there wasn't much she could do about it. She'd just been fishing, for goodness' sake.

"Hey there," she said as he got out of the car, expensive-looking sunglasses on, the kind Peter would wear. His tousled hair looked windblown, which surprisingly suited him. He gave her a wide smile.

"I'm glad I spotted you!"

"Oh?" She tilted her head, curious, but he didn't elaborate.

The office was cool as they stepped in, and she left the door open, flicked on the lights.

"I only stopped by to grab my laptop. You have good timing."

He stepped closer. "This might sound, well, a little cheesy, but I've been thinking of you since you ran out of the coffee shop last time."

"I didn't exactly run out."

"Well, left quickly, let's say." A dimple quirked, and she found herself unreasonably angry at it. Stop it, Rebecca. "Anyway, it got me thinking."

She waited, watched his face. If she wasn't mistaken, he was blushing. Even Peter hadn't done that. Was this guy for real?

"I—I'd love to take you to dinner some night. Preferably this Saturday."

"Ah—"

He held up a hand. "If you have plans, that's fine. We can go Friday or even Monday or Tuesday, if weeknights work better."

"Erik, I—"

"You're, well, you're a beautiful, successful, intelligent woman, and let's just say women like you don't often land in this part of South Carolina." The dimple deepened, and she found herself gritting her teeth, wanting to wipe that cute little grin off his handsome face.

She shook her head. No way. "I … can't."

She could have sworn she saw his jaw drop, and a thrill of triumph shot through her. For a moment, she felt like she was exacting some sort of strange revenge against Peter. Which of course was silly—this wasn't Peter, this was Erik.

"Uh, can't?"

"I'm sorry, but I've just come out of a very serious relationship. Dating is off-limits for me right now." Especially dating someone like you.

He looked genuinely disappointed. "How about as friends? I could use the company. Someone nice to talk with." He gave her a wry smile. "You have to admit there's a shortage of sophisticated dinner partners in Dahlia. It would be a good time."

"It's tempting, Erik, but I'm not ready."

He nodded. "I understand. Well, you can't blame a guy for trying."

"I hope it doesn't interfere with our business relationship. We've really appreciated having your partnership with the *Dahlia Weekly*."

He winked. "If I buy a bigger ad, would you go out with me?"

"Uh …"

"Teasing. Mostly." He slid his sunglasses back on, grinning.

"Well, at least let me walk you out."

She did, and they said goodbye at their cars. What a charmer. Peter had nothing on this guy.

And turning her key in the ignition, she drove toward Granny's house, willing her mind to stay on the road, on work, on the fish she'd caught. On anything but Erik Wennerman.

CHAPTER 20

Devon

DEVON ARRIVED AT Friday Night Giveaway just as people were starting to gather outside. A few perched on the low wall, which was much more comfortable than the actual town benches in front of the church. The benches had slats that poked into your legs when you sat, but the low wall was smooth, better for sitting.

As he pedaled up, one of the guys, Paulo, caught his eye, gave a little half-wave/nod, and another man, Sammy, held open the door and motioned him in.

"Come, come, Mista Devon, sir." Sammy's voice reminded him of music almost, like he came from far, far, away, though Devon knew he'd lived in Dahlia many years.

Mrs. Martha greeted him, checking him off on her clipboard. She came around the registration table to give him a quick hug.

"Well, hello there, Devon! How are you doing tonight?" Her cheek felt smooth and powdery, and her perfume smelled like roses, strong and sweet. He liked it.

"Great, Mrs. Martha. How are you?"

"Can't complain." She grinned, called over to the skinny older man at the bottles-and-clothing table.

"Mike, look who's nice and early tonight."

Mike waved. "Got a few minutes to help me sort?"

Devon pitched in, stacking the shampoo, mini soaps, and shaving creams just so, the way Mr. Mike liked them. Mike barely looked up as they sorted—bottles on the left, mini soaps next, down the line. His gray hair bobbed here and there with the motion.

"Hey there, sugar!" a voice called, and Devon looked up to see Marla waving at him through the opening between the fellowship hall and kitchen. "You stay out there till we get rolling, then I'm gonna need you back here with me doing dishes."

"You got it!"

He'd finished laying out the napkins and silverware and was getting ready to help Mike sort the clothes when Miss Becca arrived.

She stood in the doorway, looking nervous in her button-down shirt and jeans. She hadn't spotted him yet.

"This is the ministry night?" She fiddled with her car keys, and Mrs. Martha gave an extra big smile.

"You've come to volunteer?"

"Miss Becca!" Devon called, and he saw her face light up, and he ran to her, hugged her around the waist. "You came!"

Miss Becca smiled, then nodded at the older woman. "I'd love to volunteer if you need the help."

"Boy, do we ever!" Mrs. Martha's eyes crinkled. "Devon, can she help you get those clothes laid out? Mike, we got a new one!"

"Thank the good Lord," Mike said, waving hello.

"Probably just tonight." Miss Becca pushed up her sleeves as she filled out her nametag and got all checked in with Mrs. Martha, then followed Devon to the clothing table. "But I'm a hard worker."

"Ha, that's what I said. 'Just tonight.' But here I am, three years later, haven't missed a Friday." Mike elbowed him. "Right, Devon?"

"Right, Mr. Mike."

Miss Becca giggled, and that made him happy. He wanted her to like the giveaway, wanted her to keep coming back.

"So what can I do to help?" she asked.

"You take that end," Devon pointed toward the clothes. "Start by sorting them into men's on one side, women's on the other."

Ten minutes later, they had the clothing organized into a loose pile of men's and women's and were folding them as neat as possible. Jeans went with jeans, shirts with shirts, and the socks were in the center so they wouldn't roll off.

"Hey, you got a knack for it." Mike surveyed her work with a nod.

"Thanks." She smiled, motioned toward the bottles he'd organized. "Why all the mini bottles? Wouldn't it be more economical to give out big ones?"

Mike shook his head. "Nah, they like the little ones best. They fit better in their backpacks, and they need to carry light. One change of clothes, a few bottles to clean up, that sort of thing." He shrugged. "That, and the hotels give us this stuff for free."

"They do?"

"Most big hotels do, if you ask," Devon said. "They're supposed to throw out the used ones, you know—when people use a drop and leave it in the shower? Mr. Mike and some of his neighbors, they collect the leftovers."

Mike nodded. "Once a week or so, we go around to the hotels in Aberville, pick up our bags."

"We also ask people in town to donate any mini bottles they gather when on vacation," Martha called over from her table.

"Genius," Miss Becca said. "This place is like a machine! You do this every Friday, week after week? I'm thoroughly impressed."

Mrs. Martha clapped her hands. "It's time for our guests!"

"It's time!" Devon turned to Miss Becca, grinning. "Mrs. Martha, can I ring the bell?"

"By all means," she said, and handed him the chunky gold hand-bell. It made a big boiiiing sound, and the men and women began to stream in, talking and joking as they approached the registration table.

"Now what?" Miss Becca asked.

"Follow my lead," Mike told her, stepping toward the rear of the bottles table and motioning her to do the same on her side. "When the guests come up, smile and help with whatever they want. They can fill one of these plastic bags with whatever they want. One bag per guest."

"Guest. I like that."

"Well, it's a lot more respectful than, say, 'homeless client' or 'needy.' I mean, people are people." Mike tapped his head.

"Good point."

They all took their places, and Devon slipped into the kitchen to run food. Later he'd join Marla to help with dishes. That was his favorite part. The smell of the dish soap reminded him of the one Mama used to use, reminded him of back when she was alive and they'd do after-dinner dishes together, side by side at the sink. Plus it was fun, and Marla always let him blow bubbles at the end.

At one point he came out to refill the bread basket and saw two of the guests chatting with Miss Becca, who was laughing so hard she was red in the face. She caught Devon's eye and waved, and he waved back. He liked that she was having a good time, liked that she looked happy.

Mr. Sammy came up then and gave Miss Becca a big hand-shake, the kind that shook her whole arm, said she was "mighty welcome." Then he sat down at the piano and began to play a jazzed-up version of "Amazing Grace."

The next time Devon came out of the kitchen, he saw his new fishing friend, JJ, there with his dad. Mr. Josh had a guitar slung over his shoulder, and he was trying to show Mr. Sammy how to play while JJ and Miss Becca watched. It was a dancy, silly kind of beat, and Miss Becca was bobbing her knees to it, and she'd pulled her hair back in a ponytail. His chest felt tight, and he was just starting to feel the slightest bit jealous of JJ, standing there with her, all swaying and smiling, when they both turned, and JJ grinned, and Miss Becca motioned him over, caught him in a hug, and then suddenly everything was all right again, and he wondered why he'd felt that way to begin with. Mama always said jealousy was a downright rotten way to feel, one of the seven deadly sins for a reason.

"A tranquil heart gives life to the flesh, but envy makes the bones rot," Mama would say, from Proverbs. She'd said it the first time after Devon had complained one day about wanting the Lego ninja set he'd seen on television, the big set that came with the gold sensei, especially after one of the kids at school bragged about having it.

JJ came back to the dish room with him and Marla, helped scrub and stack dishes and run plates, and when he'd left—early, he and his dad had to be somewhere at the crack of dawn the next day, he'd told Devon—JJ had hugged him and told him to come fishing sometime soon.

"We won't be there this Sunday, but next weekend for sure," JJ'd said, and then he was gone and Devon and Marla were in their dishes groove, singing and dancing and blowing bubbles.

"Well, this is certainly where the party is!" he heard and looked over to see Miss Becca standing there, smiling and watching them fan bubbles around.

"Hey, Miss Becca! You know Miss Marla, from my school?"

"Marla Bryant, and it's good to see you, Rebecca." Marla waved. "I'd shake your hand, but I'll get you all wet."

"Good to see you!" Miss Becca smiled back. "Actually, I came to pitch in, if you need the help. They sent me to tell you it's over and time for the volunteers to eat."

"Throw on an apron and we'll make quick work of it." Marla motioned to the hooks on the wall, where some aprons hung.

Devon wrinkled a nose. "It gets pretty messy."

Soon she was following their lead, rinsing utensils and plates and setting them in the big industrial dishwasher.

"This is pretty expensive equipment for a church in a small town," she said.

"Oh, we got the dishwasher when the Chinese food place closed a few years ago," Marla said, searching the cabinets behind them for the detergent. "Figured we'd need it, and church and community members chipped in quite a lot, really on faith. That was when this ministry first got going. You were probably this big then." She smiled at Devon, held her hand low to the ground.

"Marla's first lady here, so she knows all this stuff," Devon said.

"First lady?"

Marla laughed. "He means the preacher's wife."

"Ohhhh." Miss Becca blushed. "Sorry. I don't know all the lingo."

Marla waved her hand. "No one does, don't you worry about that!"

"Do I hear my beautiful bride back here?" came a booming voice, and they all looked up to see Rev round the corner.

"And I hear my handsome husband."

"Hey, Rev!" Devon turned off the spray. "This is Miss Becca. The one I told you about."

"Well, hey there, Miss Becca." Rev smiled at Devon. "Hey, Devon."

"Nice to meet you, Reverend Bryant." Miss Becca said.

"Just Reverend is fine, or Rev. That's what most people call me, anyway." Rev leaned over, kissed his wife, and loosened his blue-green tie, pushed up his shirtsleeves. "How about we eat, and then can I pitch in, too?"

Marla giggled. "You have the best timing in the world, love."

"All done!" Devon said, set the last plate inside the washer.

"Rev has seminary on Fridays and all day Saturday," Marla explained. "Finishing his doctorate down in Columbia."

"He used to be here every single Friday, but now he usually gets here at the very end," Devon said.

"One more semester of coursework, and then it's all writing till the end. Then I can be here all the time," Rev said.

Devon tried to untie his apron, which he'd somehow managed to triple-knot. Miss Becca bent down, helped him with the knots. Then they all headed out to the front room, where the remaining volunteers were sitting at one of the long tables.

Someone passed him a plate of food piled high with fried chicken, butterbeans, cornbread, and the creamiest mac-and-cheese casserole he'd tasted in a long time, and he sat next to Miss Becca, who was digging in like she hadn't seen food in weeks.

When they were done and had cleaned up, the rest of the volunteers left, and Devon and Miss Becca brought some of the empty, half flattened boxes to the recycling bin out back while Rev and Marla finished inside.

It was twilight, Devon's favorite time, the heat of the day not so bad anymore, the sky gray and blue, with a hazy orange glow off in the distance. From somewhere, an owl hooted, like it was welcoming the night.

"There!" he said, and jumped basketball-style to toss the final flattened box inside.

He cheered like he'd made the winning shot, arms raised high in victory, when he noticed Miss Becca staring at his midsection, a funny look on her face.

He glanced down, realized too late his T-shirt had lifted up, and he was standing directly under the streetlight, which lit his bruises like his very own look-at-me spotlight.

"Oh, this?" He forced a laugh. "Don't you worry, Miss Becca. I took a really bad fall on my bike last week. I'm all better, though it hurt like crazy for a while."

He shrugged like it was nothing, all the while crossing his fingers that she'd buy it. His heart thudded like it was in his throat, and his mouth got super dry, and he didn't know whether he wanted to cry or run or hold on tight and see it through, play the game.

He shouldn't have let his guard down, should have remembered the bruises, but with Uncle T still gone on his trip, he'd felt like he was on top of the world, carefree, like everything had all been a bad dream, but for Memaw still in the bed, and he really didn't quite know what to do about that.

Miss Becca was still staring, but she had scrunched her brow now, and he saw it was more with sympathy than with suspicion. His heart thudded downward, out of his throat and back where it belonged, and he managed to swallow.

"Wanna see? It's pretty nasty," he said, started to lift his shirt like it really was all nothing, an accident like he'd said, and she crept closer.

"Ugh, poor you. That looks like it kills!"

"What does?" Marla stepped outside then, car keys jangling, Rev right behind her.

"I fell off my bike last week," he said, and he saw their faces turn to worry. "The bike's fine, though, rides like before, but I got all bruised up. The kids at camp said it could have been a lot worse. One of them took a spill not too long ago and broke his leg."

Devon grimaced, then pointed to Marla's keys.

"Time to go?"

Miss Becca pulled out her own keys. "Want me to drive you? I'm pretty sure I can fit your bike in the back. I assume you rode your bike here."

"No thanks, Miss Becca. Marla and Rev here said they'll run me home."

Marla nodded. "We've got some business out that way. Our

standing after-supper date with Miz Louree Jackson, matriarch of
Dahlia, to hear her tell it."

"Miz Louree's a shut-in," Devon said.

Miss Becca giggled. "Sounds like a prisoner."

Rev laughed, slapped his leg. The sound made a sharp clap,
echoed through the small enclosure.

"I always say the same thing." He reached over, gave Miss Becca's hand a shake. "Nice of you to join us tonight, Miss Becca. We
welcome you back every week. Hope to see you Sunday, too."

Marla drove the SUV, Devon's bike in the way back and the
to-go box for Memaw resting on his lap, while Rev leaned back,
closed his eyes. Devon was quiet on the drive, though Marla asked
a few questions about Miss Becca, and whether he thought she'd
come again, and whether she'd liked the giveaway, and whether
Devon needed anything for his bruises.

"I'm okay, but thanks."

"If you're sure, honey. We're here for you." She turned around to
look at him when she pulled up to his house, put the SUV in park.
"Like family."

"I know."

They waved when they pulled away, and he thought about that
word, family, and wished it really were so. Wished he could just
go live with them, move right into the parsonage, him and Memaw. Or even, he admitted in the private corner of his heart, just
him. Though he knew that was a wrong way to think. He needed
Memaw and Memaw needed him, and Robinsons stuck together.
He'd promised Mama. And besides, who would take care of the
memory garden if they didn't live here anymore?

He thought about JJ and his dad, remembered the last time
they'd gone fishing. Sunday. T hadn't been around, so he hadn't
stayed out so long this time, but they'd caught a few bass apiece,
and JJ's dad let them go off again to the tunnel.

"Your dad really doesn't care?" Devon had asked as they slipped through the grate, stepped inside. JJ'd told him the "keep out" signs were old, and the county had stopped using the drain like forty years ago or something.

JJ shrugged. "Nah, he said when he was a kid he had his places, too, and it's good for kids to have hidey holes. 'Course, back then he was hiding from his big sister, but whatevs."

The tunnel was cool and dark, way cooler than the hot summer day outside, and you could go high enough inside to where you could see the river but no one could see you. It felt safe, somehow. Secure. Like all the bad stuff in the world could stay out, stay far away.

To be honest, he felt that way around JJ and his dad, too. And around Rev and Marla. He couldn't remember the last time he'd felt that way—really, truly safe. Not since Mama had died, he imagined.

Now, Devon watched Marla's SUV get to the end of the street and turn. He knelt down at the memory garden after they were long gone and sat there awhile, talking with Mama in his mind. The night air felt good, the gentle breeze a caress reminding him of Mrs. Martha's powdery cheek, and he didn't even realize he was crying until he felt the wetness on his cheeks.

Then, standing from his crouch, he wheeled his bike around the back and went inside to bring Memaw her dinner.

CHAPTER 21

Rebecca

THE MONDAY AFTER GIVEAWAY NIGHT brought the most beautiful sunrise Rebecca had seen since she'd arrived in Dahlia. She'd awakened before dawn, tried to remember the barest hint of a dream but couldn't. Unable to go back to sleep, she'd given up and found herself in the kitchen, nursing a quiet cup of coffee. When the sun peeked over the trees, a giant nectarine against a hazy rose-gray sky, a gasp slipped from her. Somehow, the massive sun, the dim sky, and the faint hint of trees at the horizon made her feel timeless, reverent, and incredibly, incredibly small.

She heard the pad of slippered feet behind her. "God sure did create a masterpiece, didn't he," Granny murmured, her voice still husky with sleep.

"It's beautiful," Rebecca whispered, eyes still on the sun.

Granny filled a cup, took a chair beside her, and together they watched the sun make its slow ascent.

After a few minutes, Rebecca took a sip from her mug, the sound breaking the hush of the room. She smiled at Granny.

"Mornin', sunshine."

Granny brought her mug to her lips.

"You stole my line. Busy day today?"

"Very. We lay out the paper tomorrow, so today is finalizing—last minute stories, typing, calls to advertisers dragging feet. Oh, and read over Tiff's stories to make sure they're not so syrupy sweet." She made a face.

"Tiff's your reporter? How's she coming along—still very junior?"

Rebecca toyed with her mug. "Tiff's, well, sweet. It's a struggle to get her to think like a newshound. She loves feature stories, and she's a good writer, so I can pawn off most of those on her, but sometimes ..." She shook her head. "Her favorite color's pink, if that tells you anything."

"Your favorite color used to be pink, might I remind you."

"When I was five!"

Granny fanned a brow. "I remember a certain young woman who used to refuse to wear old clothes fishing with her Gramps and threw an all-out hissy fit when her favorite pink sneakers got soaked."

Rebecca covered her mouth. "Oh, those shoes! They were magnificent."

"And pink as the risen day."

Rebecca giggled again. "You're right. I did love pink."

They watched the sun rise higher, and Rebecca stood to refill their mugs. She remembered those mornings with Gramps, how at first she'd hated being awakened at dawn. On a weekend, of all times. But Gramps had said he'd needed help, and Granny had been insistent, so she'd gone. Those reluctant mornings ended up becoming one of her favorite things about summers in Dahlia. She missed them, missed so much of that time, and wondered why she'd never come back to visit in all those years except that once, for the funeral. It wasn't just the fishing. It was the way you could be with Gramps and not have to say anything at all. "You just be you, and let everybody else worry 'bout the rest, girl," he'd been fond of saying. His words still echoed in her ears at times. She remembered the feel of the pole in her hands, how Gramps would show her how to pull it back, just so, and barely flick it out over the water. "Easy, girl. You don't need much, just enough to do the deed," he'd say.

She thought of young JJ, the look of pride on his face when he'd landed that bass the other day. The way Josh had stood back, let his son have his moment, before helping with the net.

A flood of warmth rushed over her.

"Penny for your thoughts," Granny said, and Rebecca remembered the mugs in her hands.

"Thinking of Gramps, I guess. How much I miss him." Rebecca set the mugs on the table, took her seat. "You know, I went fishing the other day and ended up casting with my old friend JJ—well, I guess he goes by Josh Jamison now."

"Now that was a nice boy. He's turned out to be a fine man, too. And not too shabby on the eyes, if I don't say so myself."

Rebecca laughed. "He is a good guy. Though it's hard to get used to calling him 'Josh' and his son 'JJ,' I have to admit. Fishing with him made me think a lot about the old days. It's funny how you don't realize how precious something is until it's gone."

"Got that right. You know, I still hear him sometimes, your Gramps," Granny leaned back. "I hear the floorboards shift, and it sounds like him, walking through the house, like he's going to walk in here any moment and say, 'Helen, have you seen my watch?'" Granny's voice dropped in imitation.

"He was always looking for his watch! Or his slippers. What'd he call them, home shoes?"

Granny grinned, the years dropping from her face. "And his keys. That man would lose his head if it weren't latched on. I used to tease him all the time about that." She shook her head suddenly.

"I'm a silly old woman. Hearing footsteps like he was here just yesterday. It's been fifteen years this March."

"It doesn't seem that long." Rebecca closed her eyes, ticked off the years in her head. She'd been twenty-five, had flown in from New York and barely made it in time for the funeral. "You must miss him terribly."

"It's hard sometimes. It was worse at first, those initial years." Granny fiddled with the mug, voice soft. "I remember not even wanting to get out of bed." She cleared her throat. "But a good friend did the trick. Betty. Told me, 'Get through today, Helen. That's all you have to do.' And today turned into tomorrow, and tomorrow turned into the next, and soon I was out there again, doing my part. The missing never goes away. But you learn to go on, somehow."

"You always seemed so strong." Rebecca took Granny's hand. "I didn't realize how hard it was. To go on. To deal with everything."

"Oh, honey, it was so hard. But you know what? Faith kept me going. Still does. And I know he's up there, waiting for me in heaven."

Granny squeezed Rebecca's hand twice. Love you.

Love you back, Rebecca squeezed in reply.

"I'm sorry, Granny." Her grandmother's wrinkles were smooth and comforting beneath her fingers, and Rebecca squeezed tighter. "Sorry I wasn't here for you, afterwards. Not in a better way. I was so caught up in my—my own stupid little world, and I didn't realize."

She'd been a jerk. A selfish, self-absorbed jerk. And that was the plain truth. A lump began to form in her throat.

"Sweet girl, you weren't meant to be. You needed to spread your wings, do your thing. Learn to be you."

"I needed to be there for the people I love." Rebecca let out a long breath. "Granny, I mean it—I'm sorry. I love you. I learned so much from you. You and Gramps. And even if I haven't acted very grateful since you brought me here …" She squeezed Granny's hand once more, then let go. "I'm very, very thankful you did."

She meant it. Dahlia could be boring, and it drove her crazy most days, but this time with Granny, the chance to heal and get away from everything, had been exactly what she'd needed. Somehow, Granny had known that. Known her better than Rebecca knew herself, perhaps.

"Oh, girl, you are a good one. Always did have my heart. That reporter of yours? Her sweet's got nothing on yours. Even if you do say you don't like sappy stories anymore."

Rebecca made a face, and they laughed, scraped the chairs on the linoleum as they rose from the table.

As she drove to work, she passed the turn that led to Devon's side of town, which led to remembering how much fun she'd had at his church giveaway Friday. She smiled at that, at how much things had changed. A year ago, "fun" would have been a great party or restaurant, some exciting trip with friends or Peter. She frowned; now that she thought about it, she wouldn't exactly call times with Peter "fun" at all. They had gone out on the town quite a bit, which was always exciting, but it was usually for business, not pleasure. To see or be seen, or as he called it, networking.

In a million years she wouldn't have thought spending four hours folding old clothes and chatting it up with homeless guys at a church giveaway would be a good time, and yet it was the best night she'd had in ages. Even counting New York.

And to think she almost hadn't gone.

But she had, despite her misgivings, despite worries that she'd get sucked into some obligatory donation or church invite, or have to stand there all night with a cheesy way-too-wholesome smile on her face saying "oh golly" and "shucks" and commenting on the weather.

They, the volunteers and guests, had been nice. Really nice. Some wouldn't meet her eye or say a word, but others were personable, funny, like those two guys who kept her rolling with jokes all night. No wonder Devon liked it, went week after week. Plus the food was amazing.

She couldn't tell if half the people were volunteers or homeless, and maybe that was the point. The man with the musical accent, Sammy, who called her "Miss Lady" and reminded her of one of those Gullah men who'd woven her a palm basket once, down in Charleston, acted like he ran the place. Sweet, perky Mrs. Martha with the white hair and the clipboard. Mike, who had a killer dry sense of humor. She found out after that he'd lost his wife to cancer four months ago. She was half surprised Granny didn't walk in and help, though she knew Granny had another commitment that night with a couple of her longtime pals.

Devon himself was a dynamo, she thought as she turned onto Main Street, paused to let a couple cross the road. And he did it all with a smile, like work was normal and natural and expected, no big deal. He made it fun, and just being around him made her feel lighter inside. When she was eleven, she didn't think her mom would have let her in the kitchen to load the dishwasher with their expensive plates and cups, let alone bike to a church and volunteer with a bunch of poor people. She'd been coddled, she realized now. Coddled and pampered and protected from the real world.

Even his pastor was an all right guy. Rev's "welcome back anytime" had felt genuine, and the Sunday sermon actually sounded interesting. She didn't go or anything, but he'd said he was planning to preach on soccer, something about how teamwork, controlling the ball, and making the goal had everything to do with a person's faith walk. If they'd done sermons like that when she was a kid, maybe she would have stayed alert and engaged in church instead of hightailing it the first chance she had. This pastor was doing something right if he'd managed to get an eleven-year-old kid hooked on church. Even if he did use words like "faith walk."

She needed to go back and do an article about the place.

Her cell phone buzzed, and she answered as she pulled up to the newspaper office.

"Rebecca Chastain," she answered, not bothering to look at the caller ID.

"It's happened," a dramatic voice came over the line. "You do have a Southern accent."

Sarah. Rebecca almost cackled as she shifted the car into park.

"I do not have a Southern accent." Rebecca gave an exaggerated huff, grinning.

"You totally do. 'Rebecca Chastayyyyyn, how may I help yewwwwww?'" Sarah mimicked her in a high falsetto, adding at least six syllables to the words.

"Knock it off, babe," Rebecca countered in her best New York cabbie impression, and the women laughed.

"It's good to hear your voice." Sarah's own was warm across the miles. "How've you been? You sound happy. I don't think we've done much but text these last few weeks. It's been crazy here."

"Here, too! And I am happy, sort of." Rebecca looked out her car window at the newspaper office, the "open" sign already turned around. Inside, she could see Millie bustling about, making coffee and straightening up, preparing for the busy day ahead.

"What do you do all day? Do you like it? Are you going to come back with all these hometown quirks?"

Rebecca found herself wanting to tell all about Devon, and the fishing hole she'd rediscovered, and her old friend Josh and his cute little son with the freckles and crazy hair, and the James Watkins stories, but it all sounded like the kind of stereotypical Southern living Sarah would tease her about endlessly.

"Would you believe I've been fishing? I connected with an old friend, and he and his son and I caught, like, five bass in the river the other day," she summed up instead, and Sarah laughed heartily.

"I love it! Fishing! Please text me a picture of you and a worm. Better yet, post it on socials. Marisol and I had actual bets on whether you'd take up fishing or knitting. Or, what's that thing they do with the fruits and vegetables—preserving, or canning?" Sarah teased. "Oh, Rebecca, I've missed you."

"I miss you too, Sarah."

She did. Suddenly, the smells and sounds of New York came back in a rush, and she closed her eyes, remembering the last time she'd seen her friend, at their goodbye brunch at that French-fusion place in the Village.

Sarah and Marisol had done their best to act normal, like Rebecca hadn't just been in the psych ward, like she was heading off on a new adventure and not some therapist-ordered respite in the middle of nowhere. But at the end of their lunch, after Marisol had slipped off to the restroom, Sarah had pressed something into Rebecca's hand. She'd opened it to see a small yellow-crystal sun on a slim chain. Rebecca had held it up, and it sparkled in the afternoon light, throwing prisms of color around the restaurant. For hope, Sarah had told her then, hugging her hard and tight, like she was afraid Rebecca would disappear, never come back, gone for good.

Rebecca had hung the sun on her rearview mirror in the car, and she batted it now, remembering that day, remembering the feel of her friend's arms around her neck, remembering the long walk back to her apartment, where she and Granny had packed the last of her things and said goodbye to the city.

"How are you really doing?" Sarah's voice was quiet.

"Honestly, much better."

"Really?" Sarah let out a shaky laugh. "I've been worried about you, girlfriend."

"Scout's honor. I've been taking my Prozac, laying low, exercising, and steering clear of all men. Even the cute ones."

"I don't know, Mr. Fishing Buddy sounds like an eligible man."

Sarah's tone was suggestive, and Rebecca snorted. "Seriously, I even turned down a date with a mega-gorgeous man. We're talking better-looking than Peter."

"I'm impressed."

"You should be." Rebecca pictured Erik, his warm smile, the way his button-down and slender tie hung just right on his trim physique. A little shiver threatened, and she tamped it down. No dating, she reminded herself. Not for a long, long time.

As they hung up, Rebecca realized that for the first time, she'd said Peter's name like it was nothing.

For an instant, she pictured him. His dark hair, perfect teeth. His laugh. The oddest thought struck her then—Peter was like an illusion. Like a man she'd seen in a movie, or dreamed about. Not real at all. Just an idea. An idea she thought she'd been in love with.

An idea she'd almost died for. An involuntary shudder ran through her.

And giving the crystal yellow sun a last playful swing, she slid her leather bag onto her shoulder and headed into the office.

The morning flew by in a flurry of activity, as usual: Dinah on sales calls, Millie dealing with customers, Tiff finishing her stories while tap-tapping her stilettos—strappy beige sandal stilettos, for the summertime, of course—and Rebecca herself, hair top-knotted and a red pen in her hand, marking up changes to the finished pieces.

The phone rang, and Rebecca grabbed it.

"I have two things to say to you this morning, Rebecca Chastain, and I don't want any lip," the woman's gruff voice began, and Rebecca groaned inwardly.

"Mrs. Pauling?" Rebecca asked politely.

"Of course," Lib Pauling snapped. "Now, I know you're getting ready to put out this week's paper, and I want to make sure we're not going to have any of those ridiculous stories about the new banks and Dahlia's economy. I'll have you know my precious son-in-law is the president of one of those banks, and you're talking about real people when you write that garbage. And two," Lib paused for a deep breath, Rebecca waiting as patiently as she could muster. "That story on those two hikers who got lost in the state park, the one whose mama was born here? That was most excellent. Ron Stone would have been proud."

Rebecca blinked. Lib Pauling had actually told her the mythically perfect former *Dahlia Weekly* editor would have liked her article? Been proud? That was a first.

"Well, I appreciate that, Mrs—"

"Don't thank me." Maybe it was Rebecca's imagination, but Lib's voice sounded a tad less clipped than before. Softer, somehow. Then she barked, "Keep it up," and hung up.

Rebecca sat a moment, staring at the receiver in her hand. Lib Pauling was truly one of the most confusing women she'd ever met.

"Was that Mrs. Pauling?" Millie asked as she rose from her seat, the creak loud above the din of the newsroom.

"Yeah." Rebecca shook her head. "That one's hot and cold."

Millie crossed the room, filled a cup from the coffee station. "She was a lot nicer before she lost her husband a few years ago. Went through quite a spell for a time. She used to come in here and scream at the last editor all the time before he finally barred her from the office."

Lib, a widow? Still, Rebecca couldn't help herself.

"This is the nicer version?"

Millie shrugged, tried to disguise a smirk as she headed back to her desk. "In a manner of speaking."

The bell above the door tinkled, and in walked Josh Jamison, checkbook in hand.

"Well, hey there!" she said with a smile, standing to greet him. He wore jeans and a green T shirt, the logo for Jamison Contracting front and center, and a pencil was tucked behind his ear. As they hugged, she saw Dinah stop what she was doing and stare up at him, a little curve on her lips. Tiff grinned from over her shoulder, then turned back to her computer.

"Ran out for some more supplies, thought I'd swing by and pay my ad bill." He handed a check to Millie, gave her a wink before he turned back to Rebecca. "That was some time on Friday. I don't think JJ talked about anything else all weekend."

Rebecca laughed. "I don't blame him. It really was fun."

"I think we'll probably be there again this week. You going?"

Part of her wanted to beg off, make up some excuse. The other part wondered what she was afraid of. Going a couple times didn't commit her to going forever. And there was the article to do.

"I think so."

"Well, good! See you then, if I don't see you before." His grin was boyish, made him look ten years younger, and she realized she hadn't stopped smiling since he'd come in. "Bye, ladies."

He waved a general goodbye at the office, turned to go. But as he got to the door, it opened.

In stepped Erik Wennerman.

Instantly, Josh's demeanor changed. He pulled up short, stiffened.

"Jamison." Erik's smile was poised, and he stood aside, let Josh slide past.

She couldn't see the expression on his face, but the muttered "Wennerman" said it all. Josh was out the door and into his truck, gone.

She stared after him, the mood of the newsroom suddenly turned on end, like everything had gone quiet. Too quiet.

Erik approached her desk. He looked good as usual. Today he wore a burgundy and white striped shirt, and the tie was loosened, the collar unbuttoned. The slim khakis fit nicely, and today he wore a large silver watch. He carried a few folders.

It was the first time since she'd seen him last week, when he'd asked her out. Her tongue felt dry in her mouth. She forced a smile. Act natural. Just because he'd asked her out didn't mean she needed to act like a teenager. They needed the business, anyway, and she couldn't afford to push him away.

"Got a minute?"

"Absolutely." Her voice sounded warm to her ears, like she dealt with this every day of her life. Out of the corner of her eye she saw Millie watching them.

"Brought you some more of our latest plans, thought maybe you could steer me on the timing." He opened the folders on her desk, his hand faintly brushing hers as he pointed to one of the papers. "Retire in style," the one on top proclaimed in extra-large print, with a picture of a smiling older couple, each holding a tennis racquet, taking much of the space below. The company logo and contact information was at the bottom.

He looked at her under dark, thick lashes. "Think maybe you can run a little business announcement in the paper when we launch these ads? I'm thinking next week." She hesitated, and he rushed on, "We're thinking of doing two color full-pagers next week, really make a big splash."

She nodded quickly. "Sure. It'll have to be short, but we can do that."

He sat back, grinned. "I really appreciate that. Maybe you can let me take you out to lunch on Wednesday, celebrate the opening of our Aberville facility."

She opened her mouth, then shut it as quickly and stood, smiling. End of conversation.

"I'm not free Wednesday, but if you come by later in the week, we can go over the details of the ad, line up this month's schedule."

"Perfect." And he was out the door, the purr of his sleek Audi loud and powerful.

Rebecca went to the coffee machine, poured another cup.

"I don't like him," Millie said to no one and everyone, lips pressed into a thin line.

Rebecca couldn't help but laugh. "Why in the world not?"

"He's a 'player,'" the secretary pronounced, like she'd eaten bad fish and wished she could spit it out.

"Well, he's helping to keep this newspaper afloat."

"Hmpf. At what cost? Besides, it's doing better."

"I'm not sure that's quite the point."

Millie looked like she wanted to say much more, but she didn't respond, just turned back to her classifieds. The others said nothing, Tiff lost in a story, Dinah on the phone.

Rebecca took a seat, staring at the Wennerman folder, the yellow sun on the company logo nothing at all like the one dangling from the rearview mirror in her car.

CHAPTER 22

Devon

DEVON WAS STARTING to get edgy. Uncle T hadn't returned. As time passed, he found himself watching cars on the road, looking out for his uncle's brown Cadillac. Waiting. Dreading. Once he'd seen a brown car and almost wrecked his bike for real, but it was only an old Chevy, and when it passed, a big rusted panel on the side, Devon saw it looked nothing at all like T's except the color.

"Careful you don't feed your worries too much or they'll grow fat on you," Memaw used to tell him sometimes, when she'd catch him staring out the window, frowning. Uncle T didn't come around much back then, and certainly didn't bring his friends over. Memaw wouldn't have stood for that. His biggest worries then were how to stop Marquis from picking on CJ, or staying on top of his homework. Now his worries were far different. Far worse.

Though he didn't let himself worry when he could help it. The worries tended to sneak in, catch him unawares. Like now, when he was supposed to be in the recliner doing his reading log but instead kept jumping every time he heard a car door slam outside at the neighbors', or someone yell from across the way.

"Trust in the Lord with all your heart" came back to him then, and he sighed, fiddled with the pencil. He'd told Miss Becca to give it to God, and he'd meant what he'd said. For the most part, he tried to live that way, just throw himself into work and camp and church and anything else that came his way.

But sometimes like today, he'd find himself sitting there, staring out the front window, heart all tight and knotty, waiting to hear the familiar putt-putt of T's engine, or the bang of the screen door. He'd wake late at night sure he'd heard laughter or someone's hand slam down hard on the kitchen table, then realize he'd dreamed it, and T really wasn't there at all. His bruises were almost gone now, and his ribs didn't hurt whenever he lifted his arms. But he was afraid of letting his guard down, afraid to relax too deeply.

Like a caged rabbit, he didn't want to sleep for fear the wolf would come and eat him alive.

If there was one big positive it was that Memaw was doing much better. Yesterday, he'd come home from camp and found the bread on the counter instead of in the fridge where he'd left it, a knife with peanut butter in the sink. When he'd checked on her, she was sleeping, but her hair smelled like shampoo, and he knew she'd been up, been moving around the house.

He'd gone back to sleeping in his own room again, and this morning, she'd been awake when he popped in to say goodbye before camp.

"Have a good day, honey," she said, and she almost sounded like her old self.

But today she was sound asleep when he'd gotten home, and he realized that was the worst of it. The quiet. The absence of sound made him want for the sound.

That was it. He tucked the reading log in his backpack, then slipped out the door, turning the lock and pocketing his key. Five minutes later he was pedaling down Aberville Road.

For the next two hours he helped Mr. Allen stock shelves, sweep the floor, and wash the windows. After, Mr. Allen gave him a few dollars and a bag of apples.

"When you get old enough, you can come work here at the counter, like your mama did, Son," Mr. Allen said in his raspy voice, smiled. "You're a good boy, and a good worker."

"Thanks, Mr. Allen."

Devon smiled at him, but deep down, he didn't want that at all. He didn't want to work at the corner shop, didn't want to stay on in Dahlia. He wanted to go to college like the kid in the book he was reading, the one whose brother was in a gang but who'd managed to "break the cycle" and achieve his dreams. "Breaking the cycle" was one of the things they talked about a lot at camp, that and staying in school and steering clear of drugs and alcohol, saying no to abuse, telling a trusted adult when they saw something they knew was wrong.

A lot of that stuff wouldn't work at all in real life. You didn't go telling a trusted adult your uncle's dealing drugs out of your house while your sick Memaw's laying in the bed and you're trying to sneak in through the window so you don't get spotted and dragged into the whole mess. You don't tell a trusted adult unless you want the whole thing to go caving in on you and you're yanked into some Home for Kids faster than you can snap.

But college, college was one of those things that would work. He could picture himself there, on some fancy campus with his blue backpack and a nice fresh clean shirt. A girl would come up and talk to him, a pretty girl, with good teeth and eyes that smiled along with her mouth, and they'd go to football games or sit in the center of one of those campus squares they talked about in the books, where people discussed philosophy or quizzed each other for exams.

Rev told him about college sometimes. He'd met Marla there, back before he was a preacher, and they'd go get ice cream and sit and stare at books together, not a care in the world beyond an A on a paper or getting to a part-time job on time.

"Those were the days," Rev would say, shaking his head. "It'll be strange when I finally finish seminary. I'll have to go back and teach someday just 'cause I miss it!"

Devon had laughed, but privately he'd started to panic. What if Rev did leave one day, if he and Marla did move off and go teach someplace, left him far behind?

He'd be alone then, good and alone. Give it to God, he nodded to himself. No sense worrying about the future. God would provide, one way or the other.

He took the long way back, and it was almost dark when he got home. His eyes shot to the carport on reflex, and he breathed a sigh of relief, heart fluttering back to normal. No Cadillac.

And he hurried in to make him and Memaw some supper.

CHAPTER 23

Rebecca

ON WEDNESDAY, Rebecca sat in a quiet corner of the James Watkins cafeteria with ten-year-old Tamika, willing herself to be patient, to listen. The girl gazed out the window at the other kids playing. The look on her face said she'd rather be anywhere but here.

Rebecca gave the girl an encouraging smile, pen poised over the reporter's notebook.

"Tamika, how long have you been going to James Watkins?"

The girl shrugged.

"Since you started school?"

She shrugged again. Rebecca frowned.

"What grade are you in?"

Tamika's voice was so quiet Rebecca could barely hear her, leaned closer.

"Say again?"

"Going into fifth."

The girl looked completely miserable, her arms crossed tight against the electric-blue tank top. She was pretty, that much Rebecca could tell, with chocolate-brown skin and the darkest, most vivid brown eyes Rebecca had ever seen, but her looks were overshadowed by something—discomfort? fear?—that made her look far older than her years.

Rebecca infused as much warmth into her smile as she could, reached out to touch the girl's hand. Tamika flinched.

"Tamika, listen. I'm not going to ask you anything bad or scary, and you don't even have to answer my questions." Rebecca spoke quietly. "You don't even have to talk to me at all. You can go right out there to recess with your friends, if that's easier."

Tamika looked surprised.

Rebecca held her gaze. "I mean it."

The girl appeared to mull over the words, then shrugged again. "They said it might help someone else." Her voice was still soft, but at least this time Rebecca could hear her.

"It might," Rebecca said. "Well, let's start with the easy stuff. Where do you live?"

"Right out there." The girl motioned vaguely out the window, toward the rows of houses beyond the playground.

"That neighborhood?"

"Those cars," Tamika said clearly, her gaze matching Rebecca's. "My brother and Mama and me, we been sleepin' in our car the last three nights."

"Oh." Rebecca's voice went small.

"Mama said the landlord kicked us out on account a' her not paying the rent on time, but it's all right. Tonight we're s'posed to bunk at Aunt Cici's. That's Mama's best friend. Said we can stay in her guest room a little while, till her man comes home from his trip. At least I can take a shower."

For once in her life, Rebecca had no words. She could only listen, and write.

"Mama says the shelter down in Aberville won't take us, 'cause it's summer and there's no major need. If it were winter we could at least use their showers, or stay in the crisis rooms or whatever they call 'em, but if we go lookin' for a room now, they'll have to send me and Ronny to the kids' home and Mama to some women's place for getting your life on track. Anyway, Mama doesn't want to split us up, and Ronny's a crybaby anyway, and I figure the car's fine a few days, and who knows? Maybe Aunt Cici'll keep us awhile, till Mama figures out something. Mama's got an interview this morning, so who knows."

A thousand words threatened: How can you live in a car? Is it safe? How old is your brother? Does the social welfare office know? A verse came from somewhere, maybe Millie, or Granny's walls—be quick to listen, slow to speak. Rebecca bit her tongue, nodded for Tamika to go on.

She'd heard about people living in their cars, heard about kids, too. When she lived in New York, she'd encountered plenty of people on the streets, even knew a few of the guys on her block and one lady by name. Char, the woman's name had been, and Rebecca recalled her stringy hair, toothy grin, and saucy, wildly inappropriate jokes. Rebecca would give them a dollar here or there. Once, she'd even given Char a bunch of her old bras and other hand-me-down clothes. Char had made some wisecrack about the bras being good for business, and Rebecca had fooled herself into thinking Char didn't mind being on the streets. Much.

But this was the first time she'd actually talked with a homeless kid.

For the first time, Rebecca caught a glimpse of what it might be like to live that way.

In a car. With no place to shower.

And despite how Char had always come off, Rebecca knew it was no joke. Char had just been dealing with it the best way she knew how.

How would this kid end up? How would Tamika deal with it down the line? Humor? Drugs? Depression? Would she be a fighter, or would all this wear her down, kill her spirit?

After work, she swung by Smathers Grocery, "Where We Have It All," as the sign proclaimed. Granny needed beans and rice for a big pot of chili she was cooking that night.

Smathers reminded her of the small grocery/convenience shops in New York, only this place really did seem to have mostly everything. If they didn't have it, rumor had it you could ask Old Man Smathers and he'd have it for you in two days.

It was a good place, if you could get past the dingy lighting and cracking linoleum, the old-fashioned posters for cereal that didn't even exist anymore, featuring red-cheeked children with their mouths in perfect Os, saying things like "gee-whiz" and "mmm." She'd joked to Granny that Smathers Grocery was a time warp. Granny had laughed and agreed.

Rebecca walked the aisles in a daze, spent far too long trying to decide between white rice, brown rice, and jasmine. Finally she grabbed one at random, moved to the beans aisle. She couldn't stop thinking about Tamika, about how unfair life could be. In New York, there was so much wealth. The real estate prices alone boggled her mind. Some of the people she knew were absolutely rolling in dough, and yet they were some of the biggest jerks she'd ever met. And here was Tamika, ten years old, who didn't do a thing in the world to deserve a life like this.

She passed a bunch of trial-sized toiletries, and the Friday giveaway came to mind. That was the one thing that made her feel weird about that whole night—the kids. She wasn't stupid, knew there were plenty of children living at or far below poverty level, but knowing and seeing were two different things. Twice, she saw a couple of the guests come in with kids. Really young kids, their hands clutched in their mothers', who filed in, filled a bag with necessities, ate a plate of food, and left as quickly. And now there was Tamika. Tamika, whose story she'd put in the paper next week, whose tale would hopefully become a wakeup call for Dahlia, open some eyes about the way the "other half" lived.

It's just that Dahlia wasn't that kind of place, or at least, she'd never thought of it that way. It was white picket fences and gardens and people who took care of each other.

Then again, maybe this was the real Dahlia at last, not the ghost of a town from her childhood. Maybe the real Dahlia did have picket fences, but they were cracked and peeling, hung slightly ajar, and contained a homeless ministry behind them and not some cookie-cutter nuclear home with the perfect mom, dad, dog, and two-point-five kids.

She'd reached the beans aisle when her ears pricked at the words "Dahlia Weekly" and "that editor." She edged closer. They were on the next aisle, but between the cackles and high-pitched cadence she'd come to associate with Dahlia's women, she could hear much of what was said.

"No, she didn't!" one lady said, her voice sounding familiar.

"She did indeed," came the second lady. "And she even kept the preseason football photos to a two-page spread. Why, Ron Stone, bless his soul, ran that spread four full pages, and nobody, I mean nobody, dared to change a thing. Until now, and that woman."

"She's got to learn," the first woman said, and Rebecca thought she heard a tsk-tsk. A thread of rage began to snake through her.

"She does," agreed the second. "She's not gonna last two more minutes in this town if she keeps that nonsense up. Why, Maline and Jo Lynn have already canceled their subscriptions. I have a mind to, myself."

"Oh, I don't know, Diane," the first woman said, to Rebecca's surprise. "It's a good paper. Haven't you been reading those stories of all them poor kids down in that mess of a school? Or what she's been doing with the new town growth? Don't get me wrong, she does have to learn, but we shouldn't go canceling our subscriptions or we're gonna find ourselves with no paper at all. Give the girl a chance."

Woman Number One didn't know how right she was, Rebecca thought: four-and-a-half more months till PC-Day. Paper Close Day.

"Oh, Lib, you're no fun," the second woman said, and Rebecca's jaw dropped. There was only one Lib she'd heard of in this town. Lib Pauling was suddenly her great defender?

Someone cleared his throat next to her, and she startled, realizing she was clutching a can of kidney beans awkwardly to her chest.

"Need a cart, ma'am?" a kid in a green Smathers apron said, all hooded eyes and shaggy brown hair that shook a little as he spoke.

"No, no, I'm good. Just a few items." Rebecca gripped the can tighter and reached on the shelf for another. She gave a little smile, for the first time the ma'am making her feel more like a bona fide grownup than an over-the-hill, washed-up has-been. "Thanks."

He gave her a sleepy grin and sauntered off, and Rebecca rounded the corner and gave a quick little wave to the gossiping women, whom she saw do a double-take while she grabbed a loaf of French bread.

She passed the shampoo and hair aisle as she headed toward the pharmacy for Advil, and immediately a woman from Giveaway Night with an eighties-style pink fluffy scrunchie in her ponytail came to mind. Someone's discarded hand basket rested nearby, and she piled her items into the basket, then snagged several packs of more modern-looking elastic bands, bobby pins, metal barrettes, and a few trendier headbands and headwraps—some sporty, some hippie—and popped them in the basket, too. On a whim, she grabbed a few mini hairsprays and multi-packs of plastic combs in shades of pink, pale green, purple, and blue. Basic black did the trick, sure, but these were women, and no matter whether they lived in a car or some warehouse by the river, they had to appreciate a few feminine touches. Some lip balm and body sprays went in the basket, too, which was now so heavy she had to grab it with two hands as she headed toward checkout.

"Hey, Becks!" The voice came from behind her, and she set her basket on the checkout counter and turned to find Josh Jamison pushing a piled-high grocery cart her way.

"Hey, Josh," she said, then looked around for JJ. "Your son's not with you today?"

"Ever try to bring a ten-year-old with you to the grocery store?" Josh made a face, and Rebecca laughed. "Nah, he's with his Aunt Lissa and cousins. She keeps him in the summer for me."

"That's nice of her," Rebecca said as she unpacked her items, set them on the belt.

"You and your Granny doing some sort of girls' hairdo night?" Josh looked quizzically at all the combs and hair accessories as they went one by one down the belt toward the register.

She giggled. "No, these are for the Friday thing," she waved her hand, suddenly shy about mentioning it. Just because you've helped once doesn't mean you're a ministry volunteer, Rebecca. You don't want to go sounding like you're some actual do-gooder. He'll see right through it, or worse, start badgering you to do more.

"Cool," Josh said simply, pushed his cart closer.

She inspected the contents furtively, noting mostly healthy stuff: several packs of meat and chicken, some vegetables, various boxes of rice and pasta and other things, with a pack of Hostess cupcakes perched neatly on top.

He followed her gaze to the cupcakes and laughed. "Still got a weakness for 'em, though now not every day." He patted his waistline, which to her looked trim and athletic.

She made a face. "I used to love those things. I haven't had one in years, literally." She looked at him, realizing how much time had passed. "Maybe since that last summer here."

His jaw dropped. "You're kidding me. How could you not have had a Hostess cupcake since you were, like, seventeen?"

She shrugged. After high school, there was college in a new city filled with all sorts of eclectic tastes and cultures, followed by grad school and a series of internships, one in Paris. Why have a processed cupcake when she could have an éclair or cheesecake? It was like having your fill of Gruyere or baked brie, then going home to slug some Cheez Whiz from the fridge.

But Josh wouldn't let it go. "Seriously, Becks. These things are like the fruit of life. Right, Bobby?" Josh said to the checkout kid, who nodded.

"I like 'em," Bobby the clerk muttered, and Rebecca laughed and shook her head, pulled out her wallet, and paid.

"Don't leave yet. There's something I need to show you in my truck," Josh said, and it was Rebecca's turn to peer at Josh quizzically.

She waited and walked out with him, and he piled all his bags in the flatbed, then lowered the truck's tailgate and climbed up.

"Hop on," he motioned, a wide grin on his face, and she shrugged and followed suit, her own two grocery bags and leather purse going on the flatbed, too. It felt silly but rather fun to sit there, swinging her legs in her wrap dress and heels, as customers walking into the store gave them odd looks.

"Okay, close your eyes and hold out your hands," he said, and she complied, listening to the sound of a box opening and plastic crumpling before something was set in her hands. She opened her eyes to see a Hostess cupcake, glistening with sugar and cream and fakey chocolaty goodness, in her palm. Another was in his own hand.

"Cheers, old friend who's now back," Josh said in a mock serious tone and held up the cupcake in salute.

"Cheers." She giggled and took a bite.

"Good, huh?" he said around a mouthful, and she closed her eyes, nodded blissfully. Whatever had been coiled inside her began to slowly, warmly unravel.

"Insanely good!" It was true—they tasted like childhood and sugar and happy all rolled into one. Who needs Prozac?

"You're welcome," Josh said.

He gave her a grin, and she stuck her tongue out at him.

"You better share these with JJ," she teased.

"If he makes me."

They sat companionably, the afternoon sun warm on their shoulders. She swung her legs as they ate the last of their cupcakes. She was half-tempted to ask for another, but then she'd be forced to go for a second run tonight.

She looked over at him when they finished. "I've been meaning to ask you. On Monday at my office, you seemed like you had some serious issue with that guy. Erik Wennerman."

Josh shook his head, his face darkening. "Don't get me started on him."

She arched a brow. "Why? He seems like a decent enough guy."

"Well, he's not. And after what they did to Mom and Dad…"

"They?"

"Wennerman Incorporated." Josh said the word like it tasted of moldy cheese. "That family's bad news, Becks. I take it he's an advertiser? Guess I've seen their ads."

"Yeah. What'd they do to your parents?" She remembered Josh's mom and dad a little. She hadn't known them, really; her friendship with their son had been limited to casting lines on the river, but from Josh's stories, she knew they were good people, a little older, the kind who'd bring a casserole if someone was sick or spend a Saturday helping a neighbor in need repair their home. They'd had a small family farm and often sent fresh blueberries with their son to give to Rebecca for her Granny. His dad was a handyman of sorts, drove a truck that said something like "At your service." She hadn't even asked him about them.

"During the recession, Mr. Wennerman, Erik's dad, made my parents an offer they couldn't turn down. Offered to buy the farm, let them stay till they both passed on, but as soon as the ink was dry, the story changed. There was some loophole, and the attorney didn't catch it, and before you knew it, they were out on their fannies. The house was torn down to make room for the big hospital expansion, and Mom and Dad had to move to my Aunt Dell's place, out toward Aberville."

He shook his head, looked away, the cupcake wrapper balled in his hands.

Rebecca wanted to touch his arm. "Your childhood home."

"I didn't mind for me, but Mom was real broken up about it, and Dad, well, it killed his spirit. He went and talked to Mr. Wennerman about it, said the guy laughed and told him that's just business and he shoulda read the fine print." Josh's lips were tight. "Dad passed on not long after, and Mom a couple years later. They're in a better place now, but I sure would've liked their remaining days to have been smoother."

They were quiet a moment. "I'm sorry, Josh."

He waved a hand like he was clearing away smoke. "Water under the bridge now, and I don't like to be carrying all that anger inside me. It's not a Christian way to live. But sometimes a guy can't help it. Especially when you see the man responsible out and about in your own town."

"You know, a son's not necessarily always like a father."

Josh made a face. "That one is. Known him for years. He's all smoke, and his brother's just about rotten." He eyed her. "You know they buy up little newspapers, too, not only farms. Fold 'em into a chain of generic fish wrappers."

Her mouth went dry.

"Be careful is all I'm saying." He shrugged. "If something a Wennerman offers sounds too good to be true, it probably is."

She stewed all the way home, stewed up the stairs and into her bedroom, where she pulled out her laptop and typed "Wennerman Incorporated" in the search box once she was nestled in bed.

The Wennerman company website was high on branding and low on content, with slick, professional photography featuring smiling older adults with taglines much like the ad markups Erik had given her Monday. Retire in style. Enjoy the better things in life. Sophistication at its finest. You, at your best. The "Partners" page listed a number of hospitals—and, at the bottom, W Media.

Her eyes narrowed.

She did a search for "W Media," then "W Media South Carolina." A few clicks later and she struck gold.

By the time she finished reading a handful of news articles, she realized she was gripping her pen so hard her knuckles were white. Scribbled notes covered two full pages of the legal pad at her side. That lousy, lying, no-good son-of-a—

She fumbled in her purse, pulled out her cell phone. And dialed Erik Wennerman.

CHAPTER 24

Devon

THE SUN WAS HIGH AND BRIGHT as Devon and CJ slammed open the school doors and headed off, down the steps and out to the bike rack.

"See ya tomorrow," Devon said as they passed Shenise, Gabby, and Mariana, where they gathered in a tight group of girls. Gabby didn't have the braids today, he noticed, and she'd pulled her long brown hair into a high ponytail. It looked cute, he thought, and too late realized she'd noticed him staring. He shrugged and waved at the group. Shenise wiggled her fingers back.

"See ya, guys," Shenise said.

He and CJ unlocked their bikes and pedaled toward Baker Street. There was no sign of Marquis, Johnny, or Big Ty, and Devon felt a surge of relief. Marquis had been giving him extra bad looks lately, like he was looking for trouble or something. Come to think of it, he hadn't seen them for a few days, now. Maybe they'd found something else to do in the afternoons besides messing with them.

"Wanna come over to my house?" CJ asked as they made a right and then a left, heading toward home. "We can play my X-Box. Ma's working late, and she already said she won't mind."

Devon thought a moment. Memaw had been good this morning, had been sitting at the kitchen table with a bowl of cereal when he'd left for camp, almost like the old days. She had taken to wearing her faded blue bathrobe around the house all the time now instead of the housedresses she normally favored, said she had a chill, though how anyone could have a chill in the summertime was beyond him. She looked extra old these days, and her hair wasn't right, like she didn't really bother with it, but she was up, and that's what mattered. She was up and around and not laying all day in the bed like before. She was talking better, too.

"Yeah, I'll come for a little while. Gotta help Memaw, but maybe I can come for an hour or so."

"Awesome!" CJ grinned, and for a second Devon felt like a normal kid. "My cousin gave me Lego Jurassic World cause he got tired of it. It's amazing."

Devon bit back a smile as they pedaled and CJ went on and on about the game and how you could experiment with DNA and create your own dinosaurs, even. CJ was obsessed with dinosaurs, had gone around for years saying he wanted to be a paleontologist while the rest of the kids were all into firefighters or Army superheroes or whatever. They rounded the corner, still smiling as CJ went on and on about the game, until Devon noticed CJ had suddenly grown quiet and stopped talking all together.

There, ahead, were Marquis, Johnny Vasquez, and Big Ty. They were standing in the middle of the street, arms crossed and shoulder-to-shoulder, staring them down. Marquis's basketball rested at his feet. Oh, man. They were waiting. Just for them.

Almost in unison, CJ and Devon stopped pedaling, gears whirring as they coasted way, way down.

"Let's go," Devon muttered, already circling back. They could always go the long way, back down Baker toward Washington and over, cut through the trailer park and Old Mr. Sellers's backyard.

But to his surprise, CJ had stopped his bike smack in the center of the street. And now he was getting off it, setting the bike down. Standing up straight.

"CJ, what are you doing?" Devon asked in a low voice.

"I'm tired of this, Dev." As he watched, CJ began to walk toward the trio. "Sick and tired."

Marquis smirked as CJ approached. "Aw, look. Buddy boy wants to play. Miss all our fun from last summer?"

Johnny Vasquez cracked his knuckles, and Big Ty narrowed his eyes and stood, frozen, as CJ walked closer.

Devon looked around. There was no one in sight, no one within earshot. The houses looked closed up and empty, everyone either at work or inside, resting. From somewhere far off a dog barked, one of those snarling, vicious-sounding dogs, and Devon's heart began to thud.

What is he doing? Is he trying to get himself killed?

"I'm not scared of you anymore," CJ called out to them, lifting his chin. "I'm tired of running and tired of hiding. So let's get it over with. You wanna beat me up? Have your fun?"

He's gone crazy. Devon swallowed, trying to get the nerve to say something, figure out the words to stop all this, or at least hit pause. He couldn't leave CJ there alone to fend for himself, couldn't go for help and return fast enough, but if he stuck around, they'd jump him, too.

"Actually," Johnny Vasquez said, hitching his pants and tucking his bandanna into his back pocket, "that sounds like the right idea to me."

Johnny took a step back, like he was getting into some karate position or something, but Marquis had stopped smirking and was staring at CJ like CJ was from another planet.

"What are you doing?" Marquis demanded, eyes wide.

CJ said nothing, just got within three or four feet of them and stopped. For the first time, Devon realized CJ had shot up a few inches. Instead of flab, he had muscles.

"Dude, I said what do you think you're doing?" Marquis sounded both mad as all get-out and completely confused. "You do know these guys'll turn you into a human pretzel."

CJ shook his head, stared at Big Ty. "No. I don't think so."

Big Ty stared back for a long, long moment. Devon held his breath.

And then, as Devon stared, Big Ty socked Vasquez hard in the bicep.

"Oww." It was Vasquez's turn to stare.

"Leave him alone," Big Ty said in a deep voice. "We got better things to do. I'm hungry."

Devon watched as Big Ty turned on his heel and slowly walked off, headed in the direction of the corner store. Marquis shot CJ a baffled look and followed, and then Vasquez, with one last knuckle-crack, finally did the same.

After they were halfway down the street, Devon wheeled over to CJ.

"What in the world."

But CJ just smiled, like he didn't have a worry in the world.

"Have you been working out or something?" Devon asked, staring at his friend.

CJ grinned, shrugged like he was embarrassed. "Ma got an evening shift cleaning the high school, and they have a weight room for the football players."

"You've been lifting weights?"

"Uh, yeah." CJ's smile was even wider now. "Not only that, but my Ma's new boss happens to be in charge of the football program, and I heard that Big Ty might be up for some scholarship—if he can keep his nose clean and play for them."

Devon raised his eyebrows. "That's some gamble."

CJ gave him a sideways smile. "I ran into him once or twice over at the gym, lifting. Turns out we lift about the same range. Big Ty isn't such a big deal."

Devon covered his mouth, his shoulders shaking as they started to laugh.

"Man, CJ, you must have nerves of steel."

"Well, I also noticed that."

CJ pointed, and Devon looked over to see a plain black car parked in the lot next to a house two doors down. He peered closer, saw what looked to be two undercover officers inside.

"You're good."

CJ laughed as they got on their bikes, pedaled off down the street toward his house.

"You know what? I sure am."

When Devon got home an hour later, he was surprised to see Memaw sitting in the reclining chair in front of the TV set. She still had her blue robe on, but a glass of ice water with a straw was sitting on the little table beside her, and she had her feet up and was doing a crossword puzzle. It was almost like that whole dark spell, when she'd been sick and T and his friends were there and everything had turned upside down, had never even happened at all.

He grinned at her, gave her a peck as he set his backpack down. "Hey, Memaw."

She smiled back at him over her reading glasses.

"How's my sweet boy?"

"You know what, Memaw? Awesome!" And right then and there he plopped on the edge of the sofa and filled her in on CJ and what had happened that afternoon, which he still wasn't one hundred percent certain had actually even occurred, and the latest at camp, and the new Voices from James Watkins series, and even Miss Becca herself.

"You'd love her, Memaw."

Memaw's eyes were bright as she listened. "Well, bring her 'round. I hope to meet this Miss Becca of yours."

"I sure will."

Memaw reached over, squeezed his hand. "I don't tell you enough how good you do my heart," she said softly. "After your Mama passed on, I was so worried you'd lose your light, sweet boy. Oh, how I worried."

Devon squeezed her hand back, saw moisture fill her eyes and threaten to spill.

"Aw, Memaw, you don't have to worry about me."

"Sugar, I do anyway." She sniffled, felt around in her bathrobe pocket for a tissue, which she used to blow her nose. "That light of yours, it reminds me so much of your Mama's. You have such a beautiful, kind spirit in you. The spirit of the Lord, I like to say."

He swallowed, felt his throat start to burn, but in a good way.

"I love you, Memaw."

"I love you, too, child."

They sat that way a few moments, listening to the birds outside, listening to a delivery truck roar by, and then he glanced up, realized it was nearly five thirty and time to start supper.

Inspiration struck.

"Memaw, how do you feel about a good home-cooked meal tonight?" He closed his eyes and smacked his lips. "I'm talking mashed potatoes, green beans, the works. I can fry up some hamburger steaks, throw in a bit of onion, too!"

She laughed with him, the deep belly laugh he hadn't heard in ages, didn't realize how much he'd missed till he heard it again.

"Oh, sweet boy, that sounds like heaven to me."

He got to work, thawed out the meat from the icebox, found a can of green beans and had peeled all the potatoes, and was slicing onions when he noticed he was actually humming to himself, humming like Mama used to hum, that old hymn "Marching to Zion," and tapping the knife along with the beat. He giggled at himself then, realized he couldn't remember the last time he'd been this happy.

He was so caught in the melody and the tapping that he almost didn't hear it at first, the low thumping bass that grew steadily louder and louder outside.

But then he heard it, and the sound made him freeze dead in his tracks. The hair on the back of his neck prickled.

Everything was over. Everything, every little thing that had made him feel lighter than air moments before, like he was walking on clouds and had hope in the world again, was suddenly and completely gone.

Done.

Finished.

He heard the unmistakable motor, the slam of the car door, the chirp of the alarm.

Uncle T was back.

CHAPTER 25

Rebecca

SHE WAITED AT THE BISTRO TABLE in Joe Mama's at ten the next morning, clenching and unclenching her jaw. Her latte sat untouched before her, next to the stack of articles she'd printed out last night. "W Media Buys Tickersville Chronicle." "Milltown Gazette Now Part of W Media Chain." "W Media's Littleton Herald Takeover Latest in String of Small Paper Buys." Every one of them detailing how the Wennerman-led media company had swooped in on a so-called dying paper and saved it from demise.

She'd been right. Erik Wennerman's ad offer really had been too good to be true. Her neck prickled, red-hot anger still boiling. She wasn't sure who earned her rage more—him or her. How could I have been so blind?

Erik joined her then, wearing a hangdog look and carrying a large mug.

"Rebecca, it's not what it looks like," he said as he slid into the chair across from her.

She held up a hand, the other a tight fist atop the articles.

"Erik, stop." The words came out harsh, and she took a breath, reining in her anger. "You've been visiting me week after week,

213

asking me out, coming to the 'rescue' with this amazing ad deal, making me believe full well your family business is all about the retirement home industry, and you never once mentioned anything about W Media?"

His brow creased at the center and his face looked suddenly long, reminding her of the mastiff from that movie *Turner and Hooch*.

"I should have mentioned it, and I'm sorry. I see that now." He looked down, and she could have sworn his bottom lip turned down in a pout. Her eyes narrowed. "My dad owns several companies, W Media among them. But I don't have anything to do with any of them—only the homes. That's it."

"Sure you don't." Her laugh was bitter.

"I mean it! W Media's an entirely separate company, my brother and my dad and a couple of silent partners, and I have absolutely no connection. Take a look at the website, all those articles you have there." He gestured to the stack, his eyes steely. "I promise you, Rebecca. My name appears nowhere. Not a single place."

"Oh, drop the game, Erik." Her voice was tired. "Just because you're not listed as part of the team doesn't mean anything."

"It does to me." He looked hurt. "You don't have to believe me, but I am telling the truth. My focus is entirely retirement lifestyle and marketing. The only dealing I have with newspapers, or any other media for that matter, is buying ads. That's it. And truth be told, my brother and I don't have a whole lot in common besides the fact that we share parents."

His lips were tight. Either he was that good of a liar or he was telling the truth.

"I'm not stupid, Erik. I read the articles. That one paper that wouldn't sell, the one in Lark Run? You all got really dirty with that one, even started a competing newspaper in the same town, charging very little for advertising and offering the paper for free, until numbers got so bad the first paper was forced to sell out or go under entirely." She gave him a look. "I'm sure you had absolutely nothing to do with selling them ads on that one."

"There's no need to be sarcastic here. It's not fair." He was right, she realized. She could tell she'd hurt him.

Suddenly, all the steam left her. She let out a breath.

"Look, Erik, what am I supposed to think?" She gestured to the articles. "The *Dahlia Weekly* is exactly like these other papers. And here you are, buying up ads, being all charming, asking me out—"

He reached out then and seized her hands, and she let out an involuntary gasp at the touch.

"Rebecca, that is not the reason I want to go out with you."

She wanted to let go, needed to let go, but he was holding her hands tight, and his eyes were sincere.

"I like you. A lot," he said. "I can't defend my brother and dad, or their practices. I honestly don't know what their intentions are, or if they've even approached your paper. Though I will say I'm pretty sure they would have bypassed you and gone straight to the paper's owners."

She mulled that over, knew he had a point. Slipping her hands out of his, she folded them in her lap.

"It's still bullying, plain and simple." Her voice was quiet.

He gave a slight nod.

"I hear you. But I will say the Tickersville paper today is strong. W Media saved them from annihilation from the inside out. Same with the one in Milltown." His blue eyes had an edge now, but his tone was soothing. "Those communities still have their traditions, still have their connecting force, still have a fair public spotlight and First Amendment freedoms. And their employees still have jobs, which means a lot to those towns." He leveled a gaze at her. "Whether you like what my brother and dad do or not, and their ways aside, think about it, Rebecca. It's better than being gone entirely."

"But—that one paper, where they started the competing publication."

Erik chuckled. "That was downright dirty. I'll give you that."

"And yet you still sell ads for them."

He shook his head. "Oh, no. I sell for the homes."

"It's one and the same."

That hurt look again. "Not to me. And believe it or not, when they did that in Lark Run, I went to them. Told them I didn't operate that way and didn't want to be associated with a company that does business that way. Though, not to defend them, but that Lark Run paper had major problems before W Media came in. Nepotism, a major sexual harassment lawsuit costing the paper tens of thousands of dollars, even a brush with libel. Look it up. You'll find it if you dig."

She bit her lip. "But … this whole time you never mentioned once that your family had a media business."

A puppy dog look, then a devilish grin. The guy must have taken charm lessons. She found she couldn't even look away.

"Do you really think a guy wants to mention to the beautiful newspaper editor that he wants to buy ads and oh, by the way, his family just happens to own a company that buys up little newspapers like hers?"

She forced her lips not to curve, brought her hands up from her lap and curled them around her coffee cup. "Touché."

He reached across the table again, gave her hand a gentle tap with his finger.

"And I'd still love to take you out on a date."

Her cheeks flushed. No. "I can't."

"I know you think so. But maybe you have to let yourself try. Live a little."

He flashed a smile, dimples and all.

Peter sprang to mind, the way he'd courted her, the kicker being three-dozen red roses delivered to her office with a note: You only live once. Dinner tonight?

Live a little, indeed.

But no. No way. She pulled back, the wooden chair scraping on the floor, and stood. And, oddly, Josh Jamison flashed in her mind.

"I … have to get to the office. Erik—" She searched for the words, came up dry. "Thanks."

He stood with her. As he did, she noticed two teenaged girls in line for coffee swivel, look him up and down. One of them whispered something to the other, giggling.

"Seriously, Rebecca. Look it up when you get to your computer." His blue eyes were soft now, patient. "What happened in Lark Run, and me. I promise you'll find I have nothing to do with that business in the least."

She fled as quickly as she could, articles safely back in her leather bag, her lukewarm latte sloshing as she nudged open the door to leave. She held it for an older black-haired woman with a streak of white in her hair, who gave her a smile and a thanks. Josh's Bible study leader, Rebecca remembered.

She was in her car in seconds, doors locked and heart pounding. Every emotion was bubbling around inside her, and she felt like a pinball machine. Anger. Dismay. Glee. Confusion.

She rummaged in her purse for two Advil, swallowed them down with the lukewarm coffee. She didn't know what to think, whether to believe him or not. She took a long, slow, centering breath, then put her car into gear.

Time for the hunt.

CHAPTER 26

Devon

DEVON STILL HADN'T MOVED from where he was frozen, paring knife in hand. He listened as he heard a man's voice outside, talking to someone with those long pauses like he was on the phone, laughing. A low, sinister laugh.

Maybe it's not Uncle T. Maybe it's a new neighbor, or someone accidentally pulled up at the wrong house, or—

Devon squeezed his eyes shut, counted to ten. Oh, dear Lord. Please don't let it be him. Please don't …

And then the slow pound of feet on the wooden stairs outside the kitchen door, the telltale creak of the screen door, the twisting of the door handle.

I could lock it. Then he won't be able to get in. Maybe jam a chair under the handle, keep him out, get Memaw and sneak out the window …

But his feet felt like they were stuck in mud, like he was having one of those dreams he used to have, where he was in the jungle and there was a humongous lion coming straight toward him and he couldn't do anything but stand there, completely still, his feet glued to the ground, and wait as the lion ran closer and closer.

Only this time, the lion was Uncle T. And all he did was stand there—waiting for the attack, waiting for everything to end—and watch T turn the handle and step inside.

"If it ain't Saint Devon." T pocketed his cell phone, slipped off his sunglasses. The glasses were new, Devon could see, and T wore a new-looking shirt, too. A businessy kind of shirt, like Rev wore.

"Sugar, that you?" came Memaw's voice from the living room.

"Maw?" T turned to Devon, surprise written on his face. "She's out of bed?"

A wave of satisfaction—Devon knew it was pride, but he couldn't help himself—shot through him.

"She started getting better a day or two after you left," Devon said with meaning, cocked his head.

T seemed like he was about to say something more, opened his mouth, in fact, but then appeared to change his mind. He set his shiny new sunglasses on the kitchen counter and wandered out toward the living room.

"I'm glad you're doing better, Maw," Devon could hear him say in a big circus-style voice, like he was some TV announcer, not real at all, and there was the unmistakable sound of cheeks being kissed and Memaw's recliner squeaking as he imagined her trying to stand. "No, no, Maw, don't get up. You rest. Take a load off. Devon and I'll take good care of you. We got it all covered, a'ight?"

Devon didn't hear Memaw's reply, but T laughed, a snide, cutting laugh.

"I can do better than hamburger steak and canned green beans for my Maw," T said, stepping back into the kitchen. He gave Devon the once-over, muttered, "Move it, shorty. I got this."

For a moment, all Devon could think about was CJ, and the way his friend, who'd always been afraid of everything, had stood up to Marquis, Johnny Vasquez, and Big Ty not two hours ago. He closed his eyes again, took a deep breath, let it all unfold in his mind. Everything he would do: look T straight in the eyes, tell him in no uncertain terms to get out and never come back.

"You feel me, boy?" Uncle T was saying, and he opened his eyes to realize T'd been talking to him for a good minute now, and at this moment had his head swiveled to the side and was staring at him like he'd gone crazy, like Devon himself had looked at CJ earlier that day. "I said, get outta my kitchen."

He wanted the words to come so badly, burst big and strong and powerful-like from his chest, like he'd imagined so many times before. Like a battle cry. But when they came, they weren't big at all. They were soft, like a mouse, so soft T made him repeat himself.

"… I said no …"

They were out now. And he couldn't take them back.

Time stood still for a moment. And for a millisecond, Devon thought maybe Uncle T would make like Big Ty. Turn on his heel and head right back from where he came.

Except T smiled. A twisted smile, that thrummed through Devon's body like a lightning bolt.

A dead quiet settled over the room.

"What did you say?" T asked in a low voice.

But Devon couldn't repeat it. And then he was backing away, backing across the room.

And T was on him then, both his hands squeezing Devon's wrists so tight he thought they'd snap in two. T's thumbs pressed into the tender undersides hard.

Harder.

Pain seared through him.

"Look at me when I'm talking to you," T hissed, and Devon locked eyes with him, saw the anger and the rage and the cold, cold evil.

"Everything all right in there?" Memaw called from the other room.

"All good, Maw," T called over his shoulder.

With one final, painful squeeze he released Devon's arms. Devon gasped, stumbled away. For an instant he thought he'd faint dead over, but it passed, and he watched T calmly walk to the door, turn the handle, and swing it open.

"See ya, Dev. Sorry you can't stay for supper," T said loud enough for Memaw to hear.

And choking back tears, Devon scrambled to his feet and out the door.

CHAPTER 27

Rebecca

BACK AT THE OFFICE, Rebecca went straight to her laptop, typed in W Media and Erik Wennerman. Nothing, though she made sure to google Erik himself, too. He checked out okay, and she found a lot of information on several social media career profile sites, saw he had a bachelor's in marketing and two graduate degrees, one in business advertising and another in geriatric care management.

His profile picture was a professional one, and he somehow managed to look both relaxed and natural in the pose. Trustworthy. The thought came that he'd make a good politician.

A search for news articles about him brought up a couple of features, the first on a local project he and some classmates had done in grad school and the second on his vision for Aberville Estates, the largest of the Wennerman retirement communities in the area. She also found a few photos of some community and business awards he'd accepted on behalf of his father's companies. All of it was pretty vanilla, she had to admit. No shady past, no bad business deals, no complaints or poor reviews.

No connection whatsoever to media buyouts.

Frowning, she did a search for the *Lark Run Gazette*, teamed that with terms like "lawsuit," "nepotism," "libel" and "sexual harassment." Several articles, most by the daily paper in Charlotte, came up. Erik had been telling the truth—that newspaper had been going under fast on its own accord. She winced as she read how a string of young female reporters, just out of college, finally went in on a class action handled by a large firm. The paper settled, and it seemed the sale to W Media was ultimately a win-win. She cocked her head. She'd been too hard on Erik. His hangdog look and patient way of explaining settled over her, balled like a lump in her stomach.

"What's wrong?" Millie's gruff voice startled her, and she sat upright. They were alone in the newsroom—Tiff was at a zoning meeting and Dinah out making sales rounds—and Rebecca glanced at the wall clock, surprised to see it was already after two. Soon she'd need to be leaving to go meet Devon.

"It's nothing."

Millie raised a brow. "Nothing my foot."

Rebecca bit back a retort, then sighed. "I found out yesterday that the Wennermans, who've been running those huge ads in the paper for their retirement homes? They own a media company that buys small papers like ours all over this region."

Millie pursed her lips. "Coulda told ya that ages ago."

"You knew?"

"Thought you did, too. Thought that was why that Wennerman fellow's been so friendly, coming in and making googly eyes at you."

Rebecca rubbed at her temples. "It was a shock to me. And it seems Erik has nothing to do with his dad's media arm, though I sure gave him an earful a couple hours ago at the coffee shop." She frowned, gave Millie a sideways look. "You thought I was chumming up with the Wennermans about a paper sale?"

Millie shrugged. "The paper's not doing well, that Wennerman fellow's been comin' round, and I put two and two together, jumped to conclusions. Figured you were ready to cast lots with the winning team."

"Well, I had no idea. And besides, Erik told me his father and brother would likely be talking with Mr. McCafferty and Mr. Hansler, not me, anyway."

"They may well be. And I suppose working for the Wennermans would be better than no job at all, but I don't like it. Not one bit. There's something sleazy about that family, I don't care how you spin it."

Rebecca's mouth twisted. "I know what you mean."

She watched Millie a moment. The secretary's back was ramrod straight as she organized the papers on her desk. Rebecca glanced at the papers as she stood to pour another cup of coffee, saw they were classified orders.

"You're doing well with the classifieds." She tried to make her voice sound warm.

"Just doin' my job."

"No, really, Millie. You're doing great. I appreciate it." Rebecca took her seat again, sipped at the too-hot coffee.

Millie sniffed. "So're you. I'm liking that James Watkins series."

"Thanks."

Millie opened her mouth like she was going to say something more, then seemed to think better of it. A minute passed, then another. Finally, Rebecca turned back to her laptop, and the research.

But when Rebecca left for her weekly Devon interview, Millie passed her a slip of folded pale-blue paper. Rebecca opened it in the car.

"I can do all things through him who strengthens me—Philippians 4:13," Millie had written, then added, "You're doing a good job."

Rebecca kept the blue paper open on her passenger seat, read it again as she pulled up to the school. Millie's compliment surprised her; the woman hadn't exactly been friendly with her, though they'd formed a loose bond in the couple months since Rebecca had come to Dahlia. But like almost everything else she'd experienced since she'd moved here, Millie had a way of surprising her. Deep down, she suspected her gruff demeanor hid a kind heart.

She glanced in the rearview mirror and saw Devon walking toward her from the school, big blue backpack on. He had on one of those thin nylon hoodies in spite of the heat, and he seemed extra pensive today—none of the lightness she saw last week was evident. Her heart sagged. She couldn't imagine what it might be like for him at home, whether he'd even had enough to eat today. She wished she could ask him.

Why not ask?

The thought caught her off-guard. Why not, indeed? Out of fear of offending him, for one thing, though if he were truly hungry, she imagined being offended wouldn't be an issue. Or maybe out of a worry that she was being too pushy or nosy, or worse, judgmental. The kid had enough problems without worrying whether his weekly diner pal thought he was a poster child for the needy.

But as Devon slid into the car, the words tumbled out. "You doing okay?" she asked, eyes soft.

"I'm fine." He smiled at her, and she wasn't entirely sure but thought it didn't quite meet his eyes. In fact, his eyes looked sunken today, like he hadn't slept a wink. But she shifted the car into gear, tossed him a smile, and headed for Harold's.

At the diner, Rebecca made sure to order an extra burger—"just in case," she told him—and some fried cheese sticks.

"You know," the waitress, Louanne, said to her, one hip jutted out as she peered beneath her eyeglasses, "that story you did on the anniversary of the mill closing was real nice. And those kid stories, too—even though summer's winding down, I hope you keep 'em going when school starts back. They're good. My Leroy says they're his favorite part of the paper, and I don't even argue."

"Thanks, Louanne."

Louanne set down a basket of cornbread in front of them, along with a handful of those little packets of butter.

"They do this town some real good, you ask me," Louanne said, then clicked her pen and winked at Devon. "Keep it up. I can see a nice change in the paper since you've been here."

"She likes you," Devon said behind a mouthful of cornbread after Louanne walked off.

Rebecca looked at him, surprised.

"What makes you say that?"

"Dunno. You can just tell."

Their talk today was quieter, and she remembered Tamika right as Louanne delivered their food.

"Do you know I talked to a kid in your school yesterday who lives in a car? Actually lives in a car."

Devon shrugged like Tamika had. "Yeah."

"Isn't anybody doing anything about this? Like, the teachers? The school staff?"

Devon gave her a look. "If they know about it, sure. But Miss Becca, most 'a the kids don't want people to know they're living in a car. That's like asking to become a foster kid."

"You know more than one kid who lives in a car?"

"I guess. A couple. Another girl in the grade below me, for sure." He shrugged again. "They don't live there all the time or anything."

"That's—" She shook her head. "I just can't believe it."

"I know a kid. He was in my class this year. Spent all of last summer living in a tent in those woods, out behind James Watkins?" He gestured in the general direction of the school, then dunked a fry in ketchup, gobbled it down and ate two more. "Him and his whole family, too. Said it wasn't so bad, except for it being hot. And the mosquitos. Now they live near my house, in an apartment building. It was better than being split up. Least that's what he said."

Ideas were swirling: how maybe she could start a collection for Tamika's family, possibly enough for first month's rent on a house. But then what? She didn't know Tamika's mom in the least. What if the woman was a loafer, who drifted by with no desire to work? All that money would go down the drain. Or—what if she found the woman a job? A good job, where she could earn enough to support herself and her kids?

"You wanna fix it, don't you," Devon said, gazed at her, a ketchup-coated fry in his hand. "That's why you got so quiet."

Rebecca blushed. Devon was proving to be a surprisingly good mind-reader. "Probably." She switched gears. "You seem to know a lot of people, hear a lot of stories."

"I like people." He slurped at his milkshake, ate the fry.

"Why?" She didn't dislike people. It was more that she appreciated her privacy, her solitude. She imagined Devon was the kind of person who couldn't stand in line at the grocery store without chatting with the person behind him. She preferred to study the magazines and rows of candy and gum than make small talk with a stranger she'd never meet again.

"Dunno. It's not their fault they got handed a whole bunch of trash. They're dealing with it best they know how. That's what Mama always said, anyway."

"Your Mama was a wise woman."

"I know." He looked down then, and for the first time since she'd met him, she wondered if he was about to start crying. His brows pressed in tight, and she could see him swallow thickly.

Louanne's words came to mind, about keeping the stories going once school started again. They were still a couple weeks off from that, but she wondered how they could pull it off, decided to mention it. Maybe it would keep his mind off his sadness to talk.

"Say, what Louanne said about continuing the stories into the school year, what do you think about that?"

She took a bite of burger, tried to act casual.

He took a breath and then another bite of his own burger, chewed thoughtfully.

"I think it could work. I know the kids like sharing their stories."

She cocked her head. "Can you help me? I don't think I can do it without you."

He cut his eyes at her. "You can too."

"Well, maybe I could, but not as good as with your help. I mean it—can you help me? Can I count on you?"

She could tell he knew what she was doing, but he smiled anyway, nodded.

"You can count on me, Miss Becca."

She giggled, held out a hand. "Deal?"

"Deal."

As they clasped hands, his thin jacket scrunched up a little, and she glanced down at his wrist, saw a deep plummy-black splotch on the underside.

She held onto his hand a moment, peered at it. She saw his face change, shut down, the smile gone.

"Devon, did you get hurt or something?"

"No," he said too quickly. He pulled his hand back, tucked it between his legs beneath the table. "I mean, it's nothing."

Well, that was a strange reaction. She peered at him, remembered the bruises on his torso.

"It doesn't look like 'nothing.'"

"It's fine, Miss Becca, really." He gave a little laugh, started to shrug on his backpack. "Slammed it in the locker at school. Seriously—no big deal. It hurt a day or so but it's fine now, I promise."

"Can I see it?"

"Nah, come on. Let's go—I have some homework to finish tonight."

"They give homework?"

"I mean, not homework-homework. I mean like my own work I gotta do at home. That kinda homework. To help with the camp. Like, for the committee."

He's lying. Her stomach knotted. "Gotcha." She watched him carefully as she gathered the check, headed to the little counter to pay.

Waving another goodbye at Louanne, they headed to her car. He kept up a steady stream of talk all the way back to the school, some wildlife presentation the forestry service had done that day with eagle and beaver skulls, and she listened and nodded in all the right places. He kept his wrist close to his side, near the car door, so she couldn't get another peek.

A thought struck. Maybe she could get his address. If he had nothing to hide, surely he'd give it. Or if not, she could follow him home.

"You sure you don't want a ride?"

He laughed. "You ask that every week."

She stuck her tongue out. "And every week you say no." She looked at him. "But seriously, you don't live far?"

"Not far at all." He slid out.

The words were out before she could stop them. "Which street is yours?" She tried to ask it real casual-like.

"Two-twenty-one Baker," he said, thumbed that way. "Just a short ride."

She glanced over—there goes that theory—and nodded. "Yeah, I guess that's not far at all."

Two-twenty-one. That would be easy to remember; it was Granny's birthday: February twenty-first.

A beat passed, then another.

"Well, gotta go." He grinned at her, slammed the door. "Thanks!"

She watched him walk off, the wrist still close to him.

"See you tomorrow night!" she called.

What are you doing, Rebecca? Kids got bruises all the time. Her own legs had been various shades of black and blue and skinned knees until she was maybe fifteen, from climbing trees or falling off her bike.

But it wasn't the bruise that got her worried. She bit her lip, puzzled over it as she watched him unlock his bike from the rack, slide on, and pedal off.

No, it was his reaction to her questions that raised her concern. That and the jacket, which was entirely out of place in this weather. Her neck prickled. Was he being bullied? He mentioned some kids picking on him. Or something at home? He didn't talk about his home life, or at least not his current situation. When he talked about home at all it was couched in memory—Mama said this, Mama showed him that. She realized she didn't know much about his home life at all. He lived with his grandmother. Memaw, he called her. There was some on-again, off-again uncle. That was really all she knew.

Maybe she needed to make a visit, introduce herself. See for herself what was really going on. She looked at her watch, remembered she'd promised Granny she'd grab cinnamon on the way home. Granny was making some dinner for a shut-in, plus had mentioned needing her help loading meals for a church event.

Tomorrow, maybe. Tomorrow was Friday. Giveaway night. She'd volunteer again, then insist on driving Devon home after. Weather reports said it was supposed to rain over the weekend, anyway, some hurricane starting to form off the coast, and surely he'd want a ride.

And putting the car into gear, she pulled out and headed back to town.

CHAPTER 28

Devon

DEVON PEDALED DOWN BAKER STREET—past CJ's house, past Shenise and Gabby, who called hellos he ignored. Past his own house, Uncle T's car still parked outside. His eyes filled with hot tears, and he gritted his teeth, willed them gone.

When he got to the end of the street, he swiped at his face impatiently, bruised wrists still aching with the motion. Tears didn't solve anything. They didn't bring your mama back. They didn't make your uncle leave. They only burned your eyes and clouded your vision.

And right now he needed his vision. Needed to think right and clear and true. For once and for all. He'd lied to Miss Becca. Lied to her good and well. Lied, even though he knew it was wrong, knew she might be one of the only people who had the power to help. He'd done it anyway.

I can't take it anymore.

But could he? And should he, for Memaw's sake?

He thought about Memaw, about last night when he'd come home late, so late Uncle T was passed out on the couch with the TV on, so late Memaw didn't even stir when he poked his head into her bedroom and, finding her asleep and snoring softly, made his old nest out of blankets on her floor and settled down for an exhausted sleep.

He'd slept maybe two hours, then woke at four and sat there, wide awake, the light from Mrs. Brown's porch light casting a faint glow on Memaw's face.

Could he leave her? Could he just run off for good, see if Rev and Marla could take him in, protect him?

But "could" wasn't even the question.

Robinsons stick together.

He remembered when Mama had said it that last time, in the hospital bed, the hum of oxygen and the soft puffs of the machine at her bedside the only other sounds besides her voice.

"You need to take care of each other, baby," she'd told him, calmly and patiently, like her body wasn't shutting down, like they hadn't called him in for his final goodbye.

He'd promised her, then: He'd never let her down. He'd stick with Memaw and Memaw would stick with him. They were a team. For now and for always.

Only he was at the end of his rope now, and he wasn't sure he could keep his promise anymore. Would Mama want him to? Would she have told him to leave a long time ago? Or told him to tough it out, sustain, carry on the fight?

"Be strong in the Lord and in the strength of his might," she'd scrawled in the Bible, from Ephesians 6:10.

But he wasn't like her. Wasn't even like CJ. He wasn't strong at all.

If he went back, he might not make it out alive.

A thought came to him then—maybe that wasn't such a bad thing. Then he'd be with Mama again, and Jesus. Jesus had been through this and worse. Jesus understood.

He gripped the handlebar of his bike, took a deep, centering breath, and pedaled down First Street, heading to the corner store.

He needed some hard work, a few dollars from Mr. Allen, and time to think.

Plenty of time.

Uncle T's car was gone by the time he gathered his courage and headed home a couple hours later. As he walked to the house, he passed by Mama's memory garden, touched the cross at the center for comfort. Strength.

Padding up the back stairs, he put his hand on the doorknob, closed his eyes a moment. One of the psalms popped into his mind: "The Lord is on my side; I will not fear. What can man do to me?"

He found Memaw dozing in the recliner.

"Memaw," he whispered, leaned close.

He said it again and she stirred, eyes half-lidded and drowsy, then opened fully to look at him straight, like she knew and had been waiting, like she wanted him to say the words once and for all.

"Tell me, boy." Her voice was soft, and he knelt in front of her, clasped her hand.

The words wouldn't come at first, but then they did, like they were a roomful of water unleashed with the opening of a door. He told her everything—the drugs, the late-night parties, the threats. Slipped off his jacket and showed her his wrists, the still-fading bruises on his ribs.

He needed to get it all out, needed to make her see what was happening, why they needed to go.

As she listened, he saw her eyes narrow and glisten, at first with tears, but by the time he reached the end, with a rage he'd never seen before. And finally the words were done and he sat, numb and empty.

She stared back at him, her mouth opening to speak, then shutting as she appeared to consider, rethink, start again.

He swallowed. "Memaw, we—we need to go. You and me, just get up and go. We'll walk over to Mrs. Brown's, and … and you can wait there while I ride out to get Rev and Marla, and I know they'll take us in, help us make a plan, and then we'll—"

"We'll do nothing of the sort." Memaw struggled to sit upright, her eyes hard, harder than he'd ever seen from anyone, ever. "This is my house, mine and yours. And nobody, son or not, has the right to walk in here and bully his way into a takeover."

Her hands shook as she tried to stand, and Devon's eyes were wide.

"Memaw, sit back down." They needed to gather their things, go, not sit around getting angry.

He glanced at the door, stomach roiling. Any second now, Uncle T could walk in.

"No, boy, I won't sit back down." Her voice rose, harsh and pitched. "I'm tired of sitting, tired of turning a blind eye to all this."

She waved a hand as she straightened her back, slowly got to her feet, and all he could do was nod, heart pounding.

"Yes, ma'am," he mumbled.

She fumbled for her cane. "Your PawPaw and I bought this house with our own money, saved our last dime, put ever'thing we had into this place, and there ain't nobody no how, blood or no blood, gonna come in here and make me leave."

"Memaw, please—"

"Child, don't you 'Memaw please' me. I've a like to …"

The telltale crunch of tires on gravel came then, the squeak of brakes, the sound of low thrumming bass from car speakers.

Devon stiffened, his heart thudding so strong he thought Memaw must be able to see it pound through his thin jacket, but she didn't even seem to notice, just leaned heavily on her cane, going on and on about how no son of hers had a right to hurt her grandson and he had another think coming if he thought it could continue.

Every inch of his body tensed as he stood there, throat cracking, chest booming. Waiting.

Oh, Jesus, he thought as a hot shudder of terror flooded him from head to toe.

He's back.

CHAPTER 29

Rebecca

THE LATE AFTERNOON WAS SHIFTING slowly to dusk when she got home with the cinnamon and a few other items from the grocery store. As she pulled into the driveway, she saw Granny on her knees in the garden, pulling at a weed.

Rebecca set her leather briefcase and the grocery bag against the porch railing, slipped her slingbacks off, and padded over in her bare feet. The soft grass felt good beneath her toes. She wondered why she hadn't thought to do that all summer—slip off her shoes and go barefoot, feel the earth on her skin, smell the trees and the flowers and the tangy summertime air.

"Stubborn fool," she heard Granny mutter to the weed. Then Granny looked up. "Hey, sweetheart."

"Hey Gran, got your cinnamon," Rebecca said, kissing her on her hair, which was pulled back in a ponytail. A gardening hat rested on the ground nearby, along with a shovel, gloves, and a bunch of tools. She slipped on the gloves. "Here, I'll give you a hand."

"On three. One, two—" And with a tug the thick roots of the weed slid out of the earth.

"Now that's teamwork." Granny grinned. "Thanks."

"Rebecca Chastain, fixer of newspapers, friend of the orphans, and puller of weeds, at your service." She did a mock bow.

"And most wonderful granddaughter on the planet." Granny stood, collecting the tools and placing them carefully in the bucket. "Light's fading, but I sure could use a glass of tea. You want some?"

"I'd love some."

Rebecca followed Granny inside with the groceries and pulled two glasses down from the shelf. Something was cooking in the oven that made the entire kitchen smell divine—onions and meat and spices and who knew what else—and Rebecca inhaled deeply.

"Is this for us or the church?"

Granny laughed. "Both! Mrs. Stewart's son is coming to pick it up in, oh, about forty minutes." She eyed the clock, then snagged the cinnamon from the grocery bag, opened the oven and peeled back the foil to sprinkle some of the spice inside. "My secret ingredient. Got to mix a little of the sweet in to counter the savory."

"It smells amazing."

"There's enough for us to have our own supper, and then I'll bundle the rest and send it over with the Stewart boy."

"Let's fix some plates and eat al fresco, then!" Rebecca said.

Five minutes later, they were settled around the small patio table on the screened back porch, a pair of fat citronella candles casting a warm glow on their meal.

"Seen much of Devon Robinson these days?"

"We had our weekly interview this afternoon," Rebecca nodded and took a large forkful of stew. "He's a good kid. I think I get more out of our weekly time together than he does."

"He's something else." Granny shook her head. "It'll be interesting to see what he ends up doing in life. People call him the young mayor these days, you know."

"The young mayor," Rebecca mulled. "Suits him."

She eyed Granny. *I'm probably making too much of it.* He did give her his address readily.

Granny eyed her back. "You're troubled."

Rebecca shook her head. "I'm sure it's nothing. It's—well, Devon had a big bruise on his wrist today. When I asked him about it, he kind of panicked. Wouldn't let me see, said something about hurting it on his locker at school."

Granny looked thoughtful.

"Maybe he was embarrassed."

"Maybe."

"But you think it was more?"

Rebecca pursed her lips. "I don't know, Granny. This sounds dumb, but it made me wonder if there's trouble going on. Like, at home or something. Or if he's being bullied. People don't usually have bruises here." She pointed to the underside of her wrist. "A week or so ago, he had some nasty bruising on his torso, too. Said he fell off his bike, but…"

She sighed, couldn't bring herself to say the words.

"I'd hate to think he's having trouble." Granny thought a moment. "Why don't I take a look at school tomorrow, see for myself."

Relief washed over her. "Thanks. I'm probably just making a big deal out of it, but …"

"But just in case."

"Exactly."

They finished their meal in silence, then Rebecca leaned back, sipped her tea and surveyed the land beyond. Dusk had turned to twilight, and the twangy staccato of katydids began to fill the air.

"Six more weeks," Granny said.

"Huh?"

"When you start to hear the katydids again, that means six weeks till the first cold snap."

"But it's a hundred degrees outside."

Granny laughed. "This town can turn on a dime. It'll be in the hundreds one week, then we'll get a week of rain and boom: the next week we're in the eighties, then the seventies, then you wake up and it's fall."

Rebecca raised her eyebrows. "I always thought it was more subtle. In New York, seasons ease one into the next."

A flash of last fall, walking with Peter in Central Park on a rare no-work afternoon, came suddenly, and sadness flooded. Not for him, necessarily, but for all she'd once been, all she'd lost. She realized now if she did go back, it would be a different Rebecca who'd walk those streets. One who looked a little deeper at the people she passed, one who cared a little more.

"I forgot you'd not been here for fall before. You always came in the summers. Wait till you see Christmas."

They grew silent, the evening air settling around them like a shawl. If things didn't turn around at the paper, Rebecca might not even be here at Christmas. It was hard to imagine.

"You look like you have the world on your shoulders, Becca." Granny's tone was light, but Rebecca couldn't see her expression in the semi-darkness.

"I was wondering if I'd even see Christmas in Dahlia." She wasn't even sure why that bothered her. Not that she planned to stay here long-term. But for Granny's sake, not to mention her own, she wanted to say she'd been able to turn the *Dahlia Weekly* around and get it going in the right direction before she moved on to a bigger area.

"Oh, sweet girl. Surely the paper's doing better. You said so yourself earlier this week, that things were picking up. Small growth is growth, after all."

"The numbers are still dismal. And now that advertiser, Erik Wennerman, has me worried. He's been coming by, being all charming, asking me out—" She held up a hand as Granny started to speak. "No, I have no intention of dating him, or anyone, but now I'm wondering whether he's more interested in luring me and the paper to his family business."

"A retirement home?"

"No, no, I mean his family's other business. Turns out they own a media company."

Granny's eyes turned dark. "One that buys struggling papers, I presume?"

Rebecca let out a breath. "He insists he has nothing to do with it, only his dad and brother—"

"But you're suspicious."

"Very. Not to mention, Josh seems to think he's rotten."

Granny said nothing, just sipped her tea. Then she sighed.

"Would it be a bad thing? If Wennerman's company bought the paper?"

"I guess not, not in the big picture. But they're dirty, Granny."

She relayed what happened in Lark Run, Littleton, Milltown.

"Granted, those papers were sinking ships, but I'm not sure how I feel about working for people who seem to feel no shame about cutting the dying competition at the knees. I'm no stranger to buy-outs, but after what happened with the Bannister Group in New York, after all Ed's promises that my job would always be safe, look what happened. Axed without warning in spite of all I gave."

Hot tears threatened, and she was glad for the twilight, glad she could swallow them back. She was done crying over the past.

Granny reached over, clasped her hand. "It sure wasn't Christian the way they treated you. I bet all this, and now the Wennerman business, feels like a rehash of all you went through."

"Yeah."

The katydids chirped away as twilight thickened.

"Granny, can I ask you something?"

"Shoot."

"You know how people are always saying 'give it to God'—what does that mean, exactly? It's something Devon and I were talking about recently, and it's been on my mind."

She felt more than saw Granny's shoulders shift. "Ah, that's just a fancy way of saying pray about your worries instead of letting them trouble you. You make a decision to give it to the Lord, who will handle it on your behalf."

"So you get cancer and decide you're not going to waste your time stressing about it. You just say God, handle this for me?" Rebecca raised her eyebrows.

"Pretty much."

"Sounds fatalistic."

"It's not, really." Granny sighed. "More like you've decided he's in control of your ship and you're going to rely on him to take you through the storm. Like when you're on an airplane and it starts to sway—you know your pilot's going to fly you out of it because there's a vested interest."

"That's assuming God has a vested interest in us."

Granny laughed. "I'd say he does! But yes, it's making that assumption."

They grew quiet again.

"So, how do you do this, exactly? Talk to God. Give him your troubles."

"You just keep it simple. Sit down in a quiet spot and talk to God like you would anybody else."

Rebecca made a face in the darkness. "Like how? Like, hey God, it's me, Rebecca, and I know we haven't talked in a while but I have a hangnail and it hurts and can you please fix it?"

"If that's what's on your mind, sure," Granny said evenly.

"Seriously."

"Seriously! That's what I do, anyhow. For me, I like to talk to him during mundane tasks. Like doing the dishes, or chopping celery. I make a conscious effort not to get anxious and, frankly, I find it pretty liberating. And it's all right there in the Bible. Philippians 4:6: 'Do not be anxious about anything, but in everything by prayer and supplication with thanksgiving let your requests be made known to God.'"

Rebecca rolled her eyes but smiled. "You're like the walking Bible, Granny."

"Not quite, but thanks, sweetheart. You might try it sometime. Talk to him about your job, say. Or Devon."

"We'll see."

The squeak of tires sounded, followed by the crunch of gravel.

"Ah, that's Davey Stewart now." Granny got to her feet. "Help me cover this stew for him?"

That night, stretching out her legs in the four-poster bed in Granny's guest room, Rebecca turned out the light, closed her eyes, and opened her mouth. But the words wouldn't come. What would she even say—hey God, please let Devon be okay, and while you're at it, fix this paper so I won't let Granny and my whole staff down and be a complete failure?

She shook her head, anxiety building. She thought of Devon again, of the way he'd yanked his bruised wrist back, mumbled some excuse. Maybe he was embarrassed. Maybe that was all.

But maybe not.

And balling her hands into fists, she buried her head under the covers and willed her mind to shut down for the night. Tomorrow she'd deal with the paper and figure out a way to give Devon a ride home, see if she couldn't figure out what was going on.

It was hard for her to imagine someone hurting a kid like Devon—sweet, friendly, quiet, the kind of kid you couldn't imagine ever getting in trouble a day in his life. But she knew there were sickos in the world, knew people kept some pretty dark secrets. About hunger, about homelessness, you name it. Devon himself had told her that. Why not abuse?

When she slept, her dreams were filled with shadowy, deceptive figures, all of them silent. And try as she might, she couldn't get them to speak.

The next evening, Rebecca pulled up at Dahlia Community Bible Church, parked in the lot. A loose crowd of men and women were already starting to gather outside the church. Most stood in packs right outside the door, but one man stood, arms outstretched, like he wanted to catch the last rays of sun. It was one of the most gorgeous days she'd seen in Dahlia since she'd moved there, the greens extra green, the sky a deep, clear azure, with a hint of cloud cover in the east. Thanks to the hurricane brewing off the coast, the weather forecasters were calling for rain, but so far, there was none in sight, and she reveled in the beauty. Even the heat had seemed to loosen its tight grip, give a little breathing space.

As she got out of her car, she could hear someone call out to the man, but he laughed and waved the words aside. He looked free beneath the tall pines, unscripted and fully, vibrantly alive—and in almost total opposition to the way she herself felt, which after today was mostly frustrated, impatient, and worried.

Granny had called right before lunchtime, telling her Devon hadn't shown for camp.

"But don't you fret, girl. A dozen kids are out today. Some virus is going around. If he doesn't show tonight at the giveaway, you can bet that's what it is. We can go visiting tomorrow morning, bring him some chicken soup."

Work had been extraordinarily busy; otherwise she knew the hours would have dragged until the giveaway. One minute it had been nine o'clock and the next nearly four, filled with town meetings and interviews and a last-minute photo of some business donation. And all the while the tension and worry built.

But she could feel it melt from her shoulders as she hurried to the door, glancing down the street to see if Devon would be riding up on his bike. Maybe he was already there, helping with setup.

"Hey, there, Martha!" She smiled at the white-haired lady, who was straightening her papers and clipboards at the registration table. Next to the table, the menu for the night was written in neat script on a chalkboard: spaghetti and meatballs, garlic bread, and strawberry shortcake. Her stomach started to growl.

"See Devon tonight?" she asked.

Martha smiled, shook her head. "Haven't seen him yet, but go on back if you like. Can you grab me an extra bundle of ballpoint pens from Rev's office?"

"Will do." Rebecca waved at Mike, who tossed her a half-smile and a "hey" as he lined up the shampoo and body wash bottles at one table. A large pile of clothing was dumped atop another, and she imagined that's where she'd be stationed tonight. Maybe Josh and JJ would come, too, and lend a hand. She smiled as she remembered the Hostess cupcakes from the other day, the feeling of swinging her legs while perched on the back of Josh's truck. In a way, it reminded her of the man outside in the last remnants of day—alive and free.

But there was no sign of Devon in the back, either.

"I don't think he's comin', sugar," Marla told her from the prep area, shaking her head as she buttered the last of the bread and sprinkled on garlic powder. "He wasn't at camp today, either. Probably out with that nasty virus. I imagine teachers and staff are next."

"That's what Granny said." She frowned, debated whether she should leave and go check on him now—forget waiting till morning. If she were sick, though, the last thing she'd want was a friend poking their head in. She preferred to be left alone when sick, nursing chicken soup and watching old movies on TV. Then again, this was Devon. Did he even have chicken soup?

"Marla, got that bread ready?" someone hollered from the kitchen.

"Comin' now," Marla hollered back, then pushed the tray into Rebecca's hands. "Here, hon, run that to the ovens for me."

And then it was crunch time, they were in the last-minute frenzy of setup, and she didn't have time to worry about Devon as she ran food to the tables and folded and set out clothes, made sure all the utensils and plates were stacked for the guests. At six sharp the bell clanged, held by a grinning JJ, who stood by his dad at the front. She hadn't seen them come in. Her heart did a little happy dance to see them, and Josh gave her a big hello wave, then pantomimed popping a giant Hostess cupcake in his mouth, pretending to chew and swallow and then rub his belly in delight. She giggled at the thought, realized she was still smiling when she looked up and saw the woman with the pink scrunchie standing before her.

"You look like the cat who ate the canary," the lady pronounced.

"I sure feel like it." Rebecca giggled, then remembered the hair items she'd snagged at the grocery store earlier that week. "Oh, hang on a sec!"

She darted in the back to her purse, grabbed the plastic bag, and raced back, holding out a handful of the modern-style elastics in her hand, plus one of the pastel combs.

"I picked up some of these," Rebecca said, suddenly feeling shy. "I figured maybe the ladies could use them. Some of these black combs and drab colors get a little, well, depressing."

"Hey, thanks, baby doll!" The woman grinned, her tanned face creasing and showing one missing tooth, right on the side.

How old was she? Rebecca's age? Older? Rebecca couldn't tell. Time and rough living had a way of aging people far beyond their years.

"I'm Rebecca, by the way." She held out her hand.

"Shayna," the woman shook it, her dishwater blond ponytail

swinging with the motion. She shouldered her backpack more securely, took the elastics and comb. Rebecca noticed her biceps were amazing, then mentally chastised herself. Of course she's strong and fit, you idiot—she lives on the street, not in some cushy house with some cushy job. You've got to be strong to survive out there. Though what Shayna would need in order to survive left her curious.

A man came up behind Shayna, patted her arm as he dug through the men's clothing.

"Hey, Roy. Hot enough for you lately?"

"You sure are, honey," Roy said, an exaggerated leer on his face as he found a T-shirt and folded it into a tight rectangle.

Shayna gave him a look. "Baby, you know you better knock that out. You been warned."

The man just laughed. Rebecca got the impression they did this often.

When the man walked off, Rebecca couldn't help but blurt, "Do the guys do that a lot? Bother you?"

Shayna laughed, waved a hand, biceps flexing nicely. "Nah, they're more like brothers, most a' the time, anyway. It's like with dogs, you know? Gotta show 'em who's boss once, show 'em you're the Alpha, the one what's in charge, and other than a bit of teasing here and there, you ain't gotta worry 'bout it again. Usually."

That made sense, in theory. "I bet you have some stories, huh." Rebecca began to fold some of the clothes that had gotten ransacked, neatening the piles somewhat.

"Oh, girl, I got some crazy stories. You hang around me enough you'll hear 'em so often you can prob'ly tell 'em yourself!"

Rebecca grinned at her. "That a promise?"

"Maybe." Shayna grinned back. "Ooh, hey, look at these!"

She spotted a pair of overall shorts in Rebecca's hand.

Rebecca passed them across the table. "Cute!"

"They are cute. I might have to take me some of these! They got pockets, too. I love me some pockets." Shayna held the overalls to her slender frame, her shoulders bony behind the muscles. "Now if you only had a pink T-shirt to go under these, I'd be set."

"Pink's your favorite color?"

"Pink's my signature color." Shayna mimicked an old-fashioned screen siren as she daintily put a hand to her head, thrust out a hip. Rebecca couldn't help but think of Tiff. The women were light years apart on the surface, yet they shared a favorite color.

Then again, she mused, surveying the room, wasn't that the way with everybody? You take away their job, home, and social status, and it just came down to the basics, really. Are you a survivor? Do you make time for play? Do you have faith, or are you steeped in darkness?

"See ya around, girl." Shayna waved as she stuffed the overalls in her bag and moved off toward the food table as someone settled behind the big piano and began to play. A familiar Billy Joel tune filled the room.

As she continued to look around at the tables, watching people just be people, it hit Rebecca suddenly what Granny had meant when she talked about ministry with, not to, people. Maybe that's what had always bothered her about volunteering: the notion that she'd be swooping in with some Miss Fix-It persona, patronizingly saving the day as she doled out soup or canned goods, the ultimate power trip. Here's me, who has everything, doing you, the "poor" person, the supreme favor of giving you what you need. That never felt right to her.

But giveaway night was more like a giant party where people hung out and ate together, plus gathered up stuff they needed in order to live. None of the volunteers were shoving advice and judgment down anybody's throat. There was no ridiculous paternalistic power play. Even the crazy drunk guy who'd stumbled in last week and made a mess of the front entrance had simply been cleaned up and ushered to a table, where they gave him some cornbread and lemonade. No biggie. Come to think of it, she hadn't even heard the name "Jesus." People just, well, hung out with each other, whether they were a volunteer or someone who came to snag some free stuff.

Serving with, not to, Rebecca nodded absently. There is a difference. She wondered if that's how it was with other ministries, like the ones Granny helped with, or if this one was unique. Is that why Christians seemed to be doing stuff for others all the time? Because it felt human to be helpful, even when your own life wasn't exactly perfect?

She shivered, wished for a moment Devon was here, so she could share the thought with him.

"Earth to Rebecca," a voice said and nudged her.

She had been staring off into space for several minutes and now shook her head, came back to reality, and realized Josh was standing there. He had a big empty box in one arm and wore a chef's hat, which made him look both silly and cute and professional all at the same time.

She grinned at him. "Sorry, lost in thought."

"You okay?" Josh gave her a kind look, and suddenly she felt the overwhelming desire to talk to him, to ask him about Jesus and why he was so devoted, whether he actually believed the Bible, why he gave his life to Christ, and what that actually meant.

Whether, once you did give your life, it'd fill that space that always seemed to settle in her bones like a cancer. The space even Prozac didn't seem to make better.

But the moment passed as quickly as it had come. "Yeah, yeah, I'm good."

A guest walked up to browse, and she gave Josh a quick smile before turning back to the table. He waved and wandered off to the kitchen.

As busy as it had been at the start, the night wound down quickly. Rebecca piled the clothes into their cardboard boxes, stowed them in the church storage closet. She hadn't seen Josh and JJ for at least an hour, wondered if they'd gone home or were in the back. She hoped they wouldn't have gone without saying goodbye.

One of the kitchen volunteers thumbed at the spaghetti table. "Better get you some before it's gone."

"Thanks," Rebecca said, but she found she wasn't hungry. Instead, she wandered to the kitchen with a box of mini bottles. As she walked in, she almost ran straight into Millie Jeffers, who looked about as startled as she did. Whatever Millie was carrying tumbled to the ground.

"What are you doing here?" they each started to ask, then burst out laughing.

Rebecca knelt to help Millie pick up what had fallen—some empty boxes—and offered a few to her. "I'll give you a hand. Where are you headed?"

"Recycling." Millie motioned to the pile in the corner, gave Rebecca a sidelong look. Instead of the poly-blend blouses and practical pants she wore to the office, tonight Millie was wearing a faded orange T-shirt emblazoned with the words "Run4Christ" and a pair of blue jeans. She looked almost girlish, Rebecca thought, nowhere near the prim-and-proper look she'd sported earlier that day.

"So, you help with the giveaway ministry too?" Millie asked, tossed a few boxes atop the pile.

Rebecca shrugged, tossed her own boxes on. "It's my second time."

"I've been out the last few Fridays with my grands, but their mama's got the little ones tonight. I brought the oldest with me," Millie said, still looking at Rebecca curiously.

"I've been helping give out the clothes, in front," Rebecca gestured vaguely. "You're back here in the kitchen?"

"I run the soup cooker in the winter, mostly, and in the summers do backup for the line—chopping veggies, fetching, gathering, that kind of thing. My grandson was a big help."

Millie looked happier than she normally did, and Rebecca could tell she, too, enjoyed the work. It was kind of addictive, Rebecca thought, and it crossed her mind that was maybe why so many churches held drug and alcohol programs. If you've got to give over one habit, it made sense to replace it with another. The church could be a habit like anything else, she mused. It had happened that way for Granny.

"Where you off to now? Heading out?" Millie asked as Josh and JJ came out from the dishwashing room.

JJ was tugging on his dad's hand, and another boy trailed close behind.

"Hey, Miss Becca!" JJ waved, then turned back to his dad. "Pleeeeeease, Dad? His granny said it's all right."

"There's my grandson now." Millie beamed as she laid a hand on the other boy's head, a dark-haired kid about JJ's age wearing a video game T-shirt. Millie looked at Josh. "JJ's absolutely welcome to sleep over. The more the merrier."

"See? Told you." JJ gave his dad a plaintive look, and Josh held up a warning finger.

"Watch it, JJ. Respect?"

"Sorry, Dad." JJ looked down, immediately chastened. Rebecca was impressed.

Josh ruffled his son's hair, his face softening instantly. "You're forgiven." He looked at Millie. "Sure, you can sleep over, but I've gotta pick you up at nine sharp. Remember we're skipping fishing because we promised to help Aunt Lissa and Uncle Gary with the garage sale this weekend?"

"Yessir!" JJ and the other kid exchanged high-fives, and Millie laughed and ushered them toward the door.

"Gather your things, boys. Time to head on," Millie said as they walked off. She turned to wave. "See ya, Rebecca."

"See ya, Millie," Rebecca called, then elbowed Josh. "Guess you're off dad duty tonight."

"Guess so." Josh tossed her a smile. "Wanna give me a hand with these boxes?"

They grabbed the remaining boxes and brought them back out to the recycling bins, flattened them one by one, and tossed them in. The heat of the day had dissipated, and a soft breeze swept through, tickling the hair on the back of her neck. Granny was right—fall was just around the corner. Working together made it go faster, and Josh entertained her with stories of his clients and latest house projects as they worked.

"Do you have any mean clients?" Rebecca asked as she tossed the last box into the bin. "I'm starting to feel like this is the Twilight Zone, where everyone's nice and makes you apple pies just because."

Josh laughed. "You shoulda seen the battle Mrs. Crenshaw and Mrs. Stillerman had over who made me the best pie. Almost came to blows over it."

"Really?"

He stuck out his tongue. "Just messin' with you."

"Watch it, JJ. I bet I'm still stronger than you are. Remember the time I knocked you flat on your back?"

His eyes widened. "Oh, man, I remember that! Sheesh, Becks, that was low. There I was, knocked out on the banks of the Wahca by my first crush." He shook his head in mock defeat.

"Your first ... crush?" She cocked her head at him.

His face pinked in the bright streetlights. "I figured you knew. I mean, come on—the prettiest girl I'd laid eyes on and she liked to fish? How could I not crush on you?"

A crush? She thought back to those days, the kids they'd been all those years ago—him all teasing goofiness, her all awkward and aloof, bonding over cupcakes and apples on the riverbank.

"You never said." She watched him in the streetlight, marveled again at how the chubby kid with pimples and freckles and braces had turned into such a good-looking man and great dad. Sarah and Marisol would have deemed him a "hottie" for sure. She bit her lip, tried to laugh. "I never knew. Wow, we were so young."

"Yeah, we were."

"So much has happened since then."

Rebecca wanted to say more to fill the silence, but the right words wouldn't formulate in her head, let alone leave her lips. And then the door to the church banged open and there were Marla and Rev. Marla was brandishing Rebecca's purse and smiling broadly.

"Time to lock up! Y'all have anything else inside?" she asked. Rev had his hand on her elbow, helped his wife gently down the back steps into the alley.

"Nope, that's it." Rebecca took the purse, fished inside for her car keys.

"Hey, there, Jamison. Been a long time!" Rev shook hands with Josh, and they did that one-armed man-hug. "I almost called you the other day to help me with a small job at the parsonage, but I managed to rig it."

Marla good-naturedly swatted her husband. "'Rig' is generous," she said to Josh. "I think we could use your help after all."

"You asked the right man." Josh smiled, and Rebecca watched them talk shop about dimensions and tools and budget restrictions, admiring how he heard them out in full, then offered suggestions. They exchanged numbers, and Josh promised to call on Monday.

They all walked to the front, and Josh and Rebecca watched Rev and Marla hop into their separate cars.

She wanted to ask again about Devon, give Marla her number

and ask her to call if she heard anything. But she just stayed quiet. You're overreacting, Rebecca.

"Join us Sunday if you can," Rev called, and they motored off into the night.

Rebecca jangled her keys, edging toward her car.

"Well, it's getting late."

Josh wiggled his eyebrows comically. "This is what they call 'late' in the city?"

She giggled, and he looked at the sky.

"The night is young." He held out an arm, nodded for her to join. "Come. Take a walk with me."

She bit her lip, then realized that was exactly what she wanted to do—go for a walk with her old friend and let everything go. Just for a little while.

"Sounds like fun," she said, linking her arm in his.

They walked through the town toward the big gazebo at the center, and Josh told her all about the big community festivals they held there once the weather turned cooler—the back-to-school bash, the fall pumpkin fest, the turkey giveaway, the Christmas walk.

"They'd still hold the St. Patty's Day Party if Les Newman hadn't gotten everyone sick with food poisoning from the barbecue that one year. Whew, that was one rough weekend."

She put her hand to her mouth. "Oh, my."

They walked on, the soft pad of their shoes on the pavement and an occasional dog bark or car cruising by the only sounds.

"By the way, I really liked your article on that artist from this week's paper, the one who does the landscapes? I went to school with him."

"You did?" Her cheeks flushed, and she felt unreasonably happy at the compliment. The story had fallen into her pile and she'd almost given it to Tiff, but the girl was overloaded and Rebecca felt like a creative break after the weight of Tamika's story and the endless cycle of meeting coverage, which at best was tedious and at worst was nitpicky politicking. The artist, a funny but quiet man named Ralph, had one arm and was missing two fingers on his right hand, but it didn't seem to slow him down one bit. He had perfected a special painting technique, and watching him felt like she was witnessing a beautiful ballet, the colors and swirls landing on the canvas in an artful combination of realism and fantasy.

Josh smiled over at her. "You have this …" He waved a hand, laughed. "I don't even know how to say it, and I'm probably going to sound like a wacko, but this … way of catching someone's attention and making them hold onto the words, fall in love with the subject, like it's the most fascinating thing you've ever heard about, ever."

"Wow, Josh." She risked a glance, hoped her pink cheeks weren't too obvious. "I think that's the best compliment I've had in, well, I don't know how long!"

He chuckled. "Well, I mean it sincerely."

The ring of a bike bell from a side street caught her ear as they walked and she turned suddenly, hoping she'd see Devon. But it was another kid on a bike, an older kid, not Devon at all. Her heart sank, though her head knew it wasn't at all logical she'd see him out, riding around at this hour.

She looked at Josh. "JJ hasn't mentioned Devon this week, has he?"

"Not since the weekend. Why—everything okay?"

Rebecca shrugged. "It's silly, but I've been worried about him. I saw him yesterday, burgers at the diner, and I asked him about a nasty bruise on his wrist. He got kinda quiet about it, made up some story, and now he's MIA."

"Could be sick."

"That's what Marla said, that he probably had that nasty virus going around. But …"

"But you don't think so?"

Rebecca shook her head, not sure how to say it. "Granny said he had some issues at home."

Josh cocked his head. "You think Devon's being ... abused?"

Hearing him say the word aloud made it somehow sound less hysterical than it did floating around in her head. She chewed her lip, nodded.

"Maybe."

Josh frowned. "Does Marla think so?"

"We haven't talked about it. It's just been this ..." She waved her hand like she was shooing stray thoughts. "This strange theory. Call it an instinct."

He stopped walking. "God gives us instincts for a reason, Becks."

"Except when you're confusing instinct with imagination. And that could get people in serious trouble if it's unfounded." She let out a breath. "I don't know, Josh. I mean, I've been having weekly meetings with this kid for more than a month now. We talk— about real stuff, mind you. We laugh. But I don't really know him. I've never even been to his house. If he was in trouble, don't you think Marla or Rev would have clued in to it?"

He screwed up his face like he was thinking. "Maybe not. Maybe they're too close to see it." He looked at her. "Sometimes we miss the things that are right in front of our face."

He had a point.

They started walking again.

"I suppose I can call Marla tomorrow, see if she has any suspicions."

"That's a good idea. And hey, if you're worried, it can't hurt to take a drive out to his house. She might want to tag along."

"Granny and I are planning to bring him some chicken soup in the morning. Maybe Marla will want to come, too."

They reached the gazebo and stopped, and Rebecca surprised

herself by leaping up the steps and onto one of the two oversized glider bench swings. The back of the swing was cool, and the metal felt good on her skin, which was slightly warm from the walk.

Josh joined her, and the swing swayed heavily as he sat, her feet lifting off the ground. She found herself smiling, closing her eyes as she leaned back and let herself enjoy the rhythm.

She could sense Josh next to her. He was a big guy, she let herself realize. Not overweight, but tall, with broad shoulders. She imagined he'd need the strength for his work as a contractor. She remembered what he'd said about her being his first crush, wondered why she'd never thought about him that way. She opened her eyes, saw he was leaning back as she was, hands behind his head. He'd been so easy to talk to, all those years ago. Like a sounding board. She'd rant about her parents, her friends back home, whatever guy she was currently obsessed with.

And yet, a crush. Did he still have one? It had been more than twenty years. He'd become a man, had a wife, a son. Been widowed.

"You know I came here to Dahlia because I hit rock bottom." The words were out before she could help herself, but once they were she felt better. Bolder. Stronger.

He opened his eyes, nodded slowly. "I wondered."

"It wasn't good." She hesitated. "I'd been in the hospital."

He kept his eyes on her. "You don't have to tell me."

But she wanted to, found herself opening up like the old days, telling him about Peter, Alyssa, the Bannister Group.

"I'd taken too many pills. I didn't think I was trying to kill myself, didn't mean to, but looking back, I think that's exactly what I was trying to do. Take away the pain. Escape. Whatever you want to call it." A lump settled in her throat, and she swallowed, gazing out at the town, at the little sparkles of streetlight making the whole square look magical, almost like fairy lights. "I felt like I'd lost everything. They'd been my world, and I was cast aside like an afterthought."

She felt rather than saw him reach over, his skin warm as he folded his larger palm over her hand. A shiver ran through her.

"You're no afterthought." His words were soft, and she had to strain to hear him.

Turning her head, she realized how close his face was to hers. How close his lips were. It would be so easy to move her own head a fraction of an inch, turn her face up to his. To lose herself in the tumble of romance and feeling.

But this was Josh. And then what?

His eyes were locked on hers, and her heart thudded so loudly she thought he could hear it. Their fingers laced, tighter now. She wanted to kiss him, she realized, wanted to take that tumble. Felt herself leaning in, felt the heady fall begin to take over.

But she put a hand on his chest.

I can't.

"Josh—I..." She didn't even have the words. Gently, she pushed him back, slid her hand from his. Scooted back so she could turn and face him. Put some distance between them.

He nodded, but not before she saw a flash of disappointment.

"I—It's just too soon, after ..."

"It's okay, Becks. I understand."

She looked at him. "You do?"

She knit her fingers in her lap. Her left hand felt cold without his, solitary. Her heart was still hammering against her chest.

"I do." He gave a small smile. "I'm also remarkably patient."

Something about the way he said it gave her a little thrill, as if her insides had gone from solid to liquid in an instant.

A soft female laugh glided across the air, and they turned to see a couple, hand in hand, strolling across the grass, lost in each other. They were young, and Rebecca couldn't tell in the darkness, but she thought it might be Tiff and the kid from Smathers Grocery. The couple walked on by, their progress painfully slow. After what felt like hours, they were far off, down the street, their laughter an echo on the summer air.

"Thanks for trusting me." His voice was quiet.

She gave a wry smile. "Thanks for listening. I know I walk a good game, like I've got it all together, but some days that hospital room feels like yesterday. I'm a long way off from 'normal.'"

"Normal's overrated. And you're stronger than you think you are, Becks."

She could see he believed that, and looking back at him, she believed it, too. In that moment, he reminded her of Devon. Devon looked at her the same way. Like he had utter faith in her character, like he knew she was bigger than the image she projected or even the job she did. She had more to offer than skills and marketability—Ed Bannister's word. She thought of her former boss, of his grizzled sideburns and cynical grin, and for the first time in months smiled at the memory instead of winced. They'd been friends, the two of them, in spite of what had happened with her job. That was worth holding onto.

Suddenly Josh was on his feet, tugging her up. "Come on. Race you back to the cars?"

She beat him by a good three yards, smacking her hands down on her car hood in victory.

"Home free!"

He gave her a high five, jangled his keys. "See you around this weekend?"

"Hope so."

"Night, Becks."

"Night, JJ." She stuck her tongue out at him. "Josh."

He stood a respectable distance away as she got into the car, waited as she turned the key and drove off back to Granny's. Through the rearview mirror, she watched him wave as she pulled away, the memory of his warm hand covering hers a comfort as she navigated the empty streets of Dahlia, a million miles from everything she'd ever been.

CHAPTER 30

Devon

DEVON STOOD THERE, frozen in place, ears ringing from the mighty crash of Memaw's china onto the kitchen linoleum.

"Don't you dare!" Memaw's eyes were wild and she held another heavy bowl, glared at her son. The roar in Devon's ears grew louder, and he knew then the sound wasn't the plates she'd dropped in anger, knew it wasn't a car outside or anything but his own pent-up rage, threatening to boil over and destroy everything.

Only he couldn't move. Couldn't speak. Couldn't do anything but stand there and watch.

T looked like he wanted to either run or smack her something fierce. One foot was poised, as if he wanted to hightail it out of there, leave the crazy far behind. The other, the one next to his tightly balled fist, was firmly planted. As Devon watched, T's jaw clenched, and he could see the tendons in his uncle's neck tighten like long, skinny bands.

"Maw, I'm warning you…"

The roaring got louder.

"You have no right, Terrence Jackson Robinson, no right at all to come in here and warn me. I might be an old woman, but I've seen more than you've ever seen, and I'm sick and tired of—"

"That's enough."

T stepped forward, and the heavy bowl she was holding dropped, shards of white porcelain flinging across the kitchen like someone had left the blender on while making pancakes. One shot out, grazed T's leg, but he didn't seem to notice.

"Simmer down, Maw, or ..."

"Or what? You're gonna punch an old woman, punch your own mama like you hurt your nephew? Your sister's looking down from heaven right now ..."

Someone was muttering stop it, stop it now, stop it right now, but it wasn't T or Memaw, wasn't anyone else in the room as far as he could tell, and almost like he was watching the room from above he suddenly realized the words were coming from his own lips and then they were hollering and screaming and he couldn't stop himself, couldn't hold them back. The roaring in his ears exploded and he was on T now, standing between T and Memaw and screaming it out with all he had in him.

"Stop!"

And then Memaw staggered, like she'd lost all her breath in an instant.

"Maw?" T was staring at her, and Devon turned to look as Memaw sank to her knees, there among the shattered china dishes, clutching her chest.

"Memaw?" Devon had her in his arms now, and T was pushing him aside, shaking his mother's weak frame.

"Maw, what's wrong? Can you hear me?"

Wild-eyed, T turned to Devon. The look on his uncle's face was pure, murderous fury.

"Call an ambulance. Now. And then get out for good. Don't you ever come back or mark my words, boy. I'll beat you. I'll straight-up kill you."

T shouted a few things after that, but Devon didn't stick around to hear. He just ran. Ran next door to Mrs. Brown's, used her phone, then ran to the trees, where he watched, numb.

Frozen.

Waiting.

Saw the red and white van pull up, sirens wailing, and the men rush inside. Saw Ray's car, too, music blaring and two girls inside, heard T curse at him, order him to go and don't come back. Saw the stretcher with Memaw loaded into the ambulance and T get in someone's face, tell them he'd better fix his Maw or he'd pay good and well.

And then it was quiet again, and the lights were gone and T's car was gone and all he could hear, all around him, was the chirp of the katydids and the hum of the mosquitoes.

He felt at his cheeks, surprised to realize they were bone dry.

Quickly, before he could lose his nerve, he darted into the house, grabbed his backpack and his Bible, cleared the pantry out of every pop-top can and cereal bar he could get his hands on. He got his bike from around back, pedaled silently around the front, stopping an instant to kiss his fingers and touch them gently to the faded wooden cross at the center of Mama's memory garden.

He used the payphone outside Mr. Allen's store to call the hospital, not sure whether he could believe what they told him: She was alive, in intensive care, but alive.

For now.

Memaw. The tears came then, just for a moment.

But then he shut them down. He had to move, had to go, get somewhere safe, somewhere T wouldn't find him.

He knew T'd meant what he said. He'd kill him for sure, wouldn't even think twice about it. Just to make a point, 'cause he said he would. He'd seen the look on T's face as they knelt before Memaw. He couldn't ever go back. Couldn't even go to Rev or Marla, or

Miss Becca, or CJ. No one was safe—they'd get hurt if they helped him. He knew it.

Think, Devon. Think. His mouth was like cotton, his heart like a hundred racecars barreling through.

Where could he go? Where was safe?

It came to him like an answered prayer. And before he could think it through, change his mind, question it, he adjusted his backpack, put his hands on the bars, and pedaled off into the night.

CHAPTER 31

Rebecca

AT HOME THE NEXT MORNING, Rebecca waited until ten to call Marla about Devon, just in case the preacher's wife slept late on her one weekend day off. But she'd barely missed her.

"She headed out not five minutes ago with three other ladies, bound for a women's retreat," Rev Bryant said when Rebecca rang the parsonage. "She'll be back Sunday night."

She sighed. "Thanks, Rev."

"Anything I can help with?"

Rebecca hesitated; he sounded genuine. "Well, it's probably nothing, but … I guess I'm a little worried about Devon. Marla thought he might be home sick with that virus going around. I was thinking I'd drive over to his house, maybe bring him some chicken soup."

"You let him know I asked about him, tell him I'll stop by after church tomorrow if he's not there."

"Will do." She paused, wanting to say more, not sure exactly how to say it. *I'm worried about more than Devon being sick.* But the words wouldn't come.

"You need me to come with you? Or one of the ladies from the

Care Committee? I'm heading out the door to Columbia for class, but I can meet you there if you need help."

"No, no—I'll be fine. But thanks."

"All right, then." He sounded doubtful. "Hope to see you Sunday, too. You're always welcome."

She hung up and wandered downstairs, found Granny making a grocery list in the kitchen.

"Feel like taking a ride?"

Twenty minutes later, they were driving west on Aberville Road toward James Watkins. The day was beautiful, no rain in sight yet, and a tall container of homemade chicken noodle soup, courtesy of Smathers Grocery, rested on the floorboard at Granny's feet.

Granny reached over, patted her leg. "I'm sure he's fine, sweet girl."

Rebecca cut her eyes at Granny. "I'm probably going to embarrass him, showing up at his house like this."

"Pfff, nonsense. It's being neighborly."

"Well, I don't exactly have a lot of experience with that."

Devon's neighborhood was older, a mix of small, squat concrete shack-looking structures and singlewides, more than one house with a "foreclosure" sign. The cars were older, too, and rundown, some parked in the front yards.

"Baker Street." Granny read the sign aloud, pointing, and Rebecca turned left, counted the numbers dropping. There, on the right.

"Two-twenty-one. Like your birthday, Granny," she said.

The house looked well-kept and lived-in, with a front window open to let in the breeze. A clay pot with flowers stood on the porch with a cheerful mat proclaiming "Welcome."

She and Granny approached the door, and she knocked before she could lose her nerve.

A kid just a little older than Devon answered the door. He had pale skin and shaggy brown hair, a blue Dahlia Baptist T-shirt, and only one sock. In his hand was a bowl of what looked like corn puffs.

"Well, hello there, CJ," Granny said.

"Uh, hi, Miz Helen."

Rebecca peered past him. "We're looking for Devon. Devon Robinson?"

"CJ, who's at the door?" a woman's voice called, and CJ yelled back, "Nobody, Ma!"

He turned back to them.

"Sorry, you got the wrong house." He looked uncomfortable. "Devon lives up the road a ways."

He pointed, and Rebecca and Granny stared in that direction, confused.

"Is this two-twenty-one?" Rebecca asked.

"Yeah."

Granny frowned. "CJ, honey, do you happen to know Devon's house number?"

A guarded look came over CJ's face. "Uh, I don't remember. It's that way somewhere." He glanced behind him. "Gotta go. See you Monday, Miz Helen."

They got back in the car, and Rebecca looked over at Granny.

"I know Devon said two-twenty-one."

Granny pursed her lips. "Let's call Rev Bryant, see if he knows the address."

But Rev didn't answer. They cruised slowly up the street, watching the numbers rise. Three-fifteen. Four-hundred-one.

"There!" Granny pointed.

A small black sign with silvery lettering read "Robinson."

Rebecca pulled into the driveway slowly, took it in, as if trying to piece together bits of the real Devon.

The house wasn't terrible, a modest concrete one-story with a little yard. The yard was overgrown, and a brown Cadillac was parked in the carport. But unlike CJ's house, this one had an empty look, quiet, like no one lived there and hadn't for ages. The curtains were drawn, and in the back, she could barely glimpse what remained of an old chain link fence.

"Looks like someone's home," Granny said as Rebecca pulled in behind the Cadillac and turned off the ignition, mouth dry.

"Maybe it's the uncle." Rebecca made a face. "And surely his Memaw's here. I don't imagine she gets out much. Devon said she has problems with her legs, I think from arthritis."

They got out of the car with the soup, walked to the tiny front porch. From somewhere not too far away, a big dog barked. Pit bull, maybe, or Rottweiler. The kind that probably liked to attack defenseless women and their grannies who showed up unannounced and uninvited.

This is a bad idea. Her head and heart pounded in sync. Devon clearly didn't want her coming around the house, had made excuses every time she'd offered a lift home, had even given her a fake address. She was going to make him feel awkward, pressured, maybe push him away entirely.

But Josh popped into her mind then, and his words. *God gives us instincts for a reason.*

She bit her lip, gathered her nerve, and knocked quickly on the front door.

Nothing.

She knocked again, louder.

"Maybe they're asleep," Granny murmured.

They were turning to leave when they heard the sharp thwack of a door lock turning, and then the creak as the metal door opened a crack.

A man in a white tank top and blue jeans peered out behind the door chain, eyes narrowed. The house was dark behind him, and his eyes looked off somehow, as if he'd just woken up. Maybe he was sick, too. She could hear the faint hum of a television set on in the background.

"Mr. Robinson?" Rebecca's smile felt tight, and she swallowed hard, stomach clenched. "I'm Rebecca Chastain, and this is my granny, Helen Chastain. We're friends of Devon's. He missed camp Friday and we thought maybe he was sick, brought him some chicken soup."

She held out the soup container, feeling inane.

The man just stared at her, made no move to take the soup.

"I—ah." She held onto the soup and tried to smile. "Is he home?"

"Kid's asleep." His voice was cold, quiet, but with enough of an edge that Rebecca swallowed.

"Okey doke, well, would you mind telling him we stopped by?" The smile froze on her face.

Behind them, a car rolled slowly by, got to the corner, then turned and circled back. The hair on the back of her neck prickled, and she held the soup out toward him again.

He took a step back. "We don't need no charity." The word came out like he'd tasted something bad.

Rebecca felt rather than saw Granny stiffen.

"We're just friends, just trying to say hi." Rebecca's eyes widened, and she held up a hand. "No harm meant."

"He don't need no friends, neither. Specially friends like you."

Granny put a hand on her arm. Time to go. They turned, started back toward the car.

The door shut before they got off the porch, and Rebecca could hear the door lock turning back in place. She shivered, then set the soup down on the porch, left it in case.

"Wow," Rebecca muttered as she reversed out of the driveway.

Granny exhaled sharply. "Wow is right."

"I can't believe Devon lives there, with someone like that." She clutched the wheel as she drove home the way she'd come, past rickety houses and rundown yards with stories untold, stories she ached to uncover. She glanced at Granny. "I mean, did you get as much of a bad-news vibe as I did?"

Granny sighed. "I hate to say it, but yes. I did."

Silence settled over them, and they were past James Watkins and heading toward Main Street when Granny spoke again.

"I think we need to call social services."

Rebecca nodded. "I do, too. That guy had Class A drug dealer written all over him, and I wouldn't be surprised if Devon were in trouble. Real trouble."

"Me, too."

"I just wish we could talk to him. Figure out some way past the uncle."

The sound of children laughing in the streets pierced the air as they drove through Dahlia proper now, cruising past sunny, lived-in homes. Outside one, a half-dozen happy children leaped through a sprinkler, a smattering of moms watching and chatting, oblivious to the fact that five minutes away, life for another set of kids was far, far different.

"What about Rev and Marla?" Granny asked. "Surely we're not the only ones concerned about Devon. They see him a lot more than we do—maybe they have a way to check on him, or know a neighbor who can."

Rebecca nodded, squinting against the sun. "It's worth a try."

At the house, she dialed the parsonage again. Rev didn't answer, so she left a message with as much detail as she could.

"That's the best we can do for now." Rebecca sat heavily at the kitchen table.

Granny leaned over, kissed her hair. Rebecca held her close, and they stayed that way a moment, so quiet they could hear the faint tick of the kitchen wall clock.

"You know, girl, we can do one better," Granny said.

Rebecca gave a wry smile, but she held out her hands as Granny sank into the chair next to her, and they bowed their heads. Granny's words were simple—Lord, help Devon, keep him safe, shine your light of protection upon him. Help us to help him.

When Granny finished, Rebecca opened her eyes and took a breath. She wasn't sure how "giving it to God" was supposed to feel, but her chest felt lighter somehow, and her head felt clearer. She surprised herself by blinking away tears.

"I love you, Granny."

Granny smiled, still holding onto Rebecca's hands. "Love you too, girl."

They were getting out bread and tomatoes to make sandwiches when Rebecca's cell phone rang. She snagged it off the counter, hoping it was Rev calling her back, but she didn't recognize the number.

"Rebecca, this is Lib Pauling." The gruff voice made her shake her head.

"Uh, hi, Li—Mrs. Pauling."

The woman sniffed. "I have two tickets to the humane society gala tonight, but I'm not feeling well. I wondered if you and your Granny might want to go in my place."

Rebecca wrinkled her nose. The last thing she wanted to do on a free Saturday night was schmooze with dolled-up Dahlia residents, especially with worries about Devon on her mind.

"Who is it?" Granny mouthed.

Rebecca covered the mouthpiece. "Lib Pauling. Wants to know if we'd like to go to the humane society gala tonight."

A sparkle lit Granny's eyes, and before she knew it, Rebecca found herself accepting the tickets from Lib, making plans.

"It'll be fun! A girls' night out, you and me," Granny said when Rebecca hung up, and Rebecca giggled in spite of herself. "We could go shopping, buy a new dress. I don't remember the last time

I bought a new dress for a night out."

Something about Granny's wistful expression tugged at Rebecca's heart.

"You know what? Let's do it—a girls' shopping day, a nice lunch out, and a night at the gala. It does sound fun!"

She dialed Tiff to let the girl know she was off the hook for the night. Across the line, she swore she heard the reporter clap.

"Thanks, Boss!" Tiff sounded positively thrilled. "I, ah, had to turn down a date for tonight. Looks like I can call him back and say yes after all."

Rebecca was still smiling as she hung up.

CHAPTER 32

Devon

HE WANTED SO BADLY to go back, so badly to pedal to town, fish in his pocket for his last quarter, and dial the hospital.

But he couldn't risk it. Even in the dead of night, he knew T or his friends would be out there, hunting for him, ready to take him down, hurt him.

All he could do was stay where he was, safe in JJ's tunnel in the woods, his friend's secret hideaway, and pray.

It's all my fault.

He was grateful he'd brought his Bible. He wished he'd thought to bring a pen, but it didn't matter. The words washed over him like a gentle rain, and he tried to fill his mind with them, let them drown out everything else.

The Lord is my shepherd; I shall not want.

Let not your hearts be troubled, neither let them be afraid.

God is our refuge and strength, a very present help in trouble.

Jesus wept.

Devon sat there, his back against the smooth concrete, huddled against the night, grateful when the clouds shifted and the moon swept light on the pages bright enough for him to read.

When the light was gone, he hunkered down and tried his best to sleep, tried to listen to the river slosh against the rocks below the tunnel, but the dreams and the worry were too much. He knew he was weak, knew he needed to cast his worries on God and trust in his promises, but for the first time in his life he couldn't see through, couldn't see how he'd possibly get past this.

He couldn't eat, either. The cereal bar was too dry for his throat, and he found he could barely get it past his lips, let alone chew and swallow it down. The few bites he'd managed burned his stomach, threatened to spill back out.

And so he sat, rocking slowly, cold and hungry and feeling utterly, completely alone.

CHAPTER 33

Rebecca

IN SPITE OF HER WORRIES about Devon, the day had ended up being great—she and Granny had found beautiful, swingy cocktail dresses at the little boutique next to Joe Mama's, then got lattes and paninis for lunch. Rev still hadn't called back by the time Rebecca and Granny left for the gala, and Rebecca ordered herself to put it aside for the night. Devon's fine. You're overreacting. Besides, she reminded herself, they had given it to God. Didn't they need to act like they believed it?

Now it was six, and they were pulling up to Dahlia Country Club. A valet parked their car. As they stepped out, lightning lit the sky, causing the sparkles on Granny's navy blue cocktail dress to shimmer in the twilight. It wasn't raining, but Rebecca could tell it was coming. There was an electricity to the air, a low thrum warning them of what would be.

"Swanky for Dahlia," Rebecca whispered to Granny as they strolled into the ornate entryway, high heels clicking on what looked like a marble floor. A camera dangled from Rebecca's shoulder like a purse, and she clutched a tiny beaded pocketbook in the other hand.

"You can thank Victor Wennerman for that." Granny gave an arch look.

"Erik's dad? Let me guess—he financed this place, too, for all the richy-rich retirees living in his high-end retirement village?"

"Well, the renovation, anyway. It has brought needed tax dollars to the county, I will say that much. And they did do an absolutely beautiful job."

Granny was right, Rebecca thought as they walked through the entryway—gleaming floors, elegant oil paintings, polished wood and chrome everywhere she looked. Wennerman seemed to bring a class act to everything he touched, sketchy media buyouts notwithstanding.

"I wonder if he'll be here tonight," she said to Granny. "I haven't had the 'pleasure' of meeting him yet."

Her stomach took a tumble then as she realized who else she might be seeing tonight.

Erik. The humane society schmoozefest was just the sort of place a marketing man like him would be.

Maybe he won't be at the gala. Surely he was out with some beautiful woman in a bigger city tonight, not rubbing elbows here in Dahlia.

But to her dismay, the first person she saw when she walked into the main ballroom was Erik Wennerman himself, chatting and laughing with a group of other men. He wore a black tuxedo, she noticed, and he stood out against the sea of other men, who all wore sports coats or nice suits. Her stomach dropped as she realized once again how handsome he was, and how much he reminded her of Peter.

Before he could make eye contact, she steered Granny over to one of the hors d'oeuvres stations. She crossed her fingers as she focused intently on the small appetizer plates directly in front of her. Don't notice me. Maybe he wouldn't. Maybe their little confrontation in the coffee shop had been awkward enough for both of them for him to stop trying.

"Wendy Calhoun's work," Granny observed.

"Huh?"

"The ice." Granny pointed, and Rebecca looked up at the hors d'oeuvres display they stood before. To her wonder, someone had carved a rather ornate—and rather excellent—sculpture of two animals, a beagle and a kitten, frolicking in front of a giant DHS. Dahlia Humane Society. Shrimp were artfully arranged all around.

"She's Louise Calhoun's daughter." Granny snagged a shrimp. "Every year, she donates her services to the gala, produces a new creation."

Rebecca gazed at the sculpture. "These things take hours. She must be a huge animal lover."

She snapped a few photos of the ice sculpture, then some more of the crowd, making a mental note to assign Tiff a feature story on the sculptor. Then again, she thought as she clicked away, maybe she'd do the story herself. That was one thing she'd learned about coming to Dahlia—doing an occasional feature was good for her. Stretched her creativity in new ways.

She remembered the way Josh had complimented her piece on the landscape artist—and the way she'd felt when he'd said it. She had to admit, if only to herself, that she was starting to have feelings for her old friend. Real feelings. And she didn't know what to do about them.

He said she'd been his first crush, but that didn't mean he felt the same way about her now. For all she knew, he was dating someone else, someone gorgeous and fun and without the suitcase load of baggage Rebecca brought along for the ride. Well, it wasn't as if she should be dating—let alone crushing on—anyone right now, anyway.

The music started again, and she and Granny found seats at a table next to two older sisters in embellished blazers and glittery jewelry and a middle-aged couple who told them all about their work fostering service dogs. She lost sight of Erik, breathed a sigh of relief when he locked eyes with her once and gave a friendly nod-wave from across the room but made no move to come say hello. At least we can be civil. Though she wondered how long it would take for him to pull back his advertising dollars.

"Now that's a catch," one of the sisters told her in a low voice, and Rebecca startled when she realized the woman was speaking to her, had noticed her watching Erik. A faint blush warmed Rebecca's cheeks.

"Oh, no—I'm not interested in him. I just … know him from work."

"Pity." The older woman winked and leaned closer, the stones on her ears flashing brightly. "If I were your age, I'd be more than a little interested."

The other sister leaned in. "You're from the paper, right?"

Rebecca steeled herself and nodded, waiting for the criticism, but the woman smiled.

"Well, I bet you have an inside track on this storm." The woman waved an arm, bracelets jangling. "You think a hurricane is really going to hit?"

"The one off the coast?" Rebecca cocked her head. "I doubt we have anything to worry about this far inland."

The first sister sniffed. "Back during Hugo, they said the same thing. Lost my entire vegetable garden, and a tree fell on my husband's car!"

"Oh, and that poor little child died over in Charlotte from that downed tree on the house. Who ever heard of a hurricane in Charlotte? You can bet anytime they call for a storm now, we sit up and take notice."

Rebecca made a mental note to call the National Weather Service first thing Monday, rework her front-page lineup.

"Well, I haven't heard of anything that dire in store for us, but I'll certainly look into it."

"That's good, dear."

Next to her, Granny was intently asking the foster-dog couple about their latest pack. The sisters got up for dessert, and Rebecca tuned out, found herself people-watching. The humane society had hired some sort of swing band, the musicians all in their twenties and decked out in crisp charcoal suits and bowties. A few couples were on the dance floor, twirling and laughing in time to the beat.

Granny looked happy, relaxed. She wore a navy blue short-sleeved number with a lace overlay and a flouncy skirt, and the pearls at her neck and ears looked almost iridescent in the sparkling lights of the ballroom. Rebecca smiled, watching Granny giggle with the couple, glad they'd done this tonight. Granny seemed to read her mind, reached over and clasped her hand a moment.

Love you, she squeezed twice.

Love you back, Rebecca squeezed in reply.

She looked across the room to the buffet and blinked as she saw Josh Jamison, standing entirely too close to a woman with wavy red hair. Her heart did a flip-flop, and she swallowed, mouth suddenly very dry.

Josh. With a woman.

A pretty woman.

He wore a deep gray suit with a darker gray shirt, the collar un-buttoned and tie loosened a bit. His hair was tousled, and he was laughing at whatever the woman was saying.

Her heart began to thud. A flash of their almost-kiss came again, and she found her hands were now clenched. Found she couldn't keep her eyes off him. He's a single man, Rebecca. He has every right to date whoever he wishes.

And then, almost too late, she noticed he'd spotted her and was now making a beeline her way, the woman in tow.

Oh, you are kidding me. She had to get out of there. Now.

"Granny, I'll be right back." She stood, pocketbook in hand, scanned the room for a restroom.

"Becks!" She heard her name and pretended not to hear, but then he was there, and shaking hands with Granny, and she plastered a "hey buddy old pal" smile on and looked up at the woman to realize she was staring straight into the face of Josh's older sister, Lissa.

"Becks, you remember Lissa?" Josh flashed a smile, and Rebecca swallowed back a blush. He wasn't on a date. She recognized Lissa now, her thick hair and broad smile that matched her brother's.

"Wow, it's been a long time! You're all grown up now!" Lissa's smile was warm, genuine, and Rebecca found her heart thudding back to a normal rate. Josh was chatting with Granny in earnest now. "How nice to see you again! Josh told me you're back in town."

"He did?"

Lissa gave her another smile, one that seemed to see deeper than Rebecca wanted. "He certainly did."

A tall, stocky blond man in a navy suit joined them, and Lissa pulled him close.

"Gary, this is Rebecca Chastain, Josh's friend. Rebecca, this is my husband, Gary. He runs the car dealership out on the road to Aberville."

"From the newspaper." Gary had a booming, happy voice, and his handshake was big to match. "Nice to meet you. Josh told us about you."

She giggled to dispel the awkwardness, realized no one seemed to feel it but her. Josh's eyes were on her, and her palms began to itch. Air. Need some air.

"Excuse me a moment. I ... I'll be right back."

Moments later, she was pushing through the French doors at

the rear of the room, gulping deep breaths as she stepped into the evening. The door clicked shut behind her, and she walked quickly, grateful to have a moment alone to think, to collect herself.

She stepped to the edge of the patio, gripped the stone ledge, and forced her heart to settle. Behind her, the music was pulsing and peppy, and she squeezed her eyes shut, made herself count to thirty in her head. The straps on her cocktail dress felt too tight, prickly. What was going on with her?

It was too much—months of living like a relative hermit, her only entertainment reading or watching reruns with Granny, and now not one but two men interested in her, and at a swanky party to boot?

Memories of New York, of Peter, of Peter and Alyssa all rushed back, and she gritted her teeth, willed herself to rein in the flood of emotions threatening to spill. Coming tonight was a mistake. She had no business playing socialite in a swingy gold cocktail dress, not after everything. She had no business flirting, not when she had express no-dating orders from her therapist. Get it together, Rebecca.

Unexpectedly she thought about Devon, and with all her heart wished she were back home at Granny's in her snuggliest PJs, reading the next chapter in her crime novel. The breeze picked up, made her shiver, and in the distance, she could hear thunder rumble. She wrapped her arms around herself, forcing herself to breathe in through her nose, out through her mouth.

The door to the patio opened, letting in whatever swing tune the band was playing. She turned, expecting to see Josh.

"Rebecca?"

But it wasn't Josh's voice she heard.

Instead it was Erik Wennerman standing there, glass in hand and smiling at her, beckoning to the room behind him.

"Come. Dance with me!"

It was the last thing in the world she wanted. Too late, she realized she was backing away, and now her spine was pressed tight against the stone wall overlooking the river beyond.

"You can't escape that easily," he quipped, a low chuckle. But that was exactly what she wanted to do—escape, run, hightail it out of there.

Instead, she forced a laugh. "I'm not much for dancing. Rain check?"

"Nope." That dimple appeared in one cheek, and he set his glass down on the ledge, stepped closer. "I think you get to make it up to me for accusing me of being a lowlife scoundrel in cahoots with my father to take over your newspaper."

"Ah, no, I—" She wanted to go. Get out. Be anywhere but there.

"Come on." His voice was almost a purr. "One dance. You can't deny you feel something for me."

He was too close now, and she swallowed. Lightning flickered in the distance.

Erik stepped in close, took her hand, and started to tug her toward him.

"Erik, stop …" She put a hand flat on his chest, stepped decidedly back.

But he stepped even closer, yanked her hard to him, and before she knew what was happening his mouth was on hers.

Hot anger bubbled inside and she tried to wrench free, but he held on tight.

The music grew louder, and she wriggled away in time to see the patio door opening and someone stepping through.

"Hey, Becks, come on! There's a … oh!" It was Josh who stood there. He had two lemonades in his hands, and as she watched, his face flashed from shocked to angry to hurt.

She finally broke free of Erik's grip, had just opened her mouth to speak.

But Josh's look said it all.

"Sorry to interrupt," he muttered.

And then he was gone.

Erik raised a brow mischievously, reached for her arm again. In an instant, he reminded her of Peter—every false, smarmy, two-faced, upward-climbing ounce.

"So where were we?"

Rebecca shot him a glare, shoved him away.

"No thanks, Wennerman," she said over her shoulder.

But try as she might, she couldn't find Josh anywhere at the party, inside or out.

Forget it, she told herself. Focus on Granny. It's Girls' Night Out, remember?

Still, as she went to bed that night, she couldn't stop thinking about the wounded expression on Josh's face, the smile that had turned sour in an instant.

CHAPTER 34

Devon

HE THOUGHT ABOUT THEM, wondered if they'd ever been real at all or just made-up characters, his very own book he'd invented to keep him going, keep him from going cuckoo.

Maybe that was it. Maybe he was going crazy now. It didn't really matter.

He was safe there. Safe in his tunnel. T wouldn't ever find him out here.

He closed his eyes as he listened to the river slosh and splash below, tried to picture Miss Marla, her soft caramel skin, her warm arms, her scent that reminded him of vanilla and spices and everything good and right and true.

Tried to picture Rev with his crisp button-down shirts and dark, dark skin, his voice that sounded like music and his rumbly, deep belly laugh, the kind of laugh that made you want to laugh with him, that made you feel like everything was okay and you didn't need to worry about a single thing in the whole wide world.

Tried to picture Miss Becca, with her kind, caring eyes that crinkled a little at the corners, the way she leaned in when she talked, like she wanted to really touch your heart and feel what you felt, think what you thought.

Tried to picture CJ, Shenise, Gabby. Mariana. JJ and his dad. Tried to remember what they ever even talked about, what they did.

But it felt like he'd made it all up, like they hadn't actually existed at all. The pictures in his mind were flat, one-dimensional, like an old coloring book.

It was just him and his Bible, there in the tunnel. Him and God.

And right now, God felt like he was very far away.

He wouldn't let himself think about Memaw. If he did, he thought he'd break for good. It was all his fault, he realized now. If he'd just stayed quiet like he was supposed to and let Memaw and T talk it out, none of this would have happened. Memaw would be fast asleep in her bed and not in some intensive-care hospital room fighting for her life.

If she was still even alive. For all he knew, he'd killed her. Killed his very own Memaw, who he'd promised Mama he'd always take care of.

He'd let Mama down, he'd let Memaw down, and he'd let God down.

That was why God felt far-off, he realized. God was mad at him, mad because he'd stepped in and gotten in the way, taken matters into his own hands.

Devon realized his cheeks were wet, which surprised him. He hadn't cried at all, not since the bike ride, before his talk with Memaw. Before everything came tumbling down worse than he ever could have imagined.

But now the tears wouldn't stop, and he was shuddering and shaking and gasping and on his knees and there was nothing in the world he could do to hold them back.

After, he slept. When he woke, he was hungrier than he'd ever been in his life.

He dug in his backpack, found a pop-top can of ravioli, fished out the little squares with his fingers. Ate two more after that, and one of those strawberry cereal bars, and a little plastic container of applesauce, washed it all down with a juice box. Grape. His least favorite flavor, but it tasted amazing now, and he wondered why he'd never liked it before.

Then he picked up his Bible again, read it until the light faded and he collapsed into sleep once more.

CHAPTER 35

Rebecca

REBECCA AWOKE MONDAY in a mood as dark as the skies and slipped out of the house before Granny was awake. "Off to work early—text and let me know if Devon shows at camp," she scrawled on a slip of paper, taped it to the coffeemaker for Granny.

It had been a weekend of frustration on all levels—she'd texted Josh, but he hadn't replied. Rev hadn't called her back about Devon, either. To top it off, she'd made the mistake of swinging by the office Sunday to grab some paperwork and ended up opening the bank statement.

Looking at the balance again this morning had turned her mood even darker. Despite her best efforts, the paper wasn't rebounding as fast as she'd hoped. Circulation had grown three percent in the last month, and between the Wennerman ad deal and a new real estate section Dinah started, ad sales were better than they'd been in two years. But it hadn't been long enough to make a difference where it counted. Between the low balance and the nearly maxed-out credit card, they were walking on eggshells.

A few more months remained until the December 1 deadline. She didn't see how they could turn it around in time.

And who knew if the Wennerman deal would even continue after what had happened Saturday?

She navigated the streets of Dahlia in silence, peering at the quaint houses and still-closed businesses as rain blanketed the town. The wind was starting to pick up, causing the traffic lights to sway gently as she pulled up to the red light. Waiting at the light, she slid her phone from her purse, opened the Notes app, and typed "call weather service, get Dahlia angle." The hurricane was still in the ocean, and from what she'd seen on national news, it would probably only impact the coast before it shifted north, but it still deserved a story.

It was only seven as she arrived at the *Dahlia Weekly*, climbed the steps, and locked the office door behind her. She hoped to have at least a good hour to finish crafting her story on Tamika. She closed her eyes a moment, picturing the girl, how she'd crossed her thin arms across her electric-blue tank top as she'd told her story. How her big brown eyes had gazed back at Rebecca, steady and trusting, as she let the secrets spill. She wondered how many more secrets Tamika kept, what else she'd seen in her short life.

So many secrets. And Devon—what secrets was he keeping? She pictured him there in that empty-looking house with that awful uncle, pitiful and sick and alone. What other pain was he hiding?

She glanced at the framed front page to the left of her desk, the one with the first summer camp story. She'd hung it there to help remind her of what she was trying to do with the paper, and with Dahlia—use the paper to bring new awareness about the real issues facing the community—poverty and homelessness, gangs and the economy. But looking at it, she found she couldn't even think about the camp or about Dahlia without thinking of the one person who'd inspired the series in the first place: Devon.

She remembered the sad little house on Baker Street. Remembered the look on Devon's uncle's face, the undisguised hostility.

Even Granny had felt it. She shivered and looked at her watch. Another hour and a half before Granny made it to camp and gave her an update. Granny'd promised to call her friend at social services, too, have them check things out. Just in case. Surely they'd know how to get past someone like Devon's uncle.

Instincts, Josh had said Friday. And right now, her instincts were telling her something was wrong. Really wrong. She wished she could talk to Josh about it.

Instead, she slid the memory card from her camera and began to import the photos from the gala, then scrolled through, culling the ones she intended to run in the paper.

Her heart did a flip-flop as she zoomed in to crop a dressed-to-the-nines couple on the dance floor and noticed Josh Jamison in the background of the shot. He had his head thrown back and he was laughing, joy all over his face.

You're just friends, Rebecca. Only, if they really were just friends, that didn't explain why Josh had left the gala in such a hurry, and why he hadn't replied to her text. "Where'd you go?" she'd finally sent before she and Granny drove home from the gala. But all she'd gotten was silence. By Sunday her concern had turned to downright irritation. Stupid high school games. Josh should know better than to think she was involved with Erik Wennerman, of all people.

Though she hadn't exactly had the most adult reaction when she'd spotted him and Lissa together, before she'd realized it was Lissa and not some other pretty woman who'd caught his heart. Still, she'd managed to at least maintain her composure, not storm off like some petulant baby without even giving her a chance to explain. Besides, it wasn't her fault Erik had found her outside, wasn't her fault he'd backed her into a corner and tried to pull her in for a dance. Most definitely wasn't her fault he'd kissed her. Which she certainly would have informed Josh of had he given her half a moment.

Forget him. She narrowed her eyes at her computer screen. She needed to think about work and her Tamika story, not silly romance drama. She was too old for that nonsense.

She brewed a pot of coffee, and when she sat down at her computer again, a mug before her and the door sign now turned from closed to open, the words came. By the time Millie, Tiff, and Dinah arrived, she'd knocked out the first draft of the Tamika story and was well into editing the gala photos. She hadn't heard about Devon yet from Granny, but she would soon enough. For now, she'd focus on work and let faith handle the rest.

"That storm's gonna be a big'un," Millie said as the wind blew the door wide open with a crash against the racks of extra newspapers. "Weatherman said a Category Two."

Dinah closed her umbrella and flopped into her desk chair. "Channel Six said it could be bad. Boss, think we might close up early so I can board the house?"

Rebecca gave them a look. "Dahlia's what, a three-hour drive from the coast? Are you all really worried we'll see the effects of a hurricane?"

"The flooding's the real concern," Millie said, heading for the coffee maker. "You ought to talk to the weather service, see what they say."

"Waiting on a callback," Rebecca said. "But the press release looked pretty tame. A watch for the coast and Lowcountry, that's it."

"Let's hope it stays that way," Millie said.

Tiff swiveled her chair toward her boss.

"Ma'am, I mean, Miss Rebecca?" Tiff's cheeks pinked, then settled. "Can I run something by you?"

"Of course."

"I, well, I'm done with the final erosion story, with those fixes you wanted. But, well, I took a chance."

"On the erosion story?"

"No." Tiff's cheeks pinked again. This girl would be a horrible poker player. "I mean, I did a story you didn't assign. You can throw it out entirely if you don't like it," she rushed on, waving her hands for emphasis, "and I don't mind at all, but I had some free time Saturday and decided to go for it."

Rebecca's interest piqued. What could Tiff Steadman be so interested in that she'd give up her own Saturday to write about? Rebecca could feel Millie and Dinah's eyes on her.

"Just read it, okay?" Tiff said, pressed a button on the keyboard, and a moment later pages were coming out of the printer.

Tiff excused herself to the restroom, and Rebecca grabbed the pages, leaned back in her chair for a read.

"Behind the Business: Stories of the People Who Drive Dahlia's Commerce," Rebecca read silently, and she gritted her teeth. Gracious—the girl had gone ahead, despite Rebecca's "no," and done it after all! She kept reading, not sure whether she was angry or impressed.

Chuck Smathers, owner of Smathers Grocery and Convenience

By Tiff Steadman

Editor's note: This week, we begin a new series profiling some of this town's business owners, who have seen the community grow and change both economically and socially over the last decades. All of the owners featured in this series were born and raised in Dahlia.

The man behind Dahlia's oldest grocery store has seen a lot over the years. Growing up bagging eggs and cornmeal at his Grandpappy's knee, Chuck Smathers still remembers a time

when the store didn't sell milk because it came from the milk-
man, not the grocery store.

"We didn't want to step on their toes," Smathers said. "Dahl-
ia's family, and while it would have been good business to get in
on the milk market, some things just aren't right."

Rebecca marked the copy here and there with red ink, not noticing when Tiff returned to her chair. When she'd finished reading, Rebecca looked up, surprised to see Tiff was there, eyes wide
and holding her breath.

"I know you said not to, but I couldn't let it go," Tiff blurted in a
small voice. "And if it's bad, fine, no hard feelings. I just—"

"It's actually good," Rebecca said honestly. "Really good."

"Really?" Tiff's face broke into a grin, and Rebecca found herself
smiling back.

"Really. Tiff, you were right. There's a fine line between story
and advertorial when you do business features. I mean, you don't
want to give away advertising disguised as journalism. But at least
with this one, you nailed it." Rebecca passed the sheaf of papers to
Tiff. "Make these changes. I'll try to find room for it in this week's
paper."

Tiff clapped her hands like a kid, then realized what she was
doing and stopped, composed herself. She grinned up at Rebecca.

"Thanks, Boss. Oh, and there's more!"

"More?"

Tiff grabbed her notebook. "I already collected stories from
Peggy Lancaster from the gas station, and old Mr. and Mrs. Crenshaw, from that diner out on Highway Five? I just didn't write
them yet in case you didn't like it. I've got a list of at least four more
I can do easily, and maybe Millie can help with suggestions, since
she's from here and all."

Rebecca glanced at Millie, who was pretending not to listen.

"Sure, happy to help," Millie piped up before nosing back into her classifieds.

Tiff shrugged. "I figured, if you didn't like the idea, maybe it'd made a good book series, something I can work on in my spare time. But I'd really rather see it in the paper."

Rebecca shook her head incredulously. A book idea was positively brilliant. Talk about a sleeper—this girl was one surprise after another.

"I think it'd make a fine book," she told Tiff. "I think you can do both." She did some quick mental calculations. "No promises, but possibly the paper could help on the publishing end."

Tiff flushed prettily. "Thanks, Boss. Really—thanks."

"Look into alternate publication specs and pricing," Rebecca scrawled on a notepad, then stuffed it in the "after press" inbox.

She eyed the wall clock—nine sharp. Time to get rolling on the paper. She glanced at her purse, where she knew her phone was tucked. Granny had promised to text her if Devon didn't show. No telltale "ding" from the device meant good news.

Outside, thunder began in earnest, and the lights flickered. She held her breath—the last thing they needed on pre-press day was to lose power.

"Save your work, people," she called as the phone rang and the newsroom began its usual Monday morning hum of energy.

By the time the weather service woman called her back, she had finished everything except final edits on Tiff's stories and last-minute ad deals.

"Thanks for the call," Rebecca said, pulling out her notes.

"You got it." The woman sounded harried. "I'm not sure what else you need, but you can put me down as saying we're doing everything we can to prepare and make sure residents are safe, aware, and can evacuate if needed."

"Honestly, I just have a question—isn't most of the concern for the coast and the Lowcountry? So far inland, does this part of the state really need to worry?" Rebecca glanced over at Dinah. "I mean, I have one employee who's asking if she can go home early, board her house."

"Precautions save lives and property, so from my perspective, your employee's got the right idea. But truthfully, the Dahlia and Aberville areas won't see anywhere near the damage the coast will see, though there's still danger anytime you have a storm this big looming so close. I imagine you've seen the pictures."

Rebecca eyed the live radar on her computer screen, the swirling ocean storm clouds ominously large but still very far away.

"I have."

"Well, then you know as well as I do that the best thing you can tell your readers is to stay indoors and stay safe. No sense taking unnecessary chances."

"Got it." Rebecca typed as she talked. "Thanks."

They hung up, and Rebecca finished her draft, then printed it for a final read. She glanced at her purse—still no text from Granny.

Still, she fished in her purse anyway for the phone. It couldn't hurt to check in with Granny. Just in case. Besides, she wanted to see what social services had said.

But her phone wasn't in its usual pocket. She rummaged, then hauled the bag onto her lap, peered inside.

The car! She remembered with a start that she'd used the phone to type a reminder to herself at the red light that morning. She swallowed. That was three hours ago!

"You all right?" Millie called as Rebecca darted outside into the rain with her car keys, found the phone in the cup holder next to her travel mug.

Three missed texts from Granny.

None from Josh.

Rebecca slid inside the car and shut the door, held her breath as she pulled up the messages. The rain beat against the windshield, and she watched as a gust of wind knocked over a potted plant they'd forgotten to bring inside.

"Devon's not here yet," read the first, then "I called his house, no answer." The last one, not fifteen minutes ago, read, "I left a message with social services. I'm going to take a ride out to Devon's house, check on things. I'll update ASAP."

No. The last thing Granny needed to be doing was going out alone to Devon's house. Rebecca shivered, remembering Uncle T, the way he'd glared at them. The look in his eye said in no uncertain terms: Don't come back. And now here was Granny, doing just that.

She dialed Granny's cell phone.

Granny didn't answer.

"Granny, do not under any circumstances go to Devon's house," she said breathlessly as Granny's voicemail came on and instructed her to leave a message. "At least, don't go alone. I'm heading that way now and I'll go with you. Pull over and wait for me."

Rebecca jammed the car into reverse and backed out, pulling with a squeal onto Main Street. Too late, she remembered she didn't have her purse with her, let alone her umbrella—not to mention that her entire newsroom had to be wondering why their editor had run out on them in the middle of pre-production without a word.

Forget it—I'll be back before anyone can notice. She gripped the wheel as she drove toward Devon's side of town.

As she passed Dahlia Community Bible Church, her car seemed to slow of its own will. Rev Bryant. Maybe he'd go with her. If her ever-stubborn Granny had decided to ignore her phone and show up alone at Devon's doorstep to face Uncle T, it made sense to have the broad-shouldered preacher by her side to help even the playing field.

Before she could change her mind, she parked at the curb, heart racing, and headed toward the office to find Rev. It was locked. The fellowship hall door was locked, too, and the sanctuary. Great. The rain was slick on her arms, soaking her thin dress and giving her a chill.

She was rounding the corner to the parsonage when she almost bumped right into Rev.

"Rebecca Chastain!" he said in his deep baritone, holding a large black umbrella over them both.

She could have cried in relief at the sight of him, felt in fact the telltale scratchy throat and itchy eyes that said tears were next, but she didn't have time for that.

"Rev, please—I need your help," she said, and filled him in, the words tumbling out in a torrent that she couldn't seem to stop. Granny, and Devon, and Uncle T, and all her fears and worries now released.

"My friend, take a breath." He took one of her hands, his grip gentle and comforting, but she didn't want to be calm. She needed to act. Now.

"Rev, with all due respect…"

"Rebecca." The way he said it made her look straight into his eyes. "I'm on the way there myself. Marla's with your Granny. Get it together and let's go now. We'll meet at the house together."

A wave of something—comfort? Relief?—washed over her, and she found she didn't have words to even reply.

She got in her car and followed him to Devon's, all the time praying. Please, let them be okay. Let Devon be okay. Let Granny be okay.

The rain had slowed from a pelt to a drizzle, and cleared enough so that she could see Granny in the front seat of Marla's red SUV when they got to the intersection of Fourth and Baker. Marla flashed her lights at them, and they parked on the side of the road, piled in.

"Thanks for waiting, Baby," Rev said, sliding into the seat behind Marla.

Rebecca slid in behind Granny, who gave her a worried smile.

And then Marla gunned the engine, turning left on Baker for Devon's house.

CHAPTER 36

Devon

WHEN THE RAIN BEGAN TO FALL, he thought it was a dream at first. He could hear it out there, gentle at first, then louder. The wind picked up, and he was grateful he had shelter. The tunnel was dry and solid, somehow reminding him of the three little pigs. He felt like the third pig, the smart pig, who'd built his house from bricks instead of sticks or straw. If only the chill would go away.

He'd been cold since he came, bone cold in spite of it being summer, and listening to the rain and the wind howl only made him colder. It was an inside cold, the kind that started in his chest and fanned out. Even with his hands tucked into his shirt sleeves and his knees tucked up underneath, tight against his stomach, he couldn't stop the shivering. It made his wrists and his ribs ache.

By now he thought he'd have a plan, but the more time passed, the more he felt stuck in place. He wasn't sure whether that was God's way of telling him he needed to stay put or what, but now that the rain was here, he figured he might as well rest another day. Tomorrow was as good as today. And besides, he was cold and tired, and he didn't know how far he could ride, and the rain would only slow him down. Once he started pedaling, got out in

the open again, he needed to pedal hard and fast, make it somewhere else as quickly as possible before he got spotted—by Uncle
T or worse. Though he couldn't imagine what would be worse than
Uncle T, and truth be told, he didn't have a clue about where that
somewhere-else was, anyway.

He ate another cereal bar and poured some of the grape juice
into an oatmeal packet, swirled it around with his finger and
scooped it into his mouth. It was actually pretty good, and the cinnamon flecks made him think of Memaw, and the chocolate cake
he'd helped her make for last year's church homecoming. Or was it
this year's? He couldn't remember now. Everything was fading into
one big blur, memories overlapping.

He dreamed last night he was at Harold's Diner with Miss Becca and he'd been served the biggest hamburger he'd ever seen in
his life, all juicy and dripping with ketchup and mustard and mayo
and cheese, and the fries just kept coming, and he woke up sure at
first he was there. He could smell it like it was right in his hands.
His hands, in fact, were curved together, like they were gripping
the hamburger, shoveling it in. But then he couldn't smell anything
at all, nothing but this place and his own scent.

And now, he could smell the rain.

The rain smelled like dirt and copper and wood and water, reminded him of Mama's memory garden in a weird way.

He sat there in the morning light, eyes closed, smelling the rain
and remembering her face, her smile. For a moment, he thought
he felt her touch his head, caress his cheek like she used to. I miss
you, Mama.

The rain fell faster and harder now, and he swallowed nervously,
peering out the tunnel, watching the water jab at the surface of the
river like God was spraying it with pebbles.

Thumbing through the Bible, the pages slightly damp beneath
his fingers, Devon found the passage he sought: "... he will not

leave you or forsake you. Do not fear or be dismayed ..."

He said it aloud to himself, the words echoing in the space around him, said it over and over again until it filled his mind and chased away everything else.

CHAPTER 37

Rebecca

UNCLE T'S VOICE WAS A SNARL behind the door, which was open just far enough for them to see his face. "Whaddaya want."

Rebecca watched as he took them in—the tall dark-skinned preacher, his well-dressed and beautiful wife, the old woman in blue jeans and a yellow West Dahlia Leaders Summer Enrichment Camp T-shirt, and her, in her rain-drenched wrap dress.

When T's eyes settled on Rebecca, they narrowed in recognition.

"You again?"

Rev took a step forward, blocking his glare.

"I'm Reverend Mack Bryant, Devon's pastor."

T looked like he'd swallowed a jar of pickle juice, but he said nothing.

"He's been out of camp and church, and we're concerned about him," Rev said, his voice calm and controlled, but Rebecca saw him ease a foot into the door crack.

T scowled. "Man, he ain't none-a your concern."

"Beg pardon, but Devon Robinson is my concern," Rev said, then gestured to Marla, Granny, and Rebecca. "He's our concern.

He's our friend. Is he sick?"

"He's gone."

Marla frowned. "What do you mean, gone?"

"Got a hearing problem? He's. Gone." T's last word came out in a hiss.

Rebecca felt rather than saw Rev's muscles tense. Marla put a warning hand on his arm. Granny slipped her hand into Rebecca's.

"Well, where is he?"

"How would I know? Kid took off after the ambulance came."

"Ambulance!" Rebecca blurted.

"My Maw. Had'a go to the hospital." T set his chin. "He took off out the back door. Ain't seen 'im since."

T tried to shut the door, but Rev's foot blocked it.

Rebecca's throat went dry.

"When?" Rev asked. "And where's Memaw?"

"Yesterday, day before. Dunno where he went," T muttered. "Maw's at regional. Ambulance came Thursday. Now move your foot, a'ight?"

Thursday? Her hand tightened in Granny's.

"Has he taken off before?" Rev asked.

"First time for everything." A small smile threatened. "He ain't all that. He'll be back."

Rev's back stiffened. "No, sir, that's where you're wrong. He won't be back. Ladies, to the car."

Marla gunned the engine as they all slid in.

Before he got in, Rev called to T, "Mark my words. We're going to find your nephew, and if you ever see him again, it'll be to say goodbye. For good."

Thursday. Rebecca closed her eyes, tried her best to drown out the roaring in her ears. Devon's Memaw had been in the hospital since Thursday, if they could believe T, and no one had seen or heard from Devon himself in days. God gives us instincts for a reason. Why hadn't she trusted hers? She wished Josh were with her now, wished it so badly she could taste it. Where was Devon?

"Rebecca, you had burgers with him a few days ago, right?" Rev said, pulling a notepad and pen from the center console as they backed away from the house, headed to their cars.

"Thursday, at Harold's," Rebecca said, squeezed her eyes shut. All those days, all that time. Wasted. On what—etiquette? Soothed feelings?

"He wasn't at the giveaway Friday, or at camp," Marla said.

"And he wasn't at church Sunday," Rev said, making notes.

"We came by with soup Saturday and didn't see him," Granny said.

Marla pulled out her cell phone, dialed. "Hi, Diane, this is Marla Bryant from Dahlia Community Bible Church," she said in a warm voice. "Good to hear your voice, too! Listen, I'm checking in on a member. Do you have a Dolores Robinson as a patient there?" Marla nodded at them, gave a thumbs up. "Since Thursday night, you say?"

"Is Devon there too?" Rev mouthed, and Marla added, "You haven't seen her little grandson by chance, have you? Devon. He's eleven. ... No? All righty, we'll be down in a bit to visit. You be sure to send our love, now."

She hung up.

"Okay, so at least that's the truth—Memaw's in the hospital, but no sign of Devon." Marla frowned. "Now where would Devon go if not to us? Does he have any close friends who might take him in?"

They passed two-twenty-one Baker, and Rebecca remembered CJ.

"There!" Rebecca pointed as they passed. She could see her car ahead. "His friend CJ lives there."

"Good thinking, girl," Granny said. "Devon and CJ have been friends a long, long time."

"There's also Shenise," Rev said. "I know her family real well."

"And the Garcia girls, Gabby and Mariana," Marla said. "They live off Tristan Street, in the trailer park."

"But aren't they all at camp?" Granny said. "I'm sure I saw the Garcia girls this morning."

Marla stopped the car at the intersection. The rain began to fall again, soft now instead of the morning's hard pellets, but fast.

"Let's do this the smart way and divvy the labor." Rev turned to them. "Marla, you and Helen go to the school, see what you can find out from CJ, Shenise, Gabby, and Mariana, and anyone else you can think of who might have information."

"Got it," Marla said, and Granny nodded.

"Rebecca, you feel okay going to CJ's and seeing if you can find out anything there, and I'll head over to Shenise's and the Garcia house?" Rev said. "We can call each other in twenty minutes sharp and share what we've learned."

"Absolutely."

"Be safe, girl," Granny said as Rebecca opened the door to slide out of the car and into the rain.

She gripped Granny's hand, squeezed a quick I-love-you.

"I will. You, too, Granny."

CHAPTER 38

Devon

HE SHOULD HAVE LEFT when he'd had the chance, knew it with the kind of sinking clarity that settled on his heart and mind, told him in no uncertain terms: He'd made a big mistake.

The bike was gone, and his backpack with all the food, and the Bible tucked inside. Gone while he'd slept.

Help me, he wanted to yell, wanted to scream, but he wouldn't. He needed to conserve his energy, needed it for when it would really count.

He'd crawled way up in the tunnel in the night, not really sure why other than a weird feeling in the pit of his stomach. The water hadn't gotten that high, not really, but the rain wasn't letting up, and something told him he'd be safer if he climbed farther, in case the river did rise. He should have left then, not slipped on his backpack and climbed higher, he knew that now. But he hadn't wanted to leave his bike. He didn't have a chance getting anywhere far from Dahlia without it.

Now it was the least of his concerns.

He'd gone to sleep finally with the backpack as a pillow, mashed up against that metal bar against the side of the tunnel.

It was only by the grace of God that he'd awoken in time to a screaming pain in his left arm, a pain so bad it filled his brain with colors and took his breath away, and then he was past the pain and on the other side, realizing with a start that it was only the metal bar and the Lord that kept him from being swept far, far away.

All around him was water, pounding, rushing water. It was pitch black, and his arm roared with pain, but he just clung there, gripped the metal bar, afraid to do anything but breathe and hold on. Afraid even to open his eyes.

He could feel Jesus with him, Jesus's hands pressed against his own.

Keeping him steady.

Holding him in place.

God, help me!

And then the water stopped, and he came to rest again, panting and shivering and wondering how and why and where and what in the world to do now.

He supposed if it happened again he could let go, let it all go, but he didn't want to.

Wanted to fight, to live.

Wanted to see Memaw again.

He forced himself to think of her, there in the hospital bed, think of her watery eyes and her wrinkly soft hands and her fierce determination. He pictured what she must look like, imagined the color of her hospital gown—pale blue, almost as light as Miss Becca's eyes in the afternoon sunlight—imagined that Memaw had her eyes closed but was talking to him in her mind.

"Hold on, sweet boy. Hold on a little while longer."

This time, he'd listen.

He'd do as he was told.

He held on with his good arm, held on tight for who knew how long, hours maybe, and prayed.

When the water came again, he was ready.

CHAPTER 39

Rebecca

No one was home at CJ's house, or at least no one answered the doorbell. The lights were out, and no car was in the driveway.

Underneath the front porch awning, she listened. She didn't hear a TV on inside.

If Devon were home, she imagined he wouldn't go answering their door, not if he was using the house as a hideout. She glanced at the houses on either side of CJ's. They looked empty, too. It would take a quick second for her to slip around back, check the windows. If anyone saw her, she could explain. Maybe they could help, too.

Don't be stupid, Rebecca. She knew full well this wasn't the kind of neighborhood that took kindly to snooping.

But this was Devon. Devon mattered.

And it was a risk worth taking.

"Devon? You there?" she called, feeling silly. "It's me. Becca."

Nothing.

Quickly, she slipped around back, stood on her tiptoes in the rain to peer inside the windows. All the lights were out in both the rear rooms, and she even slipped inside the back screened porch, tapped at the sliding glass door. No one was home.

Back in the car, she checked her phone, saw a text from Millie. "Where did you go?"

She winced. "Family emergency. I'll be back ASAP," she typed out, hit send.

"Let me know if you need anything," came Millie's reply seconds later. "I'm here to help."

A rush of gratitude swept over her for the second time that morning.

She cruised the neighborhood for a few minutes, racking her brain. Where would an eleven-year-old kid go if he were trying to steer clear of his crazy uncle?

Devon was a resourceful kid, but he was still a kid. Still, she'd seen him riding his bike all over town, even that one time way over by her office. Josh and JJ said he'd joined them for fishing a couple times.

He could be anywhere.

She swallowed, thinking of the dark expression on Uncle T's face.

Or nowhere at all.

That was what niggled at her—what if Devon hadn't gone anywhere? What if T were lying and Devon was at home hurt?

Or worse?

Her heart thudded.

Her cell phone rang in her hands, and she almost dropped it on the car floorboard. She eased to the side of the road, answered.

It was Rev.

"Got anything?" she asked.

But there was no luck on his end, and Granny and Marla said CJ, Shenise, Gabby, and Mariana didn't seem to know anything either, or else they were phenomenal actors.

"You keep looking, see what you can turn up," Rev told her. "Maybe go to Harold's, or that corner shop where he helps Mr.

Allen. I'm heading to the police station to file a report, see if we can get a search going."

She struggled to form the words. "I'll meet you there soon. Rev … see if they can send a car to his house, too. Just in case."

Rev seemed to understand what she'd left unsaid.

"Will do," he said, voice somber. "Check in with me in a bit."

Her mouth was bone dry as she made a right onto Aberville Highway and headed toward the corner shop. Why hadn't she followed Devon home that first night, when she first saw the bruise? Why had she doubted, wondered, talked to Granny and Josh about it and not him? She'd known something was going on at home, known it in her heart, even if her head hadn't quite caught up. What do they always say—hindsight is twenty/twenty?

Come on, Devon. Where are you?

She wished she could call Josh, wished more than anything they could go back to Saturday night, wished he was there by her side. He'd know what to do, or at least be able to help. But she couldn't call him.

Now isn't the time for games, Rebecca. She needed Josh's help— for Devon's sake, if nothing else. And lifting her chin, she picked up her phone and dialed.

Josh's hello was cold, but she pushed past it.

"I need help." She could hear her voice cracking, squeezed her eyes shut tight. No tears. You need to be strong for Devon.

"Are you okay?" Instantly, his voice changed. Instead of anger, she heard concern.

Relief flooded. "It's Devon." She filled him in.

"Where are you now?" Josh asked. In the background, she could hear what sounded like a chainsaw.

"Heading to town to check the places I know he goes regularly, then to the police station to meet Rev."

"Let's meet at the station in thirty."

"No, no, it's okay—"

"Becks, two heads are better than one. This isn't a time for being polite. You know it as well as I do."

"You're right." She let out a shaky breath. "Thanks."

"We'll find him."

"I hope so, Josh."

"Don't let yourself think otherwise. See you soon."

She made the rounds quickly: the grocery, the pharmacy. The corner store, where Mr. Allen said he'd worked a couple hours Thursday evening. No one had seen him since.

"Oh, honey," said Louanne at Harold's Diner, one hand at her chest. Her eyes were wide. "Please tell me nothing's happened to that sweet boy. Billy!" she called to the cook, who was flipping burgers behind the grill. "You seen our little Devon? You know, Miss Rebecca-here's friend?"

"Sure haven't," Billy called back. "Why, is he missing?"

"No one's seen him since Thursday." Rebecca swallowed.

"And in this weather, too." Louanne cast a look at the skies outside, which were dark, then seemed to take in Rebecca anew. "Gracious, you're soaked!"

Rebecca gave a rueful smile. "Forgot my umbrella."

"Lou, give her that rain jacket from behind the counter," Billy called.

"I forgot about that! Here ya go, sugar." Louanne ducked behind the counter, produced a red and white hooded rain jacket with the name "Harold's" emblazoned in big white letters on the chest.

Rebecca slipped it on and buttoned it all the way up.

Louanne grinned at her. "Well, if that newspaper thing don't work out, least you know you can sure fit in here."

Rebecca giggled, then surprised herself by leaning over for a quick hug. Louanne hugged her back, patting her softly.

"It'll be all right, sugar. The good Lord will keep an eye on that one. We'll be praying. You let us know if they're gonna organize some sort of search, all right?"

"Yeah, Louanne's right—we'll come search if it calls for that," Billy said.

At the station, Rebecca answered Deputy Zane's questions, feeling more than a little helpless as she stared back at the balding man with the kindly eyes and stubby fingers as she sat in one of the chairs in front of his small metal desk. No, she hadn't seen Devon since she'd dropped him off at school Thursday afternoon. No, she hadn't driven him home. He hadn't wanted her to. Yes, she'd accepted that. No, she didn't know his family. No, she didn't know his interests beyond church and helping others and riding his bike. Some friend you are.

Marla and Granny had joined Rev by the time she came out of Deputy Zane's office. Granny took one look at her face and enveloped her in a hug, her skin soft and smooth and smelling like baby powder and daisies. Josh walked in then, stood beside her without a word. Rebecca saw Granny glance up at him, nod approvingly.

"Deputy Zane, think you can put the word out around town about a Dahlia-wide search for Devon Robinson?" Rev told the officer.

"Sure can," Zane said. "But we better get rolling before the storm blows in. I think three hours tops."

"On it," Rev said.

"Here." Josh slung a backpack from his shoulders, unzipped it to pull out four walkie-talkies. "Take one, pass the rest around."

Zane nodded. "Good. Use channel five, and share what you find."

Rev stood. "All righty, friends, time to spread the word: Dahlia's searching for Devon!"

News spread quickly. Rebecca and Josh headed back to the diner to tell Louanne and Billy, who clearly had their finger on the pulse of Dahlia. By the time Rebecca and Josh walked into the *Dahlia Weekly* ten minutes later, Millie already knew and was telling Tiff and Dinah.

"I take it this is your family emergency?" Millie's face was creased with worry.

"Yeah." Rebecca swallowed. "Listen, let's close up shop the rest of the day and see if we can help with the search. Tiff, can you cover it as a story? I'm too … close."

Her voice caught on the last word, and Tiff's eyes welled in sympathy.

"You got it, Boss."

"My Granny's heading back to the school to tell the other kids, see if they can help. Rev Bryant's organizing a town walk-through and has a couple members checking the hidey-holes in the fellowship hall, and his wife Marla's going to the hospital to talk to Devon's Memaw, see if she knows anything."

"I'll hit the shops, ask around, spread the word to my counterparts over in the surrounding towns," Dinah said.

"And I'll hop on the phone to all the churches, then hit some of the kid hideouts I remember from my younger years," Millie said, picking up the phone. "Maybe I'll ask my grandson, see if he has a ten-year-old perspective."

The fire scanner sounded with a warning about high gusts of wind, and Rebecca shivered. She hoped Devon wasn't out in all this.

"Be safe," she told her staff.

"We will," Tiff said, shouldering her camera and grabbing a notebook and keys.

Rebecca turned to Josh. "Didn't Devon go fishing a couple times with you and JJ? Maybe JJ has some ideas. Perhaps Devon shared some kid-to-kid information, something we wouldn't think of."

"That's a good point," Josh said. "I'll call from the truck. He's at my sister's."

Rebecca pulled up the hood on the Harold's Diner rain jacket, grabbed her keys and phone.

"Actually, how do you feel about having JJ tag along with us?" she asked when they got in the truck.

Josh glanced uncertainly at the sky, which was growing ever darker, then gave a curt nod. "He'd want to help. I know he likes Devon a whole lot. They seemed to have a good time together fishing, guy bonding, even went off ..."

Rebecca put a hand on his arm. "What?"

He put the truck in park, turned to Rebecca.

"Becks, when we were fishing, JJ and Devon went off somewhere, someplace JJ calls his secret fort. I didn't follow, never had, always figured it's good for kids to have secret places and such, but maybe ..."

The thought hit them both at the same time.

Josh picked up the phone and shifted his truck into gear.

"Lissa?" he said into the phone. "Tell JJ to be ready. There's a kid missing. Devon. I need JJ to show me his hiding place down by the river."

CHAPTER 40

Rebecca

JJ WAS WAITING OUTSIDE Aunt Lissa's when they arrived, his neon-green rain jacket a pop of color against the gray outside.

"Be careful," Lissa called from the front door, two of her four kids peeking from behind her legs.

"We will," Josh said as JJ climbed in, buckled up. "Let me know if you hear anything. And maybe call the station, let them know where we're headed."

"You got it."

They roared off, and JJ leaned forward.

"Is Dev okay, Dad? I mean, Aunt Liss said he's missing, and they showed us that video at school last year, about strangers and kidnapping and stuff, and ..."

"We think he's hiding out, buddy," Josh said, eyes trained on the road as they made a sharp left and then a right, headed toward the Wahca River.

"In all this rain?" JJ eyed the sky through the windshield. "Isn't there a hurricane coming? Aunt Lissa wouldn't even let us go to the tree house."

"That's why we have to hurry." Josh gripped the wheel, turned into the small gravel parking area near the trailhead. He picked up the walkie-talkie, explained where they were headed.

"We'll send a crew over to help," came a crackly voice in reply. "Over."

"Thanks for helping, JJ," Rebecca turned to the boy, gave what she hoped was a reassuring smile. "No one's seen him since last Thursday, and we're hoping maybe he's taking cover in that fort of yours."

"Since Thursday?" JJ looked surprised. "Like, all alone at night and everything?"

Rebecca shivered, picturing Devon in the woods alone, in the rain, with only his Bible for comfort. Did he have food? Was he scared?

"We'll find him," Josh said, glancing over, and she shook away the tears, balled her hands into fists. She hoped he was right. If they didn't find … no. She couldn't think about that.

Then they were parked and heading down the path, rain falling in patches through the canopy of trees overhead. Thunder rumbled, and she ducked instinctively as they raced through the forest, feet kicking up clumps of mud, half-pulled along by JJ.

"It's not really a fort, Dad. I mean, we call it a fort, but it's more like a tunnel," JJ shouted breathlessly as they ran.

"A tunnel?"

"I don't know what you call it. Like a pipe thing, only bigger."

They could see the river ahead now. She recognized her usual spot, the big rocks they sometimes used for seats or a picnic. Big splatters of rain pounded against the river surface, churning up the water, and they pressed on, past the rocks, under a large tree branch and left into a clearing.

The rain began to fall in earnest now, and the bitter taste of her morning coffee swam in her throat. Ahead and above, the green trees turned darker, and she had to duck to keep the water from her eyes. Months of early morning jogging didn't make her any less out of breath. JJ veered this way and that, and once a bush smacked her full-on in the face, but she kept going.

She could hear Josh's heavy footsteps behind her, and once she slipped as they rounded a curve, turned back toward the river.

The crackle of static on the walkie-talkie startled her.

"Flash flood warning, careful," someone was saying, and then they were at the riverbank again, and JJ was pointing, and she could barely see it.

"There! By the riverbank!"

She gaped, not sure she was seeing correctly. It looked like JJ was pointing to a huge metal grate and a massive concrete pipe, like a water tunnel or cavern. It sloped downward, and water poured out of the huge opening into the river.

She stopped mid-stride, grabbed his arm. "That's your fort?"

JJ nodded, eyes wide. "Yeah."

"That's a storm drain." Josh's face was pale as they watched the water churn. "Lord, I hope he's not in there."

Rebecca turned to JJ. "You guys enter through the bottom part, there? By the river?"

JJ looked from her to his dad, and Josh nodded for him to answer.

JJ stared at the ground, swallowed. "Yes, ma'am. They have signs, but there's never any water in it when we're there. It's dry, and it echoes, and there's a part so narrow you can touch the edge and flip yourself around, like a hamster wheel."

Rebecca let out a breath, eyed the drain. Everything she'd ever heard about storm drains and storms said to steer clear. She'd even done a story about an old man in New York who'd fallen down a drain chasing his dog, gotten trapped in a sudden rainstorm, and died. There was that big national story maybe a year ago, too, about the teenager out West who got swept away and drowned. Surely Devon knew better.

Only it hadn't been raining Thursday, or Friday. Hadn't started till Sunday night, in fact.

She put a hand on JJ's shoulder. "Is that the only entrance?"

"Uh-uh." He pointed. "There's an opening up there, too. I mean, it's a harder climb, and it's way better down here, but you can get in from the top. I've done it once or twice. Do you think he … ?"

Josh and Rebecca exchanged glances.

"I hope not," she finally said.

Josh motioned. "Why don't you two climb up and see about the top? I'll check over there, at the bottom."

Rebecca's mouth went dry as she glanced at the pipe's opening, the torrent of water gushing out. "You're not going in there, are you?"

"No, but I'll scoot close enough to see if I can peer in, call his name."

She looked at him a long moment. "Be safe."

He nodded. "I will." And then he was off, stepping over the river rocks, and JJ was tugging her arm and pushing her up the slope.

"Devon!" she called.

She could hear Josh shouting, too, from below them. No answer.

At the first level spot she grabbed for her walkie-talkie.

"This is Rebecca Chastain," she said, pressing the button. "We're at the Wahca River, by this big storm drain Devon knew about. We're looking to see if he's here."

"This is Deputy Zane. Do not go in," a voice crackled from the other end. "I repeat, do not enter the storm drain. It's dangerous. Over."

"We won't. Over and out."

"Miss Becca, I can't find it!" She watched as JJ scaled the river-bank, higher and higher, looked frantically around.

The mud and rain was making everything a soppy mess. She could barely see enough to get a good foothold. A moment later she was at his side, slipping in the muck as the rain continued to pour.

"Devon!" She cupped her hands over her mouth to make it louder, scanned the line of concrete sloping up from the river, looking for what she'd only seen in pictures—some sort of metal grate or opening in the ground, some cement block or cavern that had been there so long it probably blended into the scenery.

"Devon, where are you?" JJ yelled. "Devon!"

"It's Becca and JJ! Devon, you're safe! We're here to help!" she called, listening into the wind and rain for something, anything. "Devon, are you out here?"

"Becks!" she heard, peered down to see Josh waving something at them. She couldn't see very well, and he shouted something else that got drowned out.

"What's that?" JJ asked her.

"I don't know." She fiddled with the walkie-talkie again. "Josh, what do you have?"

Crackles, then silence.

"Josh, you okay? Over!"

"…. backpack … Dev … pack."

Her heart thudded as she peered down, realized what he held in his hands. Devon's blue backpack. Oh, God. She squeezed her eyes shut a moment. Please, please, please let him be okay. Please, God, I'm begging you.

She turned then, blocking everything else out, and began to search with fresh eyes.

Show me the opening. Show me how to find Devon. Please, God.

Water poured off the hood down her back, and then she saw it—a dull gray metal beneath what looked like a mound of forest brush, trees and leaves and moss and who knew what else.

An entrance.

"JJ, here! Help me!"

They tugged at the leaves and brush, then yanked at the metal grate. Once, twice. It wouldn't budge.

"Devon!" she yelled into the grate. "Devon, are you down there?"

The walkie-talkie crackled again, and she grabbed at it, pressed the button. "Josh, I found an entrance. Come help us!"

A sound came from inside the grate, and she listened, then hollered again. "Devon!"

"Devon, are you there?" JJ yelled with her. "Devon!"

And then they heard it. Faint, but there nonetheless.

"Here!" His voice sounded very far off. "Help me!"

Josh was there then, and two other men were suddenly at his side, volunteers from fire-rescue, and they were tugging and pulling at the grate, which barely moved even with their weight.

"Here, grab this," someone shouted, and they were all grabbing at a tree limb, ripping open the grate. Water poured out, and above them, she could hear sirens, heard Josh shouting for her and JJ to stay back.

"Hold on tight, Devon!" she called. "We're coming!"

A rope. Pulling. Slipping. A burly man in a muddy uniform was in the tunnel now.

"He's got him!" Josh murmured at her side.

And then there was Devon. Soaking wet and in her arms, sobbing and shaking and safe.

A cheer went up from the crowd of rescuers now gathered below and above.

Holding him, as someone wrapped them both in a huge gray blanket, she sank to her knees in the wet mud above the river and cried with relief.

Thank you, God. Oh, thank you, thank you, God.

CHAPTER 41

Devon

WHEN HE AWOKE he thought he was dreaming. Marla was there, and Miss Becca, gathered around his hospital bed. Rev, who wore a big smile and had tears in his eyes. He thought he saw Mama once, but then he blinked and she was gone, and in her place there was a woman he didn't know, a nurse, bending over him and adjusting a tube in his arm. She smiled at him, and then Marla leaned in, soothed his brow.

"You're okay," someone whispered. "You're safe."

And so he let himself sleep again, cozy and warm, wondering if he'd ever felt so good in his whole entire life.

When he woke for real they pieced together the story—how he'd run from Uncle T, run to the only place he knew he could hide and not be found. JJ's hiding spot. The tunnel. Miss Becca called it a storm drain, said he'd probably been there Friday, Saturday, and most of Sunday without a problem, but when the storm rolled in Sunday afternoon and into Monday, the rains began to fill the drain little by little.

He told them how he'd crawled in through the bottom, near the river, but then the rain started getting so bad that something made him slip on his backpack and leave his bike at the bottom, climb farther into the drain, thinking it would give him better protection if the water started to climb higher.

"That might've saved your life," Rev said, closing his eyes briefly. "Thank you, Jesus."

The rain had slowed for a while, but from what Miss Becca said, it came on hard and fast and he'd been startled out of sleep by a huge pounding wave of water, like someone had turned the drain into a ginormous water slide, like the one in CJ's Lego set they'd built last year.

"So you grabbed a handrail?" Miss Becca asked, her eyebrows creased at the center.

"Yeah, only I didn't know what it was at first, just held on and didn't let go." Devon swallowed, feeling like a big lump was in his throat. "A couple times I almost did. Almost let go, but in my head I kept hearing 'hold on.'"

His voice sounded small and weak and babyish to his own ears, but he couldn't help it. It didn't matter, anyway. He didn't know how he'd made it out.

He only had one explanation: God.

God at work through his friends.

Miss Becca took a shaky breath and squeezed his hand. "Thank God you didn't, kiddo. I don't know what we'd do if we lost you."

He closed his eyes to keep the tears back, but they oozed out anyway. Marla stroked his brow again and he just lay there, let himself be soothed.

The drain had flooded three times, if he remembered right, and he'd held on tight through it all. After the first wave of water, his arm didn't hurt as bad, though they told him it was broken. A clean break, but he'd need a cast for eight weeks. Marla said he'd be in the hospital a couple more days while doctors were rehydrating him, but other than getting out all the extra water in his lungs, he'd be okay. Memaw, too. They'd told him that, the very first day, though he still hadn't been able to see her.

As for Uncle T, apparently he didn't need to worry about him anymore. The police officer, the big heavyset one that looked like a football player, said his uncle was locked up and would be for a long time. T was facing at least five different drug charges, domestic abuse of a minor, crossing state lines with stolen goods, and a few other things he couldn't remember. He wouldn't be getting out anytime soon, if ever.

Miss Becca said she'd heard Uncle T had snitched on a few of his friends, hoping to cut some sort of deal, but it hadn't worked in his favor. And now Ray and a bunch of the other super-bad drug guys were locked up, too.

"One of the rescue workers told me, 'That Devon Robinson had his very own guardian angel,'" Miss Becca said and grinned down at him, but behind the smile he could see the worry. "You're one lucky kid."

"Amen to that. Lucky and blessed," Marla said.

"They even found your Mama's Bible." Rev shook his head. "Good thing you put it in the waterproof pocket of that backpack."

A tap sounded, and they looked up to see Miss Becca's granny peering in through the little window in the door.

"Be right back," Miss Becca said and slipped out.

When she'd gone, Marla and Rev looked at each other. Rev nodded.

Devon watched them both, a tickle of concern sliding through his belly.

"There's something else." Devon looked from one to the other.

Marla pressed her lips together, then stood from the bedside chair, perched on the bed with him.

"Dev, honey, there's something we were hoping to talk to you about." She glanced at Rev again, then let out a nervous laugh.

"Well, it's just, we've been talking to your Memaw, and—well, we have some concerns."

His heart started to pound. "Is Memaw gonna die?"

Marla's brow creased. "Oh, honey, she'll be okay, it's ..."

He saw Rev squeeze her hand, and the tickle in his belly moved higher, a burning now in his throat. She's not okay. He'd have to go to foster care now, and it was all for nothing. Everything was for nothing, and now ...

Rev cleared his throat.

"What Marla means is we think she's too old to handle some of the responsibilities of raising a young boy."

Devon squeezed his eyes shut. Don't cry. Just breathe.

Marla took a breath. "Rev and I were wondering, well ... if you'd maybe like to come live with us."

He opened his eyes. Was he hearing right?

"With you?"

"With us." She smiled at him, her voice stronger now, looked straight into his eyes. "I mean, for good."

"A family." Rev shifted closer so his face was right next to Miss Marla's.

"I know we can't replace your mama, or Memaw, but you're like a son to us," Marla said quietly. "The child we couldn't have. And we'd love to be your parents, for real."

Tears flooded his eyes in earnest, began to roll down his cheeks.

"You don't have to decide now or anything." Rev held up a hand. "We already talked to social services, and for now it'll be foster care until they get the paperwork all squared away, do what they can to try to locate your biological father, but they said if you're open to the possibility of adoption—"

"You want me?" Devon's voice cracked a bit at the end, but he didn't care.

"Oh, baby. We want you," Marla said.

And as they gathered him close for a hug, he almost thought he heard singing. Mama's singing.

Joyful and deep and true.

CHAPTER 42

Rebecca

OUTSIDE THE HOSPITAL ROOM, Granny hugged her and held up a cup of coffee.

"Figured you'd need this."

"Do I ever." Rebecca chuckled, took a sip.

"I brought you something else, too," Granny said as they walked together to the small waiting room, a pretty space with soft shafts of sunlight here and there and calming gray carpet and blue-green walls.

Granny slid the latest *Dahlia Weekly* from her pocketbook.

Rebecca scanned the headlines, a five-column photo front-and-center of a blanket-wrapped Devon in her arms outside the drain, rescue crews all around. She flipped through, shaking her head in admiration at what she'd authorized but had yet to see. Her staff had stepped up and done the entire paper in her absence, Tiff taking the lead in layout with heavy backup from Dinah. They'd done a remarkably good job—the front page was strong, the calendar layout exactly as Rebecca liked, and the high school football pre-season page was exceptional.

She didn't even realize Tiff knew her way around layout, but when the young woman confessed over the phone last night that she'd taken a few courses in college and had been sharpening her skills on the side, Rebecca decided to chance it, let them try their hand.

"Sounds like you might be underutilizing that reporter of yours," Granny said with a wry grin, and Rebecca laughed.

Granny was right. Tiff had grown a whole lot more than she'd ever expected. Perhaps she'd pegged the girl wrong from the start. Behind the stilettos, the mousy features, and the breathy voice, perhaps there was a small-town version of Rebecca, the kind of person who'd finesse her page design skills on the sly to wow her boss when she least expected it.

They reached a quiet corner in the waiting room, stood looking out the window. From the fourth floor of the hospital, they could see some of the damage the storm had done—a couple of washed out roads, a handful of trees on houses, a bit of flooding. Granny's church was taking the lead in storm recovery, and Rebecca thought she'd join in on Saturday, help some of the crews muck out the homes closest to the river that had been affected. It was nowhere near the damage they'd seen on the coast; while the hurricane had passed them by, tornados and flooding had left their mark. But it had certainly done damage.

She bit her lip as she thought of Devon in the hospital bed, beyond grateful that he'd escaped the worst of it.

"How's he doing?" Granny asked softly, looking over at her.

"Granny, I can't believe he's okay. When I saw that storm drain, saw the water pouring out …"

Rebecca shuddered, closed her eyes as she imagined what it must have been like for him. They'd found his bike two miles downstream, a mangled mess of bent metal.

"He must have been in the exact, perfect position, some cosmic stroke of luck or something, in order to survive that."

"The Lord had his hand on that boy," Granny murmured.

"Yeah, I know what you mean."

"No, Becca." Granny's voice was soft but there was an edge to it now, and she tucked a finger under Rebecca's chin, looked her square in the eye. "Hear what I'm saying. The Lord had his hand on him. For whatever reason, he kept Devon safe. He has a plan for that child, and he used all of us—you and Marla and Rev, Josh and JJ, me and everybody else—to make it happen."

Rebecca was quiet for a moment, let it all sink in. Granny was right. She knew it in her bones, knew it wasn't luck or quick thinking or anything else that had saved Devon.

It was God.

It was prayer.

For the first time in her life, she realized, she truly believed. She didn't believe halfway, or in the possibility.

She believed.

God had done this. God had answered her prayer.

He wasn't some pie-in-the-sky, mythical figure watching from the clouds. She swallowed as she let herself accept what she'd known deep down all along, but had been too full of pride to admit.

God was real.

Faith is confidence in what we hope for and assurance about what we do not see. The thought popped suddenly into her brain, and she thought she remembered it from one of Granny's framed scripture verses.

"You know what, Granny?" she said, her voice barely a whisper. "I do believe. I think you're absolutely right."

She looked at her granny, there in her cream-colored pants and white button down, clutching her pocketbook and smiling at her in surprise. Turning toward her, Rebecca held out her hands.

"You know that prayer you were talking about, the one where you invite Jesus in?" Rebecca said.

Granny let out a breathless giggle, and then so did Rebecca, and then the two of them were laughing and crying and hugging and she felt something, like a shift in the air or a warm, comforting breeze, settle on them. The most perfect joy she'd ever experienced filled her heart.

This is hope, she realized. This is what it feels like.

And there, right in their own small corner of the hospital waiting room, Granny took Rebecca's hands in her own and they sank to their knees in prayer.

"Well, hey, you two," she heard several minutes later, and she looked over to see Josh and JJ walk over from the elevator, smiling down at them like it was the most natural thing in the world to see two people on the ground in prayer. Maybe it was.

Josh had a cheerful yellow vase of fresh flowers in one hand and a handful of get-well-soon balloons in the other, and JJ had both arms around a giant plastic basket filled with candy, doughnuts, popcorn, a few tennis and baseballs, a small tackle box, one of those jumbo lollipops, and what looked like a whoopee cushion tucked in on the side.

"That looks like every boy's dream," Rebecca said, wiping her eyes as she helped Granny to her feet.

Josh laughed. "JJ picked out every last thing in that basket. Right, Son?"

He ruffled JJ's hair, and JJ grinned widely.

"Hopefully Devon's got a sweet tooth," JJ said.

"I thought we'd bring these to his Memaw," Josh held out the flowers, looked at Rebecca. "Want to join me?"

Granny gave her a sidelong look and smiled mischievously.

"Come on, JJ, let's go say hi to Devon together." She took the balloons from Josh and winked at Rebecca as she gathered her pocketbook and wrapped one arm around JJ's shoulders. "So what do you think he'll want to eat first?"

They disappeared down the hall, leaving Rebecca and Josh alone.

He nodded his chin in the direction of the room. "Shall we?"

They walked toward the room, their shoes making soft squeaks on the smooth hospital tile. She looked over at him.

"You know, this is the first time I've met Memaw."

He raised his eyebrows. "Really?"

"First time I've been out of Devon's room, actually. At first I was just too nervous, and then, well. I didn't want to let him out of my sight."

"I understand."

They stopped near the end of the hall. Four-fourteen, the sign on the closed door said, with "Robinson" scrawled in dry-erase marker below.

They were quiet a moment, looking at each other.

"Josh—I need to tell you something."

He blinked. "It's okay."

"No, hear me out." She looked down, swallowed. "There's nothing going on between me and Erik Wennerman. You didn't answer my text over the weekend, but—"

"I try not to look at my phone on Sundays …"

"Josh."

"… and, to be perfectly honest, I needed some time to think."

She bit her lip. No games. Just real. "I get that. But if you'd given me half a chance to explain, I could have told you he was trying to dance with me, Josh. I was trying my best to back away when he kissed me. And if you'd stayed two seconds longer you would have seen that."

Now it was Josh's turn to look down. "He looked awfully comfortable with you."

"That's not exactly my fault, is it? You didn't stick around to see me shove him away."

A faint flush of red crept up his cheeks.

"Fair enough." He cocked his head. "You really shoved him away?"

A giggle escaped despite her best efforts. "I did."

"Go, Becks." There was a look of admiration on his face, and she realized her own cheeks were warm, too.

Her heart was thudding. But she knew if she didn't say it all now she wouldn't say it at all, that it would drag on and on and fizzle into nothing. What was it Gramps used to say during those wood-working lessons? Sometimes you had to flip things upside down to expect different results.

She put a hand on his arm, the one with the flowers for Memaw, and stepped closer.

"Josh, you said it the other night—sometimes we miss the things that are right in front of our face. I'm not ready for dating with a capital D. I'm scarred and a little messed up, and I don't know how long it's going to take till I'm right again. But—I like you." She swallowed. "A lot. And I'm not interested in Erik or anybody else."

His eyes were steady, and he gazed back at her. "I like you, too."

"But I don't want to play stupid kid games."

He arched a brow. "You got something against Monopoly?"

Another giggle burst from her lips, and then they were both laughing, and he hugged her, arms tight and warm around her, and she knew they were okay again. A long moment passed as they stood like that, his arms around her, her head on his chest. She could hear his heart beat slow and steady, solid.

Safe.

She remembered feeling that way kneeling with Granny in the hospital waiting room earlier—secure. Protected. Like everything really, truly was going to be all right.

"Thank you, Josh," she said, looking at him. "For believing in me. For making me own up to my worries and my instincts about Devon. For making me feel … worth it."

She touched his arm again, felt a little buzz when her fingers met his bare skin. "I want to be worth it. I'm new at all this belief stuff," she waved a hand, "but I'm learning. Learning quick."

His lips curved. "Does that mean you'll finally take me up on my Bible study invitation?"

She laughed. "Yes. I'd love to."

His eyes were warm as they gazed at her. "I'm glad. And for the record?" His voice grew soft, and he looked straight into her eyes like he was seeing the real Rebecca, no walls, no façade, no mask. "You're definitely worth it."

And they pushed open the door and stepped into Memaw's room for a long-overdue introduction.

CHAPTER 43

Rebecca

BUCK MCCAFFERTY CALLED Rebecca's cell phone early Saturday morning. She took the call on the back porch, looking out at Granny's neat rows of tomato plants, which had managed to survive the storm.

"I'm guessing a call on a Saturday morning isn't going to bode well," she told the newspaper owner as she took a seat at the patio table. Granny was already up and gone, prepping the lunch at church for the storm cleanup crew. Rebecca planned to join them at ten after a quick visit to the Bryants to see Devon.

Buck sighed. "Rebecca, the numbers just aren't there. We're still a few months shy of the deadline we gave you, but Stuart and I think it's time to start talking more realistically, considering ways to gracefully close the newspaper, maybe even merge with a paper nearby."

"I imagine you've been talking with W Media."

"Them, yes, and the Charlotte paper is very interested—and they're willing to pay big bucks, even keep you all on as staff."

That was news. "Only I'm guessing they want a cookie cutter version of their own paper, but with a Dahlia stamp on it."

Buck was quiet a moment. "That's about the long and short of it."

Rebecca pursed her lips. "If our readers didn't like the hard news I was bringing them, they're certainly not going to like what the Charlotte paper serves."

"Well, W Media only wants you, which means the rest of the staff would be out of a job, plus they're not offering enough."

She pressed her lips together. Tiff would be fine, and Dinah could find work in sales about anywhere. But Millie? Rebecca shook her head.

"They both sound like lose-lose situations if you ask me." She stretched her legs, gazed out at the garden. "Buck, I don't get it—numbers are decent. Both circulation and advertising. Granted, only five percent, but that's still a gain. We're making money. Why are you so quick to bail out?"

"Truth?" Buck huffed out a breath. "Stuart doesn't have a heart for this anymore, and I don't have the capital to go it alone. That, and with my new grandbabies, I don't want to spend the best of my golden years slaving over a dying newspaper. Not to put too fine a point on it."

She thought a moment, the idea beginning to build. "What if you had a different partner?"

"Meaning?"

It had come to her in a dream last night, more like a vision where she saw herself and Buck in the newsroom, Millie and Dinah and Tiff before them, all smiling. Devon had ridden by in the dream on his bike, a brand new blue one, ringing his little bike bell. It was a wild idea, and risky. But maybe. Just maybe.

"Meaning, if I found you a new partner, an equal partner, a committed publisher/co-owner who'd front not only the money but the lion's share of the time, do you think Stuart would consider selling out his share and you'd stay on as partial owner?"

"You?" She could almost hear the wheels begin to turn in his head. "That's not a bad possibility."

She had a bit of money set aside, investments she'd let sit during the recession that were now beginning to turn around. She was still young enough that she could afford to gamble it all and still build a nice nest egg for the future if everything were lost.

It was a huge leap of faith, but suddenly, it made perfect sense. And after what had happened with Devon, it didn't feel like so much of a leap but rather a step in the right direction.

A step toward faith.

She sat straighter now, smiled confidently. "Talk numbers to me, Buck. What do you think Stuart might take to sell out his share, and how long might you commit as a co-owner?"

Buck gave her a number. She found a pen, scrawled the figure on her palm.

"And as for me, I'd say one year." His words were slow and measured, like he was thinking as he talked. But beneath the words, she could sense he, too, was excited about the idea. "I'd commit to a full year of wait-and-see, with the caveat that I could pull out if the numbers nosedive. But I'm gonna need to pray on this, talk to my wife."

"Let me do some talking and praying on my end, too, see what I can come up with."

They hung up, and Rebecca found that her hands were shaking. This might be the craziest and best idea she'd ever had.

"Wait—you'd own the paper with Buck? No more Stuart?" Millie's eyes were wide as she and the other staff gathered in their rolling chairs around Rebecca Monday morning.

Dinah eyed Tiff nervously, but Tiff just stared at her boss.

Rebecca gazed back at them. Since Saturday, she'd done a lot of praying, had a lot of honest talks with herself and with God. For the first time since she'd moved to Dahlia, she'd avoided talking to Granny about it. She wanted the choice to be all hers, was afraid that confiding in anyone, even Granny, would cloud her decision.

Now, as she spoke to her staff, there wasn't a shadow of a doubt. She felt in her bones that God wanted her to do this, that this was her next step. And she planned to do everything in her power to make it happen. No more holding back.

She was giving it all—to Dahlia, to its people, to God.

"The way I see it, we have a few options." She ticked off the choices on her fingertips. "Option one, we close down and become a branch of W Media, but you all are out of a job. They only need an editor. Option two, we get sold to the Charlotte folks, only we become the South Carolina regional branch of their operation, which doesn't do terribly much for this town, and frankly, I think it's a bad move from the town's perspective. Or three, we try it this way—I become co-owner, and we go all-out and see if we can make this ship sail like never before."

Rebecca paused to let the words sink in.

She added, "There's a Rotary Club grant we can apply for to help, and some Chamber of Commerce funding, too, but beyond that, I'm putting everything I've got on the line here—everything. If we sink, I lose it all and I'm out of a job. And so are you."

No one spoke.

Finally, Millie said, "Honestly, Rebecca, I think I'm overwhelmed. I expected you were waiting for the next ride out of here. Yet now here you are, offering to pony up gobs of money not only to save this paper but our jobs, too?"

Tiff and Dinah didn't say anything, just looked at Rebecca.

Rebecca took a breath.

"Millie, you're right. For a long time I was doing just that—

waiting for the next job to come my way so I could get as far away as I could. But I've done a lot of soul-searching. And I think the *Dahlia Weekly* doesn't deserve to get shut down because it's had a few editors, including me, who weren't worthy. I don't think the town deserves a paper that doesn't understand its readers, either. I'm not exactly sure why, but I can't seem to leave this place, can't seem to move on until I've set things right. If ever. So if you're in, and only if you're in, I want to do this thing."

Millie pursed her lips. "You're probably crazy as a loon, but if you want to throw all your savings at this newspaper, you've got my support one hundred percent." She got up, wrapped her arms around Rebecca. "I think you're doing the right thing, and I'm proud to say I'm in."

Tiff gave an excited bounce, began to clap.

"I'm in, too! I've been waiting for the right time to tell y'all this, but, well ..." Tiff's voice began to rise, became even more high-pitched, and tears pooled. "Bobby Smathers proposed! And, well, I'd love nothing more than to stay on as assistant editor of our town's paper."

Dinah's jaw dropped as the others began to talk all at once.

"Well," Dinah finally said, "I guess Smathers Grocery is our next official full-page advertiser."

Everyone giggled, and Millie, Rebecca, and Dinah gathered Tiff in a big hug.

"Congratulations, Tiff," Rebecca told her, feeling a rush of genuine care and happiness for the young woman. It was a beautiful thing watching someone come into her own.

"Thanks." Tiff blushed from ear to ear. "So, Boss, tell us what to do to help now. Can we canvas the streets, appeal to the Chamber or to Rotary on your behalf?"

"I think the first thing we can do is pray for God's guidance and hand in all of this as we move forward." Millie held out her arms.

"Rebecca, may I lead?"

Rebecca nodded, smiling, and they all joined hands as Millie began to pray.

"You're really going to do this?"

Sitting at the kitchen table that afternoon, a bowl full of string beans between them, Granny's mouth was open as she heard the whole plan from Rebecca.

Rebecca smiled at her, surprised at the peace she felt. Here she was, risking almost every penny she'd invested since she'd landed her first job, and money was the last thing on her mind. Instead, she was just hopeful she was good enough to do the job right.

"Granny, I am! And I've never been so excited in my life."

Granny shook her head, two bright spots of color on her cheeks as she broke into a grin.

"Girl, I'm—I'm thrilled to death. I don't know what to say. These last few months, with you here in the house, have meant more to me than you could ever have imagined."

"It's meant a great deal to me, too, Granny. In fact, it's hit me that I've spent my entire life chasing a dream when I think maybe I had it all right here in Dahlia, all along."

Granny's grin widened, and she gripped Rebecca's hand now.

"Your Gramps would be so proud. To think our baby girl is going to be part-owner of our town newspaper! You know, he was on the team that hired Ron Stone, back in the heyday."

"I had no idea!"

"Back then, the paper was run by a volunteer board that reported to the town council. Only later did it become a for-profit operation."

"So the town's been involved from the start?"

"Honey, it was the town that started the paper to begin with—a conglomerate of the council, the Chamber, and the churches that all teamed up to grant the initial subsidy. In the fifties, the Rotary Club played a big role in its support."

Rebecca nodded, a slow flutter filling her chest. "So they'd have an interest in funding things to keep it going."

Granny grinned. "That'd be grant money well-spent, if you ask me."

CHAPTER 44

Devon

A WEEK LATER, Devon and Miss Becca pulled up at the Baptist church in her little gray car. The day was sunny, a pretty August morning. School started back next Monday, and looking around the town, he thought it hardly seemed like there'd even been a storm. Gone were the fallen trees and the mess of branches and clutter on the roadside. The town looked new. A fresh start.

Just like he was getting.

Miss Becca parked the car, sat a moment, her shoulders still.

He leaned forward, put his good hand on her arm. "You're nervous?"

She ducked her head like she was embarrassed. "Very." She tossed him a look over the car seat. "Thanks for coming with me this morning. Are you sure you feel up to it?"

"Honestly, I'm fine."

He was. He still had the cast and a few scratches, and the bruises would take a while to heal, but he felt like a new person. Today, he and Rev and Marla were going to see Memaw in the retirement home. That man Miss Becca knew, Mr. Erik, with the extra-tan skin and extra-extra white teeth, had worked out some really neat deal. He'd heard her and Mr. Josh talking it over with Rev and Marla, didn't know what everything meant, but from what he gathered, Memaw was getting to live in some super-fantastic place, so fantastic she didn't mind one bit leaving the house she and his PawPaw had bought all those years ago.

They could even keep the house, which Memaw was putting in something she called "a trust" for him till he turned eighteen. They lined up some renters, who were supposed to move in next week.

Memaw'd hugged him at the hospital, right before his release, told him just 'cause he wasn't living under her roof anymore didn't mean she wasn't his Memaw.

"You best still come visit me," she'd said, elbowing him. "Robinsons stick together. Even across the miles."

"I promise, Memaw."

Memaw had gotten quiet then, peered at him hard.

"You know, sweet boy, what happened that night. It wasn't your fault."

Devon looked down. Fresh shame hit him like a smack. "I don't know, Memaw."

"Devon Robinson." Memaw struggled to sit upright, her hospital gown all tight and twisty. When she'd gotten settled, she held out both her hands. They shook a little, and he took them, afraid to meet her eyes.

When he finally did, he saw she was blinking hard, and behind the blinking were tears.

She took a long, slow breath. "I mean it, child. That … that thing between me and your uncle was between us. That was me and him, mother and son. Me, finally having the courage to say what I should have said a long, long time ago. What happened that night was Terrence's fault, not yours. You understand?"

Memaw's voice was hard, and he'd nodded, unable to speak.

"I said, do you understand?"

"Yes, ma'am."

She'd relaxed. "That's better. Now, fetch me one a'them blankets. The blue one. I want to catch me some beauty sleep 'fore that nurse comes in again to poke around with them needles."

He'd gotten her the blanket, switched off her light, and sat with her a few minutes.

"I love you, Memaw," he'd whispered when he got up to leave.

"I love you, too, sweet boy." She'd blown him a soft kiss. "Your mama sure would be proud of you, proud of the young man you've become."

They'd moved her into the retirement place over the weekend, and so far, so good. Rev and Marla had been taking him by to see her every day, and they even had a small worship service Sunday afternoon at the home.

Yesterday, they'd gone out to the house. It had been his first time back since he'd left, and he half-expected it to feel weird, empty, wrong. But instead, he just felt peace.

And when he'd knelt down at Mama's memory garden, he could have sworn for a moment that he smelled her in the trees around him, felt her smiling down. And he knew in his bones this was right and good.

Now, he was hoping he could help Miss Becca get the Rotary Club to give her a grant so she could keep the paper open and go from newspaper editor to newspaper owner. He had to admit it sounded pretty cool. It was good for Dahlia, plus it would mean she'd get to stay on, even help him with math after school each week—his worst subject.

Twenty minutes later, he stood at Miss Becca's side as she wrapped her speech to a close.

"Dahlia deserves a newspaper that serves its readers in the true sense of the word," Miss Becca was saying. "It deserves a newspaper invested in the community, not a cookie cutter big-shot operation that swoops in and delivers what it thinks Dahlia needs. I made that mistake when I first came here, and I learned my lesson the hard way," she said, and her cheeks got all red.

Come on, Miss Becca. You've got this.

"But thanks to a healthy dose of humble pie, I'm ready to serve Dahlia the right way. My friend Devon, here, taught me a lot about what this town means to each other. Watching you all come together to save this boy, this child of Dahlia, well…"

She trailed off, looked down at him a moment.

Devon smiled up at her, as big as he could. It felt like he had sunshine in his chest.

"Let's say it taught me a lot about the true spirit of this town," she said. "And with your help, we can make it happen."

A lady raised her hand. She had a frown on her face.

"How do we know you're going to do the right thing for this town? The clause specifies no editorial control over what your newspaper produces."

The room got quiet. In the back of the room, Devon saw Mr. Josh give Miss Becca a thumbs-up.

"You don't—you're right," Miss Becca said. Devon heard people gasp. "We can't be a newspaper worth our salt if we don't have editorial independence. But I can promise you as a person, and as a granddaughter of this town, I will do the right thing by Dahlia. And if I don't, you can give me the boot the next time grant funding comes around again."

"She's got a point," a man called from the back. "It's a one-year short-term grant, not a lifetime subsidy. Let's see what she can do with our support. This is our town paper, after all."

The Rotary president cleared his throat and looked like he wanted to duck under the table.

"Thank you, everyone, for your opinions, and thank you, Ms. Chastain. Now, if you and your friend Devon here'll step out, we'll inform you of our decision shortly."

Devon watched Miss Becca pace the front of the church as they waited.

"You know it's going to be okay one way or the other," he finally told her. "You said it yourself the other day—God has a plan for us."

She scrunched her mouth into a funny smile. "I did say that, didn't I."

"Yep. You did."

She let out a big breath and sat down next to him on the hard wooden bench.

"Well, I guess I'd better just give it to God, then."

They were a quiet a moment, and then he giggled, and she did too, and they were still laughing when a smiling man stuck his head out the door.

Miss Becca jumped. "President Vickers!"

"Congratulations," he said warmly, and Rebecca let out a squeak.

"You're kidding!" She covered her mouth with her hands.

"No joke. You're the official recipient not only of this year's Dahlia Rotary Grant but our new Special Project Business Scholarship." The man's eyes got all crinkly at the edges, and he caught Devon's eye and grinned. "I'd say you've got more than enough to get you started—not to mention advertising support from every major business in this town."

Miss Becca started crying and laughing. "I—I don't know what to say."

"Welcome to Dahlia, Ms. Chastain," the man said, and if Devon wasn't mistaken, he saw some tears in his eyes, too. "For good this time."

CHAPTER 45

Rebecca

A CHAMBER OF COMMERCE GRANT FOLLOWED the Rotary grant and scholarship, and then the ads began to pour in, slowly at first, then as the weeks turned into months, so fast Dinah could barely keep up.

"I'm drowning in paperwork!" the ad rep wailed in the newsroom on a sunny November Friday. "Not that I'm complaining, Boss!"

Rebecca laughed. "Hang in there, Dinah. Pass me some of those insertion orders. I'll pitch in."

Tiff, newly promoted to editor, started to raise a hand, then thought better. "We might think about bringing on an advertising assistant, maybe someone from the community college in Aberville who can help on a work-study or internship. They can make commission, help take the weight off Dinah, and get some real world experience."

Rebecca nodded, impressed. "I like your thinking, Madame Editor."

Tiff grinned, her newfound confidence wrapping neatly around her.

The phone rang, and Millie called out, "Rebecca, line two!"

Rebecca picked up.

"How's my favorite co-owner doing this fine morning?" Buck McCafferty sounded like a new man these days. "Numbers are booming!"

"They sure are, not to mention the stories. You should see what Tiff came up with this week. Outstanding!"

Rebecca said it loud enough for the young woman to hear, and she noted with satisfaction that Tiff's ears began to pink with pride. They should—Tiff had done a remarkable job of growing into her new position. Not only was readership up, but she'd begun winning awards, too, both for writing and photography and also for page design.

"We might think about raises after the dust begins to settle, maybe even a Christmas bonus," Buck said.

Rebecca nodded. "My sentiments exactly."

"I'll let you go—just wanted to check in and see if there was anything you needed from me. I'm off to spend a week in Alabama. Grandbaby Number Two is officially on her way!"

"That's great news!" Rebecca said, her voice warm. "Congratulations, Buck."

"Thanks, Rebecca. For that and, well. For everything. I know I've told you this before, but I'll say it again. You were right— Dahlia didn't deserve what Stuart and I were considering. What you did took a lot of guts."

Rebecca smiled at the "guts," gazed at the framed piece that now graced the wall beside her desk. "There's a lot of blood, sweat, and guts between dreams and success," it read—a Paul Bryant quote written neatly in calligraphy and matted expensively. It was a gift from her mom, who'd surprised her with an impromptu visit last month. Thanks to Devon's nudging, they were exchanging weekly phone calls, now, and Rebecca was finding she had a lot more in common with her mother than she'd ever imagined. They had a long way to go, but it was a step in the right direction.

"Thanks, Buck," she said, hanging up the phone. "You take care, now."

She looked around the room. "Hey, who's eaten?"

"I'm starved. You making a lunch run?" Dinah called out.

"My treat, as a thank you to all of you for the hard work and extraordinary talent you bring to this newspaper." Rebecca smiled at each of them in turn, her gaze settling at last on Millie, who had become absolutely indispensable these last couple of months. "Seriously—we couldn't have made it this far without each of you. So, who's up for pizza?"

Millie grinned. "Have we told you lately how much we love you?"

Rebecca laughed as she picked up the phone to order. "That never gets old."

On Sunday, she scurried into the second row at Dahlia Community Bible Church right as the front doors were closing, slipping into the seat right beside Devon. Marla squeezed her hand, gorgeous in an A-line skirt and smart emerald-green blazer, her signature chunky jewelry resplendent as always.

"We almost sent out the cavalry looking for you! I was worried you'd gotten cold feet!" Marla whispered.

Rebecca grinned at her friend. Two seats down sat Granny, right next to Josh Jamison, Lissa and her husband, and JJ. JJ waved, gave her a thumbs-up and a freckle-faced grin as the music began to play.

Josh caught her eye, too, and his smile warmed her from head to toe. After church, they had plans to go fishing, and then Josh was cooking for her and JJ for the very first time at his house. His daddy was "courting" her, JJ had said. She liked the old-fashioned, taking-it-slow sound of that.

Next to her, Devon took her other hand, closed it around his Bible.

"I want you to hold onto this today," he said into her ear as they all stood to sing. "For me, and for my mama."

Rebecca nodded and smiled down at him, lifted her voice to sing with the rest of the sanctuary.

Rev called her up when it was her turn. "Now, you all know that joining our church most certainly doesn't require giving your testimony, but today's newest member insisted. Please help me welcome one of Dahlia's favorite souls, Rebecca Helen Chastain."

She approached the altar and gave Rev a big hug, took the microphone from him. All nervousness suddenly and inexplicably disappeared as she took a breath, began.

"Anyone who knows me knows I've always been very reluctant to talk about faith, especially my own. But today wouldn't feel right without telling you my story, and how I came to be here today."

She held out the Bible and looked out into the packed sanctuary straight at her dearest friend—a young boy who'd shown her what God really looked like, helped point her to the true way. Jesus.

She cleared her throat. "My story has everything to do with Devon Robinson, the best person I've ever met and one of the people closest to my heart."

Devon gazed back at her, his eyes filling with tears.

She looked out at those gathered as she told her story, plainly and honestly. There to the left were Millie and her "grands," and behind them were Tiff and her fiancé, Bobby Smathers. Across the aisle sat Mike, Martha, and some of the others from Giveaway Night, along with their families. And in the back, slipping in now, she saw Shayna and Papa Toe.

On the altar rested a pretty ceramic pot, and inside the pot, a vivid green plant, its leaves supple and strong. Rebecca reached over for it, cradled it and the Bible in her hands.

"You see this plant, see how straight and strong its leaves have grown? I bet you never would have guessed it once used to be a tumble of ratty half-roots forgotten in my Granny's garden. But," she grinned, "just like with me, with lots of love and plenty of bright, bright Dahlia sunlight, it became what you see today: a glorious creation. As Granny is fond of saying, and I quote: 'Sometimes the worst mess of nothing sprouts the most vibrant testament to life.'"

Rebecca smiled, took a breath and locked eyes with Granny. "Thanks to your love, Granny, yours and Devon's and that of so many others in this room, I'm here today giving my own testament: to new life in Christ. You all took a chance on me. And God gave me the best gift possible. New life in him. I'm proud to be a new member of this church family."

She took her seat, Marla wrapping her in a big hug, Devon grabbing her arm tight.

Granny was family, yes. But so were these others, strangers she had come to know and love.

Strangers who'd somehow seen past her flaws and loved her anyway.

For the first time in her life, she was finally, finally home.

The End

About the Author

Jessica Brodie is an award-winning author and journalist with thousands of articles to her name and a huge heart for people and their inspiring redemption stories. She holds a master's in English and a bachelor's in communications. A native of Miami, Florida, she now makes her home in South Carolina with her husband Matt, four children, three misfit cats, and one giant German Shepherd. Find her at JessicaBrodie.com.

Book Club
Discussion Questions

1. Rebecca begins the story at her absolute lowest point after a suicide attempt, feeling like her entire life has been "nothing but an illusion." How does her journey from isolation to community reflect the broader themes of the book? What specific moments or relationships were most pivotal in her transformation?

2. The bond between Rebecca, a cynical big-city journalist, and Devon, an eleven-year-old boy, forms the heart of the story. What draws these two "kindred spirits" together despite their vastly different circumstances? How does their friendship change both characters?

3. Rebecca initially resists Granny's invitations to church and feels uncomfortable with Dahlia's openly religious atmosphere. Consider her spiritual journey throughout the book. What role does Devon play in modeling faith for her?

4. The book reveals that beneath Dahlia's wholesome exterior lie real problems like poverty, hunger, and domestic abuse. How does this contrast between appearance and reality drive the plot? What does this say about assumptions we make about communities and people based on their outward appearance?

5. Both Rebecca and Devon struggle with complicated family situations—Rebecca with her guilt and gratitude toward Granny, and Devon with his dangerous Uncle Terrence and his responsibility for Memaw. How do these family dynamics shape their characters and choices? What does the book suggest about chosen family versus biological family?

6. Rebecca's initial plan is to use the *Dahlia Weekly* as a stepping stone back to big-city journalism, but she ultimately decides to invest and stay. What changes her perspective on success and professional fulfillment? How does her evolution as a journalist mirror her personal growth?

7. Multiple characters in the story keep dangerous secrets—Devon about his home situation, Rebecca about her mental health struggles, and Erik about his family's business practices. How do these secrets both protect and harm the characters? What does the book suggest about when it's necessary to break silence and ask for help?

Acknowledgments

In many ways, this book is my own faith leap, a passion project years in the making, evolving into a gorgeous tapestry that enables me to look back at my own strange, sometimes-rocky, yet always beautiful life with a mixture of awe and inspiration.

My mom says my first toy was her old typewriter, and besides my imaginary friends—Making Butter and Teresa, who were more like playmates than actual toys—I think she's right. I still remember sitting cross-legged before that whirring, massive machine, my chubby little fingers jabbing at the keys as I spun tales of magical fascination.

I was a painfully shy girl, and for many years I lived in my own bubble. Then my sister came into this world with her never-met-a-stranger zest for life, and I learned there was much more excitement out there than I ever could have imagined. I came to crave the wide world around me, its stories and its people and its many complex layers of relationships and interactions. Most of my early decades were spent with my nose in the pages of a book—sometimes several at a time. The characters enchanted me, teaching me truths about human existence and faith that I never could have understood with my own limited perspective. A long dive into the world of theatre took that love of characters to the next level, and to this day if I weren't a writer I'm sure I'd be onstage somewhere. Maybe there's still time for that. We'll see.

My path to this place in life hasn't been easy, but looking back, I'm not sure I'd want it to be. How else could I have dreamed up such odd, enchanting, complicated people to populate the town of Dahlia had I not lived some of that tumult myself? Truly, I am blessed.

Thank you foremost to God, who sent his son Jesus to chase me down and drag me onto his path and force my feet to stay on-course, even when I wavered and doubted. I see so clearly now, and I'm sure I'll spend the rest of my life making up for those lost years.

Thank you to my family, whose love and support for my writing and world-building kept me going strong. Thank you to Matt, who insisted it was time. To Cameron and Avery, who listened to me, and to Allison and Will, who cared enough to cheer me on and believe in me. To Kathleen and Sara and Phyllis and Glenn, for unwavering encouragement no matter what. To Katy for believing this story needed to be told now, not later, for those who needed to hear before it was too late.

So many writers have supported me along the way, and their help and honesty and example have made me a better writer. I'm sure I'll leave someone out, but here's my attempt: Kevin Hall, my harshest and best journalism instructor, who taught me the true meaning of storytelling. Phil Hudgins, my mentor during my early days as a reporter, who taught me the story was never about the meeting-but about what happened at the meeting. Karen Gilfillan and Bob Fahey, who cheered me on in my earliest attempts. Marilyn Staats, Diane Thomas, Donna Warner, and Gene Wright, who ushered in my transformation and helped me to the next level. Lori Hatcher, Jean Wilund, Cindy Sproles, Tosca Lee, Lisa Wingate, and the other Christian authors and author-friends who showed me that faith-based writing can be truly excellent. Les Stobbe and to my agent Bob Hostetler, for believing in me and understanding the necessity of alternate paths.

And thanks especially to the *Advocate*, which has been a fertile and supportive place to learn (and write about!) the diverse and stirring stories of Christians across South Carolina, including the Children's Defense Fund's Freedom School, which inspired the West Dahlia Leaders Summer Enrichment Camp in *The Memory Garden*.

We're all imperfect human beings making our way into the light of Christ the best we can. My prayer is that those who read this book will find hope in that imperfection and know that all of us can find redemption and salvation, no matter what.

THE DAHLIA SERIES

The Memory Garden: Book One

The Memory Garden, the Amazon-bestselling first book in the Dahlia Series, is a gripping Southern novel following a broken journalist who finds unexpected purpose in a small town when a troubled boy's dangerous secret puts them both at risk.

Tangled Roots: Book Two

In *Tangled Roots*, Tiff Steadman thought she'd escaped her shameful past—until her recently paroled brother James arrives in Dahlia, threatening the respectable life she's carefully built. As wedding plans and buried secrets collide, these two siblings must confront the truth they've both been hiding and decide if redemption is worth the cost.

Hidden Seeds: Book Three

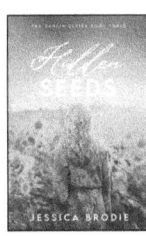

Returning to Dahlia after tragedy exposes her fiancé's betrayal, Natalie Motts rebuilds her life through art and unexpected friendship with Laney, a trafficking survivor hiding a dangerous past. When Natalie's teenage sister vanishes, Laney must choose between protecting her hard-won safety and stepping back into darkness to bring the girl home.

Book Four: Coming 2027
Marla's story . . . to be continued.

Paperback, e-book, and audiobook available.

Sign up for Jessica's Dahlia Email List and stay notified about her latest releases. Visit JessicaBrodie.com/Dahlia

www.ingramcontent.com/pod-product-compliance
Lightning Source LLC
Chambersburg PA
CBHW070909260626
47162CB00007B/2607